W9-CAT-226

ARRIVING AT THE STARTING POINT

"We're on the edge of the brain." Morrison could recognize the individual convolutions and fissures.

"Strap yourself in, Albert," said Konev. "I'll let you know if I need you."

A platelet made a head-on collision with the ship. The prow penetrated deeply and the skin of the platelet punctured. Its contents oozed out slowly, mixing with the plasma and then forming into two or three long strings that tangled with each other. They clung to a portion of the ship's hull for quite a time, trailing behind.

Morrison saw, up ahead, a milky fog that seemed to fill the blood vessel from wall to wall, pulsating and undulating. Inside it were dark granules that moved steadily from one side to the other. Morrison couldn't help but cry aloud in terror. . . .

ISAAC ASIMOV

FANTASTIC

VOYAGE II

DESTINATION BRAIN

Bantam Books by Isaac Asimov

FANTASTIC VOYAGE

FANTASTIC VOYAGE II:
DESTINATION BRAIN

ISAAC ASIMOV

FANTASTIC VOYAGE II

DESTINATION BRAIN

BANTAM BOOKS

TORONTO · NEW YORK · LONDON · SYDNEY · AUCKLAND

All characters in this book are fictional
and any resemblance to actual persons,
living or dead, is entirely coincidental.

*This edition contains the complete text
of the original hardcover edition.*
NOT ONE WORD HAS BEEN OMITTED.

FANTASTIC VOYAGE II: DESTINATION BRAIN
*A Bantam Spectra Book / published by arrangement with
Doubleday*

PRINTING HISTORY
Doubleday edition published October 1987

*The title and concept of Fantastic Voyage is from a story
originally created by Jerry Bixby and Otto Klement.*

Bantam edition / August 1988

All rights reserved.
Copyright © 1987 by Nightfall, Inc.
Cover art copyright © 1988 by Enid Hatton.
Library of Congress Catalog Card Number: 87-5334

*No part of this book may be reproduced or transmitted
in any form or by any means, electronic or mechanical,
including photocopying, recording, or by any information
storage and retrieval system, without permission in writing
from the publisher.*
For information address: Doubleday
666 Fifth Avenue, New York, NY 10130.

ISBN 0-553-27327-2

Published simultaneously in the United States and Canada

*Bantam Books are published by Bantam Books, a division of
Bantam Doubleday Dell Publishing Group, Inc. Its trademark,
consisting of the words "Bantam Books" and the portrayal of
a rooster, is Registered in U.S. Patent and Trademark Office
and in other countries, Marca Registrada, Bantam Books,
666 Fifth Avenue, New York, New York 10103*

PRINTED IN THE UNITED STATES OF AMERICA

KR 0 9 8 7 6 5 4 3 2 1

*To Dick Malina and Scott Meredith,
who made it possible.*

CONTENTS

1   NEEDED   *1*

2   TAKEN   *21*

3   MALENKIGRAD   *36*

4   GROTTO   *52*

5   COMA   *69*

6   DECISION   *90*

7   SHIP   *110*

8   PRELIMINARIES   *129*

9   ARTERY   *149*

10   CAPILLARY   *173*

11   DESTINATION   *192*

12   INTERCELLULAR   *216*

13   CELL   *238*

14   AXON   *260*

15   ALONE!   *282*

16   DEATH   *303*

17   EXIT   *321*

18   RETURN?   *344*

19   TURNAROUND   *365*

NOTES

IN 1966 my novel *Fantastic Voyage* was published. It was, actually, a novelization of a motion picture that had been written by others. I followed the plot line that existed as closely as I could, except for changing several of the more insupportable scientific inconsistencies.

I was never quite satisfied with the novel, although it did very well and is still in print in both hardcover and softcover editions, simply because I never felt it to be entirely mine.

When the opportunity arose to write another novel on the same theme—a miniaturized vessel with a crew that is inside a living human being—I agreed only on the condition that I do it entirely my own way.

Here, then, is *Fantastic Voyage II: Destination Brain.* A motion picture may be made from it, but if so, this novel will owe nothing at all to it. For better or for worse, this novel is *mine.*

CHAPTER 1

NEEDED

He who is needed must learn to endure flattery.
—*Dezhnev Senior*

1.

"PARDON me. Do you speak Russian?" said the low voice, definitely contralto, in his ear.

Albert Jonas Morrison stiffened in his seat. The room was darkened and the computer screen on the platform was displaying its graphics with an insistence that had been lost on him.

He must have been more than half-asleep. There had definitely been a man on his right when he sat down. When had that man changed into a woman? Or risen and been replaced?

Morrison cleared his throat and said, "Did you say something, ma'am?" He couldn't make her out clearly in the dim room and the flashing light from the computer screen obscured rather than revealed. He made out dark hair, straight, hugging the skull, covering the ears—no artifice.

She said, "I asked if you spoke Russian."

"Yes, I do. Why do you want to know?"

"Because that would make it easier. My English sometimes fails me. Are you Dr. Morrison? A. J. Morrison? I'm not

1

certain in this darkness. Forgive me if I have made a mistake."

"I am A. J. Morrison. Do I know you?"

"No, but I know you." Her hand reached out, touching the sleeve of his jacket lightly. "I need you badly. Are you listening to this talk? You did not seem to be."

They were both whispering, of course.

Morrison looked about involuntarily. The room was sparsely filled and no one was sitting very close. His whisper grew lower just the same. "And if I'm not? What then?" (He was curious—if only out of boredom. The talk *had* put him to sleep.)

She said, "Will you come with me now? I am Natalya Boranova."

"Come with you where, Ms. Boranova?"

"To the coffee shop—so that we may talk. It is terribly important."

That was the way it began. It didn't matter, Morrison decided afterward, that he had been in that particular room—that he had not been alert—that he had been intrigued enough, flattered enough to be willing to go with a woman who said she needed him.

She would, after all, have found him wherever he had been and would have seized upon him and would have made him listen. It might not have been quite so easy under other circumstances, but it would all have gone as it did. He was certain.

There would have been no escape.

2.

HE was looking at her in normal light now, and she was less young than he had thought. Thirty-six? Forty, perhaps?

Dark hair. No gray. Pronounced features. Heavy eyebrows. Strong jaws. Pleasant nose. Sturdy body, but not fat. Almost as tall as he was, even though she was wearing flat heels. On the whole, a woman who was attractive without being beautiful. The kind of woman, he decided, one could get used to.

He sighed, for he was facing the mirror and he saw himself there. Sandy hair, thinning. Blue eyes, faded. Thin face, thin body, stringy. Beaky nose, nice smile. He hoped it was a nice smile. But no, not a face you would want to get used to. Brenda had gotten entirely unused to it in a little over ten years, and his fortieth birthday would be five days past the fifth anniversary of the day his divorce had been made final and official.

The waitress brought the coffee. They had been sitting there, not talking but appraising each other. Morrison finally felt he had to say something.

"No vodka?" he said in an attempt at lightness.

She smiled and looked somehow even more Russian when she did so. "No Coca-Cola?"

"If that's an American habit, Coca-Cola is at least cheaper."

"For good reason."

Morrison laughed. "Are you this quick in Russian?"

"Let us see if I am. Let's talk Russian."

"We'll sound like a couple of spies."

Her last sentence had been in Russian. So had Morrison's reply. The change of language made no difference to him. He could speak and understand it as easily as English. That had to be so. If an American wished to be a scientist and keep up with the literature, he had to be able to handle Russian, almost as much as a Russian scientist had to be able to handle English.

This woman, Natalya Boranova, for instance, despite her pretence that she was not at home in English, spoke it readily and with only a faint accent, Morrison noticed.

She said, "Why will we sound like spies? There are hundreds of thousands of Americans speaking English in the Soviet Union and hundreds of thousands of Soviet citizens speaking Russian in the United States. These are not the bad old days."

"That's true. I was joking. But in that case, why do you want to speak Russian?"

"This is your country and that gives you a psychological advantage, does it not, Dr. Morrison? If we speak my language, it will balance the scales a bit."

Morrison sipped at his coffee. "As you wish."

"Tell me, Dr. Morrison. Do you know me?"

"No. I have never met you before."

"And my name? Natalya Boranova? Have you heard of me?"

"Forgive me. If you were in my field, I would have heard of you. Since I have not, I assume you are not in my field. —Should I know you?"

"It might have helped, but we'll let it go. I know you, however. In fact, I know a great deal about you. When and where you were born. Your schooling. The fact that you are divorced and that you have two daughters that live with your ex-wife. I know about your university position and the research you do."

Morrison shrugged. "None of that would be hard to find out in our computer-ridden society. Should I be flattered or annoyed?"

"Why either?"

"It depends on whether you tell me that I am famous in the Soviet Union, which would be flattering, or that I have been the target of an investigation, which might be annoying."

"I have no intention of being anything but honest with you. I have investigated you—for reasons that are important to me."

Morrison said coldly, "What reasons?"

"To begin with, you are a neurophysicist."

Morrison had finished his coffee and had absently signaled for a refill. Boranova's cup was half-empty, but she had apparently lost interest in it.

"There are other neurophysicists," Morrison said.

"None like you."

"Clearly you are trying to flatter me. That can only be because you don't know anything about me after all. Not the crucial things."

"That you are not successful? That your methods of brain wave analysis are not generally accepted in the field?"

"But if you know that, then why are you after me?"

"Because we have a neurophysicist in our country who knows your work, and he thinks it is brilliant. You have rather jumped into the unknown, he says, and you may be wrong—but if you are, you are brilliantly wrong."

"*Brilliantly* wrong? How is that different from wrong?"

"It is his view that it is impossible to be brilliantly wrong without being not altogether wrong. Even if you are in some

ways wrong, much of what you maintain will prove useful—
and you may be entirely right."

"What is the name of this paragon who has this view of
me? I'll mention him with favor in my next paper."

"He is Pyotor Leonovich Shapirov. Do you know him?"

Morrison sat back in his chair. He had not expected this.
"Know him?" he said. "I've met him. Pete Shapiro I called
him. Our people here in the United States think he's as crazy
as I am. If it turns out that he's backing me, that's just one
more nail in my coffin. —Listen, tell Pete I appreciate his
faith in me, but if he really wants to help me, please ask him
not to tell anyone he's on my side."

Boranova looked at him disapprovingly. "You are not a
very serious man. Is everything a joke to you?"

"No. Just me. I'm the joke. I've got something really great
and I can't convince anyone of it. Except Pete—I've now
found out—and he doesn't count. I can't even get my papers
published these days."

"Then come to the Soviet Union. We can use you—and
your ideas."

"No no. I'm not emigrating."

"Who said emigrate? If you wish to be an American, be an
American. But you have visited the Soviet Union in the past
and you can visit it once again and stay a while. Then return
to your own country."

"Why?"

"You have crazy ideas and we have crazy ideas. Perhaps
yours can help ours."

"What crazy ideas? I mean, yours. I know what mine are."

"It's not something to discuss until I know if you are perhaps willing to help us."

Morrison, still sitting back in his chair, was vaguely aware
of the buzz about him, of people drinking, eating, talking—
most of them from the conference, he was sure. He stared at
this intense Russian woman who admitted to crazy ideas and
wondered what kind of—

He stiffened and cried out, "Boranova! I *have* heard of
you. Of course. Pete Shapiro mentioned you. You're—"

In his excitement he was speaking English and her hand
came down on his, her nails pressing hard against his skin.

He choked it off and she removed her hand, saying,
"Sorry. I did not mean to hurt you."

He stared at the marks on his hand, one of which, he decided, was going to be slightly bruised. He said quietly in Russian, "You're the Miniaturizer."

3.

BORANOVA looked at him with an easy calm. "Perhaps a little walk and a bench by the river. The weather is beautiful."

Morrison held his lightly damaged hand in the other. There had been a few, he thought, who had looked in his direction when he had cried out in English, but none seemed to show any interest now. He shook his head. "I think not. I should be attending the conference."

Boranova smiled as though he had agreed that the weather was beautiful. "I don't think so. I think you'll find a seat by the river more interesting."

For one flashing moment, Morrison thought her smile might be intended to be seductive. Surely she wasn't implying—

He abandoned the thought almost before he had put it clearly to himself. That sort of thing was passé even on holovision: "Beautiful Russian Spy Uses Sinuous Body to Dazzle Naïve American."

To begin with, she wasn't beautiful and her body wasn't sinuous. Nor did she look as though anything of that nature could possibly be on her mind and he himself, after all, wasn't that naïve—or even interested.

Yet he found himself accompanying her across the campus and toward the river.

They walked slowly—sauntered—and she talked cheerfully about her husband Nikolai and her son Aleksandr, who was going to school and was, for some strange reason, interested in biology, even though his mother was a thermodynamicist. What's more, Aleksandr was a dreadful chess player, much to his father's disappointment, but he showed signs of promise on the violin.

Morrison did not listen. He occupied himself, instead, in trying to recall what he had heard about the Soviet interest in miniaturization and what possible connection there might be between that and his own work.

She pointed to a bench. "This one looks reasonably clean."

They sat down. Morrison stared over the river, watching, with eyes that did not really absorb it, the line of cars filing along the highway on their side and the parallel line on the highway on the other side—while sculls, looking like centipedes, plied the river itself.

He remained silent and Boranova, staring at him thoughtfully, finally said, "You do not find this interesting?"

"Find what interesting?"

"My suggestion that you come to the Soviet Union."

"No!" He said it curtly.

"But why not? Since your American colleagues do not accept your ideas, and since you are depressed over this and are seeking a way out of the dead end at which you have arrived, why not come to us?"

"Given your investigations into my life, I am sure you know that my ideas are not accepted, but how can you possibly be sure that I am all that depressed over it?"

"Any sane man would be depressed. And one has only to talk to you to be certain."

"Do *you* accept my ideas?"

"I? I am not in your field. I know nothing—or very little—about the nervous system."

"I suppose you simply accept Shapirov's estimate of my ideas."

"Yes. And even if I did not—desperate problems may require desperate remedies. What harm, then, if we try your ideas as a remedy? It will certainly leave us no worse off."

"So you have my ideas. They have been published."

She gazed at him steadily. "Somehow we don't think all your ideas have been published. That is why we want *you.*"

Morrison laughed without humor. "What good can I possibly do you in connection with miniaturization? I know less about miniaturization than you do about the brain. Far less."

"Do you know anything at all about miniaturization?"

"Only two things. That the Soviets are known to be investigating it—and that it is impossible."

Boranova stared thoughtfully at the river. "Impossible? What if I told you we had accomplished the task?"

"I would as soon believe you if you told me polar bears fly."

"Why should I lie to you?"

"I point out the fact. I'm not concerned about the motivation."

"Why are you so certain miniaturization is impossible?"

"If you reduce a man to the dimensions of a fly, then all the mass of a man would be crowded into the volume of a fly. You'd end up with a density of something like"—he paused to think—"a hundred and fifty thousand times that of platinum."

"But what if the mass were reduced in proportion?"

"Then you end up with one atom in the miniaturized man for every three million in the original. The miniaturized man would not only have the size of a fly but the brainpower of a fly as well."

"And if the atoms are reduced, too?"

"If it is miniaturized atoms you are speaking of, then Planck's constant, which is an absolutely fundamental quantity in our Universe, forbids it. Miniaturized atoms would be too small to fit into the graininess of the Universe."

"And if I told you that Planck's constant was reduced as well, so that a miniaturized man would be encased in a field in which the graininess of the Universe was incredibly finer than it is under normal conditions?"

"Then I wouldn't believe you."

"Without examining the matter? You would refuse to believe it as a result of preconceived convictions, as your colleagues refuse to believe you?"

And at this, Morrison was, for a moment, silent.

"Not the same," he mumbled at last.

"Not the same?" Again she stared thoughtfully out over the river. "In what way not the same?"

"My colleagues think I'm wrong. My ideas are not theoretically impossible in their opinion—only wrong."

"While miniaturization is impossible?"

"Yes."

"Then come and see. If it turns out that miniaturization is impossible, just as you say, then you'll at least have a month in the Soviet Union as a guest of the Soviet Government. All expenses will be paid. If there's a friend you would like to bring with you, bring her, too. Or him."

Morrison shook his head. "No thanks. I'd rather not. Even

if miniaturization were possible, it is not my field. It would not help me or be of interest to me."

"How do you know? What if miniaturization gave you the opportunity to study neurophysics as you have never studied it before—as no one has ever studied it before? And what if, in doing so, you might be able to help us? That would be our stake in it."

"How can you offer me a new way of studying neurophysics?"

"But, Dr. Morrison, I thought that was what we were talking about. You cannot really prove your theories because you cannot study single nerve cells in sufficient detail without damaging them. But what if we make a neuron as large as the Kremlin for you—or even larger—so that you can study it a molecule at a time?"

"You mean you can reverse miniaturization and make a neuron as large as you wish."

"No, we can't do that, as yet, but we can make you as small as we wish and that would amount to the same thing, wouldn't it?"

Morrison rose, staring at her.

"No," he said in half a whisper. "Are you insane? Do you think I am insane? Good-bye! Good-bye!"

He turned and strode away rapidly.

She called after him. "Dr. Morrison. Listen to me."

He made a sweeping gesture of rejection with his right arm and broke into a run across the drive, narrowly dodging the cars.

Then he was back into the hotel, puffing, almost dancing with impatience as he waited for the elevator.

Madwoman! he thought. She wanted to miniaturize *him*, attempt this impossibility on *him*. —Or attempt the possibility of it on him, which would be infinitely worse.

4.

MORRISON was still shaking when he stood at the door of his hotel room, holding the plastic rectangle of his key, breathing hard, and wondering if she knew his room number. She could find out, of course, if she were sufficiently determined. He looked down the length of the corridor each way, half-afraid he might see her running toward him, face contorted, hair flying, hands outstretched.

He shook his head. This was madness. What could she do to him? She could not carry him off bodily. She could not force him to do anything he didn't want to do. What childish terror was overcoming him?

Morrison took a deep breath and thrust his key into the door slit. He felt the small click as the key seated itself, then he withdrew it and the door swung open.

The man sitting in the wicker armchair at the window smiled at him and said, "Come in."

Morrison stared at him in astonishment, then twisted his head to look at the room number.

"No no. It's your room, all right. Do come in and close the door behind you."

Morrison followed orders, staring at the man in silent astonishment.

He was a comfortably plump man, not quite fat, filling the chair from arm to arm. He wore a thin seersucker jacket and under it was a shirt so white that it seemed to glisten. He was not yet what one might call bald, but he was clearly on the way and what remained of his brown hair was crisply curly. He did not wear glasses, but his eyes were small and had a nearsighted look about them, which might be misleading—or which perhaps meant he wore contacts.

He said, "You came back running, didn't you? I watched you"—he pointed out the window—"sitting on the bench, then get up and come toward the hotel at the double. I was hoping you would come up to your hotel room. I didn't want to sit up here all day waiting for you."

"You were here in order to watch me from the window?"

"No, not at all. That was just an accident. You just happened to walk out with the lady to that bench. Convenient, but not really foreseen. It's all right, though. If I hadn't had the view from the window, there were others watching."

By that time Morrison had caught his breath and his mind had steadied itself to the point where he asked the question that should have had pride of place in the conversation. "Who are you, anyway?"

In response the man, smiling, took a small wallet from his inner jacket pocket and let it flip open. He said, "Signature, hologram, fingerprint, voiceprint."

Morrison looked from the hologram to the smiling face. The hologram was smiling, too. He said, "All right, so you're security. It still doesn't give you the right to break into my private quarters. I'm available. You could have called me from the lobby or knocked at my door."

"Strictly speaking, you're right, of course. But I thought it best to meet you as discreetly as possible. Besides, I presumed on old acquaintance."

"What old acquaintance?"

"Two years ago. Don't you remember? An international conference in Miami? You were presenting a paper and had a hard time of it—"

"I remember the occasion. I remember the paper. It's you I don't remember."

"That's not surprising, perhaps. I met you afterward. I asked you questions, and we actually had a few drinks together."

"I don't consider that old acquaintance. —Francis Rodano?"

"That's my name, yes. You even pronounced it correctly. Accent on the second syllable. Broad *a*. Subliminal memory, obviously."

"No, I don't remember you. The name was on your identification. —I'd rather you left."

"I would like to talk to you in my official capacity."

"Apparently everyone wants to talk to me. What about?"

"Your work."

"Are you a neurophysicist?"

"You must know I'm not. Slavic languages was my major. I minored in economics."

"Then what can we talk about? I'm good at Russian, but you're probably better. And I know nothing about economics."

"We can talk about your work. As we did two years ago. —Look, why don't you sit down? It's your room and I won't really take long. If you want the chair I'm sitting on, I'll be glad to give it to you."

Morrison sat down at the side of the bed. "Let's get this over with. What do you want to know about my work?"

"The same thing I wanted to know two years ago. Is there anything to your notion that there's a specific structure in your brain that's specifically responsible for creative thought?''

"Not quite a structure. It's not something you can cut out in the ordinary way. It's a neuronic network. Yes, I think there's something to that. Obviously. The catch is that no one else thinks so because they can't locate it and have no evidence for it.''

"Have you located it?''

"No. I reason backward from results and from my analysis of brain waves and I don't seem to be convincing. My analyses are not—orthodox.'' He added bitterly, "Orthodoxy in this field has gotten them nowhere, but they won't let me be unorthodox.''

"I am told that you use mathematical techniques in your electroencephalographic analyses that are not only unorthodox, but are flat wrong. To be unorthodox is one thing; to be wrong is quite another.''

"The only reason they say I am wrong is that I cannot prove that I am right. The only reason I cannot prove that I am right is that I can't study an isolated brain neuron in sufficient detail.''

"Have you tried to study them? If you work with a living human brain, don't you leave yourself open to severe lawsuits or to criminal trial?''

"Of course. I'm not mad. I've worked with animals. I have to.''

"You told me all this two years ago. I take it, then, you have made no startling discoveries in the last two years.''

"None. But I'm convinced I'm right just the same.''

"Your being convinced doesn't matter if you can't convince anyone else. But now I have to ask you another question. —Have you done something in the last two years that has managed to convince the Soviets?''

"The Soviets?''

"Yes. What is this attitude of surprise, Dr. Morrison? Haven't you spent an hour or two in conversation with Dr. Boranova? Isn't she the one whom you just left in a great hurry?''

"Dr. Boranova?'' Morrison, in his confusion, could think of nothing better to do than play the parrot.

Rodano's face lost none of its pleasantness. "Exactly. We

know her well. We keep half an eye on her whenever she is in the United States."

"You make it sound like the bad old days," mumbled Morrison.

Rodano shrugged. "No, not at all. There is no danger of nuclear war now. We are polite to each other, the Soviet Union and we. We cooperate in space. We have a cooperative mining station on the moon and freedom of entry into each other's space settlements. That makes these the good new days. *But,* Doctor, some things don't change entirely. We keep an eye on our polite companions, the Soviets, just to make sure they stay virtuous. Why not? They keep an eye on us."

Morrison said, "You keep an eye on me, too, it would seem."

"But you were with Dr. Boranova. We couldn't help seeing you."

"That won't happen again, I assure you. I have no intention of ever being in her vicinity again if I can help it. She's a madwoman."

"Do you mean that literally?"

"Take my word for it. —Look, nothing of what she and I talked about is secret as far as I'm concerned. What she said I feel free to repeat. She's involved in some miniaturization project."

"We've heard of it," said Rodano easily. "They have a special town in the Urals devoted to miniaturization experiments."

"Are they getting anywhere as far as you know?"

"We wonder."

"She's tried to tell me they are, that they've succeeded in producing actual miniaturization."

Rodano said nothing.

Morrison, who had waited a moment to let him speak, then said, "But that's impossible, I tell you. Scientifically impossible. You must realize that. Or, since your field of expertise is Slavic languages and economics, take my word for it."

"I don't have to, my friend. There are many others who say it is impossible and yet, nevertheless, we wonder. The Soviets are free to play with miniaturization if they please, but we don't actually want them to have it unless we do also. After all, we don't know to what uses it might be put."

"To none! To none!" said Morrison fiercely. "There's no point in worrying about it. If our government really doesn't want the Soviet Union to get too far ahead in technology, it should encourage this miniaturization madness. Let the Soviets spend money on it—and time and material—and concentrate every atom of their scientific expertise on it. Everything will be wasted."

"And yet," said Rodano, "I don't think Dr. Boranova is mad or a fool, any more than I think that you are mad or a fool. —Do you know what I was thinking as I watched the two of you in so intent a conversation on the park bench? It seemed to me that she wanted your help. Perhaps she thought that with your theories on neurophysics you could somehow help the Soviet push for miniaturization. Their peculiar theories and your peculiar theories might add up to something that is not at all peculiar. Or so I think."

Morrison's lips tightened. "I told you I have no secrets to keep, so I'm telling you that you're right. Just as you say, she wants me to go to the Soviet Union and help out in their miniaturization project. I won't ask how you know that, but I don't think it's just an idle guess and don't try to persuade me it is."

Rodano smiled and Morrison went on. "In any case, I said no. I refused absolutely. I stood up and left at once—and in a hurry. You saw me hurry. That's the truth. I would have reported it if you had given me time to do so. And I'm reporting it now, as a matter of fact, to you. Nor is there any reason for you not to believe me because why, under any circumstances, would I take any part in a project that has absolutely no sense to it. Even if I wanted to work against my country, which I don't, I'm enough of a physicist not to try to do so by involving myself in anything as insane as working on a project without hope. They might as well be working on a perpetual motion machine, or antigravity, or faster-than-light travel, or—" He was perspiring freely.

And Rodano said gently, "Please, Dr. Morrison, no one doubts your loyalty. Certainly I don't. I'm not here because I am perturbed at your having had a discussion with the Russian woman. I am here because we had reason to think she might approach you and we feared you would not listen to her."

"What?"

"Now understand me, Dr. Morrison. Please understand. We would suggest—in fact, we would very much want—to have you go with Dr. Boranova to the Soviet Union."

5.

MORRISON stared at Rodano, face pale, lower lip quivering slightly. He brushed at his hair with his right hand and said, *"Why* do you want me to go to the Soviet Union?"

"Not I, personally. The United States Government wants it."

"Why?"

"For the obvious reason. If the Soviet Union is engaged in miniaturization experiments, we would like to know as much about them as possible."

"You've got Madame Boranova. She must know a great deal. Grab her and beat it out of her."

Rodano sighed and said, "I know you're joking. We can't do that these days. You know that. The Soviet Union would retaliate at once in the most unpleasant ways and world opinion would be with them. So let's not waste time with jokes like that."

"All right. Granted, we can't do anything crude. I presume we have agents attempting to dig out the details."

"The operative word, Doctor, is *attempting.* We have our agents in the Soviet Union, to say nothing of sophisticated espionage equipment both Earthside and in space, just as they have agents here. But if they and we are very good at poking around quietly, we're also very good at keeping things secret. If anything, the Soviet Union is better at it than we are. Even though these are not what you call the bad old days, the Soviet Union is still not quite an open society in our sense and they've had more than a century of practice in keeping things under the rug."

"Then what do you expect *me* to do?"

"You're different. The usual agent is sent into the Soviet Union or into some region in which the Soviet Union is operating under some cover which might possibly be penetrated. He—or she—must insinuate himself into a place where he is not really welcome and manage to elicit information that is secret. This isn't easy. He—or she—usually does not succeed and he—or she—is sometimes caught, which is always unpleasant all around. In your case, though, they're *asking* for you; they behave as though they *need* you. They will place you in the very midst of their secret installations. What an opportunity you will have.''

''But they've just asked me to go in these last two hours. How do you know so much about it?''

''They've been interested in you for quite a while now. One of the reasons I made it my business to talk to you two years ago was because they seemed interested in you even at that time and we were wondering why that should be. So when they made their move, we were ready.''

Morrison's fingers drummed on the arm of the chair, his nails making a rhythmic clicking noise. ''Let me get this straight. I'm to agree to go with Natalya Boranova to the Soviet Union, presumably to the region where they are supposedly working on miniaturization. I am to pretend to help them—''

''You needn't pretend,'' said Rodano comfortably. ''Help them if you can, especially if that means you get to know the process better.''

''All right, help them. And then give you what information I have when I return.''

''Exactly.''

''What if there is no information? What if the whole thing is one gigantic bluff or if they're only kidding themselves? What if they're following some Lysenko type down into an empty hole?''

''Then tell us *that*. We would love to know that—if it's a matter of *knowing* and not just thinking. After all, the Soviets, we are pretty certain, are under the impression that we are making progress on the matter of antigravity. Maybe we are and maybe we're not. They don't know for certain and we're not about to let them find out. Since we're not asking any Soviet scientist to come and help us, we're not giving them an easy entry. For that matter, there's some talk the Chinese are working on faster-than-light travel. Oddly enough, those are two items you mentioned as being theoretically impossible. I haven't heard that anyone's working on perpetual motion, however.''

''These are ridiculous games the nations are playing,'' said

Morrison. "Why don't they cooperate in these matters? We might as well be in the bad old days."

"Not quite. But being in the good new days does not mean we're in heaven. There is still residual suspicion and there are still attempts to take a giant step forward before someone else does. Maybe it's even a good thing. If we're driven by selfish motives of aggrandizement, as long as that doesn't lead to war, we may make more rapid progress. To stop trying to steal a march on neighbors and friends might reduce us to indolence and decay."

"So if I go and am eventually in a position to assure you, authoritatively, that the Soviets are drilling a dry hole or that they are indeed making progress of such and such a nature, then I will be helping not only the United States, but the whole world, to remain vigorous and progressive—even including the Soviet Union."

Rodano nodded. "That's a good way to look at it."

Morrison said, "I have to give you people credit. You're clever con artists. However, I don't fall for it. I favor cooperation among nations and I'm not going to play these dangerous twentieth-century games in the rational twenty-first. I told Dr. Boranova I wasn't going and I'm telling *you* I'm not going."

"Do you understand that it is your government that is asking this of you?"

"I understand that *you* are asking me and I'm refusing *you*. But if it happens that you actually represent the government's views in this, then I am prepared to refuse the government as well."

6.

MORRISON sat there, flushed, chin up. His heart was beating rapidly and he felt heroic.

Nothing can make me change my mind, he thought. What can they do? Throw me in jail? What for? They have to have a charge.

He waited for anger from the other. For a threat.

Rodano merely looked at him with an expression of quiet bemusement.

"Why do you refuse, Dr. Morrison?" he asked. "Have you no feelings of patriotism?"

"Patriotism, yes. Insanity, no."

"Why insanity?"

"Do you know what they plan to do with me?"

"Tell me."

"They intend to miniaturize me and place me in a human body to investigate the neurophysical state of a brain cell from the inside."

"Why should they want you to do that?"

"They imply it's to help me with my research, which they claim will also help *them*, but I certainly don't intend to submit to such an experiment."

Rodano scratched lightly at his fluffy hair, put it into a mild disarray, and quickly flattened it again as though anxious not to show too much pink skin.

He said, "You can't possibly be concerned over this. You tell me that miniaturization is flatly impossible—in which case, they can't miniaturize you whatever their intentions or desires."

"They'll perform *some* sort of experiment on me. They say they have miniaturization, which means they are either liars or mad, and in either case I won't have them playing games with me—either to do them pleasure, or to do you pleasure, or to do the whole American government pleasure."

"They're not mad," said Rodano, "and whatever their intentions, they know very well we'd hold them responsible for the well-being of an American citizen invited by them to their country."

"Thank you! Thank you! How would you hold them responsible? Send them a stiff note? Hold one of their citizens in reprisal? Besides, who says they'll execute me publicly in Red Square? What if they decide they don't want me to return and talk about their work on miniaturization? They'll have what they want of me—whatever that may be—and they'll decide that the American government need not benefit in their turn from any knowledge I may have gained from them. So they arrange a small accident. So sorry! So sorry! And they, of course, will pay reparations to my sorrowing family and send back a flag-draped coffin. No, thank you. I'm not the type for a suicide mission."

Rodano said, "You dramatize. You'll be a guest. You will

help them if you can and you needn't be ostentatious about learning things. We're not asking you to be a spy; we will be grateful for anything you may pick up more or less unavoidably. What's more, we will have people there who will keep an eye on you if they can. We intend to see to it that you get back safely—"

"If you can," interposed Morrison.

"If we can," agreed Rodano. "We can't promise you miracles. Would you believe us if we did?"

"Do what you will, this is not a job for me. I'm not that courageous. I'm not planning to become a pawn in some crazy chess game, with my life very possibly at stake, just because *you*—or the government—ask me to."

"You frighten yourself unnecessarily."

"Not so. Fright has its proper role; it keeps one cautious and alive. There's a trick to staying alive when you're someone like me; it's called cowardice. It may not be admirable to be a coward if someone has the muscles and mind of an ox, but it's no crime for a weakling to be one. I am not so great a coward, however, that I can be forced to take on a suicide role, simply because I fear revealing my weakness. I reveal it gladly. I am not brave enough for the role. Now, please leave."

Rodano sighed, half shrugged, half smiled, and rose slowly to his feet. "That's it, then. We can't force you to serve your country if you don't wish to."

He moved toward the door, his feet dragging a little, and then, even with his hand reaching for the doorknob, he turned and said, "Still, it upsets me a little. I'm afraid I was wrong and I *hate* to be wrong."

"Wrong? What did you do? Bet someone five bucks I'd jump at the chance to give my life for my country?"

"No, I thought you would jump at the chance to advance your career. After all, you're not getting anywhere as things are. Your ideas are not listened to; your papers are no longer published. Your appointment at your university is not likely to be renewed. Tenure? Forget it. Government grants? Never. Not after you have refused our request. After this year, you will have no income and no status. And yet you will not go to the Soviet Union, as I was sure you would as the one way of salvaging your career. Failing that, what will you do?"

"My problem."

"No. *Our* problem. The name of the game in this good new world of ours is technological advance: the prestige, the influence, the abilities that come with being able to do what other powers cannot. The game is between the two chief contestants and their respective allies; we and they, the U.S and the S.U. For all our circumspect friendship, we still compete. The counters in the game are scientists and engineers and any disgruntled counter might conceivably be used by the other side. You are a disgruntled counter, Dr. Morrison. Do you understand what I'm saying?"

"I understand that you're about to be offensive."

"We have your statement that Dr. Boranova invited you to visit the Soviet Union. Did she, really? May she not have invited you to stay in the United States and work for the Soviet Union in return for support for your ideas?"

"I was right. You are offensive."

"It's my job to be so—if I must. What if I'm right after all and you *would* jump at the chance of advancing your career. Only this is the way you intend to do it—stay here and accept Soviet money or backing in return for giving them whatever information you can."

"That is wrong. You have no evidence suggesting that and you cannot prove it."

"But I can suspect it and so can others. We will then make it our business to keep you under constant surveillance. You will not be able to do science. Your professional life will be over—entirely. —And you can avoid all that, simply by doing as we ask and going to the Soviet Union."

Morrison's lips tightened and he said, out of a dry throat, "You're threatening me in a crude attempt at blackmail and I won't capitulate. I'll take my chances. My theories on the brain's thinking center are correct and that will someday be recognized—whatever you or anyone does."

"You can't live on 'someday.' "

"Then I'll die. I may be a physical coward, but I'm not a moral one. Good-bye."

Rodano, with one last look, half-commiserating, left.

And Morrison, shaking in a spasm of fear and hopelessness, felt the spirit of defiance leak away, leaving nothing behind but despair.

CHAPTER 2

TAKEN

If asking politely is useless, take.
　　　　　　　　—Dezhnev Senior

7.

THEN I'll die, thought Morrison.

He hadn't even bothered double-locking the door after Rodano left. He sat in the chair, lost in thought, face vacant. The westering sun slanted in through the window and he didn't bother to push the contact that would opacify the glass. He simply let it slant in. In fact, he found a distant hypnotic fascination in watching the dust motes dance.

He had fled from the Russian woman in fright, but he had stood up to the American agent, stood up with the courage of —of despair.

And desperation—minus the courage—was all he felt now. What Rodano had said was, after all, true. His appointment would not be renewed for the coming year and none of the feelers he had sent out had twitched. He was poison at the academic box office and he lacked the kind of experience (or, more important, the kind of contacts) that would get him a job in the private sector, even if the quiet countervailing effort of an offended government were not taken into account.

What would he do? Go to Canada?

21

There was Janvier at McGill University. He had once expressed an interest in Morrison's ideas. Once! Morrison had not tried McGill, since he hadn't planned to leave the country. Now his plans were of no account. He might have to.

There was Latin America, where a dozen universities might welcome a northerner who could speak Spanish or Portuguese—at least after a fashion. Morrison's Spanish was poor; his Portuguese was nil.

What had he to lose? There were no family ties. Even his daughters were distant now, fading at the edges, somehow, like old photographs. He had no friends to speak of; at least none that had survived the disasters of his research.

There was his program, of course, specially designed by himself. It had been built, in the first place, by a small firm according to his specifications. Since then he had modified it endlessly on his own. Perhaps he should patent it, except that no one but he was ever likely to use it. He would take it with him, of course, wherever he went. He had it with him now, in his left inner jacket pocket, within which it bulged like an oversize wallet.

Morrison could hear the roughness of his own breathing and he realized that he was escaping from the purposeless merry-go-round of his thoughts by falling asleep over them. How could he interest others in anything, he thought bitterly, when he bored even himself?

He was aware that the sun no longer struck his window and that a gathering twilight encompassed his room. So much the better.

He became conscious of a polite buzz. It was the room telephone, he realized, but he didn't budge. Morrison let his eyes remain closed. It was probably this man, this Rodano, calling to make a final try. Let him ring.

Sleep closed in and Morrison's head lolled to one side in so uncomfortable a position that he didn't stay asleep long.

It was perhaps fifteen minutes later that he started awake. The sky was still blue, but the twilight in his room had darkened and he thought, with some guilt, that he had missed all the papers given in the afternoon. And then, rebelliously, he thought: Good! Why should I want to hear them?

Rebellion grew. What was he doing at the convention anyway? In three days he had not heard one paper that had interested him, nor had he met anyone who could do his sinking career one bit of good. What would he do the remaining three days except try to avoid the two people he had met whom he desperately did not want to meet again—Boranova and Rodano.

He was hungry. He hadn't had a proper lunch and it was almost dinnertime. The trouble was that he was in no mood to eat alone in the hotel's plush restaurant and in less of a mood to pay its inflated prices. The thought of waiting in line for a stool at the coffee shop was even less appetizing.

That decided everything. He'd had enough. He might as well check out and walk to the train station. (It was not a long walk and the cool evening air would, perhaps, help clear the miseries out of his mind.) It would take him little more than five minutes to pack; he'd be on his way in ten.

He went about the task grimly. At least he would save half the hotel bill and he would get away from a place that, he was convinced, would bring him only misery if he stayed.

He was quite right, of course, but no prescient bell in his mind rang to inform him that he had already stayed too long.

8.

AFTER quickly checking out at the desk downstairs, Morrison stepped out of the large glass doors of the hotel, glad to be free, but still ill at ease. He had carefully investigated the lobby to make sure that neither Boranova nor Rodano was in sight and now he looked up and down the line of taxis and studied the knots of people moving in and out of the hotel.

All clear—it seemed.

All clear, except for an angry government, nothing accomplished, and endless trouble ahead. McGill University seemed more attractive every moment—if he could get in.

He swung down the sidewalk in the darkening evening toward the train station, which was just too far away to be in sight. He would get home, he calculated, well past midnight and he would have no chance at all of sleeping on the train. He had a book of crossword puzzles that might occupy him— if the light were good enough. Or—

Morrison wheeled around at the sound of his name. He did this automatically, though by rights, under the conditions that prevailed, he should have hurried onward. There was no one here he wanted to speak to.

"Al! Al Morrison! Good heavens!" The voice was high-pitched and Morrison didn't recognize it.

Nor did he recognize the face. It was round, middle-aged, smooth-shaven, and decorated with steel-framed glasses. The person it belonged to was well-dressed.

Morrison at once felt the usual agony of trying to remember a person who clearly remembered him and who behaved as though they were good friends. His mouth fell open with the effort of riffling through his mind's card catalog.

The other man seemed to be aware of what was troubling Morrison and it didn't seem to bother him. He said, "You don't remember me, I see. No reason you should. I'm Charlie Norbert. We met at a Gordon Research Conference—oh, years ago. You were questioning one of the speakers on brain function and did a good job. Very incisive. So it's no wonder I remember you, you see."

"Ah yes," mumbled Morrison, trying to remember when he had last been at a Gordon Research Conference. About seven years ago, wasn't it? "That's very flattering of you."

"We had a long talk about it that evening, Dr. Morrison. *I* remember because I was so impressed by you. No reason for you to remember, though. There's nothing impressive about me. Listen, I came across your name on the list of attendees. Your middle name, Jonas, brought you right back. I wanted to talk to you. I called your room about half an hour ago, but there was no answer."

Norbert seemed to be aware of Morrison's suitcase for the first time and said in obvious dismay, "Are you leaving?"

"Actually, I'm trying to catch a train. Sorry."

"Please give me a few minutes. I've been reading about your—notions."

Morrison stepped back a little. Even expressed interest in his ideas was not enough at the moment. Besides, the other's after-shave lotion was strong and invaded his personal space, as did the man himself. Nothing the other said brought back any memory of him.

Morrison said, "I'm sorry, but if you've been reading about my notions, you're probably the only one. I hope you don't mind, but—"

"But I *do* mind." Norbert's face grew serious. "It strikes me the field isn't properly appreciative of you."

"That fact struck me a long time ago, Mr. Norbert."

"Call me Charlie. We were on a first-name basis long ago. —You don't have to go unappreciated, you know?"

"There's no compulsion about it. I just am and that's it. Well—" Morrison turned as if to leave.

"Wait, Al. What if I told you I could get you a new job with people who are sympathetic to your way of thinking?"

Morrison paused again. "I would say you were dreaming."

"I'm not. Al, listen to me—boy, am I glad I bumped into you—I want to introduce you to someone. Look, we're starting a new company, Genetic Mentalics. We've got lots of money behind us and big plans. The trick is to improve the human mind by means of genetic engineering. We've been improving computers every year, so why not our personal computer as well?" He tapped his forehead earnestly. "Where is he? I left him in the car when I saw you walk out of the hotel. You know, you haven't changed much in the years since I last saw you."

Morrison was untouched by that. "Does this new company want me?"

"Of course it wants you. We want to change the mind, make it more intelligent, more creative. But what is it we change in order to accomplish that? You can tell us."

"I'm afraid I haven't gotten that far."

"We don't expect offhand answers. We simply want you to work toward it. —Listen, whatever your salary is now, we'll double it. You just tell us your present figure and we'll go to the small trouble of multiplying it by two. Fair enough? And you'll be your own boss."

Morrison frowned. "This is the first time I've ever met Santa Claus in a business suit. Smooth-shaven, too. What's the gag?"

"No gag. —Where is he? —Ah, he moved the car to get it out of the line of traffic. —Look, he's my boss, Craig Levinson. We're not doing you a favor, Al. You'll be doing us a favor. Come with me."

Morrison hesitated only momentarily. It's always darkest before the dawn. When you're down, there's no direction but up. Lightning does strike sometimes. —He was suddenly full of old saws.

He let himself be led by the other, hanging back only slightly.

Norbert waved and called out, "I found him! This is the fellow I told you about. Al Morrison. He's the one we need."

A grave middle-aged face looked out from behind the steering wheel of a late-model automobile, whose color was something uncertain in the gathering darkness. The face smiled, teeth gleaming whitely, and the voice that belonged to it said, "Great!"

The trunk door lifted upward as they approached and Charlie Norbert took Morrison's suitcase. "Here, let me unload you." He swung it into the trunk and closed the door.

"Wait," said Morrison, rather surprised.

"Don't worry, Al. If you miss this train, there's another. If you want, we'll hire a limousine to take you home—eventually. Get in."

"Into the car?"

"Certainly." The back door had swung open invitingly.

"Where will we be going?"

"Look," said Norbert, his voice dropping half an octave and getting much softer. "Let's not waste time. Get in."

Morrison felt something hard against his side and twisted in order to see what it was.

He felt it—whatever it was—push against him. Norbert's voice was a whisper now. "Let's be very quiet, Al. Let's not make a fuss."

Morrison got into the car and was suddenly very frightened. He knew that Norbert was holding a gun.

9.

MORRISON pushed himself across the back seat, wondering if he could reach the other door and get out again. Even if Norbert had a gun, would he want to use it in a hotel parking lot with a hundred people within thirty meters? After all, even if the gun were silenced, his sudden collapse would surely draw attention.

The possibility vanished quickly, however, when a third man got into the other door, a large one who grunted as he bent himself into the car and who looked at Morrison, if not malevolently, then certainly with an expression that was free of any trace of friendship.

Morrison found himself squeezed between a man on either side and was incapable of stirring. The car moved forward smoothly and picked up speed once it moved onto the highway.

Morrison said in a choked voice, "What is this all about? Where are we going? What are you going to do?"

Norbert's voice, without the falsetto and without the synthetic bonhomie, was grim. "No need to worry, Dr. Morrison. We have no intention of harming you. We just want you with us."

"I was with you back there." (He tried to point "back there," but the man on his right leaned against him and he could not free his right hand to do so.)

"But we want you to be with us—somewhere else."

Morrison tried to sound threatening. "See here, you're kidnapping me. That's a serious offense."

"No, Dr. Morrison, let's not call it kidnapping. Let's call it being friendly in a rather forcible way."

"Whatever you call it, this is illegal. Or are you the police? If so, identify yourself and tell me what I've done and what this is all about."

"We are not charging you with anything. I told you. We just want you with us. I'd advise you to keep quiet, Doctor, and remain calm. It will be better for you."

"I can't remain calm if I don't know what's going on."

"Force yourself," said Norbert unsympathetically.

Morrison couldn't think of anything further to say that would help matters and, without actually becoming calm, fell silent.

The stars were out now. The night was as clear as the day had been. The automobile moved through traffic consisting of a thousand cars, each of which had someone behind the wheel who was going quietly about his or her ordinary business without any awareness that in a nearby car a crime was being committed.

Morrison's heart continued working overtime and his lips trembled. He couldn't help but be nervous. They said they meant him no harm, but how far could he trust them? So far, everything that this man on his left had told him had been a lie.

He tried to be calm, but to what organ of his body did he speak in order to achieve calmness? He closed his eyes and forced himself to breathe deeply and slowly—and to think rationally. He was a scientist. He *had* to think rationally.

These must be Rodano's colleagues. They were taking him to headquarters, where the pressure to force him to undertake the mission would be increased. However, they couldn't succeed. He was an American and that meant he could be treated only according to certain established rules, certain legal procedures, and certain customary modes of action. There could be nothing arbitrary, nothing improvised.

He drew another deep breath. He merely had to keep saying no and they would be helpless.

There was a small lurch and his eyes flew open.

The car had turned off the highway onto a narrow dirt road.

Automatically, he said, "Where are we going?"

There was no answer.

The automobile bumped along for a considerable distance and then turned into a field, obscure and dark. In the glow of the car's headlights, Morrison made out a helicopter, its rotors turning slowly and its motor making only the slightest purr.

It was one of the new kind, its sound waves suppressed, its smooth surface absorbing, rather than reflecting, radar beams. Its popular name was the "hushicopter."

Morrison's heart sank. If they were using a hushicopter, which were extremely expensive and quite rare, then he was being treated as no ordinary prey. He was being treated as a big fish.

But I'm *not* a big fish, he thought desperately.

The automobile stopped and the headlights went out. There was still the faint purr and a few dim violet lights, hardly visible, marked the spot where the hushicopter sat.

The large man at Morrison's right threw open the car door and, again with a grunt, lowered his head and forced his way out. His large hand reached in for Morrison.

Morrison tried to shrink away. "Where are you taking me?"

The large man seized his upper arm. "Come out. Enough talking."

Morrison felt himself half lifted, half pulled out of the car.

His shoulder hurt as it might be expected to do, considering that it had been nearly yanked out of its socket.

But he disregarded the pain. It was the first time he had heard the large man speak. The words were in English, but the accent was thickly Russian.

Morrison felt cold. These were not Americans who had him.

10.

MORRISON had entered the hushicopter—though that is not an accurate description of what took place. To enter implies a voluntary action and he had been much more nearly pushed into the vehicle.

It had pulsed its way through the darkness as he sat between the same two men between whom he had sat in the car. It was almost as though nothing had changed, although the whisper of the rotors was distinctly more hypnotic than the purr of the automobile engine had been.

After an hour—or possibly less—they came out of the darkness of the air and drifted downward toward the darkness of the ocean. Morrison could tell it was the ocean because he could smell it, was vaguely aware of the fog of droplets in the air, and because he could make out, very dimly, the dark bulk of a ship—dark on dark.

How could the hushicopter make its way out to the ocean and pinpoint a ship?—the right ship, he was sure. Even in his half-stupor of despair, Morrison's mind could not help searching for solutions. Undoubtedly, the hushicopter pilot had followed a shielded and pseudorandomized radio beam. The beam seemed random but, given the key, it could be found to have order and its source could be identified. Properly done, the pseudorandomness could not be penetrated even by quite an advanced computer.

Nor was the ship more than a temporary stopping place. He was allowed to use the head, given time for a hurried meal of bread and thick soup (which he found most welcome), and was then ushered—with the unceremonious hustle he had begun to accept as a fact of life—into a medium-sized airplane. It was a ten-seater (he counted automatically), but except for the two pilots and, sitting in the rear, the two men who had been on either side of him in the car and in the hushicopter, he was alone in the plane.

Morrison looked back at his guards, whom he just made out in the very dim light that filled the plane's interior. There was enough room in the plane so that they were not forced to hem him in. Nor did they need to do so out of fear that he might break and run for it. Here, he could break out only onto the deck of the ship. Once the plane took off, he could break out only into the open air with nothing beneath him but water of indefinite depth.

He wondered numbly why they were not taking off and then the door opened to admit another passenger. Despite the dimness, he recognized her at once.

He had met her for the first time only twelve hours before, but how could he have progressed from that first moment of meeting to the present moment in only twelve hours?

Boranova sat down in the seat next to his and said in a low voice, "I am sorry, Dr. Morrison." She was speaking in Russian.

And, as though that were the signal, the sound of the airplane's engines deepened and he felt himself pressed against his seat as the plane moved steeply upward.

Morrison stared at Natalya Boranova, trying to collect his thoughts. Dimly, he felt a desire to say something to her in a suave, imperturbable way, but there was no chance of that.

His voice was a creak and even after he cleared his throat, all he could say was "I've been kidnapped."

"That could not be helped, Dr. Morrison. I regret this. I really do. —I have my duty, you understand. I had to bring you back by persuasion if I could. Otherwise—" She let the last word hang.

"But you can't behave in this fashion. This is not the twentieth century." He choked a little in his earnest attempt to stifle his sense of indignation to the point where he could speak sensibly. "I am not a recluse. I am not a derelict. I will be missed and American intelligence is perfectly aware that we spoke and they know that you wanted me to come to the Soviet Union. They will know I have been kidnapped—they may know it already—and your government will find itself in the middle of a kind of international incident it will want no part of."

"Not so," said Boranova earnestly, her dark eyes gazing

levelly into his. "Not so. Of course your people know what has happened, but they have no objections. Dr. Morrison, the Soviet Union's intelligence operations are marked both by advanced technology and by over a century of close study of American psychology. I have no doubt that American intelligence is just as advanced. It is this equality of expertise, which is shared by several of the other geographical units of the planet, that helps to keep us in cooperation. Each of us is firmly convinced that no one else is far ahead on a road of its own."

"I don't know what you're driving at," said Morrison. The plane was arrowing through the night, speeding toward the eastern dawn.

"What concerns American intelligence most right now is our attempt at miniaturization."

"Attempt!" Morrison said with a note of sardonic amusement.

"Successful attempt. —The Americans don't know that it is successful. They don't know if the miniaturization project may not be a mask behind which something altogether different is going on. They know we're doing something. I'm sure they have a detailed map of the area in the Soviet Union where the experiments are proceeding—every building, every truck convoy. They undoubtedly have agents who are doing their best to penetrate the project.

"Naturally, we're doing our best to counter all this. We are not indignant. We know a great deal about the American experiments in antigravity and it would be naïve to take the attitude that we can probe and that the Americans can't; that we can have our successes, but the American mustn't."

Morrison rubbed his eyes. Boranova's quiet, even voice was making him realize that his ordinary bedtime was past and that he was sleepy. He said, "What has this to do with the fact that my country will bitterly resent my kidnapping?"

"Listen to me, Dr. Morrison. Understand me. Why should they? We need you, but they can't be certain why. They have no reason to suppose there is anything of value in your neurophysical notions. They must think we are following a false trail and will get nothing out of you, but they can have no objection to getting an American into the miniaturization project. If this American finds out what it is all about, the information will prove valuable to them. —Don't you think they might reason in this fashion, Dr. Morrison?"

"I don't know how they would reason," said Morrison carefully. "It is not a matter of interest to me."

"But you spoke to a Francis Rodano after you left me so suddenly. —You see, we know even that. Would you care to tell me that he did *not* suggest that you play along with us and go to the Soviet Union in order to find out what you might find out?"

"You mean he wants me to play the spy?"

"Doesn't he? Didn't he make that suggestion?"

Again Morrison ignored the question. He said, "And since you are convinced I am to be a spy, you will have me executed after I do whatever it is you want me to do. Isn't that what happens to spies?"

"You've been viewing too many old-fashioned movies, Dr. Morrison. In the first place, we will see to it that you don't find out anything important—anything at all. In the second place, spies are too valuable a commodity to destroy. They are useful as trading units for any agents of ours that may be in American hands—or in foreign hands generally. I believe that the United States takes much the same attitude."

Morrison said, "To begin with, then, I am not a spy, madame. I am not going to be a spy. I know nothing about American intelligence operations. Also, I'm not going to do anything for you."

"I'm not at all sure about that, Dr. Morrison. I think you'll decide to work with us."

"What do you have in mind? Will you starve me till I agree? Beat me? Keep me in solitary confinement? Put me in a work camp?"

Boranova frowned and shook her head slowly in what seemed to be genuine shock. "Really, Doctor, what are these things you suggest? Are we back in the days when you were loudly proclaiming us to be an evil empire and inventing horror stories about us? I don't say that we might not be tempted to use strong measures if you intransigently refuse. Necessity drives sometimes, you know. —But we won't have to. I'm convinced of that."

"What convinces you?" Morrison asked wearily.

"You're a scientist. You're a brave man."

"I? Brave? Lady, lady, what do you know about me?"

"That you have a peculiar viewpoint. That you have upheld it all this time. That you have watched your career go downhill. That you have convinced nobody. And that, despite all this, you cling to your view and do not budge from what you are certain is right. Is not this the act of a brave man?"

Morrison nodded. "Yes. Yes. It is a kind of bravery. Still, there are a thousand crackpots in the history of science who clung all their lives to some ridiculous view against logic, against evidence, against their own self-interest. I may be just another one of them."

"In that case, you might be wrong, but you would still be brave. Do you think bravery is entirely a matter of physical daring?"

"I know it is not. There are all kinds of bravery and perhaps," he said bitterly, "every one of those kinds of bravery is a mark of insanity or, at any rate, folly."

"Surely you do not consider yourself a coward?"

"Why not? In some ways, I flatter myself by saying that I am sane."

"But mad in your stubborn views concerning neurophysics?"

"I would not be surprised."

"But surely you think your views are correct."

"Certainly, Dr. Boranova. That would be part of my madness, would it not?"

Boranova shook her head. "You are not a serious man. I've said that before. My countryman Shapirov thinks you're right—or, if not right, at least a genius."

"Next best thing, certainly. Part of his madness, too."

"Shapirov's opinion is very special."

"To you, I'm sure. —Look, lady, I am tired. I am so groggy, I don't know what I'm saying. I'm not sure all this is real. I hope it isn't. Let me just—just rest a little."

Boranova sighed and a look of concern entered her eyes. "Yes, of course, my poor friend. We wish you no harm. Please believe that."

Morrison let his head bow down on his chest. His eyes closed. Dimly, he felt himself pushed gently to one side and a pillow placed under his head.

Time passed. A dreamless time.

When he opened his eyes, he was still on the plane. There

were no lights, but he knew without any doubt whatever that he was still on the plane.

He said, "Dr. Boranova?"

She replied instantly, "Yes, Dr. Morrison?"

"We're not being pursued?"

"Not at all. There are several of our own planes flying distant interference, but they have had nothing to do. Come, my friend, we want you and your government wants us to have you."

"And you still insist that you have miniaturization? That it is not madness? Or a hoax?"

"You will see for yourself. And you will see what a wonder it is, so that you will *want* to be part of it. You will *demand* to be part of it."

"And what will you be doing with it," asked Morrison thoughtfully, "assuming this is not an elaborate joke you are playing on me? Do you plan to make a weapon of it? Transport an army in a plane like this? Infiltrate each land with an invisible host? That sort of thing?"

"How revolting!" She cleared her throat as though she were tempted to spit with disgust. "Have we not enough land? Enough people? Enough resources? Have we not our large share of space? Are there not more important things to do with miniaturization? Can it be that you are so twisted and distorted that you do not see what it will mean as a research tool? Imagine the study of living systems that it will make possible; the study of crystal chemistry and solid-state systems; the construction of ultraminiaturized computers and devices of all sorts. Think further of what we might learn of physics if we can alter Planck's constant to suit ourselves. What might we not learn of cosmology?"

Morrison struggled to sit upright. He was still woozy, but there was an incipient dawn outside the plane windows and he could see Boranova very dimly.

He said, "Is that what you wish to do with it, then? Noble scientific endeavors?"

"What would your government do with it if you had it? Try to achieve a sudden military superiority and restore the bad old days?"

"No. Of course not."

"So that only you are noble and only we are terribly evil? Do you honestly believe that? —It may be, of course, that if miniaturization becomes sufficiently successful, the Soviet Union may achieve a lead in the development of a space-centered society. Think of transporting miniaturized material from one world to another, of sending a million colonists in a spaceship that would house only two or three human beings of normal size. Space will acquire a Soviet coloring, a Soviet tinge—not because the Soviet people will dominate and be masters, but because Soviet thought will have won in the battle of ideas. And what is wrong with that?"

Morrison shook his head in the dimness. "Then I certainly won't help you. Why should you expect me to? I won't fasten Soviet thought on the Universe. I prefer American thought and tradition."

"You think you do and I don't blame you for it. But we will persuade you. You will see."

"You won't."

Boranova said, "My dear friend Albert—if I may call you that. I have said that we will be admired for our progress. Do you think you will be immune? —But let us leave such discussions for another time."

She pointed out the plane window at the gray sea beneath, which was just becoming visible.

"We are now over the Mediterranean," she said, "and soon we will be over the Black Sea and then across the Volga to Malenkigrad—Smalltown, in English, eh?—and the sun will have risen when we land. That will be symbolic. A new day. New light. I predict you will be eager to help us establish this new day and I would not be surprised if you never wish to leave the Soviet Union again."

"Without your forcing me to stay?"

"We will fly you home freely if you ask us to—once you have helped us."

"I won't help you."

"You will."

"And I demand *now* that I be returned."

"Now doesn't count," said Boranova cheerfully.

And they flew the last several hundred kilometers to Malenkigrad.

CHAPTER 3

MALENKIGRAD

*A pawn is the most important piece
on the chessboard—to a pawn.*
—*Dezhnev Senior*

11.

FRANCIS Rodano was at his office early the next morning, which was Monday and the beginning of the week. That he had worked on Sunday was common enough not to surprise him. That he had slept at all during the night just completed did.

When he arrived, half an hour before the official start of the day, Jonathan Winthrop was already there. That did not surprise Rodano, either.

Winthrop walked into Rodano's office within two minutes of the latter's arrival. He leaned against the wall, the palms of his large hands hugging his elbows, his left leg crossing his right, so that the toe of his left shoe was digging into the carpet.

"You look worn-out, Frank," he said, his eyebrows hunching low over his dark eyes.

Rodano looked up at the other's shock of coarse gray hair, which routinely deprived him of any claim of his own to splendor of appearance, and said, "I feel worn-out, but I was hoping it didn't show." Rodano was very aware of having

36

gone through the morning's rituals thoroughly and carefully and of having dressed with considerable judgment.

"It shows, though. Your face is the mirror of your soul. Some agent in the field you'd have made."

Rodano said, "We're not all made for the field."

"I know. And we're not all made for desk work, either." Winthrop rubbed his bulbous nose as though he were anxious to file it down to normal size. "I take it you're worried about your scientist, what's his name?"

"His name is Albert Jonas Morrison," said Rodano wearily. There was this pretense at the Department of not knowing Morrison's name, as though everyone were anxious to emphasize that the project wasn't theirs.

"Okay. I have no objection to your mentioning his name. I take it you're worried about him."

"Yes, I'm worried about him, along with a lot of other things. I wish I could see things more clearly."

"Who doesn't?" Winthrop sat down. "Look, there's no use worrying. You've handled this from the start, and I've been willing to let you do so because you're a good man. I'm perfectly satisfied you've done all you could to make this work because one thing about you is that you understand the Russkies."

Rodano winced. "Don't call them that. You've been watching too many twentieth-century movies. They're not all Russians, any more than we're all Anglo-Saxons. They're Soviets. If you want to understand them, try to understand how they think of themselves."

"Sure. Anything you say. Have you figured out what's so important about your scientist?"

"Nothing, as far as I know. No one takes him seriously except the Soviets."

"Do you think the Soviets know something we don't?"

"A few things, I'm sure, but I haven't any notion of what they see in Morrison. It's not the Soviets, either. It's one Soviet scientist—a theoretical physicist named Shapirov. It's possible that he's the guy who worked out the method of miniaturization—if the method has really been worked out at all. Scientists outside the Soviet Union are ambivalent about Shapirov. He's erratic and, to put it kindly, eccentric. The Soviets are all gung-ho on him, however, and he's all gung-ho on Morrison, though that may just be another sign of his eccentricity. Then the interest in Morrison recently graduated from curiosity to desperation."

"Ah? And how do you know that, Frank?"

"Partly from contacts inside the Soviet Union."

"Ashby?"

"Partly."

"Good agent."

"At it too long. Needs to be replaced."

"I don't know. Let's not retire a winner."

"In any case," said Rodano, unwilling to fight the point, "there was a sudden multiplication of interest in Morrison, on whom I'd been keeping tabs for a couple of years."

"This Shapirov, I suppose, had another brainstorm about Morrison and persuaded the Russ—Soviets they needed him."

"Perhaps, but the funny thing is that Shapirov seems to have dropped out of the news recently."

"Out of favor?"

"No sign of that."

"Could be, Frank. If he's been feeding the Soviets a line of garbage about miniaturization and they've caught on to it, I wouldn't want to be in his shoes. These may be the good new days, but the Soviets have never learned to have a sense of humor about being made to look or feel foolish."

"It could be that he's gone underground because the miniaturization project is heating up. And that could also explain the sudden desperation about Morrison."

"What does he know about miniaturization?"

"Only that he's sure it's impossible."

"It makes no sense, does it?"

Rodano said carefully, "That's why we let him be taken. There's always the hope it will shake up the pieces and that they may then come together in a new way that will begin to make sense."

Winthrop looked at his watch. "He should be there by now. Malenkigrad. What a name! No news of any plane crash last night anywhere in the world, so I guess he's there."

"Yes—and just the wrong person to send, too, except he was the one that the Soviets wanted."

"Why is he wrong? Is he shaky ideologically?"

"I doubt that he has an ideology. He's a zero. All last night I've been thinking that it's all a mistake. He lacks guts and he's not very bright, except in an academic sense. I don't think he can possibly think on his feet—if he ever has to. He's not going to be smart enough to find out anything. I suspect he'll be in one long panic from beginning to end and I've been thinking for hours now that we'll never see him again. They'll imprison him—or kill him—and I've sent him there."

"That's just middle-of-the-night blues, Frank. No matter how dumb he is, he'll be able to tell us whether he watched a demonstration of miniaturization, for instance, or what it was they did to him. He doesn't have to be a shrewd observer. He need only tell us what happened and *we* will do the necessary thinking."

"But, Jon, we may never see him again."

Winthrop placed his hand on Rodano's shoulder. "Don't begin by assuming disaster. I'll see that Ashby gets the word. If something can be done, it will be done and I'm sure the Russ—Soviets will hit a sane moment and let him go if we put on enough quiet pressure when the time comes. Don't make yourself sick over it. It's a move in a complex game and if it doesn't work, it doesn't work. There are a thousand other moves on the board."

12.

MORRISON felt haggard. He had slept through much of Monday, hoping it would rid him of the worst of his jet lag. He had eaten gratefully of the food that had been brought in toward evening, had partaken even more gratefully of a shower. Fresh clothing was given him that fit rather indifferently—but what of that? And he had spent Monday night alternately sleeping and reading.

—And brooding.

The more he thought of it, the more convinced he was that Natalya Boranova was correct in her estimate that he was here only because the United States was satisfied to have him here. Rodano had urged him to go, had vaguely threatened him with further career troubles (how much deeper in trouble could he possibly get?) if he did not go. Why, then, should they object to his having been taken? They might object on principle or feel there was the danger of setting an undesirable precedent, but apparently their own eagerness to have him go had overruled that.

What, then, would be the point in demanding to be taken to the nearest American consul or in making wild threats of American retaliation?

As a matter of fact, now that the deed had been done with American connivance—surely with American connivance—it would be impossible for the United States to take open action on his behalf or express any indignation whatever. Questions would inevitably arise as to how the Soviets had managed to spirit him off and there would be no answer other than American stupidity or American connivance. And surely the United States would not want to have the world come to either conclusion.

Of course, he could see why this had been done. It was as Rodano had explained. The American government wanted information and he was in an ideal position to get it for them.

Ideal? In what way? The Soviets would not be fools enough to let him get any information they didn't want him to have and if they thought that the information he managed to get (or couldn't avoid getting) was too much, they would not be fools enough to let him go.

The more he thought of that, the more he felt that, dead or alive, he would never see the United States again and that the American intelligence community would shrug its collective shoulders and write it all off as an unavoidable miss— nothing gained but, then again, nothing much lost.

Morrison assessed himself—

Albert Jonas Morrison, Ph.D., assistant professor of neurophysics, originator of a theory of thought that remained unaccepted and all but ignored; failed husband, failed father, failed scientist, and now failed pawn. Nothing much lost.

In the depth of the night, in a hotel room in a town he didn't even know the location of, in a nation that for over a century had seemed the natural enemy of his own, however much a spirit of reluctant and suspicious cooperation might rule in the last few decades, Morrison found himself weeping out of self-pity and out of sheer childish helplessness—out of a feeling of utter humiliation that no one should think him worth struggling for or even wasting regret over.

And yet—and here a small spark of pride managed to surface—the Soviets had wanted him. They had gone to considerable trouble to get him. When persuasion had failed, they had not hesitated to use force. They couldn't possibly have been *certain* that the United States would studiously look the other way. They had risked an international incident, however slightly, to get him.

And they were going to considerable trouble to keep him safe now that they had him. He was here alone, but the windows, he noted, had bars on them. The door was not locked, but when, earlier, he had opened it, two uniformed and armed men looked up from where they had been lounging against the opposite wall and asked him if he were in need of anything. He didn't like being in prison, but it was a measure, of sorts, of his value—at least here.

How long would this last? Even though they might be under the impression that his theory of thought was correct, Morrison himself had to admit that it remained a fact that all the evidence he had gathered was circumstantial and terribly indirect—and that no one had been able to confirm his most useful findings. What would happen if the Soviets found that they, too, could not confirm them or if, on closer consideration, they found it all too gaseous, too vaporous, too atmospheric to trouble with.

Boranova had said Shapirov had thought highly of Morrison's suggestions, but Shapirov was a notorious wild man who changed his mind daily.

And if Shapirov shrugged and turned away, what would the Soviets do? If their American trophy were of no use to them, would they return him contemptuously to the United States (one more humiliation, in a way) or hide their own folly in taking him, by imprisoning him indefinitely—or worse.

In fact, it had been some Soviet functionary, some specific person, who must have decided to kidnap him and risk an incident and if the whole thing turned sour, what would that functionary do to save his own neck—undoubtedly at the expense of Morrison's?

By dawn on Tuesday, when Morrison had been in the Soviet Union for a full day, he had convinced himself that every path into the future, every alternative route that could possibly be taken, would end in disaster for him. He watched the day break, but his spirits remained in deepest night.

13.

THERE was a brusque knock at his door at 8 A.M. He opened it a crack and the soldier on the other side pushed it open farther, as though to indicate who it was who controlled the door.

The soldier said, more loudly than necessary, "Madame Boranova will be here in half an hour to take you to breakfast. Be ready."

While he dressed hurriedly and made use of an electric razor of rather ancient design by American standards, he wondered why on Earth he had been faintly astonished at hearing the soldier speak of *Madame* Boranova. The archaic "comrade" had long passed out of use.

It made him feel irritable and foolish, too, since of what value was it to brood over tiny things in the midst of the vast morass in which he found himself? —Except that was what people did, he knew.

Boranova was ten minutes late. She knocked more gently than the soldier had and when she entered said, "How do you feel, Dr. Morrison?"

"I feel kidnapped," he said stiffly.

"Aside from that. Have you had enough sleep?"

"I may have. I can't tell. Frankly, madame, I'm in no mood to tell. What do you want of me?"

"At the moment, nothing but to take you to breakfast. And please, Dr. Morrison, do believe that I am as much under compulsion as you are. I assure you that I would rather, at this moment, be with my little Aleksandr. I have neglected him sadly in recent months and Nikolai is not pleased at my absence, either. But when he married me, he knew I had a career, as I keep telling him."

"As far as I'm concerned, you are free to send me back to my own country and spend all your time with Aleksandr and Nikolai."

"Ah, if that could be so—but it cannot. So come, let us go to breakfast. We could eat here, but you would feel imprisoned. Let us eat in the dining room and you will feel better."

"Will I? Those two soldiers outside will follow us, won't they?"

"Regulations, Dr. Morrison. This is a high-security zone. They must guard you until someone in charge is convinced that it is safe not to guard you—and it would be difficult to convince them of that. It is their job not to be convinced."

"I'll bet," said Morrison, shrugging himself into the jacket they had given him, which was rather tight under the armpits.

"They will in no way interfere with us, however."

"But if I suddenly break away or even just move in an unauthorized direction, I assume they will shoot me dead."

"No, that would be bad for them. You are valuable alive, not dead. They would pursue you and, eventually, seize you. —But then, I'm sure you understand that you must do nothing that would be uselessly troublesome."

Morrison frowned, making little effort to hide his anger. "When do I get my own baggage back? My own clothes?"

"In time. The first order of business is to eat."

The dining room, which they reached by an elevator and a rather long walk along a deserted corridor, was not very large. It contained a dozen tables, each one seating six, and it was not crowded.

Boranova and Morrison were alone at their table and no one offered to join them. The two soldiers were at a table near the door and though they each ate enough for two, they faced Morrison and their eyes never left him for more than a second or two.

There was no menu. Food was simply brought to them and Morrison found he had no quarrel over the quantity. There were hard-boiled eggs, boiled potatoes, cabbage soup, and caviar, along with thick slices of dark bread. They were not given out in individual portions, but were placed in the center of the table where each person could help himself.

Perhaps, thought Morrison, they bring enough food to feed six and, since we two are the only ones here, we should only consume a third. And after a while, he had to admit that with a full stomach he felt a little mollified. He said, "Madame Boranova—"

"Why not call me Natalya, Dr. Morrison? We are very informal here and we will be colleagues for perhaps an extended period of time. The repeated 'madames' will give me a headache. My friends even call me Natasha. It could come to that."

She smiled, but Morrison felt stubbornly indisposed to be ingratiated. He said, "Madame, when I feel friendly, I will certainly act friendly, but as a victim and an involuntary presence here, I prefer a certain formality."

Boranova sighed. She bit off a sizable chunk of bread and chewed moodily. Then, swallowing, she said, "Let it be as you wish, but please spare me the 'madames.' Let me have my professional title—and I don't mean 'academician.' Too many syllables. —But I interrupted you."

"Dr. Boranova," said Morrison, more coldly than before. "You haven't told me what it is you want of me. You mentioned miniaturization, but you know and I know that that is impossible. I think that you spoke of it merely to mislead—to mislead me and to mislead anyone overhearing us. Let us drop that, then. Surely here we have no need to play games. Tell me why I am really here. After all, eventually you must, since you apparently expect me to be of some use to you and I can't be that if I am left completely ignorant of what it is that you wish."

Boranova shook her head. "You are a hard man to convince, Dr. Morrison. I have been truthful with you from the start. The project is one of miniaturization."

"I cannot believe that."

"Why, then, are you in the city of Malenkigrad?"

"Small city? Littletown? Tinyburg?" said Morrison, feeling a pleasure in hearing his own voice sound the phrases in English. "Perhaps because it is a small city."

"As I have had periodic occasion to say, Dr. Morrison, you are not a serious man. Still, you will not be in doubt long. There are a few people you should meet. One of them should, in fact, be here by now." She looked around with an annoyed frown. "So where is he?"

Morrison said, "I notice that no one approaches us. Every once in a while, the people at the other tables look at me, but then they look away if they catch my eye."

"They have been warned," said Boranova absently. "We will not waste your time with irrelevancies and almost everyone here is an irrelevancy as far as you are concerned. But some are not. Where *is* he?" She rose. "Dr. Morrison, excuse me. I must find him. I will not be gone long."

"Is it safe to leave me?" said Morrison sardonically.

"The soldiers will remain, Dr. Morrison. Please do not

give them cause to react. Intellect is not their forte and they are trained to follow orders without the painful necessity of thinking, so they might easily hurt you."

"Don't worry. I'll be careful."

She left, moving hurriedly out the door after exchanging a few words with the soldiers as she passed.

Morrison watched her go, then glanced over the dining room morosely. Having found nothing of interest, he bent his eyes upon his clasped hands on the table and then stared at the still-sizable portions of unconsumed food before him.

"Are you all through, comrade?"

Morrison looked up sharply. He had decided "comrade" was an archaism, hadn't he?

—A woman was standing, looking at him, with one balled fist on her hip in a negligent manner. She was a reasonably plump woman in a white uniform, slightly stained. Her hair was reddish-brown, as were her eyebrows, which arched disdainfully.

"Who are you?" asked Morrison, frowning.

"My name? Valeri Paleron. My function? Hardworking serving woman, but Soviet citizen and member of the party. I brought you this food. Didn't you notice me? Am I beneath your notice, perhaps?"

Morrison cleared his throat. "I'm sorry, miss. I have other things on my mind. —But you had better leave the food. Someone else is supposed to be coming here, I think."

"Ah! And the Tsarina? She will be back, too, I suppose?"

"The Tsarina?"

"You don't think we have Tsarinas any longer in the Soviet Union? Think again, comrade. This Boranova, the granddaughter of peasants and a long line of peasants, considers herself quite a lady, I'm sure." She made a sound with her lips like a long "psh-sh-sh," redolent with contempt and a touch of herring.

Morrison shrugged. "I do not know her very well."

"You are an American, aren't you?"

Morrison said sharply, "Why do you say that?"

"Because of the way you speak Russian. With that accent, what would you be? The son of Tsar Nicholas the Tyrant?"

"What's wrong with the way I speak Russian?"

"It clashes as though you learned it in school. You can hear an American a kilometer away as soon as he says, 'A glass of vodka, please.' He is not as bad as an Englishman, of course. Him you can hear two kilometers away.''

"Well, then, I'm an American.''

"And you'll be going home someday?''

"I certainly hope so.''

The serving woman nodded her head quietly, pulled out a rag, and wiped the table thoughtfully. "I would like to visit the United States someday.''

Morrison nodded. "Why not?''

"I need a passport.''

"Of course.''

"And how does a simple, loyal serving woman get one?''

"I suppose you must apply for one.''

"Apply? If I go to a functionary and I say, 'I, Valeri Paleron, wish to visit the United States,' he will say, 'Why?' ''

"And why do you want to go?''

"To see the country. The people. The wealth. I am curious how they live. —That would not be reason enough.''

"Say something else,'' said Morrison. "Say you want to write a book about the United States as a lesson to Soviet youth.''

"Do you know how many books—''

She stiffened and began to wipe the table again, suddenly absorbed in her work.

Morrison looked up. Boranova was standing there, her eyes hard and angry. She uttered a harsh monosyllable that Morrison didn't recognize but that he could have sworn was an epithet and not a very polite one, either.

The serving woman flushed dully. Boranova made a small gesture with her hand and the woman turned and left.

Morrison noticed that a man stood behind Boranova— short, thick-necked, with narrowed eyes, large ears, and a broad-shouldered, muscular body. His hair was black, longer than usual for a Russian, and it was in wild disarray, as though he clutched at it a great deal.

Boranova made no move to introduce him. She said, "Was that woman talking to you?''

"Yes,'' said Morrison.

"She recognized you to be an American?''

"She said my accent made it obvious.''

"And she said she wants to visit the United States?''

"Yes, she did.''

"What did you say? Did you offer to help her go there?"

"I advised her to apply for a passport if she wanted to go."

"Nothing more?"

"Nothing more."

Boranova said with discontent, "You must pay no attention to her. She is an ignorant and uncultured woman. —Let me introduce to you my friend, Arkady Vissarionovich Dezhnev. This is Dr. Albert Jonas Morrison, Arkady."

Dezhnev managed a clumsy bow and said, "I have heard of you, Dr. Morrison. Academician Shapirov has spoken of you often."

Morrison said coldly, "I am flattered. —But tell me, Dr. Boranova, if that serving woman annoys you so much, it should be an easy task to have her replaced or transferred."

Dezhnev laughed harshly. "Not a chance, Comrade American—which I expect is what she called you—"

"Not actually."

"Then she would have sooner or later, had we not interrupted you. That woman, I suspect, may be an intelligence operator and is one of those who keeps a close eye on us."

"But why—?"

"Because with an operation like this, no one can be trusted entirely. When you Americans are engaged in breakthrough science, are you not kept under close observation?"

"I don't know," said Morrison stiffly. "I have never been engaged in any breakthrough science that my government has been in the least interested in. —But what I was going to ask is, why does that woman act as she does if she is an intelligence agent?"

"To be a provocateur, obviously. To say outrageous things and to see what she can trip someone else into saying."

Morrison nodded. "Well, it's your worry, not mine."

"As you say," said Dezhnev. He turned to Boranova. "Natasha, have you told him yet?"

"Please, Arkady—"

"Now come, Natasha. As my father used to say, 'If you must pull a tooth, it is mistaken kindness to pull it slowly.' Let's tell him."

"I have told him we're involved in miniaturization."

"Is that all?" said Dezhnev. He sat down, pulled his chair next to that of Morrison, and leaned toward him. Morrison, with his personal space invaded, automatically withdrew.

Dezhnev came closer still and said, "Comrade American, my friend Natasha is a romantic and she is convinced that you will want to help us for love of science. She feels that we can persuade you to do gladly what must be done. She is wrong. You will not be persuaded any more than you were persuaded to come here voluntarily."

"Arkady, you are being boorish," snapped Boranova.

"No, Natasha, I am being honest—which is sometimes the same thing. Dr. Morrison—or Albert, to avoid formality, which I hate"—he shuddered dramatically—"since you won't be persuaded and since we have no time, you will do what we want by force, as you were brought here by force."

Boranova said, "Arkady, you promised you wouldn't—"

"I do not care. I have thought since I promised and I have decided that the American must know what he faces. It will be easier for us—and it will be easier for him, too."

Morrison looked from one to another and his throat tightened so that it grew difficult to breathe. Whatever it was they planned for him, he knew he would be given no choice.

14.

MORRISON continued to be silent while Dezhnev, unconcerned, proceeded to eat his own breakfast with relish.

The dining room had more or less emptied out and the serving woman, Valeri Paleron, was carrying off the remains and was wiping down the chairs and tables.

Dezhnev caught her eye, beckoned to her, and indicated that the table was to be cleared.

Morrison said, "So I have no choice. No choice in what?"

"Hah! Has Natasha not even told you that?" replied Dezhnev.

"She told me on several occasions that I was to be involved in miniaturization problems. But I know—and you know—that there is no miniaturization problem except that of trying to turn an impossibility into fact—and I certainly can't help you in that. What I want to know is what you *really* have for me to do."

Dezhnev looked amused. "Why do you think miniaturization is impossible?"

"Because it is."

"And if I tell you that we have it?"

"Then I say show me!"

Dezhnev turned to Boranova, who drew a deep breath and nodded.

Dezhnev rose. He said, "Come. We will take you to the Grotto."

Morrison bit his lip in vexation. Small frustrations loomed large. "I do not know that Russian word you've used."

Boranova said, "We have an underground laboratory here. We call it the Grotto. It is one of our poetic words, not used in ordinary conversation. The Grotto is the site of our miniaturization project."

15.

OUTSIDE an air-jet awaited them. Morrison blinked, adjusting his eyes to the sunlight. He regarded the jet curiously. It lacked the elaboration of American models and seemed little more than a sled with small seats and with a complex engine in front. It would be absolutely useless in cold or wet weather and he wondered whether the Soviets had an enclosed version for those times. Perhaps this was just a summer runabout.

Dezhnev took the controls and Boranova directed Morrison into the seat behind Dezhnev, while she took the one to his right side. She turned to the guards and said, "Go back to the hotel and wait for us there. We will take full responsibility from this point." She handed them a printed slip of paper on which she scrawled her signature, the date, and, after consulting her wristwatch, the time.

When they arrived at Malenkigrad, Morrison discovered that it was a small town in fact, as well as in name. There were rows of houses—each two stories high—with a deadly sameness about them. The town had clearly been built for those who worked on the project—whatever it was that they masked with the fairy tale of miniaturization—and it had been built without undue expense. Each house had its own vegetable garden and the streets, although paved, had an unfinished look about them.

The little craft, riding on the jets of air pushing against the ground, blew up a small cloud of dust, which was, for the most part, left behind as they progressed smoothly forward. Morrison could see that it was not comfortable for the pedestrians they passed who, one and all, took evasive action as it approached.

Morrison felt the discomfort in full when they passed an air-jet moving in the other direction and was inundated in the dust.

Boranova looked amused. She coughed and said, "Do not be concerned. We will be vacuumed soon."

"Vacuumed?" asked Morrison, coughing also.

"Yes. Not so much for us, for we can live with a little dust, but the Grotto must be reasonably dust-free."

"So must my lungs. Wouldn't it be better to have these air-jets enclosed?"

"They promise us shipments of more elaborate models and perhaps someday they will arrive. Meanwhile, this is a new town and it is built in the steppes, where the climate is arid. That has its advantages—and its disadvantages, too. The settlers grow vegetables, as you saw, and they have some animals, too, but large-scale agriculture must wait until the community is larger and there are irrigation facilities. For now, it doesn't matter. It is miniaturization that concerns us."

Morrison shook his head. "You speak of miniaturization so often and with such a straight face, you might almost trick me into believing it."

"Believe it. You will have the demonstration Dezhnev arranged."

Dezhnev said from his seat at the controls, "And I had trouble doing so. Once again I had to speak to the Central Coordinating Committee—may what is left of their gray hairs fall out. As my father used to say, 'Apes were invented because politicians were needed.' How it is possible to sit two thousand kilometers away and make policy—"

The air-jet glided smoothly forward to the rather sharp ending of the town and to the broad, low rocky massif that suddenly loomed before them.

"The Grotto," said Boranova, "is located inside that. It gives us all the room we want, frees us from the vagaries of weather, and is impenetrable from aerial surveillance, even from spy satellites."

"Spy satellites are illegal," said Morrison indignantly.

"It is merely illegal to *call* them spy satellites," shot back Dezhnev.

The air-jet banked as it made a turn, then landed in the shadow of a rocky cleft in the body of the massif.

"All out," said Dezhnev.

He moved forward, the other two following, and a door opened in the hillside. Morrison didn't see how it was done. It didn't look like a door; rather it seemed an integral part of the rocky wall. It opened just as the cavern of the Forty Thieves had with the utterance of the words "Open Sesame."

Dezhnev stepped to one side and gestured for Morrison and Boranova to move inside. Morrison went out of the brilliant morning sunshine into a rather dimly lit chamber to which his eyes took half a minute to adapt. It was no thieves' cave but an elaborately detailed structure.

Morrison felt as though he had stepped from the Earth onto the moon. He had never been on the moon, of course, but he was familiar, as was virtually everyone on Earth, with the appearance of the underground lunar settlements. This had precisely that other-worldly air about it somehow, except, of course, that gravity was Earth-normal.

CHAPTER 4

GROTTO

*Small can be beautiful: An eagle may at
times go hungry; a pet canary, never.*
— Dezhnev Senior

16.

IN a large and well-lit washroom, Boranova and Dezhnev
began to remove their outer clothing. Morrison, alarmed at
the prospect, hesitated.

Boranova smiled. "You may keep your underclothing on,
Dr. Morrison. Just toss everything else, except your shoes,
into that bin. I presume there is nothing in your pockets.
Place your shoes at the base of the bin. By the time we leave,
it will all be cleaned and ready for use."

Morrison did as he was told, trying not to observe that
Boranova had a most opulent figure, concerning which she
seemed totally unaware. Amazing, he thought, what clothes
will obscure when not designed to reveal.

They were washing now, with lavish application of soap—
faces to the ears and arms to the elbows—then brushing savagely at their hair. Again Morrison hesitated and Boranova,
reading his mind, said, "The brushes are cleaned after each
use, Dr. Morrison. I don't know what you may have read of
us, but some of us understand hygiene."

Morrison said, "All this just to go into the Grotto? Do you go through this every time?"

"Every time. That's why no one goes in just briefly. And even when staying within, there are frequent ablutions. —You may find the next step unpleasant, Dr. Morrison. Close your eyes, take a deep breath, and hold it if you can. It will take about a minute."

Morrison followed orders and found himself strongly buffeted by a swirling wind. He staggered drunkenly and collided with one of the bins. He held on tightly. Then, as suddenly as it started, it was over.

He opened his eyes. Dezhnev and Boranova looked as though they had put on fright wigs. He felt his own hair and knew he must look the same. He reached for his brush.

"Don't bother," said Boranova. "There's more we'll have to go through."

"What was that all about?" said Morrison. He found he had to clear his throat twice before he could speak.

"I mentioned that we'd have the dust vacuumed away from us, but that's only the first stage of the cleaning process. —Through this door, please." She held it open for him.

Morrison emerged into a narrow but well-lit corridor, the walls glowing photoluminescently. He lifted his eyebrows. "Very nice."

"Saves energy," Dezhnev said, "and that's very important. —Or are you referring to the technological advancement? Americans seem to come to the Soviet Union expecting everything to be kerosene lamps." He chuckled and added, "I admit we haven't caught up with you in every respect. Our brothels are very primitive compared with yours."

"You strike back without waiting to be struck," said Morrison. "That is a sure sign of an unclear conscience. If you were anxious to demonstrate advanced technology, I could point out that it would be very simple to pave the avenue going from Malenkigrad to the Grotto and to use closed airjets. We would need less of this."

Dezhnev's face darkened, but Boranova put in sharply, "Dr. Morrison is quite right, Arkady. I don't like your feeling that it is not possible to be honest without being rude. If you cannot be both honest and polite, keep your tongue on your own side of your teeth."

Dezhnev grinned uneasily. "What have I said? Of course

the American doctor is right, but is there anything we can do when decisions are made in Moscow by idiots who save small bits of money without counting the consequences? As my old father used to say, 'The trouble with economizing is that it can be very expensive.' "

"That's true enough," said Boranova. "We could save a great deal of money, Dr. Morrison, by spending on a better road and better air-jets, but it is not always easy to persuade those who hold the purse strings. Surely you have the same trouble in America."

She was motioning even as she talked and Morrison followed her into a small chamber. As the door closed behind them, Dezhnev held out a bracelet to Morrison. "Let me tie this around your right wrist. When we hold up our arms, you hold up yours."

Morrison felt his weight lighten momentarily as the chamber floor dropped.

"An elevator," he said.

"Clever guess," said Dezhnev. Then he clapped a hand to his mouth and said in a muffled tone, "But I mustn't be rude."

They stopped smoothly and the elevator door opened.

"Identification!" came a peremptory voice.

Dezhnev and Boranova raised their hands, at which Morrison did as well. Under the purplish light that suddenly suffused the elevator, the three bracelets glittered in patterns which were not, Morrison noted, exactly alike.

They were ushered down another corridor and into a room that was both warm and damp.

"We will have to have a final scrubdown, Dr. Morrison," said Boranova. "We are accustomed to this and stripping is routine for us. It is easier—and timesaving—to do it as a group."

"If you can stand it," said Morrison grimly, "I can."

"It is unimportant," said Dezhnev. "None of us are strangers to the sight."

Dezhnev scrambled out of his underclothes, stepped over to a portion of the wall where a small red knob was glowing, and placed his right thumb immediately above it. A narrow panel in the wall slid open and revealed white garments hanging flaccidly to one side. He placed his underclothes at the bottom.

He seemed utterly unabashed about being nude. His chest and shoulders were dark with hair and there was a long-healed scar on his right buttock. Morrison wondered idly how that might have come about.

Boranova did the same as Dezhnev had done and said, "Pick a light that is on, Dr. Morrison. It will open to your thumbprint and then, when you touch it again, it will close. After that it will open only to your thumbprint, so please remember your locker number and you won't have to press every locker in order to find your own."

Morrison did as he was told.

Boranova said, "If you need to use the bathroom first, you can go there."

"I'm all right," said Morrison.

With that, the room was aswirl with a damp mist of water droplets.

"Close your eyes," called out Boranova, but it was unnecessary for her to say so. The initial sting of the water forced his eyes closed at once.

There was soap in the water or, at any rate, something that stung his eyes, tasted bitter in his mouth, and irritated his nostrils.

"Lift your arms," called out Dezhnev. "You needn't circle. It comes from all directions."

Morrison lifted his arms. He knew it came from all directions. It came from the floor, too, as he could tell by the slightly uncomfortable pressure on his scrotum.

"How long does this last?" he gasped.

"Too long," said Dezhnev, "but it is necessary."

Morrison counted to himself. At the count of 58, it seemed to him that the bitterness on his lips ceased. He squinted his eyes. Yes, the other two were still there. He continued to count and when he reached 126, the water stopped and he was bathed in uncomfortably hot and dry air.

He was panting by the time that stopped too and he realized he had been holding his breath.

"What was all that *for?*" he said, looking away uncomfortably at the sight of Boranova's large but firm breasts and finding little comfort in Dezhnev's hairy chest.

"We are dry," said Boranova. "Let's get dressed."

Morrison was eager but was almost immediately disappointed by the nature of the white clothes in the locker. They consisted of a blouse and pants of light cotton, the pants held by a cord. There was also a light cap to cover the hair and light sandals. Though the cotton was opaque, it seemed to Morrison that little or nothing was truly left to the imagination.

He said, "Is this all we wear?"

"Yes," said Boranova. "We work in a clean, quiet environment at even temperature and, with throwaway clothes, we can't expect much in the way of fashion or expense. Indeed, barring a certain understandable reluctance, we could easily work in the nude. But enough—come."

And now at last they stepped into what Morrison recognized at once as the main body of the Grotto. It stretched away before him—between and beyond ornate pillars to a distance he couldn't make out.

He could recognize none of the equipment. How could he? He was entirely a theoretician and when he worked in his own field, he used computerized devices that he had designed and modified himself. For a moment, he felt a stab of nostalgia for his laboratory at the university, for his books, for the smell of the animal cages, even for the stupid obstinacy of his colleagues.

There were people everywhere in the Grotto. There were a dozen nearby and others farther off and the impression was of the interior of a human ant hill crawling with machinery, with humanity, with purpose.

No one paid any attention to the newcomers or to each other. They went about their work in silence, their steps muffled by their sandals.

Again Boranova seemed to read Morrison's mind and when she spoke it was in a whisper. "We keep our council here. None of us knows more than it is good for him—or her —to know. There must be no leaks of significance."

"But surely they must communicate."

"When they must, they will—minimally. It reduces the pleasure of camaraderie, but it is necessary."

"This kind of compartmentalization slows progress," said Morrison.

"It's the price we pay for security," said Boranova, "so if no one talks to you, it is not a personal matter. They will have no reason to talk to you."

"They'll be curious about a stranger."

"I have seen to it that they know you are an outside expert. That is all they need to know."

Morrison frowned. "How can they expect an American to be an outside expert?"

"They don't know you're an American."

"My accent will give me away at once as it did to the serving woman."

"But you will not talk to anyone, except for those to whom I will introduce you."

"As you wish," said Morrison indifferently.

He was still looking around. Since he was here, he might as well learn what he could, even if it should turn out to be trivial. When—*if*—he returned to the United States, he would surely be asked for every detail he had observed and he might as well have something to give them.

He said in Boranova's ear, "This must be an expensive place. What fraction of the national budget is expended here?"

"It's expensive," said Boranova, admitting nothing further, "and the government labors to limit the expense."

Dezhnev said sourly, "I had to work for an hour this morning to persuade them to allow a small additional experiment for your benefit—may the Committee catch the cholera."

Morrison said, "The cholera no longer exists, even in India."

"May it be reinstated for the Committee."

Boranova said, "Arkady, if these supposedly humorous expressions of yours get back to the Committee, it will do you no good."

"I'm not afraid of those pigs, Natasha."

"I am. What will happen to next year's budget if you infuriate them?"

Morrison said, with sudden impatience, but speaking even more softly, "What concerns me is neither the Committee nor the budget, but the simple question of what it is I am doing here."

Dezhnev said, "You are here to witness a miniaturization and to be given an explanation of why we need your help. Will that satisfy you, Comrade Am—Comrade Outside Expert?"

17.

MORRISON followed the other two to something that looked like a small old-fashioned train carriage on very narrow-gauge tracks.

Boranova placed her thumb on a smooth patch and a door slid open smoothly and without noise. "Please get in, Dr. Morrison."

Morrison held back. "Where are we going?"

"To the miniaturization chamber, of course."

"By railroad? How big is this place?"

"It is large, Doctor, but not *so* large. This is a matter of security. Only certain individuals can use this device and only by using it can one penetrate into the core of the Grotto."

"Are your own people so untrustworthy?"

"We live in a complex world, Dr. Morrison. Our people are trustworthy, but we do not wish to subject large numbers to temptations they need not face. And if someone persuades one of us to go—elsewhere, as we have persuaded you, it is safer if their knowledge is limited, you see. —Please get in."

Morrison entered the compact vehicle with some difficulty. Dezhnev followed him with equal trouble, saying, "Another example of senseless cheese paring. Why so small? Because the bureaucrats spend billions of rubles on a project and they feel virtuous if they save a few hundred in odd places at the cost of making hardworking people miserable."

Boranova got into the front seat. Morrison could not see how she manipulated the controls or, for that matter, if there were controls to manipulate. It was probably controlled by a computer. The carriage began to move suddenly and Morrison felt the slight backward jar that resulted.

There was a small window at eye level on either side, but not of clear glass. Morrison could see a small section of the cavern outside in a streaky, wavy, poorly focused manner. Apparently, the windows were not meant for vision, but were merely intended to reduce what might otherwise be an unacceptably tight enclosure to those with claustrophobic tendencies.

It seemed to Morrison that the individuals he could make out through the glass paid no attention to the moving carriage. Everyone here, he thought, is well-trained. To show any interest in any procedure with which you have nothing directly to do must apparently be a sign of discourtesy—or worse.

It seemed to Morrison that they were approaching the wall of the cavern and the carriage, with another small jerk, slowed. A section of the wall slid aside and the carriage, with yet another jerk, picked up speed and moved through the opening.

It grew dark almost at once and the dim light in the carriage's ceiling did little more than change night to dusk.

They were in a narrow tunnel into which the carriage fit with apparently little room to spare, except on the left side where Morrison, peering past Dezhnev, thought he could make out another pair of rails. There must be at least two such carriages, he thought, with room to pass one another in the tunnel if both were in operation.

The tunnel was as dimly lit as the carriage and it was not straight. Either it had been carved through the hill in such a way as to follow lines of least resistance in order to save money or it was curved deliberately in some dim, atavistic search for making things more secure by making them more complicated. The darkness inside and outside the carriage might serve the same purpose.

"How long will this take—uh—" asked Morrison.

Dezhnev looked at him with (in the dimness) an unreadable expression. "You don't know how to address me, I see. I do not have an academic title, so why not call me Arkady? Everyone does here and why not? My father always said, 'What counts is the person, not the name.' "

Morrison nodded. "Very well. How long will this take, Arkady?"

"Not long, Albert," said Dezhnev cheerfully—and Morrison, having been lured into first-name informality, could not object to the return.

He surprised himself a little by finding he did not wish to object. Dezhnev, even with his father's aphorisms included, seemed to be uncomplicated, at least, and, under the circumstances, Morrison welcomed a chance of refraining from the perpetual fencing match to which Boranova seemed to subject him.

The carriage could not be moving at a speed faster than a

leisurely walk, but there was a small lurch each time it took a curve on the track. Apparently, petty economies included leaving the curves unbanked.

Then, with absolutely no warning, light flooded in and the carriage ground to a stop.

Morrison blinked as he stepped out. The room they were now in was not as large as the one they had left and there was virtually nothing in it. There were only the tracks under the carriage that made a wide arc and then led back toward the section of the wall from which they had emerged. He could see another small carriage disappearing into the opening and the wall closing behind it. The carriage in which they had arrived made a slow circuit of the arc and came to rest near the wall.

Morrison looked around. There were many doors and the ceiling was comparatively low. Without definite evidence of the fact, he felt that he was in a three-dimensional checkerboard, with numerous small rooms on several levels.

Boranova was waiting for him, seeming to observe his curiosity with a touch of disapproval. "Are you ready, Dr. Morrison?"

"No, Dr. Boranova," said Morrison. "Since I don't know where I'm going or what I'm doing, I'm not ready. However, if you will lead the way, I will follow."

"That is sufficiently ready. —This way, then. There is someone else you must meet."

They passed through one of the doors and into another small room. This one was very well-lit and had its walls lined with thick cables.

In the room was a young woman who looked up when they came in, pushing aside something, that seemed, from its appearance, to be some kind of technical report. She was quite pretty in a pale and vulnerable way. Her flaxen hair was cut short but with enough of a wave in it to keep her from looking too severe. The scanty cotton uniform she wore, which Morrison already knew to be universal within the Grotto, showed her to be attractively slim and shapely enough, though without Boranova's opulence. Her face was marred or perhaps enhanced (according to taste) by a tiny mole just under the left corner of her mouth. Her cheekbones were high, her hands thin-fingered and graceful, and her expression did not appear as though she were much given to smiling.

Morrison smiled, however. For the first time since his kidnapping, it seemed to him that there might be a lighter side to this dismal situation in which he had been unwillingly plunged.

"Good day," he said. "It's a pleasure meeting you." He tried to give his Russian an educated sound and to get rid of what the serving woman had so easily detected as his American accent.

The young woman made no direct answer but, turning to Boranova, said in a voice that was slightly husky, "Is this the American?"

"It is," said Boranova. "He is Dr. Albert Jonas Morrison, professor of neurophysics."

"Assistant professor," said Morrison deprecatorily.

Boranova ignored the correction. "And this, Dr. Morrison, is Dr. Sophia Kaliinin, who is our electromagnetics expert."

"She scarcely looks old enough," said Morrison gallantly.

The young lady did not seem amused. She said, "I look, perhaps, younger than I am. I am thirty-one years old." Morrison looked abashed and Boranova cut in quickly, "Come, we are ready to begin. Please check the circuits and set matters in motion. —And quickly."

Kaliinin hurried out.

Dezhnev looked after her with a grin. "I'm glad she doesn't seem to like Americans. It cuts out a hundred million potential competitors at least. Now if she also didn't like Russians and would come to realize that I am as Karelo-Finnish as she is."

"You Karelo-Finnish?" said Boranova, forced into a smile. "Who would believe that, you madman?"

"*She* would—if she were in the proper mood."

"This would require an impossible mood." Boranova turned to Morrison. "Please do not take Sophia's behavior personally, Dr. Morrison. Many of our citizens pass through an ultrapatriotic phase and feel it to be very Soviet to dislike Americans. It is more pose than reality. I'm sure, once we begin to work together as a team, that Sophia will let down her barriers."

"I understand completely. Things are similar in my country. As a matter of fact, at the moment, I'm not very fond of Soviets—and understandably, I think. But"—and he smiled —"I could make an exception for Dr. Kaliinin very easily."

Boranova shook her head. "American like you or Russian like Arkady, there is a peculiar masculine way of thought that transcends national boundaries and cultural differences."

Morrison was unmoved. "Not that I will be working with her—or with anyone. I have grown tired of telling you, Dr. Boranova, that I don't accept the existence of miniaturization and that I cannot and will not be of assistance to you in any way."

Dezhnev laughed. "You know, one could almost believe Albert. He speaks so seriously."

Boranova said, "Observe, Dr. Morrison. This is Katinka."

She tapped a cage which Morrison, startled, now observed for the first time. Dr. Kaliinin had rather absorbed his attention till now and even after she had left he had been idly keeping his eye on the door through which she had gone, waiting for her reappearance.

He focused on the cage of wire mesh. Katinka was, apparently, a white rabbit of moderate size and placid appearance, who was munching away at greenery with the rapt concentration of her kind.

Morrison was aware of the slight scrabbling noise she made and of the rabbit odor, which he must have noted, unconsciously, earlier and ignored.

He said, "Yes, I see her. A rabbit."

"Not just a rabbit, Doctor. She is a most unusual creature. Unique. She has made history to a far greater extent than has the catalog of war and disaster that usually is thought of by that name. If we exclude such purely incidental creatures as worms, fleas, and submicroscopic parasites, Katinka is the first living creature that has been miniaturized. In fact, she has been miniaturized on three separate occasions and would have been miniaturized dozens of times more if we had been able to afford it. She has contributed enormously to our knowledge of the miniaturization of life forms and, as you can see, her experiences have in no way adversely affected her."

Morrison said, "I do not wish to be insulting, but your bare statement that the rabbit has been miniaturized three times is not really evidence that this has indeed happened. I do not mean to cast doubt upon your integrity, but, in a case like this, I think you understand that nothing less than witnessing the fact is sufficiently convincing."

"Certainly. And it is for that reason that—at considerable expense—Katinka will now be miniaturized a fourth time."

18.

SOPHIA Kaliinin swirled back in and turned to Morrison. "Are you wearing a watch or do you have anything metallic on you?" she asked crisply.

"I have no possessions on me at all, Dr. Kaliinin. Nothing but the clothes I wear, the single pocket of which is empty. Even this identification bracelet that has been put on me seems to be of plastic."

"It is merely that there is a strong electromagnetic field and metal would interfere."

Morrison said, "Any physiological effects?"

"None. Or at least none have yet been detected."

Morrison, who was waiting for them to give up their pretense of miniaturization and wondering how long they could carry on the fraud (he was growing more censorious over the matter by the minute), said, with just a touch of malice, "Might not overexposure lead to birth defects should you ever get pregnant, Dr. Kaliinin?"

Kaliinin flushed. "I have a baby. She is perfectly normal."

"Were you exposed during pregnancy?"

"Once."

Boranova said, "Is the inquisition over, Dr. Morrison? May we begin?"

"You still maintain that you will miniaturize the rabbit?"

"Certainly."

"Then go ahead. I'm all eyes."

(How foolish of them, he thought sardonically. They would soon be claiming, of course, that something had gone wrong, but where would they go from there? What was it all about?)

Boranova said, "To begin with, Dr. Morrison, would you lift the cage?"

Morrison made no move to do so. He looked from one to the other of the three Soviets in suspicion and uncertainty.

Dezhnev said, "Go ahead. It won't hurt, Albert. You won't even get your hands dirty and, after all, hands were meant to become dirty at work."

Morrison put his hands on either side of the cage and lifted. It weighed about ten kilograms, he judged. He grunted and said, "May I put it down now?"

"Of course," said Boranova.

"Gently," said Kaliinin. "Do not disturb Katinka."

Morrison lowered it carefully. The rabbit, which had momentarily stopped feeding when the cage was lifted, sniffed the air curiously and returned tentatively to its unhurried chewing.

Boranova nodded and Sophia moved to one side of the room where a bank of controls were all but hidden by the cables. She looked over her shoulder at the cage as though estimating its position, then walked over to move it slightly. She returned to the controls and closed a switch.

A whining sound made itself heard and the cage began to glitter and shimmer as though something, all but invisible, had interposed itself between it and themselves. The shimmer extended beneath the cage, separating it from the stone-top table on which it had been resting.

Boranova said, "The cage is now enclosed in the miniaturization field. Only the objects within the field will be miniaturized."

Morrison stared and a little worm of uncertainty began to stir within him. Were they going to try some clever illusion on him and make him *think* he had witnessed miniaturization? He said, "And how exactly did you produce that so-called miniaturization field?"

"That," said Boranova, "we do not intend to tell you. I think you understand what classified information is. Go ahead, Sophia."

The whine heightened in pitch and intensified somewhat. Morrison found it unpleasant, but the others seemed to endure it stolidly. In looking at them, he had taken his eyes off the cage. Now when he looked at it again, it seemed to have grown smaller.

He frowned and bent his head so as to line up one side of the cage with the vertical line of a cable on the opposite wall. He held his head steady, but the side of the cage shrank away from the reference line. There was no mistake, the cage was distinctly smaller. He blinked his eyes in frustration.

Boranova smiled narrowly. "It is indeed shrinking, Dr. Morrison. Surely your eyes tell you so."

The whine continued—the shrinking continued. The cage was perhaps half its original linear measurement.

Morrison said, with obvious lack of conviction, "There are such things as optical illusions."

Boranova called out. "Sophia, stop the process for a moment."

The whine lowered into silence and the glitter of the miniaturization field dimmed and died. The cage sat on the table as before, a considerably smaller version than it had been. Inside was the rabbit still—a smaller rabbit, but one that was proportioned in every way as the original had been, munching on smaller leaves, with smaller pieces of carrot distributed across the floor of the cage.

Boranova said, "Do you honestly think that this is an optical illusion?"

Morrison was silent and Dezhnev said, "Come, Albert, accept the evidence of your senses. This experiment consumed considerable energy and if you remain unconvinced, our clever administrators will be annoyed with all of us for wasting money. What do you say, then?"

And Morrison, shaking his head in rueful confusion, said, "I don't know *what* to say."

Boranova said, "Would you lift the cage again, Dr. Morrison?"

Again Morrison hesitated and Boranova said, "The miniaturization field has not left it radioactive or anything like that. The touch of your unminiaturized hand will not affect it, nor will its state of miniaturization affect you. You see?" And she placed her hand, flatly and gently, on top of the cage.

Morrison's hesitation was not proof against that. Gingerly, he placed his hand on either side of the cage and lifted. He exclaimed in surprise, for it could not be much over a kilogram in mass. The cage trembled in his grip and the miniaturized rabbit, alarmed, hopped to one corner of the cage and huddled there in agitation.

Morrison put the cage down and, as nearly as he could estimate, did so in its original position, but Kaliinin walked over and made a small adjustment.

Boranova said, "What do you think, Dr. Morrison?"

"It weighs considerably less. Is there some way you pulled a switch?"

"Pulled a switch? You mean replaced the larger object with a smaller while you were watching, the smaller exactly like the larger in everything but size. Dr. Morrison, *please.*"

Morrison cleared his throat and didn't press the point. It lacked plausibility even to himself.

Boranova said, "Please notice, Dr. Morrison, that not only has the size been decreased, but the mass in proportion. The very atoms and molecules of which the cage and its contents are composed have shrunk in size and mass. Fundamentally, Planck's constant has decreased, so that nothing inside has changed relative to its own parts. To the rabbit, itself, its food, and everything within the cage seems perfectly normal. The outside world has increased in size relative to the rabbit, but, of course, it remains unaware of that."

"But the miniaturization field is gone. Why don't the cage and its contents revert to ordinary size?"

"For two reasons, Dr. Morrison. In the first place, the miniaturized state is metastable. That is one of the great fundamental discoveries that make miniaturization possible. At whatever point we stop in the process, it takes very little energy to maintain it in that state. And secondly, the miniaturization field is not entirely gone. It is merely minimized and drawn inward so that it still keeps the atmosphere within the cage from diffusing outward and normal molecules outside from diffusing inward. It also leaves the walls of the cage touchable by unminiaturized hands. —But we are not finished, Dr. Morrison. Shall we continue?"

Morrison, troubled and unable to deny the direct experience, wondered for a moment if he had somehow been drugged into a kind of supersuggestibility that would make him experience whatever he was told he was experiencing. In a choked way, he said, "You are telling me a great deal."

"Yes, we are, but only superficially. If you repeat this in America, you will probably not be believed and nothing you say will give the slightest hint as to the core of the miniaturization technique." Boranova lifted her hand and Kaliinin again threw the switch.

The whine returned and the cage began once again to shrink. It seemed to be going faster now and Boranova, as though reading Morrison's mind, said, "The further it shrinks, the less mass there is to remove and the more rapidly it shrinks further."

Morrison found himself staring, in a state of near-shock, at a cage that was a centimeter across and still shrinking.

But Boranova raised her hand again and the whine died.

"Be careful, Dr. Morrison. It weighs only a few hundred milligrams now and it is a fragile object indeed to anyone on our scale. Here. Try this."

She handed him a large magnifying glass. Morrison, without saying a word, took it and held it over the tiny cage. He might not have managed to make out what the moving object within it was if he had come upon it without prior knowledge, for his mind would not have accepted such an incredibly tiny rabbit.

He had seen it shrink, however, and he stared at it now with a mixture of confusion and fascination.

He looked up at Boranova and said, "Is this really happening?"

"Do you still suspect an optical illusion or hypnotism or—what else?"

"Drugs?"

"If it were drugs, Dr. Morrison, it would be a greater achievement than miniaturization. Look around you. Doesn't everything else look normal? It would be an unusual drug indeed that would alter your sense perception of a single object in a large room of unchanged miscellany. Come, Doctor, what you've witnessed is real."

"Make it larger," said Morrison breathlessly.

Dezhnev laughed and suppressed it in a quick choke. "If I laugh, the wind may well blow away Katinka, whereupon Natasha and Sophia will both strike me with everything else in this room. If you wish it enlarged, you will have to wait."

Boranova said, "Dezhnev is right. You see, Dr. Morrison, you have witnessed a scientific demonstration, not magic. If it were magic, I could snap my finger and the rabbit would be its normal self again in a normal cage—and then you would know you were witnessing an optical illusion. However, it takes considerable energy to decrease Planck's constant to a tiny fraction of its normal value, even over a relatively small volume of the Universe, which is why miniaturization is so expensive a technique. To enlarge Planck's constant once again must result in the production of energy equal to that which had been consumed originally, for the law of conservation of energy holds even in the process of miniaturization. We cannot deminiaturize then any faster than we can dispose of the heat produced, so that it takes considerable time to do it—much more than it took to miniaturize."

For a while, Morrison was silent. He found the explanation involving conservation of energy more convincing than the demonstration itself. Charlatans would not have been so meticulous about obeying the constraints of physics.

He said, "It seems to me, then, that your miniaturization process can scarcely be a practical device. At most it would only serve as a tool, perhaps, to broaden and expand quantum theory."

Boranova said, "Even that would be enough, but don't judge a technique by its initial phase. We can hope that we will learn how to circumvent these large energy changes, how to find methods of miniaturization and deminiaturization that will be more efficient. Does all the energy-change have to pass from electromagnetic fields into miniaturization and then into heat on deminiaturization? Might not deminiaturization be somehow inveigled into releasing energy as electromagnetic fields again. That would be easier to handle, perhaps."

"Have you repealed the second law of thermodynamics?" asked Morrison with exaggerated politeness.

"Not at all. We don't expect an impossible 100 percent conversion. If we can convert 75 percent of the deminiaturization energy into an electromagnetic field—or even only 25 percent—that would be an improvement over the present situation. However, there is hope of a technique even more subtle and far more efficient and that is where *you* come in."

Morrison's eyes widened. "I? I know nothing about this. Why pick me out for your salvation? You would have done as well with a child out of kindergarten."

"Not so. We know what we are doing. Come, Dr. Morrison, you and I shall go to my office while Sophia and Arkady begin the tedious process of restoring Katinka. I will there show you that you know quite enough to help us make miniaturization efficient and therefore a commercially practical venture. In fact, you will see quite clearly that you are the *only* person who can help us."

CHAPTER 5

COMA

Life is pleasant. Death is peaceful.
It is the transition that is troublesome.
— *Dezhnev Senior*

19.

"THIS," said Natalya Boranova, "is my own portion of the Grotto."

She sat down in a rather battered armchair that (Morrison imagined) she found perfectly comfortable, having molded it to her body over the years.

He sat down in another chair, smaller and more austere, with a satin-covered seat that was less comfortable than it looked. He glanced over the surroundings with a sharp sensation of homesickness. There were ways in which it reminded him of his own office. There was the computer outlet and the large screen. (Boranova's was far more ornate than his own—the Soviet style tended toward the curlicue and Morrison felt a momentary curiosity as to the reason and then put that aside as a trivial matter.)

There was also the same trend toward disorder in the piles of printouts, the same distinct odor they gave rise to, the same occasional old-fashioned book in among the film cassettes. Morrison tried to read the title of one that was too far off and too worn to be made out. (Books always had an ancient appearance, even when they were new.) He had the impression it was an English-language book, which would not have surprised him. He himself had several Russian classics in his laboratory for an occasional brushup of the language.

Boranova said, "We are quite private here. We will not be overheard and we will not be disturbed. Later we can have lunch brought in."

"You are kind," said Morrison, trying not to sound sardonic.

Boranova seemed to take it at face value. "Not at all. And now, Dr. Morrison, I can't help having noticed that Arkady is on a first-name basis with you. He is, of course, to a certain extent an uncultured individual and is apt to presume. Still, may I ask again if, despite the conditions that brought you here, we might be pleasant and informal with each other?"

Morrison hesitated. "Well, call me Albert, then. But it will be merely a convenience and no sign of friendship. I am not likely to dismiss my kidnapping."

Boranova cleared her throat. "I did try to persuade you to come of your own free will. If necessity had not driven us so hard, we would have gone no farther than that."

"If you are embarrassed by what you have done, then return me to the United States. Send me back now and I will be willing to forget this episode and will make no complaint to my government."

Slowly Boranova shook her head. "You know that cannot be done. Necessity still drives. You will see what I mean, shortly. But meanwhile, Albert, let us talk together, without nonsense, as part of the global family of science that rises superior to questions of nationality and other artificial distinctions among human beings. —Surely by now you have accepted the reality of miniaturization."

"I must accept it." Morrison shook his head, almost regretfully.

"And you see our problem?"

"Yes. It is far too expensive in energy."

"Imagine, however, if we lower the energy cost drastically. Imagine if we can bring about miniaturization by plugging a wire into a wall socket and consuming no more energy than we would if we were heating a toaster oven."

"Of course—but apparently it can't be done. Or, at any

rate, your people cannot do it. Why all the secrecy, then? Why not publish the findings you have already made and welcome the contributions of the rest of the family of science? Secrecy seems to imply the possibility that the Soviet Union is planning to use miniaturization as a weapon of some kind, one powerful enough to make it possible for your country to find it feasible to break the mutual understanding that has led to peace and cooperation throughout the world for the last two generations."

"That is not so. The Soviet Union is not trying to establish a world hegemony."

"I hope not. Still, if the Soviet Union seeks secrecy, it is understandable that other units of the global alliance would begin to wonder if it seeks conquest."

"The United States has its secrets, has it not?"

"I don't know. The American government does not confide in me. If it *does* have secrets—and actually I suppose it does—I disapprove of that, too. But tell me why there is any necessity for secrets? What does it matter if you develop miniaturization, or we, or both of us in combination—or the Africans, for that matter? We Americans invented the airplane and the telephone, but you have both. We were the first to reach the moon, but you enjoy your full share of the lunar settlements. You, on the other hand, were the first to crack the problem of fusion power and the first to build a solar power station in space and we participate fully in both."

Boranova said, "All that you say is true. Nevertheless, for over a century, the world has taken it for granted that American technology is superior to Soviet technology. That is a constant irritant to us, and if, in something as basic and as thoroughly revolutionary as miniaturization, it is clearly established that the Soviet Union led the way, then that would be most desirable for us."

"And the global family of science that you appeal to? Are you a member of that or are you merely a Soviet scientist?"

"I am both," said Boranova with a touch of anger. "If it were my decision, then perhaps I would open our discoveries to the world. However, I do not make the decision. My government does and I owe them loyalty. Nor do you Americans make it easy for us to do otherwise. Your constant loud American assumption of superiority drives us into a defensive posture."

"But won't it spoil Soviet pride in their accomplishment to have to call upon an American such as myself to help out?"

"Well, yes, it does sour the milk a bit, but it will at least give the United States a share in the achievement, which we shall acknowledge, Albert. You will be showing yourself a true American patriot and will improve your own reputation if you help us."

Morrison smiled bitterly. "A bribe?"

Boranova shrugged. "If that is how you interpret it, I cannot stop you. But let us talk in a friendly manner and see what will come of it."

"In that case, start by giving me some information. Now that I am forced to believe that miniaturization is possible, can you tell me the basic physics behind it? I am curious."

"You know better than that, Albert. It would be dangerous for you to learn too much. How would we, then, be able to let you go back to your country? —Besides, although I can operate the miniaturization system, even I don't know the basics. If I did, our government could scarcely risk having me visit the United States."

"You mean we might kidnap you as you kidnapped me. Do you think the United States engages in kidnapping?"

"I am absolutely certain it would when necessity drove sufficiently."

"And who are the people who *do* know the basics of miniaturization?"

"That also is not something that, in general, it is safe for you to know. However, I can lift the curtain just a bit in this matter. Pyotor Shapirov is one of them."

"Crazy Peter," said Morrison, smiling. "Somehow I'm not surprised."

"You shouldn't be. I am sure you say 'crazy' only as one of your jokes, but it was he who first worked out the basic rationale behind miniaturization. Of course," she added thoughtfully, "it may very well be that that required a certain insanity—or, at any rate, a certain idiosyncracy of thought. It is also Shapirov who first suggested a method of achieving miniaturization with a minimum expenditure of energy."

"How? The conversion of deminiaturization into an electromagnetic field?"

Boranova made a face. "I was merely giving you an example. Shapirov's method is far more subtle."

"Can it be explained?"

"Only roughly. Shapirov points out that the two great aspects of the unified theory of the Universe—the quantum aspect and the relativistic aspect—each depends on a constant that sets a limit. In quantum theory it is Planck's constant, which is very tiny but not zero. In relativity, it is the speed of light, which is very great but not infinite. Planck's constant sets a lower limit to the size of energy transfer and the speed of light sets an upper limit to the speed of information transmission. Shapirov maintains, furthermore, that the two are related. In other words, if Planck's constant is decreased, the speed of light would increase. If Planck's constant were reduced to zero, then the speed of light would be infinite."

Morrison said at once, "In which case, the Universe would be Newtonian in its properties."

Boranova nodded. "Yes. According to Shapirov, then, the reason for the enormous energy consumption of miniaturization is that the two limits are uncoupled, that Planck's constant is decreased without the speed of light being increased. If the two were coupled, then energy would flow from the speed-of-light limit into the Planck's constant limit during miniaturization and in the other direction during deminiaturization, so that the speed of light would go up as miniaturization proceeded and down again during deminiaturization. The efficiency should be nearly a hundred percent. Very little energy would then be required to miniaturize and re-expansion could take place very quickly."

Morrison said, "Does Shapirov know how miniaturization and deminiaturization can be carried through with the two limits coupled?"

"He said he did."

"Said? Past tense? Does that mean he has changed his mind?"

"Not exactly."

"Then what has he done?"

Boranova hesitated. "Albert," she said almost pleadingly, "do not go too fast. I want you to think. You know that miniaturization works. You know that it is possible, but not practical. You know that it would be a boon for humanity and I have assured you that it is not meant for destructive or warlike use. Once we know that our national precedence is recognized, which we want for psychological reasons I have presented to you quite frankly, I am sure we will share miniaturization with all divisions of the globe."

"Really, Natalya? Would you and your nation trust the United States if the situation were reversed?"

"Trust!" said Boranova and sighed heavily. "It doesn't come naturally to anyone. It is the weakness of humanity that we constantly read the worst into others. Yet trust must begin somewhere or the fragile mood of cooperation we have enjoyed for so long will shatter and we will be back to the twentieth century with all its horrors. Since the United States feels so strongly that it is the stronger and more advanced nation, should it not be the first to risk the act of trusting?"

Morrison spread out his arms. "I can't answer that. I am a private citizen and do not represent my nation."

"As a private citizen you can help us, knowing that you will not be harming your own country."

"I can't possibly know such a thing, since I only have your word for it and I don't believe you represent your nation any more than I represent mine. But all this is irrelevant, Natalya. Even if I wanted to, how on Earth can I help you make miniaturization practical, when I know nothing about the subject?"

"Be patient. In a while we will have lunch. Dezhnev and Kaliinin will be through with the deminiaturization of Katinka by then and will join us, together with one other whom you must meet. Then, after lunch, I will take you to see Shapirov."

"I'm not sure about that, Natalya. You told me just a while ago that it would be dangerous for me to meet anyone who really understood miniaturization. I might learn too much and this might raise problems with my return to the United States. Why, then, should I risk seeing Shapirov?"

Boranova said sadly, "Shapirov is an exception. I promise you that you will understand this when you see him—and you will also understand why we must turn to you."

"That," said Morrison with all the conviction with which he had lately proclaimed the impossibility of miniaturization, "I will never understand."

20.

LUNCH was in a well-lit room, for strips of the walls, together with the entire ceiling, were electroluminescent. Boranova had pointed it out with obvious pride and Morrison had refrained from making invidious comparisons with the United States, where electroluminescence was widespread.

Nor did he express his amusement over the fact that despite the electroluminescence there was a small but ornate chandelier centered in the ceiling. Its bulbs contributed nothing to the light, but it undoubtedly made the room seem less antiseptic.

As Boranova had predicted, a fifth person had joined them and Morrison was introduced to someone named Yuri Konev. "A neurophysicist like yourself, Albert," said Boranova.

Konev, who was darkly handsome and who seemed to be in his middle thirties, had an air of almost gawky youth about himself. He shook hands with wary curiosity and said, "I am most pleased to meet you," in creditable English, spoken with a distinct American accent.

"You have been in the United States, I imagine," said Morrison, also in English.

"I spent two years doing graduate work at Harvard University. It gave me a splendid opportunity to practice my English."

"Nevertheless," said Boranova in Russian, "Dr. Albert Morrison does very well in our language, Yuri, and we must give him a chance to practice it here in our country."

"Of course," said Konev in Russian.

Morrison had, indeed, almost forgotten that he was underground. There were no windows in the room, but that was common enough in large office buildings even aboveground.

The meal was not an ebullient one. Arkady Dezhnev ate with silent concentration and Sophia Kaliinin seemed abstracted. She glanced occasionally at Morrison, but ignored Konev completely. Boranova watched everyone, but said very little. She seemed content to leave the floor to Konev.

Konev said, "Dr. Morrison, I must tell you that I have followed your work carefully."

Morrison, who had been eating the thick cabbage soup appreciatively, looked up with a quick smile. This was the first reference to *his* work, rather than to *their* work, since he had arrived in the Soviet Union.

"Thank you for your interest, but Natalya and Arkady call me Albert and I will have difficulty in responding to different names. Let us all be on a first-name basis for the brief time that remains before I am returned to my own land."

"Help us," said Boranova in a low voice, "and it will indeed be a brief time."

"No conditions," said Morrison in an equally low tone. "I wish to leave."

Konev raised his voice, as though to force the conversation back into the track he had chosen. "But I must admit, Albert, that I have been unable to duplicate your observations."

Morrison's lips tightened. "I have had this complaint from neurophysicists in the United States."

"Now, why should this be? Academician Shapirov is greatly intrigued by your theories and maintains that you are probably correct, at least in part."

"Ah, but Shapirov isn't a neurophysicist, is he?"

"No, he's not, but he has an extraordinary feel for what is correct. I have never known him to say, 'It seems to me that this must be right,' in which whatever he is discussing hasn't proved to be right—at least in part. He says you are probably on the road to establishing an interesting relay station."

"A relay station? I don't know what he means by that."

"It's what he said once in my hearing. Some private thought of his own, no doubt." He cast a penetrating glance at Morrison, as though waiting for an explanation of the remark.

Morrison simply shrugged it away. "What I have done," he said, "is to establish a new kind of analysis of the cephalic waves originating in the brain and to have narrowed the search for a specific network within the brain devoted to creative thought."

"There you may be a little overoptimistic, Albert. I have not satisfied myself that this network of yours really exists."

"My results mark it out quite clearly."

"In dogs and monkeys. It is uncertain how far we can extrapolate such information to the much more complex structure of the human brain."

"I admit I haven't worked with the human brain anatomically, but I have analyzed human brain waves carefully and those results are at least consistent with my creative structure hypothesis."

"This is what I haven't been able to duplicate and what American researchers may not have been able to duplicate, either."

Again Morrison shrugged. "Adequate brain wave analysis is, at best, a monumentally difficult thing at the quintenary level and no one else has given the years to the problem that I have."

"Or possesses the particular computerized equipment. You have designed your own program for the purpose of brain wave analysis, haven't you?"

"Yes, I have."

"And described it in the literature?"

"Certainly. If I achieved results with an undescribed program, they would be worth nothing. Who could confirm my results, lacking an equivalent computer program?"

"Yet I have heard, at the International Neurophysical Conference in Brussels last year, that you are continually modifying your program and complaining that the lack of confirmation stems from the use of insufficiently complex programming incapable of Fourier analysis to the proper degree of sensitivity."

"No, Yuri, that is false. Entirely false. I have modified my program from time to time, but I have carefully described each modification in *Computer Technology*. I have tried to publish the data in *The American Journal of Neurophysics*, but they haven't accepted my papers these last few years. If others confine their reading to the *AJN* and don't keep up with relevant literature elsewhere, that is not my fault."

"And yet—" Konev paused and frowned in what seemed to be uncertain thought. "I don't know if I ought to say this because it may be something else that will antagonize you."

"Go ahead. I have, in these last few years, learned to accept all kinds of remarks—hostile, sarcastic, and—worst of all —pitying. I am quite hardened to it. —This is good chicken Kiev, by the way."

"This is a guest meal," murmured Kaliinin, almost under her breath. "Too buttery—bad for the figure."

"Hah," said Dezhnev loudly. "Bad for the figure. That is

an American remark that makes no sense in Russian. My father always said, 'The body knows what it needs. That's why some things taste good.' "

Kaliinin closed her eyes in quite obvious distaste. "A recipe for suicide," she said.

Morrison noticed that Konev did not look at the young woman during this bit of byplay. Not at all.

He said, "You were saying, Yuri? About something that might antagonize me, you thought?"

Konev said, "Well, then, is it true, Albert, or not true that you actually gave your program to a colleague and that, using it in your computer, he was still unable to duplicate your results?"

"That's true," said Morrison. "At least my colleague, an able enough man, *said* he could not duplicate my results."

"Do you suspect he was lying?"

"No. Not really. It's just that the observations are *so* delicate that to attempt them while certain of failure may well lead, it seems to me, to failure."

"Might one not argue the other way around, Albert, and say that your certainty of success leads you to imagine success?"

"Possibly," said Morrison. "That has been pointed out to me several times in the past. —But I don't think so."

"One more rumor," said Konev. "This I truly hate to repeat, but it seems so important. Is it true that you have claimed that in your analysis of brain waves you have occasionally sensed actual thoughts?"

Morrison shook his head vigorously. "I have never made such a claim in print. I have said to a colleague, once or twice, that in concentrating on the brain wave analysis there are occasionally times when I seem to find thoughts invading my mind. I have no way of telling whether the thoughts are entirely mine or whether my own brain waves resonate to those of the subject."

"Is such a resonance conceivable?"

"I suppose so. The brain waves produce tiny fluctuating electromagnetic fields."

"Ah! It is this, I suppose, that made Academician Shapirov make that remark about a relay station. Brain waves are always producing fluctuating electromagnetic fields—with or without analysis. You don't resonate—if resonance is what it is—to the thoughts of someone in your presence, no matter how intensely he may be thinking. The resonance takes place only when you are busily studying the brain waves with your programmed computer. It presumably acts as a relay station, magnifying or intensifying the brain waves of the subject and projecting them into your mind."

"I have no evidence for that except for an occasional fugitive impression. That's not enough."

"It might be. The human brain is far more complex than any other equivalent piece of matter we know of."

"What about dolphins?" said Dezhnev, his mouth full.

"An exploded view," said Konev at once. "They're intelligent, but their brains are devoted too entirely to the minutiae of swimming to allow enough room for abstract thought on the human scale."

"I have never studied dolphins," said Morrison indifferently.

"Ignore the dolphins," said Konev impatiently. "Just concentrate on the fact that your computer, properly programmed, may act as a relay station, passing thoughts from the mind of the subject you are studying to your own mind. If that is so, Albert, we need *you* and no other person in the world."

Morrison said, frowning and pushing his chair away from the table, "Even if I can pick up thoughts by way of my computer—a claim I have never made and which, in fact, I deny—what can that possibly have to do with miniaturization?"

Boranova rose and looked at her watch. "It is time," she said. "Let us go and see Shapirov now."

Morrison said, "What he says will make no difference to me."

"You will find," said Boranova with a hint of steel in her voice, "that he will say nothing—but will be utterly convincing just the same."

21.

MORRISON had kept his temper well so far. The Soviets were, after all, treating him as a guest and if he could overlook the small matter of his being carried off by force, he had little of which to complain.

But what were they getting at? One by one, Boranova had introduced him to others—first Dezhnev, then Kaliinin, then Konev—for reasons he had not penetrated. Over and over, Boranova had hinted of his usefulness without actually saying what it might be. Now Konev talked of it and was equally uncommunicative.

And now they were to see Shapirov. Clearly this had to be a climax of sorts. From the first mention of him by Boranova at the convention two days ago, Shapirov had seemed to hover over the whole matter like a thickening fog. It was he who had worked out the miniaturization process, he who seemed to detect a connection between Planck's constant and the speed of light, he who seemed to value Morrison's neurophysical theories, and he who made the remark about the computer as relay station that had apparently set off Konev's conviction that Morrison—and only Morrison—could help them.

It remained for Morrison, now, to resist any blandishments or arguments that Shapirov could present. If Morrison insisted that he would not help them, what would they do when all the blandishments and arguments had failed?

Crude threat of force—or torture?

Brainwashing?

Morrison quailed. He dared not put his refusal on the basis that he *would* not. He would have to persuade them that he *could* not. Surely that was a reasonable position on which to take his stand. What could neurophysics—and a dubious, unaccepted bit of neurophysical work at that—have to do with miniaturization?

But why didn't they see that for themselves? Why did they all act as though it were conceivable that a person like himself, who had never as much as thought of miniaturization until some forty-eight hours before, could do something for them—*them*, the only experts in the field—that they could not do for themselves?

It was a rather lengthy walk along corridors and, lost in his own uncomfortable thoughts, Morrison did not notice that they were fewer in number than he had thought.

He said to Boranova suddenly, "Where are the others?"

She said, "They have work to do. We do not have forever to do what we must, you know."

Morrison shook his head. Chatty, they were not. None of them seemed to scatter information. Always close-lipped. A long-standing Soviet habit, perhaps—or something that was ground into them through their work on a secret project in which even the scientists dared not step outside the narrow limits of their immediate work.

Were they coming to him as a storybook American generalist? Nothing he had ever done, surely, would give anyone that impression. As a matter of fact, he was himself a narrow specialist, knowing virtually nothing outside of neurophysics. —This was a worsening disease of modern science, he thought.

They had entered another elevator, something he had scarcely bothered to notice, and they were now on another level. He looked around him and recognized characteristics that seemed to transcend national differences.

"Are we in a medical wing?" he asked.

"A hospital," said Boranova. "The Grotto is a self-contained scientific complex."

"And why are we here? Am I—" He stopped suddenly, as the horror of the thought smote him. Was he to be drugged or, by some other medical means, made more compliant?

Boranova had walked on for a moment, then stopped, looked back, and came toward him, saying snappishly, "*Now* what is frightening you?"

Morrison felt ashamed. Were his facial expressions that transparent? "Nothing is frightening me," he grumbled. "I am simply tired of walking aimlessly."

"What makes you think we are walking aimlessly? I said we were going to see Pyotor Shapirov. We are walking toward him now. —Come, we have only a few steps left."

They turned a corner and Boranova beckoned him to a window.

He stepped to her side and looked in. It was a room and there were a number of people present. There were four beds, but only one was occupied and it was surrounded by equipment that he did not recognize. There were tubes and glassware extending toward the bed and Morrison counted a dozen functionaries, who might be doctors, nurses, or medical technicians.

Boranova said, "There is Academician Shapirov."

"Which one?" said Morrison, his eyes traveling from one of the figures to the other and finding no one who seemed similar in appearance to the scientist he recalled having met once.

"In the bed."

"In the bed? He's ill, then?"

"Worse than ill. He is in a coma. He has been in a coma for over a month and we strongly suspect it is an irreversible state."

"I'm terribly sorry to hear that. I presume that is why you referred to him in the past tense before lunch."

"Yes, the Shapirov we know is in the past tense, unless—"

"Unless he recovers? But you just said the coma is probably irreversible."

"That's true. But neither is he brain-dead. The brain is damaged certainly or he wouldn't be in a coma, but it is not dead and Konev, who has followed your work closely, thinks that some of his thinking network is still intact."

"Ah," said Morrison, the light breaking. "I begin to understand. Why didn't you explain this to begin with? If you had wanted to consult me on such a matter and had explained, I might have been willing to come here with you voluntarily. Yet, on the other hand, if I were to study his cerebral functioning and tell you, 'Yes, Yuri Konev is right,' then what good will that do you?"

"That will do us no good at all. You don't yet begin to understand, you see, and I can't explain exactly what it is I want until you understand the problem. Do you quite realize what is buried there in the still-living portions of Shapirov's brain?"

"His thoughts, I suppose."

"Specifically, his thoughts of the interconnection of Planck's constant and the speed of light. His thoughts of a method for making miniaturization and deminiaturization rapid, low-energy, and practical. With those thoughts, we give humanity a technique that will revolutionize science and technology—and society—more than anything since the invention of the transistor. Perhaps more than anything since the discovery of fire. Who can tell?"

"Are you sure you're not being overdramatic?"

"No, Albert. Does it occur to you that if miniaturization

can be tied in with a vast acceleration of the speed of light, a spaceship, if sufficiently miniaturized, can be sent to anywhere in the Universe at many times the ordinary speed of light. We won't need faster-than-light travel. Light will travel fast enough for us. And we won't need antigravity, for a miniaturized ship will have close to zero mass."

"I can't believe all that."

"You couldn't believe miniaturization."

"I don't mean I can't believe the results of miniaturization. I mean I can't believe that the solution of the problem is permanently locked in the brain of one man. Others will eventually think of it. If not now, then next year or next decade."

"It's easy to wait when you are not concerned, Albert. The trouble is we're not going to have a next decade or even a next year. This Grotto which you see all about you has cost the Soviet Union as much as a minor war. Each time we miniaturize anything—even if it's just Katinka—we consume enough energy to last a sizable town for a whole day. Already, our government leaders look askance at this expense and many scientists, who do not understand the importance of miniaturization or who are simply selfish, complain that all of Soviet science is being starved for the sake of the Grotto. If we do not come up with a device to save on energy—an extreme saving, too—this place will be shut down."

"Nevertheless, Natalya, if you publish what is now known of miniaturization and make it available to the Global Association for the Advancement of Science, then innumerable scientists will put their minds to it and quickly enough someone will devise a method for coupling Planck's constant and the speed of light."

"Yes," said Boranova, "and perhaps the scientist who will obtain the key of low-energy miniaturization will be an American or a Frenchman or a Nigerian or a Uruguayan. It is a Soviet scientist who has it now and we don't want to lose the credit."

Morrison said, "You forget the global fellowship of science. Don't cut it up into segments."

"You would speak differently if it were an American who was on the edge of the discovery and you were asked to do something that might possibly give the credit to one of us. Do you remember the history of the American reaction when the Soviet Union was the first to put an artificial satellite into orbit?"

"Surely we have advanced since then."

"Yes, we have advanced a kilometer, but we have not advanced ten kilometers. The world is not yet entirely global in its thinking. There remains national pride to a considerable extent."

"So much the worse for the world. Still, if we are not global and if national pride is something we are expected to retain, then I should have mine. As an American, why should I be disturbed over a Soviet scientist losing credit for the discovery?"

"I ask you only to understand the importance of this to *us*. I ask you to put yourself in our place for a moment and see if you can grasp our desperation to do what we can to find out what it is that Shapirov knows."

Morrison said, "All right, Natalya. I understand. I don't approve, but I understand. Now—listen carefully, please—now that I understand, what is it you want of *me?*"

"We want you," said Boranova intensely, "to help us find out what Shapirov's thoughts—his still-living and existing thoughts—are."

"How? There's nothing in my theory that makes that possible. Even granting that thinking networks do exist, and that brain waves can be minutely analyzed, and even granting that I occasionally get a mental image, possibly imaginary, possibly an artifact—there remains no way in which the brain waves can be studied to the extent of interpreting them in terms of actual thoughts."

"Not even if you could analyze, in detail, the brain waves of a single nerve cell that was part of a thinking network?"

"I couldn't deal with a single nerve cell in anything approaching the necessary kind of detail."

"You forget. You can be miniaturized and be inside that single nerve cell."

And Morrison stared at her in sick horror. She had mentioned something like this at their first meeting, but he had put it aside as nonsense—horrifying, but nonsense, since miniaturization, he was certain, was impossible. But miniaturization was not impossible and now the horror was undiluted and paralyzing.

22.

MORRISON did not then, nor could he at any time afterward, clearly recall the events that immediately followed. It was not a case of everything going black as much as everything having blurred.

His next clear memory was that of lying on a couch in a small office with Boranova looking down at him and with the other three—Dezhnev, Kaliinin, and Konev—behind her. Those three came into focus more slowly.

He tried to struggle into a sitting position, but Konev moved toward him and placed his hand on Morrison's shoulder. "Please, Albert, rest awhile. Gather your strength."

Morrison looked from one to another in confusion. He had been upset, but he did not clearly remember what he had been upset about.

"What happened? How—how did I get here?" He looked around the room again. No, he hadn't been here. He had been looking through a window at a man in a hospital bed.

He said, puzzled, "Did I faint?"

"Not really," said Boranova, "but you weren't quite yourself for a while. You seemed to undergo a shock."

Now Morrison remembered. Again he tried to lift himself into a sitting position, more strenuously this time. He struck Konev's restraining hand out of the way. He was sitting up now, with his hands on the couch on either side of him.

"I remember now. You wanted me to be miniaturized. What happened to me when you said that?"

"You simply swayed and—crumpled. I had you placed on a stretcher and brought here. It didn't seem to anyone that you needed medication, merely a chance to rest and recover."

"No medication?" Morrison looked vaguely at his arms, as though he expected to see needle marks through the sleeve of his cotton blouse.

"None. I assure you."

"I didn't say anything before I collapsed?"

"Not a word."

"Then let me answer you now. I'm not going to be miniaturized. Is that clear?"

"It is clear that you say so."

Dezhnev sat down on the couch next to Morrison. He had a full bottle in one hand and an empty glass in the other.

"You need this," he said and half filled the glass.

"What is it?" asked Morrison, lifting his arm to ward it off.

"Vodka," said Dezhnev. "It's not medicinal, it's nourishing."

"I don't drink."

"There is a time for everything, my dear Albert. This is a time for a warming bit of vodka, even for those who do not drink."

"I don't drink out of disapproval. I *can't* drink. I have no head for alcohol, that's all. If I take two swallows of that, I will be drunk within five minutes. Completely drunk."

Dezhnev's eyebrows went up. "So? What other purpose is there in drinking? Come, if you are lucky enough to win your goal in a few inexpensive sips, thank whatever you find thankable. A very small amount will warm you, stimulate your peripheral circulation, clear your head, concentrate your thoughts. It will even give you courage."

Kaliinin's voice sounded in half a whisper, but was distinctly audible. "Do not expect miracles of a little alcohol."

Morrison's head twisted sharply and he looked at her. She did not seem as pretty as he had thought her on their first meeting. There was a hard and unforgiving look about her.

Morrison said, "I have never represented myself as a courageous man. I have never presented myself as anything that would be of help to you. I have maintained from the beginning that I could not do anything for you. That I am here at all is the result of compulsion, as you all know. What do I owe you? What do I owe any of you?"

Boranova said, "Albert, you are shivering. Take a sip of the vodka. You will not be drunk on a sip and we won't force more on you."

Almost as though to show bravery in a small way, Morrison, after a moment's hesitation, took the glass from Dezhnev's hand and swallowed a bit of the liquor recklessly. He felt a burning sensation in his throat, which passed. The taste was rather sweetish than otherwise. He took a larger sip and handed the glass back. Dezhnev took it and placed it and the bottle on a small table on his side of the couch.

Morrison tried to speak, but he coughed instead. He

waited, cleared his throat, and said breathily, "Actually, that's not so bad. If you don't mind, Arkady—"

Dezhnev reached for the glass, but Boranova said, "No. That's enough, Albert." Her imperious gesture stopped Dezhnev. "We do not want you drunk, Albert. Just a little warm so you will listen to us."

Morrison could feel the warmth rising within him, as it always had when, on rare occasions of social bonhomie, he had had some sherry or (once) a dry martini. He decided he could handle any argument she could produce.

"All right," he said, "say on," and set his lips into a firm and unyielding line.

"I don't say, Albert, you *owe* us anything and I'm sorry that all this came as such a shock to you. We are aware that you are not a reckless man of action and we tried to break it to you as gently as possible. I had hoped, in fact, that you would see what was essential on your own, without any necessity of explanation."

"You were wrong," said Morrison. "At no time would such a mad thing have occurred to me."

"You see our necessity, don't you?"

"I see *your* necessity. I don't see it as *mine.*"

"You might feel you owe it to the cause of global science."

"Global science is an abstraction that I admire, but I am not likely to want to sacrifice my highly concrete body for an abstraction that doesn't seem to exist. The whole point of your necessity is that it is Soviet science that is at stake, not global science."

"Then consider American science," said Boranova. "If you help us, that will become an eternal part of the victory. It will become a joint Soviet-American victory."

"Will my part be publicized?" demanded Morrison. "Or will the thing be announced as purely Soviet?"

Boranova said, "You have my word."

"You cannot commit the Soviet Government."

"Horrible," said Kaliinin. "He judges our government by his own."

Konev said, "Wait, Natalya. Let me talk to our American friend, man to man." He sat down by Morrison and said, "Albert, I appeal to your interest in your work. So far, you have achieved little in the way of results. You have convinced no one in your country and you don't have any chance of doing so as long as you are left with only the tools you have. We offer you a better tool, one whose worth you couldn't dream of three days ago and one which you'll never have again if you turn away from it now. Albert, you have the chance to graduate from romantic speculations to convincing evidence. Do this for us and you will become, at a bound, the most famous neurophysicist in the world."

Morrison said, "You're asking me to risk my life on an untried technique."

"That is not unprecedented. All through history, scientists have risked death to continue their investigations. They have gone up in balloons and have dipped under the seas in primitive armored spheres to make their measurements and observations. Chemists have risked dealing with poisons and explosives, biologists with pathogens of all types. Physicians have injected themselves with experimental sera and physicists, in attempting to establish a self-supporting nuclear reaction, knew well that the explosion that resulted might destroy them or, conceivably, the entire planet."

Morrison said, "You spin dreams. You would never let it be known that an American played a role. Not when you confess your desperation at the possibility that Soviet science would lose the credit."

Konev said, "Let's be honest with each other, Albert. We couldn't hide your share in this, even if we wished to. The American government knows we brought you here. We know they do. You know they do. They made no move to stop us because they want you here. Well, they will know—or at least guess—what we wanted you here for and what you did for us, once we announce our success. And they will see to it that American science, in your person, will get full credit."

Morrison sat silently, head bent, for a while. There was a flushed spot, high on each cheek, as a result of the vodka he had drunk. Without looking, he knew that four pairs of eyes were firmly fixed upon him and he suspected that four breaths were being held.

He looked up and said, "Let me ask you one question. How did Shapirov come to be in a coma?"

There was again a silence and three of the pairs of staring eyes shifted to Natalya Boranova.

Morrison, seeing that, also stared at her. "Well—" he said.

Boranova said, "Albert, I will tell you the truth, even if that would tend to defeat our aims. If we try to lie to you, you will be right not to believe anything we say. If you see we are truthful, then you can believe us in the future. — Albert, Academician Shapirov is in a coma because *he* was miniaturized, as we hope you will be. There was a small accident during deminiaturizing that destroyed part of his brain, apparently permanently. That can happen, you see, and we are not hiding it from you. Now give us the credit for utter frankness and say you will help us."

CHAPTER 6

DECISION

*We are always certain that the
decision we have just made is wrong.*
— Dezhnev Senior

23.

Now, finally, Morrison rose, feeling a trifle unsteady on his feet—whether from the vodka, from the general tension of the day, or from this last revelation he did not know or care. He stamped his feet a little, as though to firm them, then deliberately walked the length of the small room and back.

He faced Boranova and said in a harsh voice, "You can miniaturize a rabbit and nothing seems to happen to it. Did it occur to you that the human brain is the most complex bit of matter we know and that, whatever else might survive, the human brain might not?"

"It did," said Boranova stolidly, "but all our investigations have shown us that miniaturization does not in the least affect the interrelationships within the object being miniaturized. In theory, even the human brain would not be affected by miniaturization."

"In theory!" said Morrison with contempt. "How is it possible that, based on theory alone, you would experiment with Shapirov, whose brain you seem to value so highly? And having failed with him, to your enormous loss, how can you

90

be so mad as to propose experimenting with me to recover that loss? You'll simply fail with me, too, and I cannot accept that."

Dezhnev said, "Don't speak nonsense. We are not mad. Nothing we did was lightly undertaken. The fault was Shapirov's."

Boranova said, "In a way, it was. Shapirov had his eccentric ways. 'Crazy Peter' I believe you call him in English and that is perhaps not so far off. He was intent on having the miniaturization experience. He was getting old, he said, and he would not, like Moses, reach the Promised Land without entering it."

"He might have been forbidden to do so."

"By me? *I* would forbid Shapirov? You can't be serious."

"Not you. Your government. If the miniaturization process is so precious to the Soviet Union—"

"Shapirov threatened to abandon the project altogether if he did not have his way and that could not be risked. Nor is our government quite so high-handed as it once was in its pressures on troublesome scientists. It must take world opinion into greater account now, as your government must. It is the price of global cooperation. Whether that is for the better or for the worse, I cannot say. In any case, Shapirov was eventually miniaturized."

Morrison muttered, "Absolutely mad."

"No," said Boranova, "for we did not move without precautions. Despite the fact that every exercise in miniaturization is costly and sends shivers through the Central Coordinating Committee, we insisted on a careful approach. Twice we miniaturized chimpanzees and twice we brought them back and could detect no changes in them—either as a result of minute studies of their behavior or by magnetic resonance imaging of the brain."

"A chimpanzee is not a human being," said Morrison.

"Something we were aware of," said Boranova gravely. "Therefore, we miniaturized a human being next. A volunteer. Yuri Konev, to be precise."

Konev said, "It had to be me. It was I who felt most strongly that the human brain would not be affected. I am the neurophysicist of the project and it was I who made the necessary calculations. I would not ask another human being to risk his sanity on my calculations and my certainty. Life is one thing—we all lose it sooner or later. Sanity is quite another."

"So brave," whispered Kaliinin, looking at her fingertips, "the deed of a true Soviet hero." Her lip trembled, as though on the brink of a sneer.

Looking firmly at Morrison, Konev said, "I am a loyal Soviet citizen, but I did not do it for nationalist motives. They would be, in this case, irrelevant. I did it as a matter of decency and of scientific ethics. I had confidence in my analysis and of what worth was my confidence if I would not risk myself on it? And it is a matter of something else, too. When the history of miniaturization is recorded, I will be listed as the first human being ever to have been subjected to the process. That will eclipse the deeds of a great-granduncle of mine who was a general fighting the German Nazis in the Great Patriotic War. And I would be pleased with that, not out of vainglory but out of a belief that the conquests of peace should always be held superior to victories in war."

Boranova said, "Well, putting ideals to one side and passing on to the facts— Yuri was miniaturized twice. First, he was taken down to about half his height and was restored in perfect order. Then he was miniaturized to the size of a mouse and again was restored in perfect order."

Morrison said, "And then Shapirov?"

"And then Shapirov. He was by no means easy to control even this far. He argued vociferously for the chance to be the first person miniaturized. After Konev's first venture into the small, it was all we could do to persuade him to wait for a second and more drastic attempt. After that we could control him no more. Not only were we forced to miniaturize him, but he swore that he would abandon the project and somehow make his way out of the country to begin a miniaturization project elsewhere if we did not miniaturize him to a greater extent than we had Konev. We had no choice. If 'Crazy Peter,' as you call him, were mad enough to speak of emigrating, that would go beyond what the government would be willing to allow even in these days. We didn't want him in prison, so we miniaturized him to the size of a cell."

"And that passed the limits of safety, did it?"

"No. We have every reason to think he was in perfect order, even miniaturized so far. He was being brought back and then at one point in the deminiaturization there was a misadventure. Deminiaturization took place a trifle too quickly and the temperature rose slightly in Shapirov's body. It had the effect of a high fever—not enough to kill him, but enough to damage his brain permanently. It might have been reversed if we could have attended to him at once, but deminiaturization had to be completed and that took time. It was an appalling catastrophe and all that we can hope for is the chance to salvage what we need from what is left of his brain."

"There may be another misadventure, as you call it, if I were to be miniaturized. Isn't that so?"

"Yes," said Boranova, "that is so. I don't deny it. There have been failures and misadventures throughout the history of science. Surely you need no reminder that there were deaths of cosmonauts in space both on the American and Soviet sides. That did not prevent our present settlement of the moon—and of space itself—as a new home for humanity."

"That may be so, but all advances in space were made by volunteers. No one was launched into space against his will. And I am not volunteering."

Boranova said, "You need not be so frightened of it. We have done our best to make it as safe as possible and, by the way, you will not go alone. Konev and Shapirov *did* go alone and as bare as the rabbit, for they, like the rabbit, were in a miniaturization field that was encased in air. You, on the other hand, will be in a ship, a kind of modified submarine. It, too, has been miniaturized and deminiaturized without harm. It is a little less expensive to carry through the process with an inanimate object because it can stand a rise in temperature more easily. In fact, such a rise serves to test for the ruggedness and stability of all its components."

"I am not going, Natalya, either alone or with the Red Army."

Boranova ignored the remark. "With you on the ship," she said, "will be we four. Myself, Sophia, Yuri, and Arkady. That is why I have introduced each of them to you. We are all partners in this greatest of all exploring trips. We will not be crossing an ocean or penetrating the vacuum of space. We will instead enter a microscopic ocean and penetrate the human brain. Can you be a scientist—a neurophysicist—and resist that?"

"Yes. I *can* resist that. And easily. I will not go."

Boranova said, "We have your software, your program. You always carry it with you and you had it with you when you were brought here. We will have a computer on board the ship for you, one that is the exact model of the one you use in your laboratory. It should not be a long trip. We will all be miniaturized, taking our chances along with you. You will take your computer readings and record the sensations you receive and then we will all be deminiaturized and your part will be done with. Say that you will join us. Say you will do it."

And Morrison, fists clenched, said stubbornly, "I will not join you. I will not do it."

Boranova said, "I am so sorry, Albert, but that is the wrong answer. We will not accept it."

24.

MORRISON felt his heart racing again. If this was going to be a straightforward contest of wills, he was not sure he was up to coping with this woman who, despite all her apparent softness, seemed made of alloy steel. Moreover, she had behind her the full apparatus of the Soviet Union and he himself was alone.

He said desperately, "Surely you know this whole thing is a trumped-up romantic notion. How do you know there is any connection between Planck's constant and the speed of light? All you have is some statement by Shapirov. Isn't that correct? Did he give you any details? Any evidence? Any explanations? Any mathematical analysis? —It was nothing more than a statement—an imaginative speculation—wasn't it?"

Morrison tried to sound confident. After all, if Shapirov had given them anything substantive, they would not now be trying the desperate trick of rifling his brain for something useful. He held his breath, waiting for the response.

Boranova looked at Konev then said, with a shade of reluctance, "We will continue our policy of telling the flat and unadorned truth. We have nothing but some remarks Shapirov made, as you've guessed. He enjoyed keeping things to himself until he could spring them on us fully dressed, so to speak. He was more than a little childish in this respect. Perhaps that was an aspect of his eccentricity—or of his genius—or of both.''

"But how can you tell, under those circumstances, that such an unsupported speculation would have any validity whatever?"

"When Academician Pyotor Shapirov said, 'I feel it will be thus and so,' that is how it turned out to be."

"Come on. Always?"

"Almost always."

"Almost always. He could have been wrong this time."

"I admit that. He could have been."

"Or if he had some notion which would really prove of use, it might have been localized in the part of the brain which has been destroyed."

"That is conceivable."

"Or if the notion is useful and is still in the intact portion of the brain, I might not be able to interpret the brain waves properly."

"That may well be."

"Putting it all together: Shapirov's suggestion may be wrong and, even if it isn't, it might be out of reach or, even if it isn't, I might not be able to interpret it. Considering that, what are the chances of success? And can't you see that we will be putting our lives into danger for something we will almost certainly fail to get?"

"Considering the matter objectively," said Boranova, "it would seem the chances are very small. However, if we do not hazard our lives, the chances of obtaining anything at all are zero—flat zero. If we *do* risk our lives, the chances of success are very small, admittedly, but they are *not* zero. Under the circumstances, we must take the risk, even though the best we can say for our chances of success are that they are not zero."

"For me," said Morrison, "the risk is too great and the chances of success are too small."

Boranova placed one hand on Morrison's shoulder and said, "Surely that is not your final decision."

"Surely it is."

"Think about it. Think about the value to the Soviet Union. Think about the benefits to your own country that will result from your acknowledged participation, to the needs of global science, to your own fame and reputation. All this is in favor of doing it. Against it are your personal fears. These are understandable, but all achievement in life requires the overcoming of fear."

"Thinking about it won't change my mind."

"Think about it until tomorrow morning, anyway. That's fifteen hours and it's all we can spare you. After all, balancing fears against hopes can keep one irresolute for a lifetime and we don't have a lifetime. Poor Shapirov might linger on in coma for a decade, but we don't know how long what is left of his brain will retain his ideas and we dare not wait very long at all."

"I can not and will not concern myself with your problems."

Boranova seemed to hear none of his denials and refusals. She said in her unfailingly gentle voice, "We will not attempt to persuade you further right now. You may have a leisurely dinner. You may watch our holovision programs if you wish, view our books, think, sleep. Arkady will accompany you back to the hotel and if you have any more questions, you need only ask him."

Morrison nodded.

"And, Albert, remember, tomorrow morning you must give us your decision."

"Take it now. It will not change."

"No. The decision must be that you will join us and help us. See to it that you come to that decision—for come to it you must—and it will be easier for all of us if you do so gladly and voluntarily."

25.

IT proved to be a quiet and thoughtful dinner for Morrison and not a very filling one—for he found he could only pick at his food. Dezhnev seemed quite unaffected by the other's lack of appetite and reaction. He ate vigorously and spoke incessantly, drawing on what was apparently a large stock of funny stories—in all of which his father played a key role—and was clearly delighted to try them out on a new audience.

Morrison smiled faintly at one or two, more because he recognized from the other's raised voice that a punch line had been advanced than because he heard them with any interest at all.

Valeri Paleron, the waitress who had served them at breakfast, was still there at dinner. A long day—but either that was reflected in her wages or it was required by her extracurricular duties. Either way, she glowered at Dezhnev each time she approached the table, perhaps (Morrison thought distantly) because she disapproved of his stories, which tended to be disrespectful of the Soviet regime.

Morrison did not particularly enjoy his own thoughts. Now that he was considering the distant possibility of getting away from the Grotto—from Malenkigrad—from the Soviet Union—he was beginning to feel a perverse disappointment at what he might be missing. He found himself daydreaming just a little on the matter of miniaturization, of using it to prove the worth of his theories, of triumphing over the smug fools who had dismissed him out of hand.

He recognized the fact that, of all the arguments presented by Boranova, only the personal one had shaken him. Any reference to the greater good of science, or of humanity, or of this nation or that was just idle rhetoric. His own place in science was something more. *That* seethed within him.

When the serving woman passed near the table, he stirred himself to say, "How long must you stay on, waïtress?"

She looked at him without favor. "Until you two grand dukes can bring yourselves to stir out of here."

"There's no rush," said Dezhnev as he emptied his glass. His speech was already slurred and his face was flushed. "I am so fond of the comrade waitress, I could stay on for as long as the Volga flows, that I might gaze on her face."

"As long as I don't have to gaze at yours," muttered Paleron.

Morrison filled Dezhnev's glass and said, "What do you think of Madame Boranova?"

Dezhnev gazed at the glass owlishly and did not offer to lift it immediately. He said with an attempt at gravity, "Not a first-class scientist, I am told, but an excellent admin—ministrator. Keen, makes up her mind quickly, and absolutely incorr—corruptible. A pain in the neck, I should think. If an administrator is incorr— too infernally honest, it makes life hard in so many little ways. She is a worshipper of Shapirov, too, and she thinks him incorr— no, incompre— no, incontrovertible. That's it."

Morrison was not sure of the Russian word. "You mean she thinks he's always right."

"Exactly. If he hints that he knows how to make miniaturization cheap, she's sure he can. Yuri Konev is sure of it, too. He's another of the worshippers. But it's Bora—Boranova who'll send you into Shapirov's brain. One way or another, she'll send you there. She has her ways. —As for Yuri, that little shaver, he's the real scientist of the group. Very brilliant." Dezhnev nodded solemnly and sipped at his refilled drink gently.

"I'm interested in Yuri Konev," said Morrison, his eyes following the lifting of the glass, "and in the young woman, Sophia Kaliinin."

Dezhnev leered. "A fine young piece." Then sadly, shaking his head, "But she has no sense of humor."

"She's married, I take it."

Dezhnev shook his head more violently than the occasion seemed to require. "No."

"She said she had had a baby."

"Yes, a little girl, but it isn't the signing of the marriage book that makes one pregnant. It's the game of bed—married or not."

"Does the puritanical Soviet Government approve of this?"

"No, but its approval was never asked, I think." He burst into laughter. "Besides, as a scientist at Malenkigrad, she has her special dispen—pensations. The government looks the other way."

"It strikes me," said Morrison, "that Sophia is much interested in Yuri Konev."

"You see that, do you? It takes little shrewdness. She is so interested that she has made it quite clear that her child was the result of Yuri's collaboration in that little game I spoke of."

"Oh?"

"But he denies it. And very vigorously, too. I think it is rather humorous, in a bitter way, that he remains compelled to work with her. Neither one can be spared from the project and all he can do is pretend she doesn't exist."

"I noticed that he never looks at her, but they must have been friendly once."

"Very friendly—if she is to be believed. If so, they were very discreet about it. But what's the difference? She doesn't need him to support the child. Her salary is a large one and the day-care center takes loving care of her daughter when she is at work. It is just a matter of emotion with her."

"What split them up, I wonder?"

"Who knows? Lovers take their disputes so seriously. I myself have never let myself fall in love—not poetically. If I like a girl, I play with her. If I get tired, I move on. It is my good fortune that the women I engage are as prag—pragmatic—isn't that a good word?—as I am and make little fuss. As my father used to say, 'A woman who doesn't fuss has no faults.' Sometimes, to be truthful, they grow tired before I do, but even then, so what? A girl who is tired of me is not much good to me and, after all, there are others."

"I suppose Yuri is much like that, too, isn't he?"

Dezhnev had emptied his glass again and he held out his hand when Morrison made a move to refill it. "Enough! Enough!"

"Never enough," said Morrison calmly. "You were telling me about Yuri."

"What is there to tell? Yuri is not a man to fly from woman to woman, but I have heard—" He stared blearily at Morrison. "You know how one hears—one tells another who tells another and who is to know whether what comes out of the funnel is anything like what went in. But I have heard that when Yuri was in the United States, being educated Western-style, he met an American girl. In went La Belle Americaine, they say, and out went poor little Soviet Sophia. Perhaps that was it. Perhaps he came back different and perhaps he still dreams of his lost love across the sea."

"And is that why Sophia is so ill-disposed to Americans?"

Dezhnev stared at the glass of vodka and sipped a little of it. "Our Sophia," he said, "has never liked Americans. This is not surprising." He leaned toward Morrison, his breath heavy with food and drink. "Americans are not a lovable people—if I may say so without offense."

"I'm not offended," said Morrison evenly, as he watched Dezhnev's head sink slowly and come to rest on his bent right arm. His breathing grew stertorous.

Morrison watched him for half a minute or so, then raised his hand to beckon the serving woman.

She came at once, her ample hips swinging. She stared at the unconscious Dezhnev with rather more than half a sneer. "Well, do you wish me to get a large pair of tongs and use them to carry our prince here to his bed?"

"Not just yet, Miss Paleron. As you know, I'm an American."

"As everyone knows. You have but to say three words and the tables and chairs in this room nod to each other and say, 'An American.' "

Morrison winced. He had always been proud of the purity of his Russian and this was the second time the woman had sneered at it.

"Nevertheless," he said, "I have been brought here by force, against my will. I believe it was done without the knowledge of the Soviet Government, which would have disapproved of and prevented the action if they had known. The people here—Dr. Boranova, whom you have referred to as the Tsarina—have acted on their own. The Soviet Government should be told of this and they will then act speedily to return me to the United States and prevent an international incident that nobody would want. Don't you agree?"

The waitress put her fists on her hips and said, "And of what matter is it to anyone either here or in the United States as to whether I agree or not? Am I a diplomat? Am I the reincarnated spirit of Tsar Peter the Great Drinker?"

"You can see to it," said Morrison, suddenly uncertain, "that the government learns of it. Quickly."

"What is it you think, American? That I have but to tell my lover, who is on the Presidium, and all will be well for you? —What have I to do with the government? What's more— and in all seriousness, Comrade Foreigner—I do not wish you to talk to me in this fashion again. Many a fine, loyal citizen has been hopelessly compromised by foreign blabbermouths. I will, of course, report this to Comrade Boranova at once and she will see to it that you do not insult me in this fashion again."

She left in a flounce and with a scowl and Morrison stared after her in dismay. And then his head whirled in surprise and astonishment when he heard Dezhnev's voice saying, "Albert, Albert, are you satisfied, my child?"

Dezhnev's head was raised from his pillowing arm and, though his eyes were a little bloodshot, his voice seemed to have lost its fuzziness. He said, "I wondered why you were so anxious to fill my glass, so I gobbled a little and let myself collapse. It was all very interesting."

"You are not drunk?" said Morrison, goggling at the other in wonder.

"I have been more sober in my life, certainly," said Dezhnev, "but I am not unconscious, nor have I been. You nondrinkers have an exaggerated idea of the speed with which an accomplished Soviet citizen will fall unconscious with drink—which shows the dangers of being a nondrinker."

Morrison still found himself in a state of disbelief over the failure of the waitress to cooperate. "You said she was an intelligence operator."

"Did I?" Dezhnev shrugged. "I think I said I suspected she was, but suspicions are often wrong. Besides, she knows me better than you do, my little Albert, and was probably under no illusion that I was drunk. I'll bet you ten rubles to a kopeck that she knew I was listening with both ears. What would you have her say in such circumstances?"

"In that case," said Morrison, taking heart, "she will have heard what I said and will nevertheless inform your government of the state of affairs. Your government, to avoid an international incident, will then order me set free, probably with an apology, and you people here will have some tall explaining to do. You had better free me and send me back to the United States of your own accord."

Dezhnev laughed. "You waste your time, my clever intriguer. You have too romantic a notion of our government. Conceivably, they may be willing to let you go someday but, regardless of possible embarrassment, not before you have been miniaturized and—"

"I don't believe anyone in authority knows you kidnapped me. They cannot approve once they find out."

"Maybe they don't know and maybe they will grind their teeth when they find out—but what can they do? The government has invested too much money in the project to let you go before you have had your chance to make it practical, so that it will repay all that has been spent—and more in addition. Well? Doesn't that seem logical to you?"

"No. Because I won't help you." Morrison felt his heart harden once again. "I will not allow myself to be miniaturized."

"That will be up to Natasha. She will be furious with you, you know, and will have no pity. You realize that you callously attempted to have everyone in the project thrown into the government's bad graces, have some of us retired—or worse. And this, after we had treated you with perfect consideration and kindness."

"You kidnapped me."

"Even that was done with perfect consideration and kindness. Were you hurt in any way? Mistreated? Yet you have tried to harm us. Natasha will repay you for that."

"How? Force? Torture? Drugs?"

Dezhnev turned his eyes up to the ceiling. "How little you know our Natasha. She doesn't do such things. I might, but she wouldn't. She's as much a gentle chicken-heart as you are, my wicked Albert—in her own way. But she will force you to go along with us."

"Well? How?"

"I don't know. I can never quite make out how she does it. But she manages. You will see." His smile developed a wolfish edge. And when Morrison saw that smile, he finally realized there was no escape.

26.

THE next morning Morrison and Dezhnev returned to the Grotto. They entered a large windowless ceiling-lit office, which Morrison had not seen before. It was clearly not Boranova's and it was very impressive, as anything with an ostentatious waste of space is bound to be.

Boranova sat behind a bulky desk and on the wall behind her was a portrait of the Soviet Executive, looking grave. In the corner to her left was a water cooler and in the one on the right a microfilm cabinet. On the desk was a small word processor. That was all. The room was empty otherwise.

Dezhnev said, "I have brought him, you see. The mischievous fellow tried to use the charming Paleron to effect an escape by intriguing with the government behind our back."

"I have received the report," said Boranova quietly.

"Please leave, Arkady. I wish to be alone with Professor Albert Morrison."

"Is that safe, Natasha?"

"I think so. Albert is not, in my opinion, a man of violence. —Will I be safe, Albert?"

Morrison spoke for virtually the first time that day. "Let's not play games," he said. "What is it you want, Natalya?"

Boranova gestured with her hand peremptorily and Dezhnev left. When the door closed behind him, she said, "Why have you done this? Why have you tried to intrigue with someone you thought was an intelligence agent watching us? Have we treated you so badly?"

"Yes," said Morrison angrily, "you have. Why can't any of you get it through your head that hijacking me to the Soviet Union is not something I am likely to appreciate? Why do you expect gratitude of me? Because you didn't break my head in the process? You probably would have—if my head, unbroken, hadn't been valuable to you."

"If your head, unbroken, hadn't been valuable to us, we would have left you in peace. You know that and you know the necessity that drove us. We have explained it carefully. If you were simply trying to get away, I would understand, but your method of attempted escape might have destroyed our project and perhaps us as well—if you had succeeded. You hoped our government would disapprove of our actions and be appalled. If that were so, what do you think would have happened to us?"

Morrison's lips tightened and he looked sullen. "I could think of no other way of escaping. You speak of driving necessities. My needs drive me, too."

"Albert, we have tried every reasonable way to persuade you to help us. There has been no force, no threats of force, no unpleasantness of any kind after you had arrived there. Isn't that true?"

"I suppose so."

"You suppose so? It *is* true. But it has all failed. You still refuse to help us, I think."

"I still refuse and I shall continue to refuse."

"Then I am forced, very much against my will, to take the next step."

A bit of fear stirred within Morrison and he felt his heart

skip a beat, but he tried desperately to sound defiant, "Which is?"

"You want to get home, to go back to America. Very well, if all our persuasiveness fails, you shall return."

"Are you serious?"

"Are you surprised?"

"Yes, I'm surprised, but I accept. I take you at your word. When will I leave?"

"The very moment we settle upon the story we're going to tell."

"Where's the problem? Tell the truth."

"That would be a little difficult, Albert. It would embarrass my government, which would have to deny having given permission for my action. I would be in serious trouble. It would be unreasonable for you to expect me to do that."

"What can you say instead?"

"That you came here at your own request, in order to help us with our projects."

Morrison shook his head vehemently. "That would be at least as difficult for me as admitting the kidnapping would be for you. These may be the good new days, but old habits die hard and the American public would be more than a little suspicious of an American scientist who went to the Soviet Union to help them with their projects. Old competitions remain and I have my reputation to think of."

"Yes, there is that difficulty," admitted Boranova, "but from my point of view, I would rather you had the difficulty than that I did."

"But I won't allow it. Do you suppose I will hesitate to tell the truth in full detail?"

"But, Albert," said Boranova quietly, "do you suppose anyone would believe you?"

"Of course. The American government knows that you asked me to come to the Soviet Union and that I refused. I would have had to be kidnapped to get here."

"I'm afraid your American government won't want to admit that, Albert. Would they want to say that Soviet agents had plucked an American out of his comfortable hotel room and carried him off by land, sea, and air without the forces of American law being aware of this? Considering modern American high-tech, of which your people are all so proud, that would argue either incompetence or a little inside treason on the part of your intelligence. I think your government would prefer to have the world believe you went to the Soviet Union voluntarily. —Besides, they *wanted* you to go to the Soviet Union voluntarily, didn't they?"

Morrison was silent.

Boranova said, "Of course they did. They wanted you to find out as much about miniaturization as possible. You're going to have to tell them you refused to be miniaturized. All you'll be able to report will be that you watched a rabbit undergo miniaturization, which they will consider to have been a bit of flimflam on our part. They will consider that we carefully hoodwinked you and you will have failed them badly. They will not feel bound to support you."

Morrison revolved the matter in his mind. He said, "Do you really intend to leave me in the position of being considered a spy and a traitor by my people? Is that what you're going to try to do?"

"No, indeed, Albert. We will tell all the truth we can. In fact, we would like to *protect* you, even though you showed no signs of wanting to protect us. We would explain that our great scientist Pyotr Shapirov is in a coma, that he had spoken highly of your neurophysical theories shortly before this tragedy had befallen him. We therefore called on you and asked you to use your theories and your expertise to see if you could bring him out of his coma. You can't object to that. It would hold you up to the world as a great humanitarian. Your government might well support this view. It would certainly protect them against possible embarrassment—and our government as well. And it is all almost true."

"What about the miniaturization?"

"That is the one place where we must avoid the truth. We can't mention that."

"But what would keep *me* from mentioning it?"

"The fact that no one would believe you. Did you accept the existence of miniaturization until you saw it with your own eyes? Nor would your government want to spread the feeling that the Soviet Union has attained miniaturization. They would not want to frighten the American public until such time as they were certain the Soviet Union had the process and, better yet, that they had the process as well. — But there you are, Albert. We will send you home with an innocuous story that doesn't mention miniaturization, doesn't embarrass either my country or yours, and relieves you of any suspicion of being a traitor. Are you satisfied?"

Morrison stared at Boranova uncertainly and rubbed his thin sandy hair till it stood up in vague tufts. "But *why* will you say you are sending me back? That has to be explained, too. You can't very well say that Shapirov recovered with my help unless he actually recovers so that you can produce him. Nor can you say that he died before I could get to him unless he actually does die soon, as otherwise you would have to explain why he is still in a coma or why, perhaps, he has come back to life. You can't hide the situation forever."

"That *is* a problem that worries us, Albert, and it is clever of you to see it. After all, we are sending you back within a few days of your arrival—and why? The only logical reason, I'm afraid, is that we have found you to be a charlatan. We brought you here in high hopes for our poor Shapirov, but in no time at all it turned out that your views were incoherent nonsense and, with bitter disappointment, we sent you back. That will do you no harm, Albert. Being a charlatan is not the same as being a spy."

"Don't play the innocent, Natalya. You can't do that." He had turned white with anger.

"But it makes sense, doesn't it? Your own peers don't take you seriously. They laugh at your views. They would agree with us that your neurophysical suggestions are incoherent nonsense. We'd be a little embarrassed for having been so credulous as to take you seriously, but it was really Shapirov who thought highly of you and he was, unbeknown to us, on the edge of a stroke and total mental breakdown, so that one could scarcely blame him for his mad admiration of you."

Morrison's lips trembled. "But you can't make a clown out of me. You can't ruin my reputation so."

"But what reputation are you talking about, Albert? Your wife has left you and some people think it was because having your career founder on your mad ideas was the last straw for her. We have heard that your appointment is not to be renewed and that you have not managed to find another place. You are finished as a scientist in any case and this story of ours would merely confirm what already exists. Perhaps you can find some other way of making a living—outside of science. You would probably have had to do that anyway, even if we had never touched you. There's that consolation."

"But you're lying and you know you're lying, Natalya. Have you no code of ethics? Can a respectable scientist do this to an honorable brother scientist?"

"You were unmoved by abstractions yesterday, Albert, and I am unmoved by them today in consequence."

"Someday scientists will discover I was right. How will you look then?"

"We may all be dead by then. Besides, you know that that is not the way it works. Franz Anton Mesmer, though he discovered hypnotism, was considered a fraud and a charlatan. When James Braid rediscovered hypnotism, he got the credit and Mesmer was *still* considered a fraud and charlatan. Besides—are we truly lying when we call you a charlatan?"

"Of course you are!"

"Let's reason it out. Why do you refuse to venture into an experiment of miniaturization which may enable you to establish your theories and which is likely to increase your knowledge of the brain by whole orders of magnitude? Such refusal can only arise through your own certain knowledge that your theories are wrong, that you are either a fool or a fraud or both, and that you don't want this established beyond a doubt, as it would be if you subjected yourself to miniaturization."

"That is not so."

"Do you expect us to believe that you refuse miniaturization simply because you are frightened? That you turn down a chance at knowledge, glory, fame, victory, vindication after years of scorn—all because you are scared? Come, we can't think so little of you, Albert. It makes much more sense to believe you are a fraud and so we will have no hesitation in saying you are."

"Americans won't believe a Soviet libel against an American scientist."

"Oh, Albert, of course they will. When we release you, with our explanation, it will be in all your American newspapers at once. They will be full of it. They are the most enterprising in the world and the 'freest,' as you are all so fond of saying, meaning they are a law unto themselves. They pride themselves on it and never tire of flaunting that in the eyes of our own more sedate press. This will be such a lovely story for them: 'American Faker Fools Stupid Soviets.' I can see the headlines now. In fact, Albert, you may make a great deal of money on your American lecture circuit. You know: 'How I Made Jerks of the Soviets.' Then you can tell them all the ridiculous things you persuaded us to believe before we caught on to you and the audiences will laugh themselves into hysterics.''

Morrison said in a whisper, "Natalya, why do you do this to me?"

"*I?* I am doing nothing. *You* are doing it. You want to go home and since we've failed to get you to accept miniaturization, we have no choice but to agree. Once, though, we agree to send you home, then, step by step, everything else must logically follow."

"But in that case, I can't go home. I can't have my life destroyed beyond repair."

"But who would care, Albert? Your estranged wife? Your children, who no longer know you and can always change their names anyway? Your university, which is firing you? Your colleagues, who laugh at you? Your government, which has abandoned you? Take heart. No one would care. An initial raucous laugh across the whole country and then you would be forgotten forever. You'll die without an obituary notice eventually, except for those papers who might not object to the tastelessness of bringing back that old joke for one more spurt of laughter to follow you to your grave."

Morrison shook his head in despair. "I can't go home."

"But you must. Unless you are willing to help us, which you're not, you can't stay here."

"But I can't go home on your terms."

"But what is the alternative?"

Morrison stared at the woman, who was looking at him with such mild concern. He whispered, "I accept the alternative."

Boranova looked at him for a long minute. "I do not wish to be mistaken, Albert. Put your agreement into clear language."

"It's either consent to be miniaturized or consent to be destroyed. Isn't that it?"

Boranova thrust out her lips. "That's a harsh way of putting it. I prefer that you look at it this way. Either you agree to help us by noon or you will be on a plane to the United States by 2 P.M. What do you say? It is now nearly 11 A.M. You have over an hour to decide."

"What's the use? An hour won't change anything. I'll be miniaturized."

"*We* will be miniaturized. You will not be alone." Boranova reached out and touched a contact on her desk.

Dezhnev entered. "Well, Albert. You stand there looking so sad, so crumpled, that it strikes me you have decided to help us."

Boranova said, "You need make no sardonic remarks. Albert will help us and we will be grateful for his help. His decision was a voluntary one."

"I'm sure it was," said Dezhnev. "How you squeezed it out this time, Natasha, I can't say, but I knew you would. — And I must contratulate you, too, Albert. It took her quite a bit longer than I thought it would."

Morrison could only stare at the two vacantly. He felt as though he had swallowed an icicle whole—one that didn't melt but that, instead, reduced the temperature of his abdomen to the freezing point.

Certainly, he was shivering.

CHAPTER 7

SHIP

*No voyage is dangerous to the one
who waves good-bye from the shore.*
            —*Dezhnev Senior*

27.

MORRISON felt numb all through lunch and yet in a way the pressure was off. There were no determined voices pressing on him, no intensity of explanations and persuasions, no smiles of intent, no heads closing in.

Of course, they made it quite clear, in a cool businesslike way, that he would no longer leave the Grotto till the deed was done and that from the Grotto there was, of course, no escape.

And then every once in a while a thought swirled into his mind—

He had actually agreed to be miniaturized!

They took him to a room of his own in the Grotto where he could view book-films through a viewer provided for his personal use—even English-language book-films if he wanted the inner familiarity of home to pass the next few hours. So he sat there with a book-film unreeling through the viewer strapped on his eyes and somehow it left his mind totally untouched.

He had actually agreed to be miniaturized!

He had been told that he could do as he pleased until someone came for him. He could do as he pleased, that is, provided he did not please to leave. There were guards everywhere.

The feeling of terror had, Morrison was aware, much diminished. That was the use of numbness and, of course, the more one repeats a sentence in one's mind, the more it loses meaning. *He had actually agreed to be miniaturized.* The more it rang in his mind like the tolling of a bell, over and over, the more the horror of it faded. —And left a mere vacuum of non-sensation in its place.

He was distantly aware that the door of his room had opened. Someone, he presumed dully, had come for him. He removed his viewer, lifted his eyes languidly, and, for just a moment, felt a mild spark of interest.

It was Sophia Kaliinin, looking beautiful even to his bleared senses. She said in English, "A good afternoon to you, gentleman."

He grimaced slightly. He would rather hear Russian than English delivered with quite so distorted an accent.

He said sullenly in Russian, "Please speak in Russian, Sophia."

His Russian might be as distressing to her, for all he knew, as her English was to him, but he didn't care. He was here by their doing and if his shortcomings troubled them, that was their doing, too.

She shrugged slightly and said in Russian, "Certainly—if that is what pleases you."

Then she stared at him for a thoughtful while. He met that stare easily enough for, at the moment, he did not much care what he did and looking at her was not much different to him than looking at something else would have been—or looking at nothing would have been. The momentary impression of beauty that had come with her entrance had faded.

She said finally, "I understand that you have now agreed to accompany us on our venture."

"Yes, I have."

"That is good of you. We are all grateful. In all honesty, I did not think you would do so, since you are an American. I apologize."

Morrison said with a far-off touch of regret and anger,

"The decision to help you was not voluntary. I was persuaded—by an expert."

"By Natalya Boranova?"

Morrison nodded.

"She is very good at persuading," said Kaliinin. "Not very kind, usually, but very good. I, too, required persuasion."

"Why you?" said Morrison.

"I had other reasons—ones that were important to me."

"Indeed? What were they?"

"—But unimportant to you."

There was a short uncomfortable pause.

"Come, the task I have been given is to show you the ship," said Kaliinin.

"The ship? How long have you been planning this? Have you had time to build a ship?"

"For the specific purpose of testing Shapirov's brain from within? Of course not. It was meant for other, simpler purposes, but it is the only thing we have that we can use. —Come, Albert, Natalya thinks it will be wise for you to become acquainted with it, see it, feel it. It is possible that the down-to-earthness of the technology will reconcile you to the task."

Morrison held back. "Why must I see it now? Can't I have time to grow accustomed to the whole subject of personal miniaturization?"

"That is foolish, Albert. If you had more time to sit in your room and brood, you would have more time to feed your—uncertainty. Besides, we have no time. How long do you suppose we can allow Shapirov to lie there deteriorating, with his thoughts diminishing with each moment? The ship embarks on its journey tomorrow morning."

"Tomorrow morning," muttered Morrison, his throat dry. Foolishly, he looked at his watch.

"You have few enough hours, but we'll keep track of the time for you so you need not consult your watch. Tomorrow morning the ship enters a human body. And you will be on the ship."

Then, without warning, she slapped his cheek hard. She said, "Your eyes were beginning to turn upward. Were you planning to faint?"

Morrison rubbed his cheek, grimacing with pain. "I wasn't planning anything," he mumbled, "but I might have fainted without planning it. Have you no gentler way of breaking the news?"

"Have I really caught you by surprise, when you already know that you have agreed to be miniaturized and it is self-evident that we have no time?"

She gestured peremptorily, "Now come with me."

And Morrison, still rubbing his cheek and seething with rage and humiliation, followed.

28.

IT was back to the miniaturization area—back to the busy people, each concerned with their own affairs and paying no attention to one another. Through them all, Kaliinin walked with an erect carriage and maintained the aristocratic air that arises automatically when all defer to you.

She was one of the leading lights, Morrison could see (his hand still resting lightly on his cheek, which felt inflamed and which he hesitated to expose), and all who crossed or even neared her path nodded their heads in a kind of rudimentary bow and stepped a little backward, as though to make sure not to impede her patch. No one acknowledged Morrison's presence at all.

On, on, through one room after another—and everywhere the feel of pent-up energy held in bare check.

Kaliinin must have sensed it too, familiar as she must be with it, for she muttered to Morrison with a certain pride, "There's a solar power station in space, a major part of whose output is reserved for Malenkigrad."

And then they were upon it before Morrison had a true chance to realize what he was looking at. It was not a very large room and the object within it was not of impressive bulk. Indeed, Morrison's first impression was that it was a piece of artwork.

It was a streamlined object not much larger than an automobile, certainly shorter than a stretch limousine, though taller. And it was transparent!

Automatically, Morrison reached out to feel it.

It was not cold to the touch. It felt smooth and almost moist, but when he removed his hand, his fingertips were perfectly dry. He tried it again and as he ran his fingertips across the surface, they seemed to stick slightly, but they left no sweaty mark. On impulse, he breathed upon it. There was the shadow of condensing moisture on the transparent material, but it disappeared quickly.

"It is a plastic material," said Kaliinin, "but I don't know its composition. If I knew, it would probably come under the head of classified information anyway, but whatever it is, it is stronger than steel—tougher and more resistant to shock—kilogram for kilogram."

"Weight for weight, perhaps," said Morrison, for the moment his scientific curiosity drowning his uneasiness, "but such a thickness of plastic material could not possibly be as strong as the same thickness of steel. It could not be as strong, volume for volume."

"Yes, but where are we going?" said Kaliinin. "There will be no pressure differential inside and outside the ship; there will be no meteroids or even cosmic dust against which we must protect ourselves. There will be about us nothing but soft cell structure. This plastic will be ample protection and it is light. The two of us could perhaps lift it if we tried. That is what is important. As you can well understand, we must be sparing of mass. Every additional kilogram consumes considerable electromagnetic energy in miniaturization and delivers considerable heat in deminiaturization."

"Will it hold a large enough crew?" said Morrison, peering inside.

"It will. It is very compact, but it can hold six and we will only be five. And it contains a surprising amount of unusual gadgetry. Not as much as we would like, of course. The original plans— But what can we do? There are always pressures for economy, even unwarranted ones, in this unjust world."

Morrison said with a twinge of strong uneasiness, "How much pressure for how much economy? Does everything work?"

"I assure you it does." Her face had lit up. Now that the settled melancholy had left (temporarily only, Morrison felt sure), Kaliinin was unmistakably good-looking. "Everything in it has been tested exhaustively, both singly and all together. Zero risk is impossible of attainment, but we have a reasonably close to zero risk here. And all with virtually no metal. What with microchips, fiber optics, and Manuilsky junctions, we have all we want in a total of less than five kilograms of devices all together. That is why the ship can be so small. After all, voyages into the microcosm are not expected to last for more than some hours, so we don't need sleeping arrangements, cycling equipment, elaborate food and air supplies, anything other than quite simple devices for excretory functions, and so on."

"Who'll be at the controls?"

"Arkady."

"Arkady Dezhnev?"

"You seem surprised."

"I don't know why I should. I presume he's qualified."

"Completely. He's in engineering design and he's a genius at it. You can't go by the way he sounds— No, you *can* go by the way he sounds. Do you suppose any of us could endure his crude humor and affectations if he weren't a genius at something? He designed the ship—every part of it—and all its equipment. He invented a dozen completely new ways of lowering mass and introducing compactness. You have nothing like it in the United States."

Morrison said stiffly, "I have no way of knowing what the United States may have or may not have in unusual devices."

"I am sure they don't. Dezhnev is an unusual person, for all his love of presenting himself as a boor. He is a descendant of Semyon Ivanov Dezhnev. You have heard of him, I suppose."

Morrison shook his head.

"Really?" Kaliinin's voice turned icy. "He is only the famous explorer who, in the time of Peter the Great, explored Siberia to its easternmost centimeter and said there was a stretch of sea separating Siberia and North America decades before Vitus Bering, a Dane in Russian employ, discovered the Bering Strait. —And you don't know Dezhnev. That's so American. Unless a Westerner did it, you never heard of it."

"Don't see insults everywhere, Sophia. I haven't studied exploration. There are many American explorers that I don't know—and that you don't, either." He shook his finger at her, again remembering her slap and rubbing his cheek once more. "This is what I mean. You find things to feed hate on —inconsequential things you should feel ashamed to grub up."

"Semyon Dezhnev was a great explorer—and not inconsequential."

"I'm willing to admit that. I am glad to learn of him and I marvel at his achievement. But my not having heard of him is not a fit occasion for Soviet-American rivalry. Be ashamed of yourself!"

Kaliinin's eyes fell, then lifted to his cheek. (Had she left a bruise there? Morrison wondered.) She said, "I'm sorry I struck you, Albert. It need not have been that hard, but I didn't want you to faint. At that moment, I felt I would have no patience to deal with an unconscious American. I did let unjustified anger guide me."

"I'll grant you meant well, but I, too, wish you had not struck so hard. Still, I will accept your apology."

"Then let us get into the ship."

Morrison managed a smile. Somehow he felt a little better dealing with Kaliinin than he would have with Dezhnev or Konev—or even Boranova. A pretty woman, still quite young, does somehow distract a man's mind from his troubles more effectively than most things would. He said, "Aren't you afraid I might try to sabotage it?"

Kaliinin paused. "Actually, I'm not. I suspect you have enough respect for a vessel of scientific exploration to avoid doing it any damage whatever. Besides—and I say this seriously, Albert—the laws against sabotage are excessively severe in the Soviet Union and the slightest mistake in handling anything in the ship will set off an alarm that will have guards here in a matter of seconds. We have strict laws against guards beating up saboteurs, but sometimes they tend to forget themselves in their indignation. Please don't even think of touching anything."

She put a hand on the hull as she spoke and presumably closed a contact, though Morrison didn't see how it was done. A door—a rectangle curved at the edge—opened. (The door's own edge seemed to be double. Would it also act as an air lock?)

The opening was compact. Kaliinin, entering first, had to stoop. She held out a hand to Morrison. "Careful, Albert."

Morrison not only stooped, but turned sideways. Once inside the ship, he found that he could not quite stand upright. When he bumped his head gently, he looked up at the ceiling, startled.

Kaliinin said, "We'll be doing our work sitting down for the most part, so don't be concerned about the ceiling."

"I don't think claustrophobes would like this."

"Are you claustrophobic?"

"No."

Kaliinin nodded her relief. "That's good. We have to save space, you know. What can I tell you?"

Morrison looked around. There were six seats, in pairs. He sat down in the one nearest the door and said, "These are not exactly roomy, either."

"No," admitted Kaliinin. "Weight lifters could not be accommodated."

Morrison said, "Obviously, this ship was built long before Shapirov went into his coma."

"Of course. We've been planning to have miniaturized personnel invade living tissue for a long time. That would be necessary if we wished to make truly important biological discoveries. Naturally, we expected that we would work with animals at the start and study the circulatory system in fine detail. It is for that project that this ship was built. No one could possibly have guessed that when the time came to carry out the first such microvoyage, the subject would not only be a human body but Shapirov himself."

Morrison was still studying the interior of the ship. It seemed bare. Detail was surprisingly difficult to make out in the situation of transparency-on-transparency and miniaturization of the old-type—ordinary, but microscopic—components.

He said, "There will be five on the ship: you and I, Boranova, Konev, and Dezhnev."

"That's right."

"And what will each of us be doing?"

"Arkady will control the ship. Obviously, he knows how to do that. It's the child of his hands and mind. He'll be in the left front seat. To his right will be the other male, who has a complete map of the neurocirculatory pattern of Shapirov's brain. He will be the pilot. I will sit behind Arkady and I will control the electromagnetic pattern of the ship's surface."

"An electromagnetic pattern? What's that for?"

"My dear Albert. You recognize objects by reflected light, a dog recognizes objects by emitted odor, a molecule recognizes objects by surface electromagnetic pattern. If we're going to make our way as a miniaturized object among molecules, we must have the proper patterns in order to be treated as friends rather than foes."

"That sounds complicated."

"It is—but it happens to be my life study. Natalya will sit behind me. She will be the captain of the expedition. She will make the decisions."

"What kind of decisions?"

"Whatever kind are necessary. Obviously, those can't be predicted in advance. As for you, you will sit to my right."

Morrison rose and managed to shift his position along the narrow aisle on the door side of the seats and move one seat back. He had been in Konev's seat and now he was in what would be his own. He could feel his heart pounding as he imagined himself in that same seat on the following day, with the miniaturization process in progress.

He said in a muffled voice, "There is only one man, then—Yuri Konev—who was miniaturized and deminiaturized and was unharmed by the process."

"Yes."

"And he mentioned no discomfort in the process, no sickness, no mental disturbance?"

"Nothing of the sort was reported."

"Would that be because he is a stoic? Would he feel it would be beneath the dignity of a hero of Soviet science to complain?"

"Don't be foolish. We are not heroes of Soviet science and the one you speak of certainly isn't. We are human beings and scientists and, in fact, if there were any discomfort that we felt, we would be compelled to describe it in full detail, since it might be that with modifications of the process we could remove that discomfort and make future miniaturizations less difficult. Hiding any part of the truth would be unscientific, unethical, and dangerous. Don't you see that—since you are a scientist yourself?"

"Yet there may be individual differences. Yuri Konev survived untouched. Pyotr Shapirov did not—quite."

"That had nothing to do with individual differences," said Kaliinin impatiently.

"We can't really tell, can we?"

"Then judge for yourself, Albert. Do you think we would

take the ship into miniaturization without a final testing—with and without human beings aboard? This ship was miniaturized, empty, during the course of this past night—not to a very great extent, but enough to know that all is well."

At once Morrison struggled upward to get out of his seat. "In that case, if you don't mind, Sophia, I want to get out before it is tested with human beings aboard."

"But, Albert, it's too late."

"What!"

"Look out the ship at the room. You haven't once looked outside since you got in, which, I suppose, was a good thing. But look out now. Go ahead. The walls are transparent and the process is complete for now. Please! Look!"

Morrison, startled, did so and then, very slowly, his knees bent and he seated himself again. He asked (and even as he did so, he knew how foolish he must sound), "Do the ship's walls have a magnifying effect?"

"No, of course not. Everything outside is as it always is. The ship and I—and *you*—have been miniaturized to about half our linear dimensions."

29.

MORRISON felt dizziness overcome him and he bent his head between his knees and breathed slowly and deeply. When he lifted his head again, he saw Kaliinin watching him thoughtfully. She was standing in the narrow aisle, leaning slightly against a seat's armrest to allow the ceiling to clear her head.

"You might have fainted this time," she said. "It would not have disturbed me. We are being deminiaturized now and that will be more time-consuming than the miniaturization, which took no more than three or four minutes. It will take an hour or so for us to get back, so you will have ample time to recover."

"It was not a decent act to do this without telling me, Sophia."

"On the contrary," said Kaliinin. "It was an act of kindness. Would you have entered the ship as freely and as easily as you did if you had suspected that we would be miniaturized? Would you have inspectd the ship as coolly if you had known? And if you had been anticipating miniaturization, would you not have developed psychogenic symptoms of all sorts?''

Morrison was silent.

Kaliinin said, ''Did you feel anything? Were you even aware that you were being miniaturized?''

Morrison shook his head. ''No.''

Then, driven by a certain shame, he said, ''You've never been miniaturized before any more than I have, have you?''

''No. Before this day, Konev and Shapirov have been the only human beings to have undergone miniaturization.''

''And you weren't at all apprehensive?''

She said, ''I wouldn't say that. I was uneasy. We know from our experience with space travel that, as you said earlier, there are individual differences in reaction to unusual environments. Some astronauts suffer episodes of nausea under zero gravity and some do not, for instance. I couldn't be sure how I would react. —Did you feel nausea?''

''I didn't until I found out we had been miniaturized, but I suppose feeling queasy now doesn't count. —Who planned this?''

''Natalya.''

''Of course. I needn't have asked,'' he said drily.

''There were reasons. She felt we couldn't have you break down once the voyage began. We couldn't be expected to deal with hysteria on your part once we began miniaturizing.''

''I suppose I deserve that lack of confidence,'' said Morrison, his eyes looking away in embarrassment from those of Kaliinin. ''And I imagine she assigned you to come with me for the precise purpose of distracting my attention while all this was going on.''

''No. That was my idea. She wanted to come with you herself, but with her, by now, I thought you might be anticipating trickery.''

''Whereas with you, I might be at my ease.''

''At least, as you say, distracted. I am still young enough to distract men.'' Then, with a touch of bitterness, ''Most men.''

Morrison looked up, eyes narrowing. ''You said I might be anticipating trickery.''

''I mean, with Natalya.''

''Why not with you? All I see now is that everything outside seems enlarged. How can I be sure that that is not an illusion, something designed to make me think I have been miniaturized and that it is harmless—merely so that I step quietly into the ship tomorrow?"

"That's ridiculous, Albert, but let's consider something. You and I have lost half our linear dimension in every direction. The strength of our muscles varies inversely with their cross-sections. They are now half their normal width and half their normal thickness, so that they have half times half or one fourth the cross-section and, therefore, the strength they would normally have. Do you see what I mean? Do you understand?"

"Yes, of course," said Morrison, annoyed. "That is elementary."

"But our bodies as a whole are half as tall, half as wide, and half as thick, so that the total volume—and mass and weight as well—is half times half times half or one eighth what it was originally. —*If* we are miniaturized, that is."

"Yes. This is the square-cube law. It's been understood since Galileo's time."

"I know, but you haven't been thinking about it. If I were to try to lift you now, I would be lifting one eighth your normal weight and I would be doing so with my muscles at one quarter their normal strength. My muscles compared to your weight would be twice as strong as they would appear to be if we were not miniaturized."

And with that, Kaliinin thrust her hands under his armpits and, with a grunt, lifted. Up he moved from his seat.

She held him so while she gasped twice and then she lowered him. "It's not easy," she said, panting a bit, "but I could do it. And since you may be telling yourself, 'Ah yes, but this is Sophia, probably a Soviet weight lifter,' then do it to me."

Kaliinin seated herself in the seat before him and held out her arms to either side and said, "Come, stand up and lift me."

Morrison rose to his feet and into the aisle. He moved forward, turned, and faced her. The slight bending enforced on him by the low ceiling made it an uncomfortable position. For a moment, he hesitated.

Kaliinin said, "Come, seize me under the arms. I use deodorant. And you needn't be concerned about possibly touching my breasts. They have been touched before this. Come— I'm lighter than you are and you're stronger than I am. Since I have lifted you, you should have no trouble at all lifting me.''

Nor did he. He couldn't lift with his full strength because of his slight, uncomfortable stoop, but he automatically applied the force he judged, through years of experience, would be suitable for an object her size. She floated upward, however, almost as though she were weightless. Despite the fact that he had been somewhat prepared for the possibility, he almost dropped her.

"Do you consider that an illusion?" Kaliinin asked. "Or are we miniaturized?"

"We are miniaturized," said Morrison. "But how did you do it? I never saw you make a move that looked as though you might be using miniaturization controls."

"I didn't. It's all done from outside. The ship is equipped with miniaturization devices of its own, but I wouldn't dare use them. That would be part of Natalya's job."

"And now the deminiaturization is being controlled from outside, too, isn't it?"

"That's right."

"And if the deminiaturization gets slightly out of hand, our brains will be damaged as Shapirov's was—or worse."

"That's not really likely," said Kaliinin, stretching her legs out into the aisle, "and it doesn't help to think about it. Why not just relax and close your eyes?"

Morrison persisted. "But damage *is* possible."

"Of course it's possible. Almost anything is possible. A three-meter-wide meteorite may strike two minutes from now, penetrate the mountain shell above us, flash into this room, and destroy the ship and us and perhaps the entire project in a few flaming seconds. —But it's not likely."

Morrison cradled his head in his arms and wondered whether—if the ship started warming—he could feel the heat before his brain proteins denatured.

30.

WELL over half an hour had passed before Morrison felt convinced that the objects he could see outside the ship were shrinking and were receding perceptibly toward their normal size.

Morrison said, "I am thinking of a paradox."

"What's that?" said Kaliinin, yawning. She had obviously taken her own advice about the advisability of relaxing.

"The objects outside the ship seemed to grow larger as we shrink. Ought not the wavelengths of light outside the ship also grow larger, becoming longer in wavelength, as we shrink? Should we not see everything outside turn reddish, since there can scarcely be enough ultraviolet outside to expand and replace the shorter-wave visible light?"

Kaliinin said, "If you could see the light waves outside, that would indeed be how they would appear to you. But you don't. You see the light waves only after they've entered the ship and impinged upon your retina. And as they enter the ship, they come under the influence of the miniaturization field and automatically shrink in wavelength, so that you see those wavelengths inside the ship exactly as you would see them outside."

"If they shrink in wavelength, they must gain energy."

"Yes, *if* Planck's constant were the same size inside the miniaturization field as it is outside. But Planck's constant decreases inside the miniaturization field—that is the essence of miniaturization. The wavelengths, in shrinking, maintain their relationship to the shrunken Planck's constant and do not gain energy. An analogous case is that of the atoms. They also shrink and yet the interrelationships among atoms and among the subatomic particles that make them up remain the same to us inside the ship as they would seem to us outside the ship."

"But gravity changes. It becomes weaker in here."

"The strong interaction and the electroweak interaction come under the umbrella of the quantum theory. They depend on Planck's constant. As for gravitation?" Kaliinin shrugged. "Despite two centuries of effort, gravitation has never been quantized. Frankly, I think the gravitational change with miniaturization is evidence enough that gravitation cannot be quantized, that it is fundamentally nonquantum in nature."

"I can't believe that," said Morrison. "Two centuries of failure can merely mean we haven't managed to get deep enough into the problem yet. Superstring theory nearly gave us our unified field at last." (It relieved him to discuss the matter. Surely he couldn't do so if his brain were heating in the least.)

"Nearly doesn't count," said Kaliinin. "Still, Shapirov agreed with you, I think. It was his notion that once we tied Planck's constant to the speed of light, we would not only have the practical effect of miniaturizing and deminiaturizing in an essentially energy-free manner, but that we would have the theoretical effect of being able to work out the connection between quantum theory and relativity and finally have a good unified field theory. And probably a simpler one than we could have imagined possible, he would say."

"Maybe," said Morrison. He didn't know enough to comment beyond that.

"Shapirov would say," said Kaliinin, warming to the task, "that at ultraminiaturization, the gravitational effect would be close enough to zero to be utterly ignored and that the speed of light would be so great that it might be considered infinite. With mass virtually zero, inertia would be virtually zero and any object, like this ship, for instance, could be accelerated with virtually zero energy input to any speed. We would have, practically speaking, antigravity and faster-than-light travel. Chemical drive, he said, gave us the Solar System, ion drive would give us the nearer stars, but relativistic miniaturization would give us the whole Universe at a bound."

"It's a beautiful vision," said Morrison, ravished.

"Then you know what we're looking for now, don't you?"

Morrison nodded. "All that—if we can read Shapirov's mind. And if he really had something there and wasn't merely dreaming."

"Isn't the chance worth the risk?"

"I am on the point of believing so," said Morrison in a low voice. "You are terribly convincing. Why couldn't Natalya have used arguments of that sort, rather than those she did use?"

"Natalya is—Natalya. She is a highly practical person, not a dreamer. She gets things done."

Morrison studied Kaliinin as she sat, now in the seat to his left, looking straight ahead with an abstracted look that gave her profile the appearance of an impractical dreamer, at that —but perhaps not one who, like Shapirov, dreamed of conquering the Universe. With her, it was something closer to home perhaps.

He said, "Your unhappiness is not my business, Sophia, as you've said—but I have been told about Yuri."

Her eyes flashed. "Arkady! I know it was he. He is a— a—" She shook her head. "With all his education and all his genius, he remains a peasant. I always think of him as a bearded serf with a vodka bottle."

"I think he's concerned about you in his own way, even if he doesn't express himself poetically. Everyone must be concerned."

Kaliinin stared at Morrison fiercely, as if holding her words back.

He prodded her gently, saying, "Why don't you tell me about it? I think it will help and I am a logical choice, being the outsider of the party—I assure you I am trustworthy."

Kaliinin looked at him again, this time almost gratefully.

"Yuri!" she spat. "Everyone may be concerned, except *Yuri*. He has no feelings."

"He must have been in love with you at one time."

"Must he? I don't believe it. He has a—a"—she looked up and spread her hands, which were shaking, as though groping for a word and having to settle for something inferior— "vision."

"We're not always masters of our own emotions and affections, Sophia. If he has found another woman and dreams of her—"

"There's no other woman," said Kaliinin, frowning. "None! He uses that as an excuse to hide behind! He loved me, if at all, only absently, because I was convenient at hand, because I satisfied a vague physical need, and because I was also involved in the project, so that he didn't have to lose much time dallying with me. As long as he had this project firmly in hand, he didn't mind having me—quietly, unobtrusively—at odd moments."

"A man's work—"

"Need not fill every moment of time. I told you he has a vision. He plans to be the new Newton, the new Einstein. He wants to make discoveries so fundamental, so great, that he will leave nothing for the future. He will take Shapirov's speculations and turn them into hard science. Yuri Konev will become the whole of the natural law and everyone else will be commentary!"

"Might that not be considered an admirable ambition?"

"Not when it makes him sacrifice everything and everyone else, when it makes him deny his own child. I? What do I matter? I can be neglected, denied. I am an adult. I can take care of myself. But a baby? A child? To deny her a father? To refuse her? To reject her? She would distract him from his work, she would make demands on him, she would consume a few moments of time here and there—so he insists he is not the father."

"A genetic analysis—"

"No. Would I drag him to court and force a legal decision upon him? Consider what his denial implies? The child is not a virgin birth. Someone *must* be the father. He implies—no, he *states*—that I am promiscuous. He has not hesitated to give it as his opinion that I do not know the father of my child since I am lost among the numerous possibilities. Shall I labor to make a man as low as he is the legally proved father of my child against his will? No, let him come to me and admit he is the father and apologize for what he has done—and I may allow him a glance, now and then, at the child."

"Yet I have a feeling you still love him."

"If I do, that is my curse," said Kaliinin bitterly. "It shall not be my child's."

"Is that why you have had to be persuaded to undertake this miniaturization?"

"And work with him? Yes, that is why. But they tell me I cannot be replaced, that what we may do for science lies far above and beyond any conceivable personal feeling—any anger, any hate. Besides—"

"Besides?"

"Besides, if I abandon the project, I lose my status as a Soviet scientist. I lose many privileges and perquisites, which do not matter, and so does my daughter—which matters a great deal."

"Did Yuri have to be persuaded, too, to work with you?"

"He? Of course not. The project is all he knows and sees. He does not look at me. He does not see me. And if he dies in the course of this attempt—" She held out her hand in appeal to him. "Please understand that I do not for a moment believe that this will happen. It is just a stupidly romantic notion that I torture myself with for the love of pain, I suppose. If he should die, he would not even be aware that I would die with him."

Morrison felt himself tremble. "Don't talk like that," he said. "And what would happen to your daughter in that case? Did Natalya tell you that?"

"She did not have to. I know that without her. My daughter would be reared by the state, as the child of a Soviet martyr to science. She might be better off so." Sophia paused and looked around. "But it's beginning to look quite normal out there. We should be out of the ship soon."

Morrison shrugged.

"You will have to spend much of the rest of the day being medically and psychologically examined, Albert. So will I. It will be very boring, but it has to be done. How do you feel?"

"I'd feel better," said Morrison in a burst of honesty, "if you hadn't talked about dying. —Listen! Tomorrow, when we make the trip into Shapirov's body, how far will we be miniaturized?"

"That will be Natalya's decision. To cellular dimensions at the very least, obviously. Perhaps to molecular dimensions."

"Has anyone ever done that?"

"Not to my knowledge."

"Rabbits? Inanimate objects?"

Kaliinin shook her head and said again, "Not to my knowledge."

"How, then, does anyone know that miniaturization to such an extent is possible? Or that, if it is, any of us can survive?"

"The theory says it is and that we can. So far, every bit of experimentation has fit in with the theory."

"Yes, but there are always boundaries. Wouldn't it be better if ultraminiaturization were tested on a simple bar of plastic, then on a rabbit, then on a—"

"Yes, of course. But persuading the Central Coordinating Committee to allow the energy expenditure would be an enormous task and such experiments would have to be dribbled out over months and years. We have no time! We must get into Shapirov immediately."

"But we're going to be doing something unprecedented, crossing into an untested region, with only the maybes of theory to—"

"Exactly, exactly. Come, the light is flashing and we must emerge and accompany the waiting physicians."

But for Morrison the marginal euphoria of a safe deminiaturization was seeping away. What he had experienced today was in no way indicative of what he must face the next day.

The terror was returning.

CHAPTER 8

PRELIMINARIES

*The greatest difficulty comes
at the start. It's called "getting ready."*
—Dezhnev Senior

31.

LATER that evening, after a long—and tedious—medical exam, he joined the four Soviet researchers for dinner. The Last Supper, Morrison thought grimly.

Sitting down, he burst out, "No one told me the results of my examination!" He turned to Kaliinin. "Did they examine you, Sophia?"

"Yes, indeed, Albert."

"Did they tell *you* the results?"

"I'm afraid not. Since it is not we who pay them, I suppose they don't feel they owe us anything."

"It doesn't matter," said Dezhnev jovially. "My old father used to say, 'Bad news has the wings of an eagle, good news the legs of a sloth.' If they said nothing, it was because they had nothing bad to report."

"Even the bad news," said Boranova, "would have been reported to me—and only to me. I am the one who must decide who will accompany us."

"What did they tell you about me?" asked Morrison.

"That there is nothing important wrong with you. You will

129

be coming with us and in twelve hours the adventure will begin."

"Is there anything unimportant wrong with me, then, Natalya?"

"Nothing worth mentioning, except that you display, according to one doctor, a 'typical American bad temper.'"

"Huh!" said Morrison. "One of our American freedoms is that of being bad-tempered when doctors show a typical Soviet lack of concern for their patients."

Nevertheless, his apprehension over the state of his mind ebbed and, as it did so, inevitably the apprehension over his impending miniaturization rose higher.

He lapsed into silence, eating slowly and without much of an appetite.

32.

YURI Konev was the first to rise from the dinner table. For a moment he remained standing, leaning forward over the table, a slight frown on his intense, youthful face.

"Natalya," he said, "I must take Albert to my office. It is necessary that we discuss tomorrow's task and prepare for it."

Boranova said, "You will remember, please, that we must all have a good night's sleep. I don't wish you to forget the passage of time. Do you want Arkady to go with you?"

"I don't need him," said Konev haughtily.

"Nevertheless," said Boranova, "there will be two guards at your office door and you will call out if you need them."

Konev turned from her impatiently and said, "I won't need them, Natalya, I'm sure. Come with me, Albert."

Morrison, who had been watching them both from under lowered eyebrows, rose and said, "Is this going to be a long trip? I'm tired of being shuttled from point to point in the Grotto."

Morrison knew well he was being ungracious, but it didn't seem to bother Konev, who responded just as ungraciously, "I should think a professor would be used to plunging back and forth across a university campus."

Morrison followed Konev out the door and together they tramped along the corridor in silence. Morrison was aware that at a certain point two guards fell in behind them. He heard additional footsteps keeping time with his own. He looked back, but Konev did not.

Morrison said impatiently, "Much longer, Yuri?"

"That is a foolish question, Albert. I have no intention of walking you past our destination. When we get there, we will be there. If we are still walking, it is because we are not there yet."

"I should think, with all this walking, you might arrange golf carts or something of the sort for the corridors."

"Anything to allow the muscles to atrophy, Albert? Come, you are not so old that you cannot walk or so young that you must be carried."

Morrison thought, If I were that poor woman with his child, I would shoot off fireworks to celebrate his denial of fatherhood.

They reached Konev's office at last. At least Morrison assumed it was his office when Konev barked the word "Open" and the door slid smoothly open in response to his voiceprint. Konev strode through first.

"What if someone imitates your voice?" asked Morrison curiously. "You don't have a very distinctive voice, you know."

Konev said, "It also scans my face. It will not respond to either separately."

"And if you have a cold?"

"One time when I had a bad one, I could not get into my office for three days and I finally had to have the door opened mechanically. If my face were bruised or scarred by accident, I might also have trouble. Still, that is the price of security."

"But are the people here so—inquisitive—that they would invade your privacy?"

"People are people and it is not wise to overtempt even the best of them. I have things here unique to myself and they may be viewed only when I decide to allow it. This, for instance." His slim hand (very well-cared-for and manicured, Morrison noticed—he might neglect other things for his work, but not himself) rested on an extraordinarily large and thick volume, which, in turn, rested on a stand that had been clearly designed for it.

"What is that?" asked Morrison.

"That," said Konev, "is Academician Shapirov—or at least the essence of him." He opened the book and flipped the pages. Page after page (all of them, perhaps) were filled with symbols arranged in diagrammatic fashion.

Konev said, "I have it on microfilm, of course, but there are certain conveniences to having it in a printed volume." He patted the pages almost lovingly.

"I still don't understand," said Morrison.

"This is the basic structure of Shapirov's brain, translated into a symbolism of my own devising. Fed into the appropriate software, it can reconstitute a three-dimensional map of the brain in intimate detail on a computer screen."

"Astonishing," said Morrison, "if you are serious."

"I am serious," said Konev. "I have spent my entire career on this task: translating brain structure into symbols and symbols into brain structure. I have invented and advanced this science of cerebrography."

"And you used Shapirov as your subject."

"By incredible good fortune, I did. Or perhaps it was not good fortune, but merely inevitable. We all have our small vanities and it seemed to Shapirov that his brain was worth preserving in detail. Once I began working on this field under his direction—for there was the feeling that we might someday want to explore animal brains at least—he insisted on having his own brain analyzed cerebrographically."

Morrison said with a sudden excitement, "Can you get his theories out of the recorded cerebral structure of his brain?"

"Of course not. These symbols record a cerebral scanning that was carried through three years ago. That was before he had evolved his recent notions and, in any case, what I have preserved here is, unfortunately, only the physical structure and not the thoughts. Still, the cerebrograph will be invaluable to us in tomorrow's voyage."

"I should think so—but I have never heard of this."

"I'm not surprised. I have published papers on this, but only in the Grotto's own publication—and these remain highly classified. No one outside the Grotto, not even here in the Soviet Union, knows of them."

"That is bad policy. You will be overtaken by someone else who will publish and who will be granted priority."

Konev shook his head. "At the first sign that significant advances in this direction are being made elsewhere, enough of my early work will be published to establish priority. I have cerebrographs of canine brains that I can publish, for instance. But never mind that. The point is that we have a map of Shapirov's brain to guide us, which is a matter of incredible good fortune. It was made without the knowledge that we might need it someday to guide us through that very cerebral jungle."

Konev turned to a computer and, with practiced flips of his wrist, inserted five large discs.

"Each one of these," he said, "can hold all the information in the Central Moscow Library without crowding. It is all devoted to Shapirov's brain."

"Are you trying to tell me," said Morrison indignantly, "that you could transfer all that information, all of Shapirov's brain, into that book you have here?"

"Well, no," said Konev, glancing at the book. "In comparison with the total code, that book is only a small pamphlet. However, it does hold the basic skeleton, so to speak, of Shapirov's neuronic structure and I was able to use it as a guide by which to direct a computer program that mapped it out in greater detail. It took months for the best and most advanced computer we have to do the job.

"And even so, Albert, all we have reaches merely to the cellular level. If we were to map the brain down to the molecular level and try to record all the permutations and combinations—all the conceivable thoughts that might arise from a particular human brain like Shapirov's; all the creativity, actual and potential—I suppose it would take a computer the size of the Universe working for a much longer time than the Universe has existed. What I have, however, may be enough for our task."

Morrison, entranced, asked, "Can you show me how it works, Yuri?"

Konev studied the computer—which was turned on, as one could tell by the soft whisper of its cooling mechanism—then pushed the necessary keys. On the screen there appeared the side view of a human brain.

Konev said, "This can be viewed at any cross-section." He pressed a key and the brain began to peel as though it were being continually sliced by an ultrathin microtome some thousands of slices per second. "At this rate," he said, "it would take an hour and fifteen minutes to complete the task, but I could stop it at any chosen point. I could also cut off thicker slices or cut off one thick calculated slice to bring me at once to any wanted cross-section."

As he spoke, he demonstrated. "Or I could orient it in another direction or rotate it along any axis. Or I can magnify it to any extent down to the cellular level, either slowly or, as you see, quickly." As he said this, the material of the brain spread outward in all directions from a central point—dizzyingly—so that Morrison was forced to blink his eyes and then look away.

Konev said, "This is now at the cellular level. Those small objects are individual neurons and if I expanded the image still further, you would see the axons and dendrites. If one wishes, we could follow a single axon through the cell into a dendrite and across a synapse to another neuron and so on, traveling, by computer, through a brain three-dimensionally. Nor is the matter of three demensions just a manner of speaking. The computer is outfitted for holographic imaging and it can present a three-dimensional appearance quite literally."

Morrison said challengingly, "Then why do you need miniaturization? Why do you need to send ships into the brain?"

Konev briefly allowed a look of contempt to cross his face. "That is a foolish question, Albert, and I suppose it is inspired only by your fear of miniaturization. You are groping for any excuse to eliminate it. What you see here on the screen is a three-dimensional mapping of the brain, but *only* three-dimensional. It has caught it at what is, essentially, an instant of time. In effect, we see unchanging material—dead material. What we want to be able to detect is the living activity of the neurons, the changing activity with time. We want a four-dimensional view of the electric potentials that rise and fall, the microcurrents that travel along the cells and cell fibers, and we want to interpret them into thoughts. That's your task, Albert. Arkady Dezhnev will manipulate the ship along the routes I have chosen and you will give us the thoughts."

"On what basis have you chosen the routes?"

"On the basis of your own papers, Albert. I have chosen the regions you had decided must represent the neuronic network for creative thought and, using this book, with its coded representation of Shapirov's brain as my initial guide,

I calculated centers where more or less direct pathways could be found to several portions of the network. I then located them more accurately on the computer and it is to one or more of those centers that we will penetrate tomorrow."

Morrison shook his head. "I'm afraid I can't guarantee that we will be able to determine actual thoughts, even if we find the centers in which thinking takes place. It's as though we might reach a place where we can hear people's voices, but if we don't know the language, we are still left in ignorance of what they are saying."

"We can't know that in advance. The varying electric potentials in Shapirov's mind must resemble those in ours and we may simply be aware of his thoughts without knowing how we are aware. In any case, we can't tell unless we go in and try."

"In that case, you will have to be ready for possible disappointment."

"Never," said Konev with the utmost seriousness. "I intend to be the person to whom the human brain will finally yield its secrets. I will solve, completely, the ultimate physiological mystery of humanity, perhaps of the Universe—if we are the most advanced thinking devices that exist anywhere. —So we will work together, you and I, tomorrow. I want you to be ready for it, to help guide me by studying carefully the brain waves we encounter. I want you to interpret Shapirov's thoughts and, most particularly, his thoughts on combining quantum theory and relativity so that trips such as ours tomorrow can become routine and we can begin the study of the brain in all earnestness."

He stopped and stared at Morrison intently, then said, "Well?"

"Well, what?"

"Does none of this impress you?"

"Of course it impresses me, but . . . I have a question. Yesterday when I watched the rabbit being miniaturized, there was a pronounced whine during the process—and a rumble when it was deminiaturized. There was nothing of the sort when I was subjected to it—or I would have known what was happening."

Konev raised a finger. "Ah. The noise is apparent when you are in real space, but not when you are in miniaturized space. I was the first to realize that was so when I was miniaturized and I reported it. We still don't know why the miniaturization field seems to stop sound waves when it doesn't stop light waves, but then we expect to learn new aspects of the process as we go on."

"As long as we don't discover fatal aspects," muttered Morrison. "Are you afraid of nothing, Yuri?"

"I'm afraid of not being able to complete my work. That would be true if I died tomorrow or if I refused to undergo miniaturization. Being stopped by death, however, is only a small possibility, but if I refuse to undergo miniaturization, then I am stopped certainly. That is why I much prefer to risk the former than take the latter way out."

"Does it bother you that Sophia will be undergoing miniaturization with you?"

Konev frowned. "What?"

"If you don't remember her first name, it may help if I refer to her as Kaliinin."

"She is part of the group and will be on the ship. Yes."

"And you don't mind?"

"Why should I?"

"After all, she feels you have betrayed her."

Konev frowned darkly and a dull flush rose to his face. "Has her madness gone so far as to force her to confide her incoherencies to strangers? If she weren't needed on this project—"

"I'm sorry. She didn't sound incoherent to me."

Morrison didn't know why he was pushing the matter. Perhaps he felt diminished at fearing a task the other so ardently welcomed and he therefore wished to diminish in turn. "Were you never her—friend?"

"Friend?" Konev's face mirrored his contempt. "What is friendship? When I joined the project, I found her here; she had joined a month earlier. We worked together, we were new and untried together. Of course, there was what one might call friendship, a physical need for intimacy. What of it? We were young and unsure of ourselves. It was a passing phase."

"But it left something behind. A child."

"That was not my doing." And his mouth closed with a snap.

"She says—"

"I have no doubt she would like to saddle me with the responsibility, but it won't work."

"Have you considered genetic analysis?"

"No! The child is adequately cared for, I imagine, and even if genetic analysis seemed to indicate I might be the parent, I would refuse all efforts to tie me to the child emotionally, so what would the woman have to gain?"

"Are you so coldhearted?"

"Coldhearted! What do you imagine I have done—corrupted a young, innocent virgin? She took the initiative in everything. In the sad story that I suppose she told you, did she happen to mention that she'd been pregnant before, that she had had an abortion some years before I met her? I don't know who the father was then or who it is now. Perhaps neither does she—either time."

"You are being unkind to her."

"I am *not*. She is being unkind to herself. I *have* a mistress. I *have* a love. It is this project. It is the human brain in the abstract, its study, its analysis, and all that that might lead to. The woman was, at best, a distraction—at worst, a destruction. This little talk we are having—that I did not ask for—that she goaded you into undertaking, no doubt—"

"She did not," interjected Morrison.

"Goads are not necessarily noticed. This discussion may cost me a night's sleep and make me that much less sharp tomorrow when I will need all my sharpness. Is that your intention?"

"No, of course not," Morrison said quietly.

"Then it is surely hers. You have no idea in how many different ways she has attempted interference and how often she has succeeded. I don't look at her, I don't speak to her, yet she will not leave me alone. Her imaginary wrongs seem as fresh in her mind as they were when I first broke away. Yes—I *do* mind her being on the ship with me and I have said so to Boranova, but she says that both of us are needed. — Are you satisfied?"

"I'm sorry. I didn't mean to upset you so."

"What *did* you mean? Simply to have a quiet conversation? 'Say, what about all those betrayals and dirty tricks you have committed?' Just a friendly talk?"

Morrison remained silent, bowing his head slightly against the other's rage. Three out of five on the ship—himself and the two ex-lovers—would be laboring under a sense of un-bearable wrong. He wondered if, on careful questioning, Dezhnev and Boranova would prove similarly disabled.

Konev said harshly, "You had better go. I brought you here to bury your fear of the project by providing you with a blaze of enthusiasm. Obviously, I have failed. You are more interested in prurient gossip. Go, the guards outside this door will take you to the quarters assigned you. You will need to sleep."

Morrison sighed. Sleep?

33.

YET on this, his third night in the Soviet Union, Morrison slept.

Dezhnev had been waiting outside Konev's room with the guards, his broad face grinning and his large ears all but flapping with merriment. After the shadowed intensity of Konev's personality, Morrison found himself welcoming Dezhnev's chatter on all subjects but the morrow's miniaturization.

Dezhnev urged a drink on him. "It is not vodka, not alcohol," he had said. "It is milk and a little sugar and flavoring. I stole it from the commissary where it is used, I think, for animals, because all those officials find human beings more easily replaceable than the animals. It is the curse of over-population. As my father used to say, 'To get a human being takes a moment of pleasure, but to get a horse costs money.' But drink. It will settle the stomach. I promise you."

The drink was in a can which Morrison punctured. He poured it into a cup that Dezhnev proffered and it tasted fairly good. He thanked Dezhnev almost cheerily.

When they got to Morrison's room, Dezhnev said, "Now the important thing for you to do is to sleep. Sleep well. Let me show you where everything is." And as he did so, he rather resembled a large and slightly unkempt mother hen. With a hearty "Good night. Be sure to get plenty of sleep," Dezhnev left the room.

And Morrison slept. Almost as soon as he worked himself into his favorite position—stomach down, left leg bent, knee outward—he began to feel sleepy. Of course, he had little sleep the last two nights, but he suddenly guessed that there had been a mild sedative in the cup into which he had poured the drink. Then came the thought that perhaps Konev should take such a sedative. Then—nothing.

When he woke, he could not even remember having had any dreams.

Nor did he wake of his own accord. Dezhnev was shaking him, as cheerful as he had been the evening before, as wide awake, and even as spruced up as it was possible for that animated haystack to be.

He said, "Awake, Comrade American, for it is time. You must shave and wash. There are fresh towels, combs, deodorants, tissues, and soap in the bathroom. I know because I have delivered them myself. Also a new electric razor. And on top of that, new cotton clothes for you to wear with a reinforcement in the crotch so you will not feel so exposed. They actually have them, the rotten bureaucrats, if you know how to ask—with a fist." And he raised his fist while twisting his face into a look of ferocity.

Morrison stirred and sat up on the bed. It took him a moment to place himself and to weather the shock of realization that it was Thursday morning and that miniaturization was just ahead.

Half an hour or so later, when Morrison stepped out of the bathroom again—satisfactorily bathed, dried, deodorized, shaved, combed, and reaching for his two-piece cotton uniform and his slippers—Dezhnev said, "Satisfactory elimination, my lad? No constipation?"

"Quite satisfactory," said Morrison.

"Good! I don't ask out of idle curiosity, of course. I am not fascinated by excrement. It is just that the ship is not ideally suited for such things. Better we all go in empty. I didn't trust to nature, myself. I took a bit of a laxative."

"How long will we stay miniaturized?" asked Morrison.

"Perhaps not long. An hour if we are very lucky, perhaps twelve if we're not."

"But, look," said Morrison. "I can count on a well-behaved colon, but I can't go for twelve hours without urinating."

"Who can?" asked Dezhnev jovially. "Each seat in the ship is equipped for the eventuality. There is a recess, a removable cover. A built-in toilet, so to speak. I designed it myself.

But it will be a struggle and, if you're sensitive, embarrassing. Someday, though, when the energy-free miniaturization process is a fact, we can build ocean liners for miniaturization and live in them like tsars of old.''

''Well, let's hope the expedition is not unnecessarily extended.'' (He found it odd that, for a moment, his apprehension shifted from fears of death or mental disability to the details of how to manipulate the toilet lid and how to proceed as unobtrusively as possible. —It occurred to him that there must have been many grossnesses and indelicacies involved in the great exploratory trips of the past, items that had gone undetailed and, therefore, unnoted.)

He was in his cotton clothes and had stepped into his slippers when Dezhnev, dressed in slightly larger versions of the same (also with refinement in the crotch), said, ''Let us now go to breakfast. We will have good food, high calories, and low bulk, for there will be no eating on board the ship. There'll be water, of course, and fruit juices, but no real beverages of any kind. The sweet Natasha made a terrible face when I suggested we might need a drop of vodka now and then. There were a lot of uncalled-for comments about sots and drunkards. Albert, Albert, how I am persecuted—and unjustly, too.''

Breakfast was indeed plentiful, but not exactly filling. There was gelatin and custard, thick slabs of white bread with butter and marmalade, fruit juices, and several varieties of pills to be sluiced down.

The talk over the breakfast table was moderately animated and, for the most part, dealt with the local chess tournament. There was no mention of the ship or of miniaturization. (Was it bad luck to mention the project?)

Morrison did not object to the direction of comment. He even made a few comments about his own adventures as a chess player of marked lack of renown.

And then, all too soon, the table was being cleared and it was time—

They left for the ship.

34.

THEY walked in single file, with space between themselves. Dezhnev was first, then Kaliinin, then Boranova, then Morrison, and finally Konev.

Almost at once, Morrison understood the purpose. They were on view and they were being individualized. Along the edges of the corridor were men and women—employees of the project, obviously—watching eagerly. They, at least, must know what was going on, even if the rest of the Soviet Union (let alone the world) did not.

Drezhnev, in front, waved eagerly to the right and left, rather in the fashion of a kindly and popular monarch, and the crowds responded appropriately, shouting, waving, and calling out his name.

Each name was called at various times, for obviously each prospective crew member was known to all. The two women were restrained in their acknowledgement and Konev (as Morrison could see when he looked behind him) was, not unexpectedly, moving along, eyes forward and unresponsive.

And then Morrison was surprised when he distinctly heard the cry, in English, "Hurrah, the American!"

He looked in the direction of the outcry and automatically waved, at which, just as automatically, there was a loud and enthusiastic shout and the words were picked up until "Hurrah, the American!" drowned out all else.

Morrison found himself unable to maintain his earlier sullen resignation. He had never been the object of mob jubilation and he took to it immediately and without trouble, waving and grinning madly. He caught Boranova's gravely amused expression and saw Dezhnev pointing his finger at him in an ostentatious that's-the-American gesture, but allowed neither action to disturb him.

And then they passed out of the line of observers and into the large room in which Shapirov was resting in his mental cocoon of coma. The ship was also in the room.

Morrison looked around with astonishment. He said, "There's a camera crew out there."

Kaliinin was now standing next to him. (How beautiful her breasts are, Morrison thought. They were veiled but not hidden by the thin cotton and he could see why Konev had referred to her as a distraction.) She said, "Oh yes, we'll be on television. Every significant experiment is carefully recorded and there are reporters at each occasion so that it might be described. There was even a camera present when you and I were miniaturized yesterday, but we kept it out of sight since you weren't to know you were to undergo the process."

"But if this is a secret project—"

"It will not always be secret. Someday, when we have reached full success, the details of our progress will be revealed to our people and to the world. —Sooner, if it seems some other nation is making progress on its own in the same direction."

Morrison shook his head. "It isn't good, this primary concern with priority. Progress would be much faster if additional brains and resources were put on the job."

Kaliinin said, "Would you willingly give up priority in your own field of research?"

Morrison was silent. It was the obvious retort.

Kaliinin, noting this, said with a shake of her head, "I thought so. It is easy to be generous with someone else's money."

Boranova, meanwhile, was talking to someone whom Morrison judged to be a reporter, one who was listening eagerly. Morrison transferred his attention and found himself listening eagerly, too.

Boranova was saying, "This is the American scientist, Albert Jonas Morrison, who is a professor of neurophysics, which is, of course, Academician Konev's field. He is here serving as both an American observer and as an assistant to Academician Konev."

"And there will be five who will be on the ship?"

"Yes. And there will never be so remarkable a five again—or so remarkable an event—if miniaturization lasts a million years. Academician Konev is the very first human being ever to have undergone miniaturization. Dr. Sophia Kaliinin is the first woman and Professor Albert Morrison is the first American ever to have undergone miniaturization. Kaliinin and Morrison represent the first multiple miniaturization and were the first to be miniaturized in the ship. And as for today's voyage, this will represent the first miniaturization of five human beings at once and it will be the first occasion on which a miniaturized ship and its crew will be inserted into a living human being. The human being into whom we will be inserted is, of course, Academician Pyotr Shapirov, who was the second human being to be miniaturized and the first to be a casualty of the process."

Dezhnev, who was suddenly at Morrison's side, whispered hoarsely into his ear, "There you are, Albert. You are now an indelible footnote in history. You might have imagined until now that you were a failure, but not so. No one can take from you the fact that you were the first American ever to be miniaturized. Even if your countrymen work out the miniaturization process on their own and miniaturize an American, that American can be no better than second."

Morrison had not thought of that. He was tasting this newfound and permanent personal statistic (if the Soviets would someday release Natalya's statement, undistorted and unrewritten) and he found it savory.

Yet he was not satisfied. "It is not what I want to be remembered for."

"Do a good job on this journey we are to take and you will end up being known for much more," said Dezhnev. "Besides, as my old father used to say, 'It is good to be at the head of the table, even if only one other sits with you and there is but a bowl of cabbage soup to share.'"

Dezhnev stepped away and now Kaliinin was again at Morrison's side. She tugged at his sleeve and said, "Albert."

"Yes, Sophia?"

"You were with *him* after dinner last night, weren't you?"

"He showed me a map of Shapirov's brain. Marvelous!"

"Did he say anything about me?"

Morrison hesitated. "Why should he have?"

"Because you are a curious man, trying to escape your own private devils. You would have asked."

Morrison winced at her characterization of him. He said, "He defended himself."

"How?"

"He mentioned an earlier pregnancy—and—and abortion. It was not something I would believe, Sophia, unless you admitted it."

Kaliinin's eyes became bright with gathering tears. "Did he—did he describe the circumstances?"

"No, Sophia. Nor did I ask."

"He might have told you. I was forced when I was seventeen. It had undesirable consequences and my parents took legal measures."

"I understand. Perhaps Yuri chooses not to believe this."

"He may choose to think that I asked for it, but it is all on the record and the rapist is still in prison. Soviet law is hard on offenders of this type, but only if the situation can be thoroughly proven. I recognize the fact that women can falsely accuse men of rape, but this was not one of those situations and Yuri knows it. How cowardly of him to state the fact without the extenuation."

Morrison said, "Nevertheless, now is not the time to be concerned about this, although I understand how deeply it must affect you. We will have a complicated job to do inside the ship and it will need all our concentration and skill. I assure you, though, that I am on your side and not on his."

Kaliinin nodded and said, "I thank you for your kindness and sympathy, but don't be afraid of me. I will do my job."

At this point, Boranova called out, "We are now to enter the ship in the order in which I call your names: Dezhnev—Konev—Kaliinin—Morrison—and myself."

Boranova moved immediately into position behind him and murmured, "How do you feel, Albert?"

"Terrible," said Morrison. "Did you expect any other answer?"

"No," said Boranova. "But, nevertheless, I expect you to do your work as though you *didn't* feel lousy. Do you understand?"

"I will try," said Morrison through stiff lips and, following Kaliinin, he entered the ship a second time.

35.

ONE by one, they had to adjust themselves into their seats in the arrangement that Kaliinin had described the day before. Dezhnev was front left at the controls, Konev front right, Kaliinin mid-left, Morrison mid-right, and Boranova rear left.

Morrison blinked his eyes and blew his nose into a tissue he found in one of his pockets. What if he needed more tissues than had been supplied him? (A silly thing to worry about, but it was a more comfortable worry than some he might have.) His forehead felt damp. Was that because of the closeness? Would five people breathing—hyperventilating, perhaps—into a skimpy volume raise the humidity to maximum? Or would there be sufficient ventilation?

He thought suddenly of the first astronauts of a century before—even more constricted, more helpless—but going into a space that was somewhat known and understood, not into a microcosm that was utterly virgin territory.

Yet, as Morrison sat down, he felt the edge of terror dulled. He had, after all, been in the ship before. He had even been miniaturized and deminiaturized and was none the worse for it. It didn't hurt.

He looked around to see how the others were taking it. Kaliinin, to his left, looked coldly blank. A rather icy loveliness. It might have been impressive that she was showing no fear, no anxiety, but (as she had said of him) she was probably sitting there fighting her private devils.

Dezhnev was looking back, perhaps trying to weigh reactions as Morrison was, and very likely for different reasons. Morrison was trying to bolster what little inner courage he could find by borrowing from that of others, whereas Dezhnev (Morrison thought) was weighing responses in order to measure the possible success of the mission.

Konev faced directly forward and Morrison could see only the back of his neck. Boranova was just seating herself and was straightening her flimsy cotton costume.

Dezhnev said, "Friends. Fellow-travelers. Before we can leave, we must each inspect our equipment. Once we start, telling me something doesn't work is not going to strike me as an uproarious joke. As my father used to say, 'The truly wise trapeze artist does not inspect his nails in mid-jump.' It will be my job to make sure that the ship's controls are in order, as I am particularly certain they are, since I designed them myself and supervised the construction.

"As for you, Yuri, my friend, your cereb-whatever-you-call-it—or your brain map, as anyone with sense would call it —has been transferred point for point into the software of your computer behind the plate before you. Please make sure that you know how to operate the plate and then see if the brain map is functional in all respects.

"Sophia, my little dove, I don't know what it is you do except that you make electricity, therefore make sure you can make it in the style you will find suitable. Natalya," his voice lifted slightly, "are you all right back there?"

Boranova said, "I am perfectly all right. Please check Albert. He needs your help most."

"Of course," said Dezhnev. "I have left him for last, so that he can get my full attention. Albert, do you know how to operate the panel before you?"

"Of course not," Morrison snapped. "How should I know?"

"In two seconds, you will know. This contact is to open and that contact is to close. Albert, open! —Ah, you see, it slides open noiselessly. Now close! Perfect. Now you know. —And have you seen what is inside the recess?"

"A computer," said Morrison.

"Perfect again, but do me a favor and see if it is a computer equivalent to *yours*. Your programmed software is in the recess to the side. Please check it out, make sure it fits the computer, and make sure it works as it is supposed to work. I will rely on you to tell me if it is working properly. Please! If you have any doubts, any suspicion, the tiniest hint that something is not just so, we will delay until it is fixed to your entire satisfaction."

Boranova said, "Please, Arkady, no dramatics. There is no time."

Dezhnev ignored her. "But if you tell me that something is wrong that really isn't wrong, my good Albert, Yuri will find out, I assure you, and neither he, nor I, nor anyone will be pleased. So if it occurs to you that inventing a trouble may delay the trip or even cancel it, let it unoccur to you at once."

Morrison could feel his face flushing and he hoped that it would be interpreted as the result of a generous anger over the thought that he might be dishonest in this fashion and not as guilt over a foiled plot.

Actually, as he hovered over his computer, he thought again of what his design and repeated redesign of his program had done. Now and then, these most recent designs of his had brought him—feelings. It was not something he could identify, but it felt as though his own thought centers were being directly stimulated by the brain waves he was analyzing. He had not reported these, but he had occasionally talked about it and the word had gotten out. Shapirov had called his program a relay station because of that—if Yuri was to be believed. Well, then, how could he now check if *that* were working well, when at best he had had the sensation only a few times and at unpredictable occasions?

Or might it all be simply the will-to-believe, the same will that had led Percival Lowell to see canals on Mars?

He realized that it hadn't actually even occurred to him to try to stymie the voyage by saying his program wasn't working. Dearly as he longed to avoid the risk, he could not do so at the cost of vilifying his program.

And then there was suddenly cause for a bit of fresh panic within Morrison's heart. What if the program had been damaged somehow in transit? How could he persuade them that there was truly something wrong and that he was not simply pretending?

But it all worked beautifully, at least as far as he could tell without it being in actual contact with a skull behind which an active brain existed.

Dezhnev said, as he watched Morrison's hands working, "We have placed new batteries in it. *American* batteries."

"Everything is working properly," said Morrison, "as far as I can see."

"Good. —Is everyone satisfied with the equipment? Then lift your pretty rears from your seats and check the sliding panels there. Do they work? Believe me, you would all be very unhappy if they didn't."

Morrison watched Kaliinin open and close the panel (covered with a thin layer of upholstery) that she was sitting on. His own worked similarly when he imitated her motions.

Dezhnev said, "It will take solid wastes, too, within reason, but let us hope we will have no occasion to check that out. In case the worst comes to the worst, there is a small roll of tissue just under the edge of your seat, where you can reach it easily. As we miniaturize, everything loses mass, so excretions would float. There will, however, be a downward current of air to prevent that. Don't let the draft startle you. There is a liter of water in a tiny refrigerator under the side of your seat. It is only for drinking. If you get dirty or sweaty or smelly, just make up your mind to stay that way. No washing until we get out. And no eating. If we lose a few ounces, so much the better."

Boranova said dryly, "If you lost seven kilograms, Arkady, so much the better. And we would consume less energy in the miniaturization."

"The thought has occurred to me at times, Natasha," replied Dezhnev coolly. "I will now test the controls of the ship and if all responds properly, as I'm sure it will, we will be ready to begin."

There was what seemed to Morrison to be a tense wait in utter silence, except for a soft whistle between the teeth on the part of Dezhnev, as he bent over his controls.

Then Dezhnev sat up, wiped his forehead with his sleeve, and said, "All is well. Comrade Ladies, Comrade Gentleman, and Comrade American, the fantastic voyage we face is about to begin." He fixed an auditor in his left ear, raised a tiny microphone before his mouth, and said, "All is operational within. Is all operational outside? —Very well, then, wish us good fortune, comrades all."

Nothing seemed to happen and Morrison cast a quick look at Kaliinin. She was still immobile, but she seemed to be aware of Morrison's head turning toward her, for she said, "Yes, we are miniaturizing."

The blood roared in Morrison's ears. This was the first time he was *consciously* miniaturizing.

CHAPTER 9

ARTERY

If the current flow is taking you
where you want to go, don't argue.
　　　　　　　　　—Dezhnev Senior

36.

MORRISON'S eyes remained, for the most part, focused on the recess before him, on the computer, and on the software he had inserted. The software—the one material object of the long ago.

Long ago? It was less than a hundred hours ago that he was half dozing his way through a dull talk on his last day at the conference and wondering whether there was any way to save his position at the university. And now a hundred subjective years had passed in those hundred objective hours and he could no longer clearly visualize the university at all or the life of sad frustration he had been leading there toward the end.

He would have given a great deal to have broken out of the dull cycle of useless striving a hundred hours ago. He would give a great deal more—a *great* deal more—to break back into it now, to wake up and to find the last hundred hours (or years) had never taken place.

He glanced through the transparent wall of the ship, there at his right elbow, his eyes half-closed as though he were really reluctant to see anything. He *was* reluctant. He did not want to see anything larger than it should be. It would interfere with his wild hope that the miniaturization process had broken down or that the whole thing had—somehow—been an illusion.

But a man walked into his view—tall, over two meters tall. But then, perhaps he was actually that tall.

Others appeared. They couldn't *all* be that tall.

He shrank down into his seat and looked no more. It was enough. He knew that the miniaturization process was going its inexorable way.

The silence inside the ship was oppressive, unbearable. Morrison felt he had to hear a voice, even if only his own.

Kaliinin, at his left side, was the one to whom he could speak most easily and she might be the best of a difficult choice, perhaps. Since Morrison did not want Dezhnev's misplaced jocularity, or Boranova's one-dimensional concentration, or Konev's dark intensity, he turned to Kaliinin's frozen sorrow.

He said, "How will we get into Shapirov's body, Sophia?"

It took a while, it seemed, for Kaliinin to hear him. When she did, her lips moved pallidly and she said in a whisper, "Injection."

Then, as though with a supreme effort, she apparently decided that she must be companionable, so she turned to him and said, "When we are small enough, we will be placed into a hypodermic needle and injected into Academician Shapirov's left carotid artery."

"We'll be shaken up like dice," said Morrison, appalled.

"Not at all. It will be complex, but the problems have been thought through."

"How do you know? This has never been done before. Never in a ship. Never in a hypodermic needle. Never into a human body."

"True," said Kaliinin, "but problems like this—much simpler ones, of course—have been planned for a long time and we have had extended seminars over the last few days on *this* mission. You don't think that Arkady's announcements before miniaturization began—the ones about toilet tissue and so on—were new to us, do you? We have heard it all before, over and over. It was for your benefit, actually, since you have attended no seminars, and for Arkady's, too, since he loves his moment in the sun."

"Tell me, then, what will happen?"

"I will explain events as they occur. For now we do nothing until we are in the centimeter range. It will take another twenty minutes, but not everything will be so slow. The smaller we get, the faster we can miniaturize, in proportion. —Have you felt any bad effects yet?"

Morrison mentally subtracted the rapid beating of his heart and the panting of his lungs and said, "None." Then, feeling that to be an unduly optimistic remark, he added, "At least so far."

"Well, then?" said Kaliinin and closed her eyes as though to indicate that she was tired of talking.

Morrison thought that might not be such a bad idea and closed his as well.

He might have actually fallen asleep or he might simply have gone into a protective state of semiunconsciousness, withdrawing from reality, for it seemed that no time had passed when he was brought to by a slight jar.

He opened his eyes wide and found himself a centimeter or so above the seat. He had the odd sensation of drifting with each vagrant puff of wind.

Boranova had moved over to the seat behind him and placed her hands on his shoulders. She pushed down gently and said, "Albert, put on your seat belt. Sophia, show him how. I'm sorry, Albert—we should have gone over all of this —everything—before we started, but we had little time and you were nervous enough as it was. We did not wish to reduce you to utter helplessness by flooding you with information."

To his own surprise, Morrison had not been feeling helpless. He had rather enjoyed the sensation of sitting on air.

Kaliinin touched a spot on her seat edge between her knees and a belt around her waist flipped away. It had not been there, Morrison was sure, when he had closed his eyes and now it was again no longer there, for it disappeared, with a snap, into a recess in the seat to her left. She twisted toward Morrison and said, "This, here to your left, is your belt ejector." Morrison couldn't help noticing that, now unbound, she lifted up from her seat slightly as she moved toward him.

She pressed the ejector—a somewhat darker circle in a

light background—and a flexible network of clear plastic shot out with a faint hiss, wrapped itself about him, and buried its triple tip into the seat at his other side. He found himself held, elastically, in a kind of lacework.

"If you want to free yourself, there is the belt release there, just between your knees." Kaliinin leaned farther toward him to indicate the place and Morrison found the pressure of her body against his to be pleasurable.

She did not seem to be aware of it and, having completed her task, she pulled herself back into her chair and rebelted herself.

Morrison glanced quickly around, squeezing upward and forward as far as the belt would let him, and peered, with difficulty, over Konev's shoulder. All five were belted.

He said, "We've miniaturized to the point where we have very little weight, is that it?"

"You only weigh about twenty-five milligrams now," said Boranova, "so that you might as well consider yourself weightless. Then, too, the ship is being lifted."

Morrison looked at Kaliinin accusingly and Kaliinin shrugged slightly and said, "I told you I'd describe things as they happened, but you seemed to be asleep and I thought it wiser to let you stay that way. The jar of the clamp woke you and lifted you out of the seat."

"The clamp?" He looked to one side. He had been conscious of a shadow on both sides, but walls were supposed to be opaque and he had dismissed the sensation. Now he suddenly remembered that the ship's walls were transparent and realized that the light on either side was blocked.

Kaliinin nodded. "A clamp is gripping us and helping to keep us steady so that we are not shaken up unnecessarily. It looks enormous, but it is a very small and delicately padded clamp. And we are being put into a small tank of saline solution. We are also being held steady by an airstream being sucked upward into a blunt nozzle. That pushes us against the nozzle so that, with the clamps, we are held three ways."

Morrison looked out again. Objects outside the ship that might have been visible through portions of the wall not blocked by the clamp or by the overhead nozzle were, nevertheless, not visible. Morrison could see occasional shifting of light and shadow and realized that whatever existed out there was too large to make out clearly with his tiny eyes. If the

photons that approached the ship were not themselves miniaturized as they entered the field, they would behave as
though they were long radio waves and he would have seen
nothing at all.

He felt the ship suddenly jar again as the clamps withdrew,
although he couldn't actually see them withdraw. One moment they were there and the next they weren't. The movement—on his scale—was too rapid to see.

Then he felt himself rising slightly against the belt that
bound him in and he interpreted that as a downward movement of the ship. There followed a slow bobbing sensation.

Dezhnev pointed to a dark horizontal line that moved
slowly up and down against the wall of the ship and said with
satisfaction, "That's the surface of the water. I thought the
motions would be worse. Apparently, there are engineers in
this place who are almost as good as I am."

Boranova said, "Actually, engineering has little to do with
it. We're being held in place by surface tension. That will
only work while we're at the surface of a fluid. It will not
affect us once we're in Shapirov's body."

"But this ripple effect, Natasha? This up-and-down movement. Is that affecting it at all?"

Boranova was studying her instruments and, in particular,
a small screen on which a horizontal line seemed to be playing out forever, without budging from the center. Morrison,
twisting and lifting until his back ached, could just make it
out.

Boranova said, "It's as steady as your hand when you are
sober, Arkady."

"No better than that, eh?" Dezhnev's laugh boomed out.

(He sounds relieved, thought Morrison uneasily and wondered what the "it" was that Dezhnev had felt might be
affected.)

"What happens now?" asked Morrison.

Konev spoke for the first time, as far as Morrison could
remember, since miniaturization had begun. "Must everything be explained to you?"

Morrison answered with spirit. "Yes! You have had everything explained to you. Why should I not have it explained as
well?"

Boranova said quietly, "Albert is perfectly correct, Yuri.
Please hold your temper and be reasonable. You will need

his help soon enough and I hope he will not be so discourteous as to snap at you."

Konev's shoulders twitched, but he said nothing in reply.

Boranova said, "The cylinder of a hypodermic syringe will pick us up, Albert. It will be under remote control."

And, as though that cylinder were waiting to hear her say so, a shadow encased them from behind, swallowing them almost at once. Only in front was there a circle of light visible for a moment and then that disappeared, too.

Boranova said calmly, "The needle has been clamped on. Now we will have to wait a while."

The interior of the ship, which had become quite dark, was suddenly suffused with a white light, rather softer and more restful than before, and Boranova said, "From now on there will be no more light from the outside until our journey is over. We will have to rely on our own internal illumination, Albert."

Puzzled, Morrison looked around for the source of the light. It seemed to be in the transparent walls themselves.

Kaliinin, interpreting his glance, said, "Electroluminescence."

"But what is the source of power?"

"We have three microfusion engines." She looked at him proudly. "Of a type that's the best in the world." Then she repeated, "In the *world.*"

Morrison let it go. He had the impulse to talk of the American microfusion engines on the latest space vessels, but what would be the point? Someday the world would be freed of its nationalist fervors, but that day had not yet arrived. Still, as long as those fervors did not express themselves in violence or threat of violence, matters were bearable.

Dezhnev, leaning back in his seat with his arms behind his neck and apparently addressing the gently illuminated wall before him, said, "Someday what we will do is expand a hypodermic syringe, place that around a full-sized ship, and miniaturize the whole thing. Then we won't have this small-scale maneuvering."

Morrison said, "Oh, can you do the other thing, too? What do you call it? Maximization? Gigantization?"

"We don't call it anything," said Konev crisply, "because it can't be done."

"Maybe someday, though."

"No," said Konev. "Never. It is physically impossible. It takes a lot of energy to miniaturize, but more than an infinite amount to maximize."

"Even if you hooked it up to relativity?"

"Even so."

Dezhnev made an inelegant sound with his lips. "That for your physically impossible. Someday you will see."

Konev relapsed into indignant silence.

Morrison said, "What is it we are waiting for?"

Boranova said, "The last-minute preparation of Shapirov and then the moving up of the needle and its insertion into the carotid."

As she spoke, the ship was jarred forward.

"Is that it?" asked Morrison.

"Not yet. They were merely removing the air bubbles. Don't worry, Albert. We'll know."

"How?"

"Why, they'll tell us. Arkady is in contact with them. It's not difficult. Radio wave photons miniaturize as they cross the boundary from there to here and deminiaturize as they cross in the other direction. There's very little energy involved—even less than in the case of light."

Dezhnev said, "It's time to move up to the base of the needle."

"Then go ahead," said Boranova. "We might as well test the motive power under miniaturization."

There was a gathering rumble that reached a low peak and then settled down into a buzzing murmur. Morrison twisted his head in order to look as nearly backward as he could against his restraining belt.

Water was churning behind them as though paddle wheels were turning. In the absence of any real reference point outside, it was impossible to judge how quickly they were moving, but progress seemed slow to Morrison.

"Are we moving much?" he asked.

"No, but we don't need to," said Boranova. "There's no use wasting energy trying to move faster. After all, we're pushing against normal-sized molecules, which means high viscosity on our scale."

"But with microfusion motors—"

"We have many energy needs for matters other than propulsion."

"I'm just wondering how long it will take us to get to key points in the brain."

"Believe me," said Boranova grimly, "I'm wondering, too, but we will have an arterial current taking us as close as possible."

Dezhnev cried out, "We're there! See?"

Right ahead, in the forward light beam of the ship, a round circle could be seen. Morrison had no trouble translating that into the base of the needle.

On the other end of that needle, they would find Pyotr Shapirov's bloodstream and then they would actually be within a human body.

37.

MORRISON said, "We're too large to go through the needle, Natalya."

He felt a peculiar amalgam of emotions at the thought. Uppermost was a feeling of hope that perhaps the whole experiment had failed. This might be as small as they could get and it wasn't small enough. They would have to deminiaturize and it would all be over.

Under that thought, well-hidden, was a little sigh of disappointment. Having come so far, might it not be as well to get into the body and experience the interior of a nerve cell? Ordinarily, being no darer of dangers, no scaler of heights, Morrison would have turned away in horror at the thought— he *did* turn away in horror—but having miniaturized, having reached this point, having survived the fright so far, was it possible that he might want to go farther?

But above these contradictory urges came a bit of realism. Surely these people were not such fools as to deal with a ship that could not be reduced to a size that would pass through the needle it was supposed to pass through. No conceivable stupidity in these very intelligent people could reach that pitch.

And Boranova, as though she were resonating with that thought, said, almost indifferently, "Yes, we are too large now, but we will not stay too large. That is my job here."

"Yours?" said Morrison blankly.

"Of course. We have been reduced to this point by our

central miniaturization device. Now the fine adjustments will be made by me."

Kaliinin murmured, "That is one of the things we must save our microfusion motors for as much as possible."

Morrison looked from one to another. "Do we have enough energy on board ship for further miniaturization? Surely the impression I got was that a vast quantity of energy was needed for—"

"Albert," said Boranova, "if gravitation were quantized, then it would take the same enormous amount of energy to reduce a mass by half, regardless of the original value of that mass. To reduce the mass of a mouse by half would take the same energy as was required to reduce the mass of an elephant by half. —But the gravitational interaction is not quantized and, therefore, neither is mass loss. That means that the energy required for mass loss decreases with that loss—not entirely in proportion, but to an extent. We have so little mass now that it takes much less energy to miniaturize further."

Morrison said, "But since you've never miniaturized anything as large as this ship through so many orders of magnitude, you are depending on the extrapolation of data obtained for a much different size range."

(They're not speaking to an infant, he thought indignantly. I am their equal.)

"Yes," said Boranova. "We are taking the chance that the extrapolation *will* hold, that something new and unexpected will *not* surprise us. Still, we live in a Universe that faces us with uncertainties now and then. That can't be helped."

"But we all face death if something goes wrong."

"Didn't you know that?" said Boranova calmly. "Have you been uneasy about this fantastic voyage of ours simply for the pleasure of being uneasy? But we are not alone in this. If things go wrong and the stored energy of miniaturization is released, it will not only destroy us, but it may damage the Grotto to some extent. I'm sure that many an unminiaturized person out there is holding his or her breath and wondering if he or she will survive an explosion. You see, Albert, even those who are not undergoing the risks of miniaturization are not altogether safe."

Dezhnev turned and grinned widely. Morrison noted that

one of his upper molars was capped and did not match the rather yellowish tint of his other teeth.

Dezhnev said, "Concentrate on the thought, my friend, that if something goes wrong, you will never know. My father used to say, 'Since we all must die, what better can we ask for than a quick and sudden death?' "

Morrison said, "Julius Caesar said the same thing."

Dezhnev said, "Yes, but we won't even have time to say, 'Et tu, Brute.' "

"There will be no death," said Konev sharply, "and it is foolish to speak of it. The equations are correct."

"Ah," said Dezhnev. "There was a time of superstition when people relied on the protection of God. Thank Equations we now have Equations to rely on."

"Not funny," said Konev.

"I didn't mean to be funny, Yuri. —Natasha, they're ready out there for us to proceed."

Boranova said, "Then there will be no further need to speculate. Here we go."

Morrison gripped his seat tightly, preparing himself, but he felt nothing happen. Up front, though, the round circle he had made out expanded and grew dimmer and dimmer as it moved very slowly backward until it could no longer be made out.

"Are we moving?" he asked automatically. It was the kind of question one was unable to refrain from asking, even though the answer was obvious.

"Yes," said Kaliinin, "and we are expending no energy in doing so. We are not battling the water molecules. We are being carried along by the water flow in the needle as the cylinder presses in slowly."

Morrison was counting to himself. It kept his mind more efficiently occupied than studying the second hand of his watch would have done.

When he reached a hundred, he said, "How long will it take?"

"How long will *what* take?" asked Kaliinin.

"When do we reach the bloodstream?"

Dezhnev said, "A few minutes. They are going very slowly, just in case there is some kind of microturbulence. As my father once said, 'It is slower, but better, to creep along the downward path than to leap over the cliff.' "

Morrison grunted, then said, "Are we still miniaturizing?"

Boranova answered from behind him. "No. We are down in the cellular range and that is far enough for our needs now."

Morrison was surprised to find that he was trembling. After all, so much was happening and so many new things existed to think about that he had somehow lacked the room to remain in terror. He was *not* terrified, at least not to an acute stage—yet for some reason he continued to tremble.

He attempted to will himself to relax. He tried to let himself droop, but that required more than an effort of will. It needed gravitational pull and there was none to speak of. He closed his eyes and slowed his breathing. He even tried humming, under his breath, the choral singing from Beethoven's *Ninth Symphony.*

Finally he felt himself forced into comment on the matter. "I'm sorry," he said. "I seem to be shaking."

Dezhnev snickered. "Aha! I wondered who would be the first to mention it."

Boranova said, "It's not you, Albert. We are all shaking slightly. It's the ship."

Morrison was at once elevated into fright. "Is something wrong with it?"

"No. It's just a matter of size. It's small enough to feel the effect of Brownian motion. You know what that is, don't you?"

It was a purely rhetorical question. Boranova would surely expect a high school student of physics to know what Brownian motion was, let alone Morrison, and yet Morrison found himself explaining it in his own mind—not in words, but as a flash of concept.

Every object suspended in a liquid is bombarded on all sides by the atoms or molecules of the liquid. These particles strike randomly and therefore unevenly, but the unevenness is so small compared to the total that it is unnoticeable and has no measurable effect. As an object grows smaller, however, the unevenness becomes greater among the smaller and smaller number of particles striking the object in a given time. The ship was small enough now to respond to the slight excesses of collisions—first in one direction, then in another —randomly. It moved slightly in consequence, a random trembling.

Morrison said, "Yes, I should have thought of that. It will get worse if we continue to become smaller."

"Actually, it won't," said Boranova. "There will be other counteracting effects."

"I don't know of any," said Morrison, frowning.

"Nevertheless, there will be such effects."

"Leave it to the Equations," said Dezhnev in an affectedly pious tone. "The Equations know."

Morrison said, "I think this could make us seasick."

"It certainly would," said Boranova, "but there is a chemical treatment for that. We have been dosed with the same chemical that cosmonauts use against space sickness."

"Not I," said Morrison indignantly. "Not only haven't I been treated, I haven't even been forewarned."

"We told you as little as possible of the discomforts and dangers out of concern for your comfort, Albert. As for treatment, you consumed your dose with your breakfast. —How do you feel?"

Morrison, who had begun to feel a bit squeamish with all this talk about sickness, decided that he felt fine. Astonishing, he thought, the tyranny exerted over the body by the mind.

He said in a low voice, "Tolerable."

"Good," said Boranova, "because we are now in Academician Shapirov's bloodstream."

38.

MORRISON stared through the transparent wall of the ship.

Blood?

His first impulse was to expect redness. What else?

He peered out, squinting his eyes slightly, but could see nothing, even in the gleaming light of the ship. He might as well have been in a rowboat, drifting down the calm surface of a pond on a dark and cloudy night.

Morrison's thoughts suddenly veered. In the absolute sense, the light within the ship had the wavelength of gamma rays—and very hard gamma rays at that. Yet the wavelengths were the result of miniaturizing ordinary visible light and to the equally miniaturized retinas and optic lobes of the people within the ship they were still light rays and had the property of light rays.

Outside, just beyond the hull of the ship, where the miniaturization field ended, the miniaturized photons enlarged to ordinary light-wave photons and those that were reflected back to the ship were miniaturized again when the field boundary was crossed. The others might be accustomed to this paradox-ridden situation, but to Morrison the attempt to grasp the effect of a miniaturized bubble within a sea of normality was dizzying. Was the boundary visible, marking off the miniaturized from the normal? Was there a discontinuity somewhere?

Following his line of thought, he whispered to Kaliinin, who was bent over her instrument, "Sophia, when our light leaves the miniaturization field and expands, it must give off heat energy, and when it's reflected back into the ship it must absorb energy in order to be miniaturized and the energy must come from us. Am I right?"

"Perfectly, Albert," said Kaliinin without looking up. "Our use of light results in a small but steady loss of energy, but our motors can supply that. It is not a significant drain."

"And are we really in the bloodstream?"

"Never fear. We are. Natalya will probably dim the internal lights in a while and you'll see the outside more clearly then."

Almost as though that were a signal, Boranova said, "There! Now we can relax for a few moments." The lights dimmed.

At once, objects outside the ship came dimly into view. He could not make them out clearly yet, but they were immersed in something heterogeneous, something with objects floating in it, as would be true of blood.

Morrison stirred uneasily, straining at the constraint of his seat belt. He said, "But if we are in the bloodstream, which is at a temperature of thirty-seven degrees Celsius, we'll—"

"Our temperature is conditioned. We'll be quite comfortable," said Kaliinin. "Really, Albert, we've thought of these things."

"Perhaps you have," said Morrison, slightly offended, "but I haven't been privy to those thoughts, have I? How can you condition the temperature when you don't have a cold sink?"

"We don't have one here, but there's outer space, isn't there? The microfusion motors give off a thin drizzle of subatomic particles which, under miniaturized conditions, have a mass of very nearly zero. They therefore travel at virtually the speed of light, penetrating matter as easily as neutrinos do and carrying off energy with them. In less than a second they are in outer space, so that the effect is of transferring heat from within the ship into outer space and we keep cool. Do you see?"

"I see," muttered Morrison. It was ingenious—but perhaps obvious, after all, to those used to thinking in terms of miniaturization.

Morrison noticed that the controls of the ship, immediately under Dezhnev's hands, were luminous, as were the instruments before Kaliinin. He struggled to raise himself in his seat and managed to see a corner of the computer screen in front of Konev. It contained what Morrison thought might be a map of the circulatory system of the neck. For a moment, before his body ceased its fight against the webbing of the belt and he sank down into his seat again, he saw a small red dot on the screen, which, he deduced, was a device to mark the position of the ship in the left internal carotid artery.

He was panting a little from his effort and had to wait a few moments to regain control of his breath. The recess in which his own computer rested was illuminated and he shielded that bit of light from his face by raising his left hand. Then he looked out.

Far in the distance, Morrison could see something that looked like a wall, a barrier of some sort. It receded, then approached, then receded again, over and over, rhythmically. Automatically, he looked at his watch for a few seconds. It was clearly the pulsation of the arterial wall.

He said to Kaliinin in a low voice, "Obviously the passage of time is not affected by miniaturization. At least the pulsation of the heart is just what it ought to be, even though I view it with miniaturized eyes and time it with a miniaturized watch."

It was Konev who answered. "Time isn't quantized apparently, or at least it isn't affected by the miniaturization field, which may be the same thing. That's convenient. If we had to take a shifting time flow into account, things might become unbearably complicated."

Morrison silently agreed and turned his thoughts in other directions.

If they were inside an artery, and if the ship were merely being swept forward by the current, the forward movement would have to be in spurts, one spurt for each contraction of the distant heart (the very distant heart—on the scale of their present size). And if *that* were so, he ought to feel those spurts of motion.

He closed his eyes and tried to hold as still as possible, to move not at all except for the trembling of the Brownian motion—which, after all, he could in no way control.

Ah, he could feel it. A slight but distinct push backward as the spurt started, a slight push forward as it came to an end.

But why was the spurt not more energetic? Why was he not yanked backward and forward in a sickening fashion?

And then he thought of the mass he no longer possessed. With his remaining mass so tiny, his inertia was similarly tiny. The viscosity of the normal fluid of the bloodstream exerted an enormous cushioning effect, so that the spurts were all but lost in the Brownian motion.

And, ever so slightly, Morrison felt himself relax. He felt something inside himself untighten a bit. The miniaturized environment was unexpectedly benign.

He looked through the ship's transparent hull again, his eyes focusing on the volume between himself and the arterial wall. He could see bubbles, faintly outlined. No, not bubbles, but things of substance—many of them. Some turned slowly and changed apparent shape as they did so, so they were not spheres. They were disks, he now realized.

The truth burst in on him and shamed him. Why was he so slow in identifying them, since he knew he was in a bloodstream? —But then he knew the answer to that, too. He could not really conceive of himself as being in a bloodstream; it was too easy to suppose he was in a submarine making its way through an ocean. He would naturally expect to see the familiar sights of an ocean and would be foolishly puzzled at anything he saw that did not fit his assumption.

He would see the red corpuscles of the blood—the erythrocytes—and fail to recognize them.

Of course, they weren't red but faintly yellowish. Each one absorbed some shortwave light to produce that color. Get them in bulk, though, millions and billions of them, and they would absorb enough such light to appear red—in arterial blood, anyway, and they were in an artery now. Once the cells withdrew the oxygen carried by the red corpuscles, the individual corpuscle would seem faintly bluish, and, in bulk, blue-purple.

He watched the erythrocytes with interest and saw them quite clearly now that he had recognized them for what they were.

They were biconcave discs, the centers depressed on each side. To Morrison, they were enormous, considering that, under normal conditions, they were microscopic, perhaps seven and a half micrometers in diameter and a little over two micrometers thick. Now here they were, swollen objects the size of his hand.

There were many of them in sight and they had a tendency to pile together in roulettes. These weren't static, however. Some corpuscles would peel off the roulettes and others would add on and there were always some single corpuscles in view. Those that were in sight tended to stay in sight; they weren't moving relative to the ship.

"I take it," said Morrison, "that we're simply going with the flow."

"That's right," said Kaliinin. "It saves energy."

But, at that, the red corpuscles weren't entirely stationary relative to the ship. Morrison noticed one corpuscle drifting slowly toward the ship, carried perhaps by a bit of microturbulence or by a random push of Brownian motion. The corpuscle flattened slightly and momentarily against the plastic of the ship and then rebounded.

Morrison turned to Kaliinin. "Did you see that, Sophia?"

"The red corpuscle nudging us? Yes."

"Why didn't it miniaturize? Surely it entered the field."

"Not quite, Albert. It bounced off the field, which extends a small distance beyond any miniaturized object, such as our ship, in every direction. There's a certain repulsion between normal matter and miniaturized matter, and the greater the extent of miniaturization, the stronger the repulsion. That's why very tiny objects such as miniaturized atoms or subatomic particles go through matter without interacting with it. It's also that which keeps the miniaturized state metastable."

"How do you mean?"

"Any miniaturized object is always surrounded by normal matter, unless it is in deep space. If nothing served to keep normal matter out of the field, such matter would forever be miniaturizing and, in the process, absorbing energy from the miniaturized object. The drain would be significant and the miniaturized object would quickly deminiaturize. In fact, it would be impossible to induce miniaturization in the first place, since the energy crammed into the miniaturizing object would leak away at once. What we would then be trying to do, in effect, would be to miniaturize the entire Universe. —Of course, the repulsion isn't extremely strong at our size. If a red corpuscle collided with sufficient force, the colliding surface might undergo some miniaturization."

Morrison turned back to the view and, almost at once, something that was obviously a shredded red corpuscle drifted into view.

"Ah," said Morrison, "is that an example of one that approached us too forcefully?"

Kaliinin bent toward Morrison to get a better view in the direction he was pointing. She shook her head. "I don't think so, Albert. Red corpuscles have a limited life of about a hundred and twenty days. The poor things wear out and break down. In the volume of blood we can see, several dozen would break down every minute, so that torn and damaged red corpuscles would be a common sight. —And that is a good thing, too, for it means that if we were to use our power and rush through the bloodstream, breaking up a few red corpuscles, or even a few million, it would make no difference to Shapirov. We couldn't possibly break down red corpuscles at a rate even approaching that of natural breakdown."

Morrison said, "What about platelets?"

"Why do you ask?"

"That must be a platelet I see there." He pointed. "It's lentil-shaped and only half the size of the red corpuscles."

A pause and then Kaliinin nodded. "Ah yes, I see it now. That's a platelet. There should be one of them to every twenty red corpuscles."

That was about right, Morrison thought. If he were on a carousel, reaching out for rings as he passed, and each red corpuscle were an ordinary iron ring, the occasional platelet would represent the coveted brass ring.

Morrison said, "My point, Sophia, is that platelets are more fragile than red corpuscles and when they break they start the clotting process. If we break a few, we'll start a clot forming in the artery. Shapirov will then have another stroke and surely die."

Boranova, who had been listening to the exchange between Morrison and Kaliinin, interposed at this point. "In the first place," she said, "platelets are not as fragile as all that. They can strike us lightly and rebound without harm. The danger of another stroke lies at the arterial wall. The platelets are moving much faster relative to the inner wall of the carotid artery than they are relative to us. And the inner wall of the artery may be layered with cholesterol and lipid plaques of all kinds. That surface is therefore much rougher and uneven than the smooth plastic hull of our ship. It's at the arterial wall that the clots might form—not here. And even that isn't too enormous a danger. A single platelet—or even a few hundred of them—might be broken and still be insufficient to start the clotting process in a way that doesn't damp out. Massive quantities of platelets must break to turn the trick."

Morrison watched a platelet that vanished, now and then, behind the numerous red corpuscles. He wanted to see if it would make contact with the ship and, if it did, what would happen. The platelet, however, did not oblige but remained at a distance.

It then occurred to Morrison that the platelet appeared to be as large as his hand. How could that be if they were half the diameter of the red corpuscles and the red corpuscles were themselves as large as his hand? His eyes sought out a red call and, sure enough, it seemed considerably larger than his hand.

He said, troubled, "The objects out there are getting larger."

"We're still miniaturizing, obviously," called out Konev, apparently annoyed at Morrison's seeming inability to draw the proper conclusion from an observed fact.

Boranova said, "That's right, Albert. The coronary is narrowing as we progress and we want to keep pace with it."

"We don't want to get stuck in the pipe," said Dezhnev genially, "by being too fat." Then, as another thought struck him, he added, "You know, Natasha, I've never been this thin in my life."

Boranova said, unmoved, "You are as fat as ever, Arkady, on the scale of Planck's constant."

Morrison was in no mood for airy banter. "But how far do we miniaturize, Natalya?"

"Down to molecular size, Albert."

And all of Morrison's apprehensions surged up again.

39.

MORRISON felt foolish at his failure to realize at once that they were still miniaturizing and, at the same time, bitterly resentful at Konev for making it plain he recognized that folly. The trouble was that all these others had been living and thinking miniaturization for years and he himself, a newcomer to the concept, was still trying to cram it into his reluctant brain. Couldn't they sympathize with his difficulties?

He studied the red corpuscles moodily. They were distinctly larger. They were wider across than his chest and their boundaries were becoming less sharp. Their surfaces quivered, as though they were canvas bags full of syrup.

He said in a low voice to Kaliinin, "Molecular size?"

Kaliinin looked quickly at him, then turned away and said, "Yes."

Morrison said, "I don't know why that should bother me, considering the small size to which we have already miniaturized, but there's something rather frightening about being as small as a molecule. How small a molecule, do you suppose?"

Kaliinin shrugged. "I don't know. That's up to Natalya. A virus molecule, perhaps."

"But this sort of thing has never been tried."

Kaliinin shook her head. "We're charting unknown territory."

There was a pause and then Morrison said uneasily, "Aren't you afraid?"

She looked at him furiously, but continued to whisper. "Of course I'm afraid. What do you think I am? It isn't sensible not to be afraid when you have rational reason for it. I was afraid when I was violated. I was afraid when I was pregnant and deserted. I've spent half my life being afraid. Everyone does. That's why people drink as much as they do, to wipe out the fear that grips them." She was virtually hissing through clenched teeth. "Do you want me to be sorry for you because *you're* afraid?"

"No," muttered Morrison, taken aback.

"There's nothing remarkable about being afraid," she went on, "as long as you don't *act* afraid—as long as you don't let yourself be twisted into doing nothing because of fear, into having hysterics because of fear, into failing—" She interrupted herself in a bitter, whispered self-accusation. "I've had hysterics in my time." Her glance flickered in the direction of Konev, whose back was straight, stiff, and motionless.

"But now," she went on, "I intend to do my part, even if I am half-dead with fear. No one will tell from my actions that I'm afraid. And that had better be your case, too, Mr. American."

Morrison swallowed hard and he said, "Yes, of course," but it sounded very unconvincing, even to him.

His eyes flicked backward, then forward. There was no use whispering in these close quarters. There was no whisper so low it would not be overheard.

Boranova, behind Kaliinin, was obviously busy with her miniaturization mechanism, but there was a tiny smile on her face. Approval? Contempt? Morrison couldn't tell.

As for Dezhnev, he turned his head and called out, "Natasha, it is continuing to narrow. Should you hasten the miniaturization?"

"I'll do what is needed, Arkady."

Dezhnev's eye caught Morrison's and he winked, with a grin. "Don't believe little Sophia," he said, pretending to whisper. "She is not afraid. Never afraid. She just doesn't want you to be alone with your uneasiness. She has a very soft heart, our Sophia, as soft as her—"

"Keep quiet, Arkady," said Sophia. "Surely your father must have told you that it is not wise to beat the empty teapot you call your head with the rusty spoon you call your tongue."

"Ah," said Dezhnev, rolling his eyes, "that was harsh. What my father *did* say was that no knife could be honed as sharp as a woman's tongue. —But, Albert, seriously, reaching molecular size is nothing. Wait until we have learned to attach relativity to quantum theory and then, with a tiny puff of energy, we will reduce ourselves to subatomic size. *Then* you will see."

"What will I see?" said Morrison.

"You would see instant acceleration. We would simply take off—" He removed his hands from the controls momentarily in order to make a whizzing gesture with them, accompanied by a shrill whistle.

Boranova said calmly, "Hands on the controls, Arkady."

"Of course, my dear Natasha," said Dezhnev. "A moment of excusable drama, no more." Then to Morrison, "Instantly we would go at nearly the speed of light, the much faster speed of light under such conditions. In ten minutes we could be across the Galaxy, in three hours at the Andromeda, in two years at the nearest quasar. And if that's not fast enough, we can get smaller still. We have faster-than-light travel, we have antigravity, we have everything. The Soviet Union will lead the way to it all."

Morrison said, "And how would you guide the flight, Arkady?"

"What?"

"How would you guide it?" said Morrison seriously. "As soon as the ship swoops down to the proper sizelessness and masslessness, it will, in effect, radiate outward at hundreds of light-years per second. That means that if there were trillions of ships, they would shoot out in every direction with spherical symmetry—like sunlight. But since there would be only one ship, it would move outward in one particular direction, but in an absolutely unpredictable one."

"That's a problem for the clever theoreticians—like Yuri."

Konev had not indicated any interest in the conversation up to that point, but now he snorted loudly.

Morrison said, "I'm not sure that it's wise to develop the traveling and carelessly assume the steering. Wouldn't your father say: 'A wise man does not build the roof of a house first.'"

"He might," said Arkady, "but what he once did say was this: 'If you find a gold key without a lock, don't throw it away. The gold is also sufficient.'"

Boranova stirred in her seat behind Morrison and said, "Enough with the saws and sayings, my friends. —Where are we, Yuri? Are we making progress?"

Konev said, "In my opinion we are, but I would like the American to support my judgment, or correct it."

"How can I do either?" snapped Morrison. "I'm strapped in."

"Then unstrap," said Konev. "If you float a bit, at least you can't float very far."

For a moment, Morrison fumbled at his seat belt, having forgotten the location of the appropriate contact. Kaliinin's hand moved quickly and he was free.

"Thank you, Sophia," he said.

"You will learn," she replied indifferently.

"Lift yourself so that you can see over my shoulder," said Konev.

Morrison did so and, inevitably, pushed too hard against the back of the seat ahead. As a result of his insignificant inertia, he moved upward explosively and struck his head against the roof of the ship. Had this happened at the same speed under unminiaturized conditions, he might well have suffered the blinding pain of a concussion, but the very lack of mass and inertia that had sent him shooting upward had bounced him back almost at once with no sensation of pain and virtually none of pressure. He was as easy to stop as he had been to start.

Konev clicked his tongue. "Gently. Just lift your hand upward edgewise, turn it slowly, then push it down flatwise, *slowly*. Do you get it?"

Morrison said, "I understand."

He followed Konev's suggestion and moved up slowly. He caught at Konev's shoulder and stopped himself.

Konev said, "Now, look here at the cerebrograph. Do you see where we are at this moment?"

Morrison found himself looking at an enormously complex network, with a distinct three-dimensional effect. It consisted of sinuous rills branching outward in such a way as to form an exceedingly intricate tree. In one of the larger branches there was a small red dot, moving slowly and progressively.

Morrison said, "Can you give me a broader view so that I can place this section?"

Konev, with another click of his tongue, one that might have signified impatience, expanded the view. "Does this help?"

"Yes, we're on the edge of the brain." He could recognize

the individual convolutions and fissures. "Where do you plan to go?"

The picture magnified somewhat. Konev said, "We'll curve off here into the interior of the neuronic layer—the gray matter. And where I'd like to head for, by this route"—he named the areas in Russian rapidly and Morrison struggled to translate them in his mind into English—"is this area here which, if I have read your papers correctly, is a crucial node of the neuronic network."

"No two brains are exactly alike," said Morrison. "I can pin down nothing with certainty, all the more so if the particular brain in question is one I have never studied. Still, I would say the area you're heading for looks hopeful."

"Good, as far as that goes. And if we get to my destination, will you be able to tell more accurately whether we are at a crossroads where several branches of the network meet or, if not, in what direction and how far such a crossroads might be?"

"I can try," said Morrison cautiously, "but please remember that I have made no guarantees as to my abilities in this connection. I have not offered you any promises. I have not volunteered—"

"We know that, Albert," said Boranova. "We ask only that you do what you can."

"In any case," said Konev, "that's where we're going as a first approximation and we'll get there before long, even though the current is slowing. We are, after all, almost down to capillary size. —Strap yourself in, Albert. I'll let you know if I need you."

Morrison managed to operate the seat belt without any help, proving that even small triumphs can be sweet.

Almost to capillary size, he thought, and looked out through the walls of the ship.

The vessel wall was still at a comfortable distance, but it had changed in appearance. Earlier, the steadily pulsating walls had been rather featureless. Now, however, Morrison could make out no pulsing and the walls were beginning to look faintly tiled. The tiling, Morrison realized, consisted of the cells that made up the thinning walls.

He could not actually get a clear look at the tiling, either, for the red corpuscles were in the way. They were now soft bags nearly the size of the ship. Occasionally, one ballooned past the ship at close quarters and was pushed elastically inward at the point of contact, without undergoing any visible harm.

One time a small smear was left behind. Perhaps the contact had been just a little too forceful and a line of miniaturized molecules had been formed against the hull, Morrison thought. The smear lifted off quickly, however, and dissolved in the surrounding fluid.

The platelets were another story, since by their very nature they were much more fragile than the red corpuscles.

One made a head-on collision with the ship. Or perhaps it had been slowed by a collision with a red corpuscle so that the ship had overtaken it. The prow of the ship penetrated deeply and the skin of the platelet punctured. Its contents oozed out slowly, mixing with the plasma and then forming into two or three long strings that tangled with each other. They clung to a portion of the ship's hull for quite a time, trailing behind.

Morrison waited to see any evidence of a clot forming. None did.

Minutes later Morrison saw, up ahead, a milky fog that seemed to fill the blood vessel from wall to wall, pulsating and undulating. Inside it were dark granules that moved steadily from one side to the other. To Morrison, it looked like a malignant monster and he couldn't help but cry aloud in a moment of terror.

CHAPTER 10

CAPILLARY

*If you want to know whether
water is boiling, don't test it by hand.*
—Dezhnev Senior

40.

DEZHNEV turned his head, startled, and said, "It's a white cell, Albert, a leucocyte. It is nothing to be bothered about."

Morrison swallowed and felt distinctly annoyed. "I know it's a white cell. It just caught me by surprise. It's bigger than I thought it would be."

"It's nothing," said Dezhnev. "A piece of pumpernickel, really, and no bigger than it should be. We're just smaller. And even if it were as big as Moscow, so what? It's just floating along in the bloodstream as we are."

"As a matter of fact," said Kaliinin gently, "it doesn't even know we're here—I mean, that we're anything special. It thinks we're a red corpuscle."

Konev seemed to be addressing the air in front of him in an abstracted sort of way, saying, "White cells do not think."

A flash of resentment crossed Kaliinin's face, flushing it slightly, but her voice remained even. "By saying 'think,' Albert, I am merely using a figure of speech. What I mean is that the white cell's behavior toward us is that which it would display toward a red corpuscle."

173

Morrison cast another look toward the large billowing cell up ahead and decided that, harmless or not, he found its appearance distasteful. He looked with much appreciation at the contrast made by Kaliinin's pretty high-cheekboned face, and wondered why she had never had that little mole under the left corner of her lip removed. Then he wondered if it didn't add just the right trifle of piquancy to a face that might otherwise be considered too pretty to possess character.

That moment of beside-the-point speculation effectively removed the uneasiness that the white cell's appearance had introduced and Morrison returned, in his mind, to Kaliinin's statement.

"Does it act as though we're a red corpuscle because we're the right size for it?"

"That may help," said Kaliinin, "but it's not the real reason. You judge a red corpuscle to be a red corpuscle because you see it. The white cell judges a red corpuscle to be one because it senses the characteristic pattern of the electromagnetic pattern on its surface. White cells are trained—that is just another figure of speech—let us say, adapted—to ignore that."

"But this ship doesn't have the electromagnetic pattern of a red corpuscle. . . . Ah, but I guess you've taken care of that."

Kaliinin smiled in gentle self-satisfaction. "Yes, I have. It is my specialty."

Dezhnev said, "That is it, Albert. Our little Sophia knows, completely in her head"—he tapped his right temple—"the exact electromagnetic pattern of every cell, every bacterium, every virus, every protein molecule, every—"

"Not quite," said Kaliinin, "but those I forget, my computer can supply. And I have a device here that can use the energy of the microfusion motors to place positive and negative electric charges on the ship in whatever pattern I choose. The ship has the charge pattern of a red corpuscle on itself as best as I can duplicate it, and that is close enough to cause the white cell to react—or, rather, not to react—accordingly."

"When did you do that, Sophia?" asked Morrison with interest.

"When we were reduced to the size that would make us a potential object of interest for a white cell or for the immune apparatus generally. We don't want antibodies swarming over us, either."

A thought occurred to Morrison. "Since we're talking about being reduced in size, why hasn't the Brownian motion gotten worse? I should think it would batter us more as we got smaller."

Boranova put in from behind, "So it would if we were unminiaturized objects of this size. Since we are miniaturized, there are theoretical reasons that prevent Brownian motion from getting very bad. It's nothing to worry about."

Morrison thought about it, then shrugged. They weren't going to tell him anything they thought might make him too knowledgeable in the matter of miniaturization and what did that matter? The Brownian motion had *not* grown worse. In fact, it had grown less troublesome (or was he just getting used to it?) and he had no objection to that. That made it, as Boranova said, nothing to worry about.

His attention shifted back toward Kaliinin. "How long have you been training in this field, Sophia?"

"Since my graduate days. Even without Shapirov's coma, we all knew the time would come when a trip through a bloodstream would become necessary. We've been planning something like this for a long time and we knew that this skill of mine would be needed."

"You might have planned an automated crewless ship."

"Someday, perhaps," said Boranova, "we will, but not yet. We cannot, even now, make the automation equivalent to the versatility and ingenuity of a human brain."

"That's true," said Kaliinin. "An automated pattern maker would place us in the red corpuscle pattern as a way of following the path of least resistance, and it would do little more than that. After all, it would be a useless expense and perhaps an impractical exercise altogether to try to instill in an automated pattern maker the ability to change appropriately in response to all sorts of improbable conditions. When I am present, however, I have the capacity to do almost anything. I can change the pattern to meet an unlikely emergency, to test the value of something earlier unthought of, or simply to suit a whim. —For instance, I could change the ship's pattern to that of an *E. coli* bacterium and the white cell would attack at once."

"I'm sure of that," said Morrison, "but don't do it, please."

"No fear," said Kaliinin. "I won't."

But Boranova's voice sounded in sudden—and uncharacteristic—excitement. "On the contrary, Sophia, do that!"

"But, Natalya—"

"I mean it, Sophia. Do it. We haven't tested your instrument under field conditions, you know. Let's try it."

Konev muttered, "That's a waste of time, Natalya. Let us first get to where we're going."

Boranova said, "It won't do us any good to get there—if we can't enter a cell. Here is an immediate opportunity at hand to see if Sophia can control the behavior of a cell."

"I agree," said Dezhnev boisterously. "This has been a remarkably uneventful trip so far."

"That's the best kind, I should think," said Morrison.

But Dezhnev held up a disapproving hand. "My old father used to say: 'To want peace and quiet above all else is to hope for death.'"

"Go ahead, Sophia," Boranova said firmly. "We waste time."

Kaliinin hesitated a bare moment—the time required, perhaps, to remember that Boranova was captain of the ship—then her hand flickered over the controls of her device and the configurations upon the television screen altered markedly. (Morrison admired, in an apprehensive sort of way, the speed with which she did it.)

Morrison lifted his eyes to the white cell ahead, and for a moment he saw no change. And then it seemed as though a fit of trembling overtook the monster and Dezhnev whispered, "Aha, it recognizes the presence of its prey."

At the extreme forward end of the white cell, its substance seemed to bulge toward and all around them in an uneven circle. At the same time, the substance in the center retreated as though it were being sucked in. Morrison envisioned a monster's jaws preparing for a meal.

Konev said, "It works, Natalya. That creature ahead is preparing to envelop and engulf us."

Boranova said, "So it is. Very well, Sophia, restore us to the red cell mode."

Again Kaliinin's fingers flickered and the configurations on the screen returned (as nearly as Morrison's memory could judge) to what they had earlier been.

This time, however, the white cell remained unaffected. Its outer rim was shooting past the ship, which was now heading into the deep central concavity.

41.

MORRISON was appalled. The entire ship was encased by something that looked precisely like fog—a gritty granular fog, within which a multilobed object, faintly denser than the rest, writhed its way around them. Morrison knew that this must be the nucleus of the white cell.

Konev snapped out angrily, "Apparently, once the white cell gears itself for engulfment, the rest is automatic and nothing will stop it. —What now, Natalya?"

Boranova replied quietly, "I admit I hadn't expected this. The fault is mine."

"What's the difference?" said Dezhnev, frowning. "It's no matter. What can this blob do to us? It cannot crush us. It is not a boa constrictor."

Konev said, "It can try to digest us. We're in a food vacuole right now and digestive enzymes are pouring in around us."

"Let them pour," said Dezhnev. "I wish them the joy of the attempt. The ship's wall is not digestible to anything a white cell has. After a while, it will reject us as indigestible residue."

"How will it know?" asked Kaliinin.

"How will it know what?" snapped Dezhnev.

"How will it know we are indigestible residue? It was spurred into activity by our bacterial charge pattern."

"Which you removed."

"Yes, but as someone remarked, the white cell, once stimulated, apparently has to go through its whole cycle of activity. It is not a thinking device; it is entirely automatic." Kaliinin was frowning now and looking around at the others. "It seems to me that the white cell will continue trying to digest us until it is given the appropriate stimulus that will put its engulfment mechanism into reverse and allow it to eject us."

Boranova said, "But we now have the charge pattern of a red corpuscle again. Don't you think that would stimulate rejection? It doesn't eat red cells."

"I think it's too late for that," said Kaliinin a little diffidently, as though nervous about standing up to Boranova. "The red corpuscle pattern keeps it unengulfed, but once it *is* engulfed by some means, it would seem that the pattern alone is insufficient to spark ejection. After all, here we are; we are *not* being ejected."

Her eyes—all five pairs of eyes, in fact—uneasily surveyed the wall of the ship. They were trapped in the cloudy cell.

"I think," Kaliinin went on, "that there's a charge pattern to the kind of indigestible residue left by the bacteria the white cell is designed to engulf and that that alone would be a trigger for ejection."

"In that case," said Dezhnev, "give it the pattern it wants, Sophia, my little chicken."

"Gladly," said Kaliinin, "if you will tell me what it is because I don't know. I can't just try patterns at random. The number of possible patterns is astronomical."

"As a matter of fact," said Konev, "can we be sure the white cell ejects anything at all? Perhaps indigestible residue becomes part of its granular material and remains within it until it is removed and dismantled in the spleen."

Boranova said sharply (perhaps weighed down with the knowledge that she was responsible for their present situation, thought Morrison), "There is no point in babbling. Is there a constructive suggestion?"

Dezhnev said, "I can turn on the microfusion motors and bore a way out of the white cell."

"No," said Boranova sharply. "Do you know the direction which we are heading at this moment? Inside this food vacuole we may be slowly turning or the vacuole itself may be drifting through the cell's substance. If you smash your way outward, you may damage the wall of the blood vessel and the brain itself."

Konev said, "For that matter, white cells can wiggle out of a capillary, working their way between the cells that make up the capillary wall. Since the path we have taken has led us into an arteriole branch that has narrowed to just about capillary size, we can't even be sure that we're still in the bloodstream."

"Yes, we can," said Morrison suddenly. "The white cell can pinch itself small, but it can't pinch *us* small. If it squeezes out of the vessel, it would be forced to leave us behind. — And that would be a good thing, except that it hasn't done it."

"There you are," said Dezhnev. "I should have thought of it sooner. Natasha, make us bigger and crack the white cell open. Give it indigestion like it has never had."

Again a sharp negative from Boranova. "And crack the blood vessel open, too? The blood vessel is fairly small now, not much wider than the white cell."

Kaliinin said, "If Arkady will get in touch with the Grotto, someone there might have an idea."

There was silence for a moment and then Boranova said in a half-strangled way, "Not just yet. We have done something foolish—well, *I* have—and you know as well as I do that it would be better for all of us if we didn't need help."

"We can't wait forever," said Konev restlessly. "The fact is that I don't know where we are by now. I can't rely on the white cell drifting with the bloodstream or with maintaining any given speed, for that matter. Once we are lost, it may take considerable time to locate ourselves and we may need help from the Grotto to do it, too. In that case, how do we explain being lost?"

Morrison said, "How about the air-conditioning?"

There was a pause and Boranova said, "What do you mean, Albert?"

"Well, we're sending miniaturized subatomic particles out of the ship and into interplanetary space. They carry heat away from the ship, I was told, so that we remain cool even in the all-pervasive warmth of the body we're in. That coolness must be something the white cell is not designed to tolerate. If we turn up the air-conditioning and become colder still, there may come a time when the white cell will be uncomfortable enough to eject us."

Boranova mulled this over and said evenly, "I think—possibly—that might work."

Dezhnev said, "Don't bother thinking. I've turned up the air-conditioning to maximum. Let's see if anything happens besides all of us getting frostbite."

Morrison watched the fog outside. He was well aware that he was as tense as the others. He was not in agony over an unfortunate decision—an ill-advised experiment. Nor was he biting his nails over the fate of Shapirov and yet—

Tapping his own emotions, it occurred to him that having come thus far, having been miniaturized and finding himself in a small cerebral arteriole, he suddenly had an urge to check out his theories. Had he come this far in order to turn back and spend the rest of his life holding up an imaginary thumb and forefinger nearly in contact and saying in the depth of his mind, "Missed it by that much"?

Very well, then. He had passed from desperately not wanting to attempt the project to a definite reluctance to abort it.

Dezhnev's voice broke in on his thoughts. "I don't think this little animal likes what's happening."

Morrison was conscious of a biting chill, and shivered as he became aware that the thin cotton uniform he wore was a totally inadequate shield against this sudden onset of winter.

And perhaps the white cell "thought" this, too, for the fog thinned and a rift appeared in it. Then, in another moment or two, the surroundings were clear and the white cell was a ball of fog to their rear, drifting away—or perhaps crawling away—amoebalike, from an unpleasant experience.

Boranova said (sounding a little dumbfounded), "Well, it's gone."

Dezhnev waved both hands high in the air. "A toast—if we had a small swallow of vodka with us—to our American hero. It was an excellent suggestion."

Kaliinin nodded at Morrison and smiled. "It was a good idea."

"As good as mine was bad," said Boranova, "but at least we know that your technique can do what it should, Sophia—as long as we know enough. And as for you, Arkady, ease the air-conditioning intensity before we all catch pneumonia. —So you see, Albert, we have already done well to take you with us."

"Perhaps," said Konev tightly, "but in the meanwhile, I think the white cell took us on an excursion. We are not where we were and I do not know exactly where we are."

42.

BORANOVA'S lips tightened and she asked with some difficulty, "How can you not know where we are? We were inside the white cell only a few minutes. It couldn't have moved us into the liver, could it?"

Konev seemed at least equally upset. "No, we're not in the liver, *Madame.*" (He came down heavily on the honorific, giving it the French pronunciation.) "But I suspect the white cell, dragging us with it, has turned into a branching capillary so that we are now out of the mainstream of the arteriole—which was not yet quite a capillary—that we were carefully following."

"Which capillary did it turn into?" asked Boranova.

"That is what I don't know. There are a dozen capillaries it might have turned into and I don't know which one it was."

"Doesn't your red marker—" began Morrison.

"My red marker," said Konev at once, "works by dead reckoning. If I know where we are and the speed at which we're progressing, it will move along with us, turning when I tell it to turn."

"You mean," said Morrison incredulously, "it only marks your position insofar as you know your position—no more than that?"

"It is not a magical marker, no," said Konev freezingly. "It acts to mark our place and keep track of it, lest we lose it in the confusion of the three-dimensional complexity of the bloodstream and the neuronic networks, but we have to guide it. At this stage, it's not complex enough to guide itself. In an emergency, we can be located from outside, but that's a time-consuming process."

It seemed to be time for someone to ask a classically foolish question and that someone turned out to be Dezhnev. He said, "Why should the white cell have turned off into a capillary?"

Konev turned red. Speaking so rapidly that Morrison could hardly make out the Russian, he said, "And how should I know that? Am I privy to the thought processes of a white cell?"

"That's enough," said Morrison sharply. "We're not here

to fight with each other." (He noted the quick look that Boranova had shot toward him and he chose to interpret it as representing gratitude.)

"Actually," he went on, "the solution is simple. We're in a capillary. Very well. The current is at a creeping pace in capillaries, so where is the difficulty in making use of the famous microfusion engines? If you put them into reverse, we will just back out of this capillary and eventually—not a very long eventually, either—we will be back at the junction point and in the arteriole again. Then we continue onward until we get to the proper turnoff and into the proper capillary. We'll have lost a little time and spent a little power, that's all."

Morrison's statement was greeted with solemn stares. Even Konev, who generally spoke—when he did—with his face steadfastly forward, turned now, his angry frown concentrated on Morrison.

Morrison said uneasily, "Why are you all looking at me like that? It's a perfectly natural course of procedure. If you had been driving a car and accidentally turned into a narrow alley and found it the wrong one, wouldn't you back out?"

Boranova was shaking her head. "Albert, I'm sorry. We have no reverse."

"What?" Morrison stared at her blankly.

"We have no reverse. We have only a forward drive. Nothing more."

Morrison said, "How is it possible to— No reverse gear at all?"

"None."

Morrison looked around at the other four faces and then burst out, "Of all the stupid, incompetent, maddening situations. It's only in the Sov—" He stopped.

Boranova said, "Finish the thought. You were going to say that it's only in the Soviet Union that such a situation would be allowed to arise."

Morrison swallowed, then said grumpily, "I was going to say that, yes. It might be an ill-tempered statement, but I'm angry—and the statement may be true, at that."

"And do you think we're not angry, Albert?" said Boranova with her glance level upon him. "Do you know how long we've been working on a ship like this? Years! Many years! Since miniaturization first seemed to become a practical possibility, we have been thinking of entering a blood-

stream someday and exploring the working mammalian body
—if not the human body—from within.

"But the more we planned and the more we designed, the
more expensive the project grew, and the more stubborn the
budgeteers in Moscow became in response. I can't blame
them; they had to balance the expense of this project against
other expenses in areas that were far less problematical than
miniaturization was. So, as a result, the ship grew simpler and
simpler in concept, as we cut out first this, then that, then the
other thing. Do you remember when you Americans were
building your first shuttles? What you planned and what you
got?

"In any case, we ended up with an unpowered craft, fit for
observation only. We planned to enter the bloodstream and
let the current carry us where it would. When we had all the
information we could get, we would slowly deminiaturize.
This would kill the animal which we had been studying—it
would only be an animal, of course, but even so some of us
agonized over that. That was all this ship was planned for.
Nothing more. We had no way of knowing that we would
suddenly be faced with a situation in which we had to invade
a human body, in which we had to get to a specific spot in the
brain, in which we would have to emerge without killing the
body. In which we *had* to—and all we had was this ship,
which was not meant for the job at all."

The anger and contempt on Morrison's face had vanished
into a frown of concern. "What did you do?"

"We worked as fast as we could. We improved the microfusion motors and a few other things, frightened that at any
moment Shapirov would die, and equally frightened—or
more so—that our hurry would cause us to make some fatal
mistake. Well, I don't think we made any fatal mistakes, but
still the microfusion motors we ended up with were to be
used for acceleration only when absolutely necessary—they
had originally been designed only for lighting, air-conditioning, and other low-energy uses. Of course, we lacked the
time to do a complete job, so—no reverse gear."

"Didn't anyone point out that there might just be a chance
you would want to go into reverse?"

"That would mean more money and there was none to be
had. After all, we had to compete with space, which was a
going concern, with the realistic needs of agriculture, com-

merce, industry, crime control, and half a hundred other departments of government all clutching at the national purse. Of course we never had enough."

Dezhnev sighed and said, "And so here we are. As my good father used to say: 'Only simpletons go to fortune-tellers. Who else would be in such a hurry to hear bad news?' "

"Your father is telling me nothing I don't know, Arkady. At least with that remark. —I'm afraid to ask, but can we simply turn the ship?" Morrison asked.

Dezhnev said, "You are wise to be afraid. In the first place, the capillary is too narrow. The ship has no room to turn."

Morrison shook his head impatiently. "You don't have to do it in the ship's present size. Shrink it a bit. Miniaturize it. You're going to have to miniaturize anyway before getting inside a cell. Do it now and turn it."

Dezhnev said mildly, "And in the second place, we can't turn it any more than we can go backward. We have a forward gear and that is all."

"Unbelievable," whispered Morrison to himself. Then aloud, "How could you consent to begin this project with so inadequate a ship?"

Konev said, "We had no choice and we were not counting on playing games with white cells."

Boranova, her face expressionless, her voice toneless, said, "If the project fails, I will take full responsibility."

Kaliinin looked up and said, "Natalya, assigning blame will not help us. Right now, we have no choice. We must go ahead. Let us move on, miniaturize if we have to, and find some likely cell to enter."

"Any cell?" said Konev in a stifled fury, and addressing no one. "Any cell? What good will that do?"

"We might find something useful anywhere we go, Natalya," said Kaliinin.

When Konev made no response, Boranova said, "Is there any objection to that, Yuri?"

"Objection? Of course there's objection." He did not turn, but his very back seemed stiff with anger. "We have ten billion neurons in the brain and someone is suggesting that we wander among them blindly and choose one at random. It would be an easier task to drive along Earth's roads in an automobile and randomly choose some human being on the wayside in the hope that he might be a long-lost relative.

Much easier. The number of human beings on Earth is a little more than half the number of neurons in the brain."

"That is a false analogy," said Kaliinin, carefully turning her face toward Boranova. *"We* are not engaged in a blind search. We are looking for Pyotr Shapirov's thoughts. Once we detect them, we need only move in the direction in which the thoughts strengthen."

"If you can," said Morrison, shaking his head. "If your single forward gear happens to be carrying you in the direction in which the thoughts weaken, what do you do then?"

"Exactly," said Konev. "I had plotted out a course that would have taken us directly to an important junction in the particular neuronic network that is related to abstract thought—according to Albert's researches. The *bloodstream* would have carried us there and whatever tortuous path it took, the ship would have followed. And now—" He lifted both his arms and shook them at the unresponsive Universe.

"Nevertheless," said Boranova, her voice strained, "I don't see that we have any choice but to do what Sophia suggests. If that fails, we must find a way out of the body and perhaps try again another day."

"Wait, Natalya," said Morrison. "There just may be another way to remedy the situation. Is it at all possible for one of us to get outside the ship and into the bloodstream?"

43.

MORRISON did not expect an affirmative answer. The ship, which had seemed to him earlier to be a marvelous example of high technology, had now shrunk in his imagination to a stripped-down scow of which nothing at all could be expected.

It seemed to him best, from any practical standpoint, to do as Kaliinin had suggested—to try any brain cell they could reach. But if that failed, it would mean getting out of the body and trying again, as Boranova had just said, and Morrison did not feel he would be physically capable of going through this again. He would try any wild scheme to prevent that.

"Is it possible to get out of this ship, Natalya?" he asked again as she looked at him, dazed. (The others were no more responsive.) "—Look, don't you understand? Suppose you want to collect samples? Do you have a dredge, a scoop, a net? *Or* can someone get outside and go scuba diving?"

Boranova finally seemed to overcome her surprise at the question. Her heavy eyebrows lifted into an attitude of wonder. "You know, we do. One diving suit for reconnoitering, the plans say. It should be under the back row seats. Under here, in fact."

She unclasped herself and went into a slow float, then managed to pull herself into a horizontal position, her light cotton clothing billowing.

"It's here, Albert," she said. "I presume it has been checked—I mean, against gross errors. There would be no leaks, no obvious flaws. I don't know that it's been field-tested."

"How could it be?" said Morrison. "I take it this is the first time the ship—or anything—has been in a bloodstream."

"I imagine it must have been checked in warm water adjusted to the proper viscosity. —I blame myself for not checking on this, but of course there was no thought at any time of anyone leaving the ship. I had even forgotten the suit existed."

"Do you at least know if the suit has an air supply?"

"Indeed it does," said Boranova with some asperity. "And it has a power supply that makes it possible for it to have a light of its own. You mustn't think of us as utter incompetents, Albert. —Though," she said with a rueful shrug, "I suppose we—or, at least, I—have given you some reason to think so."

"Does the suit have flippers?"

"Yes, on both hands and feet. It is meant for maneuvering in fluid."

"In that case," said Morrison, "there is perhaps a way out."

"What are you thinking of, Albert?" asked Kaliinin.

Morrison said, "Suppose we miniaturize a bit further so that the ship can turn easily without scraping the capillary walls. Someone then gets into the suit, moves outside the ship—assuming you have an air lock of some sort—and, propelling himself by means of the flippers, turns the ship. Once the ship is turned, the person gets back into the ship, which is now facing in the correct direction. The motor is started and we push our way back against the feeble capillary current to the joining with the arteriole and thus back to our original path."

Boranova said thoughtfully, "A desperate remedy, but our condition, too, is desperate. Have you ever done any scuba diving, Albert?"

"Some," said Morrison. "That's why I thought of this."

"And none of us have—which is why *we* didn't think of it. In that case, Albert, unclasp yourself and let us get this suit on you."

"On *me?*" Morrison sputtered.

"Of course. It is your idea and you're the one with experience."

"Not in the bloodstream."

"No one has experience in the bloodstream, but the rest of us don't even have it in water."

"No," said Morrison savagely. "This thing is *your* baby—you four. I've done the thinking that got you out of the white cell and I've just done the thinking that could get you out of your present fix. That's my share. *You* do the doing. One of you."

"Albert," said Boranova. "We're all in this together. In here, we are neither Soviets nor Americans; we are human beings trying to survive and to accomplish a great task. Who does what depends on who can do what best, and nothing more."

Morrison caught Kaliinin's eye. She was smiling very slightly and Morrison thought he could read admiration in that smile.

Groaning softly at the folly of being influenced in so childish a manner by a hunger for admiration, Morrison knew he would agree to this madness of his own suggestion.

44.

BORANOVA had the suit out. Like the ship itself, it was transparent, and, except in the head portion, it lay wrinkled and flat. To Morrison, it looked unpleasantly like a life-sized caricature of a human being drawn in outline by a child.

He reached out to touch it and said, "What is it made of? Plastic wrap?"

Boranova said, "No, Albert. It is thin, but it is not weak and it is exceedingly tough and inert. No foreign material will cling to it and it should be perfectly leakproof."

"*Should* be?" echoed Morrison sardonically.

Dezhnev interrupted. "It *is* leakproof. I seem to recall it was tested some time ago."

"You *seem* to recall it."

"I blame myself for not having checked it personally in going over the ship, but I, too, forgot its existence. There was no thought—"

Morrison bitterly exclaimed, "I'm sure your father must have told you once that self-blame is a cheap penalty for incompetence, Arkady."

Dezhnev replied, raspingly, "I am not incompetent, Albert."

Boranova cut in, "We will have our fights when this is all over. Albert, there is nothing to worry about. Even if there were a microscopic leak, the water molecules in the plasma outside are far larger in comparison to the suit than they would be under normal conditions. A leak in a normal suit might let in normal water molecules, but that same leak in a miniaturized suit would not allow those same water molecules, now giants in comparison, to enter."

"That makes sense," muttered Morrison, looking for solace.

"Of course," said Boranova. "We can insert a standard oxygen cylinder right here—small size, but you won't be out there for long—an absorption canister for carbon dioxide here, and a battery for the light. So, you see, you will be equipped."

"Just the same," said Konev, turning to look at Morrison dispassionately, "you had better do it as quickly as possible. It's warm out there—thirty-seven degrees Celsius—and I don't think the suit has a cooling mechanism."

"No cooling mechanism?" Morrison looked at Boranova questioningly.

Boranova shrugged. "It is not easy to cool an object in an isothermal medium. This entire body, which is as large as a mountain to us, is all at a constant temperature of thirty-seven. The ship itself can be cooled by means of the microfusion engines. We can't build an equivalent device into the suit, but then, as we keep saying, you won't be out for very long. —Still, you had better take off the suit you're wearing now, Albert."

Morrison demurred. "It's not heavy, just a thin layer of cotton."

"If you perspire with it on," said Boranova, "you will be sitting in wet clothes when you return to the ship. We have no spare clothing we can offer you."

"Well, if you insist," Morrison said. Then he removed his sandals and tried to strip his one-piecer off his legs, something which proved surprisingly difficult in his nearly weightless state.

Boranova, noting his discomfort, said, "Arkady, please help Albert into the suit."

Dezhnev worked his way, with difficulty, over the back of his seat to where Morrison floated, in a cramped posture, against the hull of the ship.

Dezhnev helped Morrison into the legs of the suit one at a time, though the two, working together, were scarcely less clumsy than Morrison alone had been. (Everything about us, Morrison thought, is designed to work in the presence of gravity.)

Dezhnev maintained a running commentary as they struggled. "The material of this suit," he said, "is precisely that of the ship itself. Entirely secret, of course, though, for all I know, you have a similar material in the United States—also secret, I am sure." He paused on a small note of inquiry.

"I wouldn't know," muttered Morrison. His bare leg worked its way into a sheath of thin plastic. It didn't stick to his leg, but moved smoothly along, yet it somehow gave the impression of being cold and wet without, in reality, being either. He had never encountered a surface quite like that of the plastic suit and he didn't know how to interpret the sensation.

Dezhnev said, "When the seams close, they become virtually a single piece of material."

"How do they open again?"

"The electrostatics can be neutralized once you're back in the ship. For now, most of the exterior of the suit has a mild negative charge, balanced by a positive one on the inner surface. Any portion of the suit will cling to any positively charged area on the ship's surface, but not so strongly that you can't pull loose."

Morrison said, "What about the rear end of the ship where the engines are?"

"You need not be concerned about them. They are working at minimum power for our cooling and illumination and any particles emerging from them will pass through you without noticing your presence at all. The oxygen cylinders and waste absorption work automatically. You will produce no bubbles. You need only breathe normally."

"One must be grateful for *some* technological blessings."

Dezhnev frowned and said darkly, "It is well-known that Soviet spacesuits are the best in the world and the Japanese are second."

"But this is not a spacesuit."

"It is modeled on one in many ways." Dezhnev made as though to pull the headpiece down.

"Wait," said Morrison. "What about a radio?"

Dezhnev paused. "Why would you need a radio?"

"To *communicate.*"

"You will be able to see us, and we will be able to see you. Everything is transparent. You can signal to us."

Morrison drew a deep breath. "In other words, no radio."

Boranova said, "I am sorry, Albert. It is really only a very simple suit for small tasks."

Morrison said sourly, "Still, if you do a thing, it's worth doing well."

"Not to bureaucrats," said Dezhnev. "To them, if you do a thing, it's worth doing cheaply."

There was one advantage of irritation and annoyance, thought Morrison; it did tend to wipe out fear. He said, "How do you plan to get me out of the ship?"

Dezhnev said, "Right where you're standing, the hull is double."

Morrison turned sharply to look and, of course, went floundering. He could not seem to remember for three seconds running that he was essentially weightless. Dezhnev helped him control his body at some cost to himself. (We must look like a pair of clowns, Morrison thought.)

Morrison found himself staring, at last, at the indicated portion of the hull. Now that his attention was drawn to it, it did seem faintly less transparent than the other portions, but that might well have been his imagination.

Dezhnev said, "Hold still, Albert. My father used to say:

'It is only when a child has learned to hold still that it can be considered a creature of sense.' "

"Your father was not considering zero-gravity conditions."

"The air lock," said Dezhnev, ignoring Morrison's comment, "is modeled on the type we have in our lunar surface enclosures. The inner layer of the lock will peel back, then move around you and seal. Most of the air between the layers will be sucked out—we can't afford to waste air—which will give you a strange feeling, no doubt. Then the outer layer will peel open and you will be outside. Simple! —Now, let me close your helmet."

"Wait! How do I get back?"

"The same way. In reverse."

Now Morrison was closed in completely and a definite claustrophobic sensation helped unsettle him, as the coldness of fear began to wipe out the saving sensation of anger.

Dezhnev was pushing him against the hull and Konev, having managed to turn about in his seat, was helping. The two women remained calmly in their seats and were staring intently.

Morrison did not for a moment feel that they were staring at his body; he wished they were, in fact. That would be relatively benign. He was absolutely certain they were watching to see if the air lock would work, if his suit would work, if he himself would remain alive for more than a few minutes once he was outside the ship.

He wanted to cry out and call off everything, but the impulse to do so remained only an impulse.

He felt a slippery motion behind him and then the whipping of a transparent sheet before him. It was like the seat belt clasping itself around his waist and chest, but here the sheet enclosed him entirely, head to toe, side to side.

It clung to him more and more tightly, as the air between was pumped out. The material of his suit seemed to strain outward as the air inside it pushed against the developing vacuum outside.

And then the outer layer of the hull behind him whipped away and he felt a soft thrust that sent him tumbling outward and into the blood plasma within the capillary.

He was out of the ship and on his own.

CHAPTER 11

DESTINATION

Going there may be most of the
fun—but only if you get there in the end.
—*Dezhnev Senior*

45.

IMMEDIATELY, Morrison felt the enveloping warmth and gasped. As Konev had said—the temperature was 37 degrees Celsius. It was the heat of a sweltering summer day and there was no escape. No shade, no breeze.

He looked around, getting his bearings. Clearly, Boranova had miniaturized the ship further while he had clumsily clambered into the suit. The tiled wall of the capillary was farther away. He could see only a bit of it, for between himself and the wall was a huge cloudy object. A red corpuscle, of course. Then a platelet went slipping between the red corpuscle and the wall, but very slowly.

All of them—red corpuscle, platelet, himself, the ship—were moving along with the small creeping current within the capillary, if one judged by the slow drifting motion of the tilings in the wall.

Morrison wondered why he felt the Brownian motion as little as he did. There was indeed the sensation of movement and the other objects in sight appeared to tremble. Even the tile marks of the capillary walls seemed to shift somehow, in a rather peculiar manner.

But there was no time to be keenly analytical. He had to get things done and get back within the ship.

He was a meter or so from the ship. (A meter? Purely subjective. How many micrometers—how many millionths of a meter was he separated from the ship in real measurements? He didn't pause to try to work out an answer to the question.) He twiddled his flippers to get back to the ship. The plasma was distinctly more viscous than seawater—unpleasantly so.

The heat continued, of course. It would never stop while the body he was in remained alive. Morrison's forehead was getting moist. —Come, he had to get started.

His hand reached out to the place where he had left the ship, but it touched nothing. It was almost as though it were pushing into a soft rubbery cushion of air, although his eyes told him there was nothing between that portion of the hull of the ship and his suited hand except, at best, a film of fluid.

A moment of thought and he saw what was happening. The outer skin of his suit carried a negative electric charge. So did that portion of the hull he was touching. It was repelling him.

There were other portions of the hull, however. Morrison slid his hands along until he was aware of touching the plastic. That was not in itself enough, however, for his hands moved along the area as though it were infinitely slippery.

And then, almost with a click, his left hand froze. It had passed a region of positive charge and remained in place. He tried to pull free first by a gentle backward push and then more frantically. He might as well have been riveted to the spot. He felt farther along with his right hand. Anchor that and he might be able to pull his left hand free.

Click. Anchored now by his right hand, he pulled at his left. Nothing happened. He clung to the hull, crucified there.

Drops of perspiration rolled down his forehead and collected in his armpits.

He shouted uselessly, wiggling his legs in an ecstasy of effort.

They were looking at him, but how could he gesture to his trapped hands? The red corpuscle that had been companion to the ship since he had emerged from it drifted closer and nudged him against the hull. His chest, however, did not cling. Luckily, it was not up against a positively charged region.

Kaliinin was looking toward him. Her lips were moving, but he could not lip-read—not Russian, at any rate. She did something with her computer and his left arm pulled free. Presumably, she had weakened the intensity of the charge.

He nodded his head in what he hoped would be interpreted as a gesture of thanks. Now it would only be necessary to work his way back, positively charged area by positively charged area, until he reached the rear of the ship.

He began the motion and found himself more or less pinned, but not so much this time by the harsh pull of the electromagnetic interaction as by the soft, pillowy push of the red corpuscle.

"Get back!" shouted Morrison, but the red corpuscle knew nothing of shouts. Its role was purely passive.

Morrison thrust at it with his hands and used his leg flippers to push harder. The elastic surface film of the red cell gave and bellied inward, but resisted more strongly, the more it gave until, finally, Morrison was pushing uselessly and, as he tired, was forced back against the ship.

He paused to catch his breath, which was difficult, hot and sweat-drenched as he was. He wondered whether he would be disabled first by dehydration or by the fever which would surely come over him if he could not get rid of the heat his own body was producing—and all the more so because of the effort he was making to free himself of the red corpuscle.

He lifted his arm again and brought it down, the plastic flipper held edgewise. It sliced through the pellicle of the corpuscle, puncturing it like a balloon. The surface tension of the film pulled the opening wider and wider. Matter exuded —a thin cloud of granules—and the red corpuscle began to shrink.

Morrison felt as though he had killed an inoffensive living creature and experienced a pang of guilt—then decided that there were trillions of others in the circulatory system and that a red corpuscle only had 120 days of functioning anyhow.

Now he could pull back toward the rear.

No fog collected on the inner surface of his suit. Why should it? The surface was as warm as he was and nothing would cling to the plastic anyway. What would have been fog was probably collecting as little pools of sweat in this corner and that of the suit, rolling around as he did.

He was back at the rear now, back where the ship's streamlining failed because the jets of each of the three microfusion engines broke the smooth lines. Here he was as far from the center of gravity of the ship as possible. (With luck, the other four would move as close to the front of the ship as they could. —He wished he had thought to make that explicit before getting into the suit.) What he had to do was to find positively charged areas that would hold his hands back and then—push!

He was feeling a little dizzy. Physical? Psychological? The effect was the same, either way.

He took another deep breath and blinked his eyes as perspiration leaked into them (there was no way he could brush it away and again he felt a spasm of fury against the fools who had designed a suit only microscopically better than none at all).

He found the handholds against the hull and paddled his feet. Would this work? The mass he was trying to turn was only micrograms in quantity, but he had at his disposal—what? Microergs? He knew that the square-cube law gave him a tremendous advantage, but how much efficiency could he put into his push?

But the ship moved. He could tell that by the motions of the tiling on the capillary wall. He could now reach that wall with his feet, so the ship must be lying across the capillary. He had turned it 90 degrees.

When his feet touched the capillary wall, he pushed with perhaps injudicious savagery. If he were to punch a hole in the wall, the results might be incalculably bad, but he was aware he had little time left and he could not think beyond that. Fortunately, his feet rebounded as though they had sunk into spongy rubber and the ship turned a bit faster.

—Then stuck.

Morrison looked up blearily, squinting and willing himself to see. (He was almost past the ability to breathe in the squalid damp heat of the suit's interior.) It was another red corpuscle. Surely it was another red corpuscle. They were as closely spaced in capillaries as—as cars on a busy city street.

This time he did not wait. The flipper on his right hand

came down at once, carving open a vast swath, and this time he did not spend a microsecond of worry over the murder of an innocent object. His legs worked again and the ship moved.

He hoped it was shifting in the same direction as before. What if he had managed to twist himself upside down in his mad attack on the red corpuscle and he was simply pushing the ship back into the wrong direction? He was almost beyond caring.

The ship was now parallel to the long axis of the capillary. Gasping, he tried to study the tiles. If they were moving forward toward the prow of the ship, then the ship was moving backward with the current and it was facing the junction of the arteriole.

He decided it was. *No, he didn't care.* Right way, wrong way, he had to get back into the ship.

He was not ready to sell his life for success.

Where? Where?

His hands were sliding along the walls of the ship. Sticking here. Sticking there.

Vaguely he saw the dim figures on the other side of the wall. Motioning. He tried to follow the gestures.

They were fading out.

Up? Signaling up? How could he clamber up? He had no strength.

His last truly sane thought, for a while, was that he needed no strength. Up meant no more than down for a weightless, massless body.

He wriggled upward, forgetting why, and a fog of darkness came down upon him.

46.

THE first thing Morrison sensed was cold.

A wave of cold. Then a touch of cold.

Then light.

He was staring at a face. For an interval of time, he did not grasp the fact that it was a face. It was just a pattern of light and shade at first. Then a face. —Then the face of Sophia Kaliinin.

She said softly, "Do you know me?"

Slowly, creakily, Morrison nodded.

"Say my name."

"Sophia," he croaked.

"And to your left?"

His eyes turned, and had difficulty focusing, then he turned his head. "Natalya," he said.

"How do you feel?"

"Headache." His voice sounded small and far away.

"It will go away."

Morrison closed his eyes and surrendered to the peace of nonstruggle. Just to do nothing was the highest good. To feel nothing.

Then he felt a cool stroke over his groin and his eyes opened again. He discovered that the suit had been removed and he was naked.

He felt arms holding him down and heard a voice say, "Don't worry. We can't give you a shower. There's no water for that. But we can use a damp towel. You need to be cooled —and cleaned."

". . . undignified," he managed, struggling over the syllables.

"Foolish. We'll dry you now. A little deodorant. Then back into your one-piece." Morrison tried to relax. It was only when he felt cotton against his body that he spoke again. He asked, "Did I turn the ship properly?"

"Yes," said Kaliinin, nodding her head vigorously, "and fought off two red corpuscles most savagely. You were heroic."

Morrison said hoarsely, "Help me up." He pushed down with his elbows against his seat and, of course, drifted into the air.

He was brought down.

"I forgot," he muttered. "Well, strap me in. Let me sit and recover."

He fought down the dizzy feeling, then said, "That plastic suit is worthless. A suit for use in the bloodstream of a warm-blooded animal must be cooled."

"We know," said Dezhnev from his seat at the controls. "The next one will be."

"The next one," spat Morrison bitterly.

"At least," said Dezhnev, "you did what was necessary and the suit made that possible."

"At a cost," said Morrison, who had slipped into English in order to express his feelings more accurately.

"I understood that," said Konev. "I lived in the United States, you know. If it will make you feel better, I'll teach you how to say every one of those words in Russian."

"Thanks," said Morrison, "but they taste better in English." He licked his dry lips with a dry tongue and said, "Water would taste still better. I'm thirsty."

"Of course," said Kaliinin. She held a bottle to his lips. "Suck at it gently. It won't pour when it has no mass to speak of. —Slowly, slowly. Don't waterlog yourself."

Morrison drew his head away from the bottle. "Do we have enough water?"

"You must replace what you lost. We'll have enough."

Morrison drank more, then sighed. "That's much better. —There was something I thought of when I was out in the capillary. Just a flash. I wasn't sufficiently myself to understand my own thought." He bent his head and covered his eyes with his hands. "I'm not sufficiently myself to remember it now. Let me think."

There was silence in the ship.

And then Morrison said with a sigh and a rather massive clearing of his throat. "Yes, I remember it."

Boranova sighed also. "Good, then you have your memory."

"Of course I have," said Morrison pettishly. "What did you think?"

Konev said coldly, "That a loss of memory might be an early sign of brain damage."

Morrison's teeth clicked as his mouth snapped shut. Then he said, feeling a chill in the pit of his stomach. "Is that what you thought?"

"It was possible," said Konev. "As in Shapirov's case."

"Never mind," said Kaliinin insinuatingly. "It didn't happen. What was your thought, Albert? You still remember." It was half-confident statement, half-hopeful question.

"Yes, I do remember. We're pushing upstream now, aren't we? So to speak?"

"Yes," said Dezhnev. "I'm using the motors—expending energy."

"When you reach the arteriole, you'll still be heading upstream and you can't turn. You'll be heading back the way you came. The ship will have to be turned again from out-side. It can't be me. Do you understand? —*It can't be me!*"

Kaliinin put her arm around his shoulder. "Shh! It's all right. It won't be you."

"It won't be-anyone, Albert, my friend," said Dezhnev jovially. "Look ahead. We're coming to the arteriole now."

Morrison looked up and felt a twinge of pain. He must have grimaced, for Kaliinin put a cool hand on his forehead and said, "How is your headache?"

"Getting better," said Morrison, shaking her hand off rather querulously. He was peering forward and relieved to find that his vision seemed normal. The cylindrical tunnel up ahead was widening somewhat and beyond an elliptical lip he could see a distant wall in which the tiling was much less pronounced.

Morrison said, "The capillary comes off the arteriole like the branch of a tree at an oblique angle. We go through that opening up ahead and we'll be pointed three quarters of the way upstream—and once we nudge the far wall, we'll bounce off and be moving fully upstream."

Dezhnev chuckled. "My old father used to say: 'Half an imagination is worse than none at all.' —Watch, little Albert. See, I will wait until we are almost at the opening and I will throttle down the motor so that we make our way up the current very slowly. Now our ship sticks its snout out of the capillary—a little more—a little more—and now the main stream of arteriole blood catches us and pushes against the nose and turns us—and I push out a little more—and it turns us a bit more—and I come out the whole way—and behold I've been turned, I am heading downstream once more, and I cut the motors."

He grinned triumphantly. "Wasn't that well-done?"

"Well-done," said Boranova, "but impossible without what Albert had done first."

"True enough," said Dezhnev, waving his hand. "I give him full credit and the Order of Lenin—if he will take it."

Morrison felt infinite relief. He would *not* have to go out again. He said, "Thank you, Arkady." Then, rather bash-fully, he added, "You know, Sophia, I'm still thirsty."

At once she handed him the bottle, but he hesitated. "Are you sure I'm not drinking more than my share, Sophia?"

"Of course you are, Albert," said Kaliinin, "but more than

your share *is* your share. Come, water is easily recycled. Besides, we have a small additional supply. You did not fit into the air lock neatly. An elbow stuck well out and we had to crack the inner layer and pull it in—which meant the entry of some plasma. Not much, thanks to its viscosity. It's been miniaturized of course and is being recycled now."

"Once miniaturized, it can't amount to more than a droplet."

"That's all it does amount to," said Kaliinin, smiling, "but even a droplet is an extra supply and since you brought it in, you deserve an extra supply. Logic is logic."

Morrison laughed and sucked up additional water greedily, squeezing it out of the flexible container astronaut-style. He was beginning to feel comparatively normal—more than that. He was feeling the kind of dreamy contentment that comes from being freed from the intolerable.

He tried to concentrate, to gain some sense of reality. He was still in the ship. He was still the size of a bacterium, more or less. He was still in the bloodstream of a man in a coma. His chance of living another few hours was still problematical. —And yet, even as he told himself all this, he nevertheless couldn't flog himself out of the feeling that the mere absence of unbearable heat, the mere being with others, the mere existence of a woman's care was, in itself, a touch of heaven.

He said, "I thank not only Arkady but all of you for pulling me in and caring for me."

"Don't bother," said Konev indifferently. "We need you and your computer program. If we had left you out there, the project would be a failure, even if we found the right cell."

"That may be so, Yuri," said Boranova, clearly indignant, "but at the time we were bringing Albert in, I did not think of that, but only of saving his life. I cannot believe that even you were cold-blooded enough to feel no anxiety for a human being who was risking his life to help us, except insofar as we needed him."

"Obviously," muttered Konev, "plain reason is not wanted."

Plain reason was certainly what Morrison wanted. Since the mention of brain damage, he had been testing himself, thinking, trying to come to conclusions. He said, "Arkady, when the microfusion engines are working, you are converting miniaturized hydrogen into miniaturized helium, and some of the helium escapes along with miniaturized water vapor or other materials designed to produce thrust.''

"Yes," said Arkady warily. "And if that is so, what follows?"

"And the miniaturized particles—atoms and less—simply escape through Shapirov and through the Grotto and through the Earth and end in outer space, as you told me."

"Again—what follows?"

"Surely," said Morrison, "they do not stay miniaturized. We are not initiating a process, are we, in which the Universe will gradually be filled with miniaturized particles as humanity proceeds to make use of miniaturization more and more?"

"If we did, what harm? All human activity for billions of years could not add a significant quantity of miniaturized particles to the Universe. But it is not so. Miniaturization is a metastable condition, which means that there is always a chance that a miniaturized particle will snap out, spontaneously, to true stability, that is, to the unminiaturized state." (Out of the corner of his eye, Morrison saw Boranova raise a warning hand, but Dezhnev was always hard to stop when in oral flood.)

"Naturally," he went on, "there is no predicting when a particular miniaturized particle will snap out of it, but it is a good wager that almost all will be beyond the moon when it happens. As for the few—there are always a few—who snap out of miniaturization almost at once, Shapirov's body can absorb them—"

He then seemed to see Boranova's gesture, which had grown peremptory, and he said, "But I'm boring you. As my old father said on his deathbed: 'My proverbs may have bored you, but now you can look forward to hearing them no more, so that you will mourn me less and, therefore, suffer less.' The old man would have been surprised—and disappointed, perhaps—to know how much we children mourned him, even so—but I think I won't risk it with my companions in this ship—"

"Exactly," snapped Konev, "so please stop, especially since we are now approaching the capillary that we should be entering. Albert, lean over and study the cerebrograph. Do you agree?"

Kaliinin, carefully addressing Boranova, said, "Albert is in no condition to be badgered with cerebrographs."

"Let me try," said Morrison, struggling with his seat belt.

"No," said Boranova with authority. "Yuri can make this decision his own responsibility."

"Then I so make it," said Konev, looking sullen. "Arkady, can you get near the wall on our right and catch the current that turns into the capillary?"

Arkady said, "I've been racing the red corpuscles and I have caught one that is drifting toward the right wall. It will push us—or the small eddy that is pushing it will also push us. —Ah, you see, it is taking place, just as it did in the previous cases where we had to branch off. Each time I managed to use the natural current correctly." A broad grin creased his happy face as he said, "Applause, everybody. Say, 'Well-done, Arkady.'"

Morrison obligingly said, "Well-done, Arkady," and into the capillary the ship went.

47.

MORRISON had recovered sufficiently to be tired of invalidism. Outside the transparent hull of the ship, the wall of the capillary was strongly tiled and seemed fairly close on all sides. It looked very much like the other capillary, the one in which he had turned the ship around.

He said, "I want to see the cerebrograph."

He flung open his seat belt, the first really decisive movement he had made since returning to the ship, and stared rebelliously at the perturbed Kaliinin as he did so.

He pushed himself gently upward into a float, holding himself in position to look over Konev's shoulders by repeated corrections—first up, then down. He said, "How do you know you *are* in the right one, Yuri?"

Konev looked up and said, "Counting and dead reckoning. See here. If we cut down the scale of the cerebrograph, this is the arteriole we've been following off the carotid. We took this branch and that one, and then it's a matter of counting the capillaries as they branch off on the right.

"We had our run-in with the white cell right here and in the time the white cell had at its disposal, this capillary was the only one it could reasonably have reached. Once we were turned around and got back to the arteriole, we followed its narrowing structure and matched what we saw against the cerebrograph. The pattern of branch points outside matched almost exactly the pattern described by the cerebrograph and that alone assures me we were following the right path. Now we have gone into this capillary."

Morrison's left hand slipped off the smooth texture of the back of Konev's seat and his attempt to make up for that twisted him into a comic handstand on the outspread fingers of his right hand. He labored to right himself even as he thought, savagely, that another improvement that must be introduced in later versions of the ship would be handholds on the seats and in other strategic areas.

He said, panting, "And where will this capillary take us?"

Konev said, "Directly to one of the centers which you believe to be a crossroad for the processes of abstract thought. —Let's cut down the scale of the cerebrograph again. Right here."

Morrison nodded. "Please remember that I've located them in human beings only indirectly, judging from my findings in animal brains. Still, if I'm correct, that should be the superior external skeptic node."

Konev said, "According to you, there should be eight such nodes, four on each side. This one, however, is the largest and most intricate on the left side and therefore stands the best chance of giving us the data we need. Am I right?"

"I think so," said Morrison cautiously, "but please remember that my reasoning has not been accepted by the scientific community."

"And do you begin to doubt it now, too, Albert?"

"Caution is a reasonable scientific attitude, Yuri. My concept of the skeptic node makes sense in the light of my observations, but I have never been able to test the matter directly —that's all—and I do not wish it said later that I misled you."

Dezhnev snickered. "Skeptic node! No wonder your countrymen are skeptical of the whole notion, Albert. My father used to say: 'People are ready enough to laugh at you. Don't make funny faces in order to encourage them.'—Why didn't you call it 'thought node' in simple Russian? It would have sounded much better."

"Or 'thought node' in simple English," said Morrison patiently. "But science is international and one uses Greek or Latin when possible. The Greek word for 'thought' is 'skeptis.' It has given us 'skeptical' both in English and in Russian to indicate a habitual doubting attitude. That's because the very act of doubt implies thought. Surely you all know that the most efficient way of accepting the foolish dogmas foisted on us by social orthodoxy is to refrain from thinking."

There was an uncomfortable silence at that, whereupon Morrison (having left it there for just long enough, out of a faint malice—he owed them that much) said, "As human beings in all nations know."

The atmosphere lightened perceptibly at once and Dezhnev said, "In that case, we will see how skeptical we need be of the skeptic node, when we reach it."

"I hope," said Konev with a scowl, "that you don't think this is something to joke about, you clown. That node is where we can hope to detect Pyotr Shapirov's thoughts. Without that, this venture will come to nothing."

Dezhnev said, "To each his own job. I will take you there, with my expert handling of the ship. Once there, you will get the thoughts—or Albert will, if you cannot. And if you do as well with the thoughts as I do with the ship, you will have nothing to be unhappy about. My father used to say—"

"Your father is better off where he is," said Konev. "Don't dig him up again."

"Yuri," said Boranova sharply, "that was an unbearably rude remark to make. You must apologize."

"That's all right," said Dezhnev. "My father used to say: 'The time for offense is when a man, once he has cooled down, repeats an insult he has offered in his rage.' —I am not sure that I can always follow that advice, but in honor of my father, I will pass over Yuri's stupid remark this time." He bent over his controls, his face grim.

Morrison had listened to the altercation (just Konev being nasty—obviously because he was under a great strain) with only half an ear. His mind slipped back to something else, to Dezhnev's carefree chatter and Boranova's warning hand.

He lowered himself into his seat, clasping himself in for stability, and turned his head toward Boranova. "Natalya! A question!"

"Yes, Albert?"

"Those miniaturized particles released into the normal, un-miniaturized Universe—"

"Yes, Albert?"

"Eventually, they deminiaturize."

Boranova hesitated. "As Arkady told you, they do."

"When?"

She shrugged. "Unpredictably. Like the radioactive breakdown of a single atom."

"How do you know?"

"Because it's so."

"I mean, what experiments have been conducted? Nothing has ever been miniaturized to the extent that we are now miniaturized, so surely you can't know what happens to such miniaturized particles by direct observation."

Boranova said, "We've observed events at miniaturizations we have reached and in that way determined what seem to be the laws of behavior of miniaturized objects. We extrapolate—"

"Extrapolations aren't always trustworthy when they go well outside the realm of direct study."

"Granted."

"You compared spontaneous deminiaturization to radioactive breakdown. Is there a half-life of deminiaturization? Even if you can't tell when a particular miniaturized particle will deminiaturize, can you tell when half of a particular large quantity of them will?"

"We have half-life figures and we think they are expressions of first-order kinetics, as radioactive half-lives are."

Morrison said, "Can you generalize from one type of particle to another?"

Boranova pursed her lips and, for a moment, seemed lost in thought. Then she said, "It would seem that the half-life of a miniaturized object varies inversely with the intensity of miniaturization and also with the normal mass of the object."

"So that as we are miniaturized to smaller and smaller sizes, the less time we are likely to remain miniaturized, and the smaller we are to begin with, the less time we are likely to remain miniaturized."

"That's right," replied Boranova stiffly.

Morrison looked at her gravely. "I admire your integrity, Natalya. You're not anxious to tell me things. You don't volunteer information. Still, you draw the line at misinforming me."

Boranova said, "I am a human being and I tell lies on occasion out of necessity or out of defects in my emotions or personality. But I am also a scientist and I would not twist scientific fact for any but the most compelling reasons."

"Then what it amounts to is this. Even this ship, although it is much more massive than a helium nucleus, has a half-life."

"A very long one," put in Boranova quickly.

"But the fact that we are so intensely miniaturized has curtailed this very long half-life."

"Still leaving it long."

"And what about the individual components of the ship? The molecules of water that we drink, the molecules of air we breathe, the individual atoms that make up our body? They could have—must have—very short—"

"No!" said Boranova forcefully, seeming to find relief in being able to deny something. "The miniaturization field overlaps where it deals with particles sufficiently close together, and that are at rest, or nearly at rest, relative to each other. An extended body—such as the ship and everything it contains—is treated as a large but single particle and has a half-life of deminiaturization to match. There miniaturization differs from radioactivity."

"Ah," said Morrison, "but when I was out of the ship and out of contact with it, could it be that I was then a separate particle with a much smaller mass than the ship and its contents and that I had a miniaturization half-life much smaller than we have now?"

"I'm not sure," said Boranova, "whether the distance between yourself and the ship was great enough to make you a separate body. Possibly it did, for the time you were not in contact."

"And I then had a shorter half-life—much shorter."

"Possibly—but then you were out of contact only a matter of minutes."

"Well, then, what is the half-life of this ship at the present level of miniaturization?"

"We can't really speak of the half-life of a single object."

"Yes, because half-lives are statistical. For any particle, deminiaturization can come, spontaneously, at any time, even after a very short time and even though the half-life of a large number of similar particles would be quite long."

"For spontaneous deminiaturization to come after a very short time when the statistical half-life is long is extremely improbable."

"But not impossible, is it?"

"No," said Boranova. "It is not impossible."

"So we can suddenly deminiaturize in five minutes, or even in one minute, or even as I take my next breath."

"In theory."

"Did you all know?" His eyes darted around the ship. "Of course you all knew. Why was I not told?"

Boranova said, "We are volunteers, Albert, working for science and for our nation. We know all the dangers and accept them. You have been forced into this and you don't have the motives that drive us. It seemed possible that if you knew all the dangers, you would have refused to enter the ship voluntarily under any persuasion or that, being brought on board ship by force, you would be altogether useless to us out of sheer—" She paused.

"Out of sheer fright, you were going to say," said Morrison. "Surely I have a right to be afraid. There is reason for fear."

Kaliinin interrupted, her voice a little shrill. "It is time to stop harping on Albert's fear, Natalya. It is he who left the ship in an inadequate suit. It is he who turned the ship around at the risk of his life. Where was his fear then? If he felt it, he bottled it inside and didn't let it prevent him from doing what had to be done."

Dezhnev said, "And yet it was you who did not hesitate to say, in the past, that Americans were all cowardly."

"Then I was wrong. I was speaking unfairly and I ask Albert's pardon."

It was at this point that Morrison caught Konev's eye. The man was twisting around in his seat and glowering at him. Morrison did not pretend to be a master at reading facial expressions, but felt that he could, at a glance, tell what was ailing Konev. The man was jealous—furiously and quite impressively jealous.

48.

THE ship continued its slow way along the capillary toward the destination Konev had marked out: the skeptic node. It was not depending on the current now, which was slow indeed. The engines were going, as Morrison could tell, in two different ways. First, it steadied the ship to have it move along actively, rather than drift passively, and it further deadened the already surprisingly small effect of Brownian motion. Second, the ship was overtaking one red corpuscle after another.

In most cases these were nudged to one side and the red corpuscles then rolled backward between the ship and the wall. Occasionally, a red corpuscle would be met too near dead-center and it would then be pushed forward for a while until it burst. The debris would flow backward, leaving the ship's hull unmarked. With at least five million corpuscles in every cubic millimeter of blood, it didn't matter how many were disrupted and Morrison had become hardened to the carnage.

Morrison deliberately thought of the red cells, rather than of the chance of spontaneous deminiaturization. He knew there was no appreciable chance of exploding outward in the next few moments and, even if it happened, it would simply mean blackout. Death by fried brain would take place so quickly that there would be no conceivable way of sensing it.

Not long before, he had been heating much more slowly in the bloodstream itself. He had *felt* himself dying. After that, instantaneous death had no terrors.

But he preferred to think of other things just the same.

Konev's look! What was seething within him and tearing him apart? He had abandoned Sophia with the utmost cruelty. Did he really think the child was not his? People needed no reason to come to an emotional conclusion and the suspicion of being wrong just bolted the conclusion defensively and immovably in place. Pathological. Think of Leontes in *The Winter's Tale.* Shakespeare always got these things right. Konev would push her away and hate her for the wrong he had done her. He would push her into another man's arms and hate her for being pushed—and be jealous in addition.

And she? Did she know of the jealousy and play upon it? Would she deliberately turn to Morrison, an American, to tear Konev into strips? Tenderly patting the American with the wet towel. Defending him at every step. With Konev, of course, a witness to everything.

Morrison's lips tightened. He didn't like to be a tennis ball, batted from one to another in order to produce maximum pain.

It was none of his business, after all, and he shouldn't take sides. But how was he going to not take sides? Sophia Kaliinin was an attractive woman who reacted with silent sorrow. Yuri Konev was a frowning nasty man who reacted with a compressed boiling of anger. He could neither help liking Sophia nor help disliking Yuri.

He then noted Boranova staring at him gravely and wondered if she were misinterpreting his thoughtfulness and silence. Did she feel he was brooding about the possibility of death by miniaturization—which he was manfully trying not to do?

It seemed so, when Boranova suddenly said, "Albert, none of us are reckless. I have a husband. I have a son. I want to go back to them alive and I intend to get us all back alive. I want you to understand that."

"I'm sure your intentions are good," said Morrison, "but what can you do against a possibility of deminiaturization that is spontaneous, unpredictable, unstoppable?"

"Spontaneous and unpredictable, I agree, but who said unstoppable?"

"Can you stop it, then?"

"I can try. We each have our jobs here. Arkady maneuvers the ship. Yuri directs it to the destination. Sophia gives the ship its electric pattern. You will study the brain waves. As for me, I sit back here and make decisions—my major decision up to now was a mistake, I admit that—and I watch the heat flow."

"The heat flow?"

"Yes. Before the deminiaturization takes place, there is a small evolution of heat, characteristic in pattern. It is that emission that is destabilizing; it is what tips the delicate balance and, after a small delay, starts the process of deminiaturization. When that happens, if I am fast enough, I can intensify the miniaturization field in such a way as to reabsorb the heat and re-establish the metastability."

Morrison said dubiously, "And has that ever been done—actually been done under field conditions—or is it simply theory?"

"It has been done—under much smaller intensities of miniaturization, of course. Still, I have trained at this and my reflexes are sharpened. I hope not to be caught short."

"Was it spontaneous deminiaturization that put Shapirov into a coma, Natalya?"

Boranova hesitated. "We don't really know whether it was an unfortunate encounter with the laws of nature or human error—or both. It may have been a slightly greater wobble from the metastable point of equilibrium than usual and nothing more than that. It is not something I can analyze in detail with you, for you don't have the needed background in the physics and mathematics of miniaturization, nor would I be permitted to give you that background."

"I understand. Classified material."

"Of course."

Dezhnev broke in. "Natasha, we have reached the skeptic node—or so Yuri says."

"Then come to a halt," ordered Boranova.

49.

COMING to a halt took a while.

Morrison noted, with some mild surprise, that Dezhnev did not seem concerned in the process. He was checking his instruments but was making no effort to control the motion of the ship.

It was Kaliinin who was deeply involved now. Morrison looked to his left, studying her as she bent over her instrument, her hair falling forward but not long enough to get in her way, her eyes intent, her slim fingers caressing the keys of her computer. The graphic patterns on the screen she was watching made no sense to Morrison, of course.

"Arkady," she said, "move forward just a little."

The feeble current in the capillaries barely stirred the ship. Dezhnev supplied a small burst of power. (Morrison felt his almost massless body move slightly backward, since there wasn't sufficient inertia to give it a real jerk.) The nearest red corpuscles between the ship and the farther wall of the capillary drifted backward.

"Stop, stop," said Kaliinin. "Enough."

"I can't stop," said Dezhnev. "I can only cut the motors and that I've done."

"It's all right," said Kaliinin. "I have it now," then added the all-but-inevitable saving afterthought of "I think." —Then: "Yes, I do have it."

Morrison felt himself sway forward very slightly. Then he noted the nearby red corpuscles, together with an occasional platelet, drift forward and pass by lazily.

In addition, he became aware of a total cessation of the Brownian motion, that faint tremble he had grown so used to that he was able to ignore it—until it stopped. Now its absence was noticeable and it produced the same sensation within Morrison as the sudden cessation of a continuous low hum would have. He stirred uneasily. It was as though his heart had stopped, even though intellectually he knew it had not.

He asked, "What's happened to the Brownian motion, Sophia?"

She replied, "We're affixed to the wall of the capillary, Albert."

Morrison nodded. If the ship was one piece with the capillary wall, so to speak, the bombarding water molecules that produced the Brownian motion would lose their effect. Their impacts would work toward moving an entire section of comparatively inert wall, instead of a tiny ship the size of a blood platelet. Naturally, the trembling would cease.

"How did you manage to affix the ship, Sophia?" he asked.

"The usual electrical forces. The capillary wall is partly protein, partly phospholipid in character. There are positively and negatively charged groups here and there. I had to detect a pattern sufficiently compact, and then produce a complementary pattern on the ship; negative where the wall is positive and vice versa. The trouble is that the ship is moving with the current, so that I have to detect it a little ahead and produce the complementary pattern before we pass it. I missed three such occasions and then we hit a region where there were no suitable patterns at all, so I had to get Arkady to move us ahead a bit into a better region. —But I made it."

"If the ship had a reverse gear," said Morrison, "there would have been no problem, would there?"

"True," said Kaliinin, "and the next ship will have one. But for now, we have only what we have."

"Quite so," put in Dezhnev. "As my father used to say: 'On tomorrow's feast, we can starve today.'"

"On the other hand," said Kaliinin, "if we had a motor that could do all we would want it to do, we would have a strong impulse to use it lavishly and that might not be so good for poor Shapirov. And it would be expensive besides. As it is, we used an electric field which is more sparing of energy than a motor would be and the price is only a little more work for me—and what of that?"

Morrison was quite certain she wasn't talking for his benefit. He said, "Are you always so philosophical?"

For a moment, her eyes widened and her nostrils tightened, but only for a moment. Then she relaxed and said with a small smile, "No, who could be? But I try."

Boranova interjected, impatiently, "Enough chat, Sophia. —Arkady, you are clearly in touch with the Grotto. What's the delay?"

Arkady held up a large hand, half twisting in his seat to present its palm toward Boranova. "Patience, my captain. They want us to stay exactly where we are for two reasons. First, I'm sending out a carrier wave in three directions. They are locating each and using them to locate us in order to see if the location they determine jibes with what Yuri says it is by dead reckoning."

"How long will that take?"

"Who can say? A few minutes, at any rate. But then my carrier waves are not very intense and the location must be precise, so they may have to repeat the measurement several times and take a mean and calculate limits of error. After all, they have to be correct, for as my father used to say: 'Almost right is no better than wrong.'"

"Yes, yes, Arkady, but that depends on the nature of the problem. What is the second reason we are waiting?"

"They're going through some observations on Pyotr Shapirov. His heartbeat has become slightly irregular."

Konev looked up, his mouth falling open slightly and his thin cheeks looking gaunt under his high cheekbones. "What! Do they say it's anything *we're* doing?"

"No," said Dezhnev. "Do not become a tragedian. They say nothing of the sort. And what can we be doing to Shapirov that is of any importance? We are merely a red corpuscle among red corpuscles in his bloodstream, one among trillions."

"Well, then, what's wrong?"

"Do I know?" said Dezhnev, clearly irritated. "Do they tell me? Am I a physician? I just maneuver this vessel and they pay me no mind except as a pair of hands on the controls."

Kaliinin said with a touch of sadness, "Academician Shapirov clings but weakly to life in any case. It is a wonder that he has remained in stable condition so long."

Boranova nodded. "You are right, Sophia."

Konev said savagely, "But he must continue to remain so. He can't let go now. Not *now*. We haven't made our measurements yet."

"We will make them," said Boranova. "An irregular heartbeat is not the end of the world, even for a man in a coma."

Konev pounded the arm of his seat with a clenched fist. "I will not lose a moment. —Albert, let's begin."

Morrison was startled. He said, "What can be done here in the bloodstream?"

"A neural effect may be felt immediately outside the nerve cell."

"Surely not. Why would the neurons have axons and dendrites to channel the impulse if it was going to spread and weaken into space beyond? Locomotives move along rails, telephone messages along wires, neural impulses—"

"Don't argue the case, Albert. Let's not accept failure by some fine process of reasoning. Let's *test* the matter. See if you can detect brain waves and if you can analyze them in the proper fashion."

Morrison said, "I'll try, but don't order me around in that bullying tone."

"I'm sorry," said Konev, not sounding sorry at all. "I want to watch what you do." He unclasped himself, turned in his seat, holding on tightly, muttering, "We must have more *room* the next time."

"An ocean liner, certainly," said Dezhnev. *"Next* time."

"What we have to do first," said Morrison, "is to discover whether we can detect anything at all. The trouble is, we are surrounded by electromagnetic fields. The muscles are rich in them and each molecule, almost, is the origin point of a—"

"Take all that as known," said Konev.

"I am only filling in the time while I carry my device through some necessary steps. The neural field is characteristic in several ways and by adjusting the computer to eliminate fields without those characteristics, I leave only what the neurons produce. We blank out all microfields like so and we deflect the muscle fields in this manner—"

"In what manner?" demanded Konev.

"I describe it in my papers."

"But I didn't see what you did."

Wordlessly, Morrison repeated the maneuver slowly.

"Oh," said Konev.

"And by now we should be detecting only neural waves if any are present here to detect—and there aren't."

Konev's right fist clenched. "Are you sure?"

"The screen shows a horizontal line. Nothing else."

"It's quivering."

"Noise. Possibly from the ship's own electric field, which is complex and not entirely like any of the natural fields of the body. I've never had to adjust a computer to filter out an artificial field."

"Well, then, we have to move on. —Arkady, tell them we can wait no longer."

"I can't do that, Yuri, unless Natasha tells me to. She's the captain. Or had you forgotten?"

"Thank you, Arkady," said Boranova coldly. "You, at least, have not. We'll forgive Konev his lapse and put it down to overzealousness in pursuit of his work. —My orders are not to move until the Grotto gives us the word. If this mission fails because of anything that goes wrong with Shapirov, there must be no opportunity for anyone to say it was because we did not follow orders."

"What if some disaster happens because we *did* follow orders? That can happen, too, you know." Konev's voice rose to near-hysteria.

Boranova replied, "The fault will then lie with those who gave the orders."

"I can find no satisfaction in apportioning blame, whether

to myself or to anyone else. It is results that count," said Konev.

"I agree," said Boranova, "if we are dealing with finespun theory. But if you expect to continue working on this project past the time of a possible catastrophe, you will find that the manner of allotting blame is all-important."

"Well, then," said Konev, stuttering slightly in his passion. "Urge them to let us move as soon as possible and then we'll —we'll—"

"Yes?" said Boranova.

"And then we'll enter the cell. We must."

CHAPTER 12

INTERCELLULAR

In life, unlike chess, the game continues after checkmate.
        —Dezhnev Senior

50.

A HEAVY silence fell upon the five shipmates. Konev's silence was the least quiet. He was quivering with unrest and his hands would not keep still.

Morrison felt a dim sympathy. To have reached the destination, to have done just as planned, through difficulties, to imagine one's self at the point of snatching success, and to have to fear that it will be moved away from the eagerly grasping fingers even now—

He knew the feeling. No longer quite as sharply perhaps, as once, now that he was ground down and dulled by frustration, but he remembered the early occasions— Experiments that raised hope, but were somehow never quite conclusive. Colleagues who smiled and nodded, but were never convinced.

He leaned forward and said, "Look, Yuri, just watch the red corpuscles. They're creeping ahead, one after the other, steadily—and that means the heart is beating and is doing so fairly normally. As long as the red corpuscles move steadily ahead, we're safe."

Dezhnev said, "There's the blood temperature, too. I've

got it monitored at all times and it will have to start dropping slowly, but with determination, if Shapirov lets go. Actually, the temperature is at the upper edge of normal."

Konev grunted, as though scorning consolation and pushing it to one side, but it seemed to Morrison that he was noticeably quieter after that.

Morrison sank back in his seat and let his eyes close. He wondered if he was experiencing hunger and decided that he was not. He also wondered if there was a distinct sensation of bladder pressure. There wasn't but that did not relieve him much. One could always postpone eating for a considerable length of time, but the necessity of urination did not lend itself to quite the same flexibility of choice.

He was suddenly aware that Kaliinin had addressed him but he had not been listening. "Pardon me. What did you say?" he asked, turning toward her.

Kaliinin looked surprised. She said softly, "I ask your pardon. I interrupted your thoughts."

"They were worth interrupting, Sophia. I ask *your* pardon for being inattentive."

"In that case, I asked what it is you do in your analysis of brain waves. I mean, what is it you do that is different from what others do? Why was it necessary for us—" She paused, clearly uncertain as to how to proceed.

Morrison finished her thought without difficulty. "Why was it necessary for me to be abstracted forcibly from my country?"

"Have I made you angry?"

"No. I presume you did not advise the action."

"Of course not. I knew nothing of it. In fact, that is why I am asking you my question. I know nothing about your field except that there are electroneural waves; that electroencephalography has become an intricate study, and an important one."

"Then if you ask me what is special about my own views, I'm afraid I can't tell you."

"Is it secret, then? I thought it might be."

"No, it is *not* secret," said Morrison, frowning. "There are no secrets in science, or there should be none—except that there are struggles for priority so that scientists are sometimes cautious about what they say, and I am guilty of that, too, sometimes. In this case, though, I mean it literally. I can't tell you because you lack the basis for understanding."

Kaliinin considered, her lips compressed as though in aid to thought. "Could you explain a bit of it?"

"I can try, if you're willing to hear simple assertions. I can't very well describe the entire field. —What we call brain waves are a conglomeration of all sorts of neuronic activity— sense perceptions of various kinds, stimuli of various muscles and glands, arousal mechanisms, coordinations, and so on. Lost among all these are those waves that control, or result from, constructive and creative thought. Isolating those skeptic waves, as I call them, from all the rest is an enormous problem. The body does it without any difficulty, but we poor scientists are, for the most part, at a total loss."

"I'm having no difficulty understanding this," said Kaliinin, smiling and looking pleased. (She is remarkably pretty, thought Morrison, when she manages to get rid of her air of melancholy.)

"I haven't gotten to the hard part yet," he said.

"Please do, then."

"About twenty years ago, it was demonstrated that there was what seemed a random component in the waves that no one had ever picked up because the instruments that had been used until then did not pick up what we now call 'the twinkle.' It's a very rapid oscillation of irregular amplitude and intensity. That's not a discovery I made, you understand."

Kaliinin smiled again. "I imagine that twenty years ago you would have been too young to make the discovery."

"I was an undergraduate then, making the discovery that young women were not entirely unapproachable, which is by no means an unimportant thing to find out. In fact, each person may have to rediscover it now and then, I think. —But never mind that.

"A number of people speculated that the twinkle might represent thought processes in the mind, but no one managed to isolate it properly. It would come and go, be detectable at times and not at others, and the general feeling was that it was artifactitious, a matter of working with instruments that were too delicate for the thing they were measuring so that one picked up what was, essentially, noise.

"I thought not. In time I developed a computer program

that made it possible for me to isolate the twinkle and to demonstrate it was always present in the human brain. For that I got some credit, though few people were able to duplicate my work. I used animals for types of experimentation that were too dangerous to perform on human beings and used the results to further sharpen my program of analysis. But the sharper I made the analysis and the more significant I thought the results, the less others were able to duplicate them and the more they insisted that I was misled by my animal experimentation.

"But even isolating the twinkle was a long way from demonstrating that it was a representation of abstract thought. I have amplified it, intensified it, modified my program over and over, and have convinced myself that I am studying thought, the skeptic waves themselves. Still, no one can duplicate the crucial points of my work. I have, on several occasions, allowed someone to use my program and my computer —the sort of thing I'm using now—and they invariably fail."

Kaliinin was listening gravely. She said, "Can you imagine why no one can duplicate your work?"

"The easiest explanation is that there is something wrong with me, that I am a crank—if not a madman. I believe that some of my colleagues suspect that to be the answer."

"Do *you* think you're a madman?"

"No, I don't, Sophia, but even I waver sometimes. You see, after you isolate the skeptic waves and amplify them, it is conceivable that the human brain itself might become a receiving instrument. The waves may transfer the thoughts from the thinker you are studying directly to you. The brain would certainly be an extraordinarily delicate receiver, but it would also be an extraordinarily individual one. If I improved my program so that I could sense the thoughts better, that would mean I improved it to suit my own individual brain. Other brains might not be affected and, in fact, might be less affected, the closer I adjusted it to mine. It would be like a painting. The closer a painting is made to look like me, the less it looks like anyone else. The more I can make my program produce sensible self-consistent results, the less anyone else can."

"Have you actually sensed thought?"

"I'm not sure. There are times I have thought I did, but I'm never quite convinced it's not my imagination. Certainly no one else—with my program or any other—has sensed anything. I have used the twinkle to track down the skeptic nodes in the brains of chimpanzees and from that reasoned out where they would be in human brains, but that is not accepted either. It is considered the overenthusiasm of a scientist oversold on his own unlikely theory. And even using leads into the skeptic nodes—on animals, of course—I couldn't be sure."

"With animals it would be difficult. Have you published these—sensations of yours?"

"I haven't dared," said Morrison, shaking his head. "No one would accept such subjective findings. I've mentioned it in passing to several people—foolish of me—and the news spread and merely convinced my colleagues all the more firmly that I am, shall we say, unstable. It was only last Sunday that Natalya told me that Shapirov took me seriously, but he is considered, at least in my country, to be unstable, too."

"He is not," said Kaliinin firmly, "or was not."

"It would be nice to think he wasn't, obviously."

Konev, from in front of Morrison, said suddenly, without turning around, "It was your sensations of thought that impressed Shapirov. I know! He discussed it with me. He said on a number of occasions that your program was a relay station and he would like to try it himself. If you were *inside* a neuron, a key neuron of the skeptic node, things would be different. You would sense thoughts unmistakably. Shapirov thought so and I think so. Shapirov thought it possible you might even have sensed thoughts unmistakably as it was, but were not ready to let the world know. Is that so?"

How they harped on secrecy, all of them, thought Morrison. Then he caught the look on Kaliinin's face. Her mouth was partly open, her eyebrows drawn together, her finger hovering near her lips. It was as though she wanted to ask him to be quiet with a kind of agonizing intensity, without quite daring to do so openly.

But then he was distracted by Dezhnev's voice, joyfully loud. "Enough babble, my children. The Grotto has located us and we are, to their enormous astonishment, exactly where we say we are."

Konev threw up both hands and his voice sounded almost boyish. "Exactly where *I* say we are."

Dezhnev said, "Let us have communal responsibility. Where *we* say we are."

"No," said Boranova. "I ordered Konev to make the decision on his own responsibility. The credit is therefore his."

Konev was not mollified. He said, "You would not have so quickly demanded communal responsibility, Arkady Vissarionovich"—he used the patronymic in a style long out of fashion in the Soviet Union, as though to emphasize the fact that Dezhnev was the son of a peasant, among whom, only, the style remained in fashion—"had we proved to be in the wrong capillary."

Dezhnev's smile became an uncomfortable one and his somewhat yellow upper incisors caught at his lower lip.

Boranova said in her masterful contralto, cutting off any retort Dezhnev might have made, "And Shapirov. What of him?"

"That," said Dezhnev, "has passed. An injection of some sort steadied the heartbeat."

Konev said, "Well, then, are we ready to go?"

"Yes," said Boranova.

"In that case—out of the bloodstream at last."

51.

BORANOVA and Kaliinin were bent over their instruments. Morrison watched them for a few moments, but, of course, knew nothing of what was going on. He turned to Dezhnev, who sat in a relaxed position (unlike Konev, whose body was tense, almost ridged with muscle), and said, "What will be done, Arkady? We can't very well just blast our way out of a blood vessel in the brain."

"We'll sneak out once we're small enough. We're miniaturizing again. Look around you."

Startled, Morrison did. He realized that every time the outside world seemed to stabilize, he quickly learned to take it for granted and to pay no attention to it.

The current had picked up speed. Or, rather, it hadn't but the ship had shrunk in size once more and objects moving by took correspondingly less time to pass, so that the mind, insisting on considering the ship's size unchanged, interpreted what was seen as a faster current.

A red cell passed by, moving as it had (or seeming to move as it had) in the carotid artery, but despite its speed, it billowed past for a long time, like a quivering whale passing a rowboat. It had grown faint indeed. It was almost transparent now and its edge was fuzzy with Brownian motion. There was a grayish dimness about it, so that it looked like an angry thundercloud spreading its way over the heavens. It had lost most of its oxygen by this time, of course, giving it up to the avid brain cells which, without motion or visible signs of life, consumed one quarter of all the oxygen carried by the blood to the various organs of the body. For all that the brain seemed to simply sit there, sense perception, response, and thought, all of it coordinated with a complexity that nonhuman computer could come within an astronomical distance of duplication—might never duplicate—did not come cheap.

To make up for the spreading of the red cells, the platelets, and the comparatively rare white cells that had grown into monsters that were now too large to grasp, the blood plasma was becoming far less featurelessly liquid.

It had started to turn grainy and now the grains were slowly expanding as they shot past with gradually increasing speed. Morrison knew he was looking at protein molecules and, after a while, it seemed to him that through their whirling and flexing he could make out the helical arrangements of their atoms in fuzzy manner. Some had a miniature forest of lipid molecules partially encasing them.

He was becoming aware also of movement, not the tremble of Brownian motion but a lurching that was becoming more pronounced.

He turned his head to look out the other side at the capillary wall to which they were attached.

The tiling was gone—or at least one tile (or cell, as he might as well think of it now) had expanded to the point where it was the only one to be seen. Slipping off behind was the bulge of the nucleus of the cell, large and thick and growing larger and thicker.

The ship lurched as part of it slid away from the wall and then lurched again as it slid back.

"What's happening?" said Morrison, looking at Kaliinin, who shook her head impatiently. She was totally absorbed in her work.

Dezhnev said, "Sophia is trying to neutralize the ship's

electric charge here and there so that it lets go before the tension damages the wall. And she has to find new areas of attachment to keep from losing the wall altogether. It's not easy, having to miniaturize and, at the same time, staying attached to the wall."

Morrison said, alarmed, "How far will we miniaturize?"

His words were overborne by Kaliinin's shrill command. "Arkady, move it forward. Gently! Just put forward pressure on the ship."

"Yes, Sophia—but tell me when to stop." To Morrison, he added, "My father used to say: 'Between not enough and too much is a hair's breadth.'"

"More, more," said Kaliinin. "All right. Now we'll try." The ship seemed to stick and strain and then it suddenly slid forward and Morrison felt himself thrust gently back against his seat.

"Good," said Kaliinin. "Just a little less now."

The cell came to an end. Beyond it was another cell. Thin cells, as cells went, a mere film of cells, fitted together to make a tiny tube, with the ship and its crew of five clinging to the inner surface by minute attractions of electric charge.

The space between the adjoining cells seemed ropy, with cables stretching from inside one cell to the other. They were not all intact and there were stumps visible like the remains of a felled forest. It seemed to Morrison that there were narrow gaps in that felled forest, but he couldn't see clearly from the angle at which he viewed them.

He said again, "How far will we miniaturize, Arkady?"

"Eventually to the size of a small organic molecule."

"But what would the chances be of spontaneous deminiaturization at that size?"

"Appreciable," said Dezhnev. "Much more than it was when we were the size of a red corpuscle or even of a blood platelet."

"Still not enough to worry about," said Boranova. "I assure you."

"Exactly," said Dezhnev and raised his hand slightly with the first two fingers crossed so that Morrison could just see it and Boranova, farther back, could not. That American gesture had become universal and Morrison, knowing exactly what it meant, felt himself growing cold inside.

Dezhnev was looking straight ahead, but he might have

sensed Morrison's grimace or heard his soft grunt. He said, "Don't worry about it, young Albert. It is always wise to have but one worry at a time and right now let us worry about squeezing out of the blood vessel. —Sophia, my loved one."

"Yes, Arkady," she said.

"Weaken the field in the rear of the ship and when I move grope for one ahead."

"I will do so, Arkady. Didn't your father once say: 'There is no point in trying to teach a thief to steal'?"

"Yes, he did. Steal, then, little thief, steal."

Morrison wondered whether Dezhnev and Kaliinin were deliberately being lighthearted in the face of the possibility of sudden death as a way of cheering him up? Or were they showing contempt for his cowardice? He chose the former. Surely when an action might equally well be interpreted as friendly or hostile, one might as well choose the friendly. Perhaps Dezhnev's father would have agreed. With that thought, he felt cheered.

The ship's rear seemed to be hanging loosely and to remain several centimeters (several picometers in real measure?) from the wall of the capillary. Morrison studied it closely and could see the serried ranks of protein and lipid molecules that made up that wall.

He thought, What are we doing ignoring this? Here is our opportunity to study tissues with greater precision than the best scanning electron microscope can—and to study them while alive; to see not only position but living change and motion. We have passed through the bloodstream and narrowed in on a capillary wall without looking at anything in any real scientific sense. We are only passing through, with no more interest than we would show if we were in a subway, barreling through an underground tunnel. —All to study oscillations that might be produced by thought . . . and might not.

The ship was inching along (an old word, thought Morrison suddenly, antedating the metric system, but he'd never heard anyone say "centimetering along") as though it were somehow feeling its way. Perhaps, between Dezhnev's motors and Kaliinin's flickering electric fields, that was precisely what it was doing.

"We're approaching the junction, little Sophia," said

Dezhnev in a curiously tight voice. "Make sure your hold is firm in front, while I move forward another meter or so."

"I suspect from the appearance and electrical behavior," said Kaliinin, "that we have a clump of arginines toward the junction. That represents a strong region of positive charge and I can handle that as smoothly as sour cream."

But Boranova said sternly, "No overconfidence, Sophia. Keep a firm watch. If you miss and the ship tears loose, there will be much to do over."

"Yes, Natalya," said Sophia, "but with all respect, the warning is not really needed."

Dezhnev said, "Sophia, do exactly what I say. Keep only the prow of the ship attached to the wall, but strongly. Release everything else."

"Done," said Sophia faintly.

Morrison found himself holding his breath. The rear of the ship had spun away from the wall, but it held in front. The bloodstream caught the detached rear end and pushed the ship into a position at right angles to the current, while the capillary wall, where the ship still held, moved outward like a pimple.

Morrison said tightly, "Watch out. We'll pull a section out of the wall."

"Quiet, all!" thundered Dezhnev. —Then, in an ordinary voice, "Sophia, I shall increase the engine push slowly. Get yourself in position to break all remaining attraction. The ship is to be entirely neutral—but not until I say so."

Sophia cast a quick look toward Boranova, who said in her quiet way, "Do exactly as you're told, Sophia. For this, Arkady's word is absolute."

Morrison imagined he felt the ship straining forward. The section of the capillary wall to which it was attached stretched farther and farther.

Sophia said urgently, "Arkady, either the field will snap or the wall will."

"Another moment, dear one, another moment. —*Now.*"

The wall snapped back and the ship bounded forward in a great leap that rocked Morrison gently backward. The forward end of the ship buried itself in the cement stuff between the two cells of the capillary wall.

52.

FOR the first time, Morrison was aware of the laboring of the microfusion engines. There was a subliminal throbbing as the ship worked its way through the joint with what seemed increasing difficulty. There was nothing to see up ahead. The thickness of the capillary wall, very thin though it was in normal terms, was far thicker than the length of the ship.

The ship was now totally immersed in the joint and Dezhnev, beads of sweat on his forehead, turned his head and spoke to Boranova. "We're using up energy faster than we should."

Boranova said, "Then stop the ship and let's consider."

Deshnev said, "If I do that, there is a chance that the natural elasticity of this material will pop us out of the joint and back into the bloodstream."

"Slow the engines down, then. Choose a level that will be enough to keep us in place."

The throbbing came to an end.

Dezhnev said, "The joint is exerting considerable pressure on the ship."

"Enough to crush us, Arkady?"

"Not now. But who can say for the future if the pressure continues?"

Morrison burst out. "This is ridiculous. Didn't someone say we're the size of a small organic molecule?"

"We're the size of a glucose molecule," said Boranova, "which is made up of twenty-four atoms altogether."

"Thank you," said Morrison freezingly, "but I know how many atoms there are in a glucose molecule. As it happens, small molecules drift through the capillary walls constantly by diffusion. Diffusion! That's the way the body works. Why aren't we diffusing through?"

Boranova said, "Diffusion is a statistical proposition. There are twenty-four billion trillion glucose molecules in the bloodstream at any given time. They move around randomly and some manage to hit in such places and in such ways as to move through a joint, or to move into the membrane of a capillary wall cell, into the cell, and out the other side. A very small percentage succeed at any given second, but that is enough to ensure proper tissue functioning. However, by chance, a particular glucose molecule may remain in the bloodstream for a month without diffusing. Can we wait a month for a chance to do its work?"

"That's no argument, Natalya," said Morrison impatiently. "Why don't we simply do deliberately what a real glucose molecule would do by chance? Especially now, when we're part way through the joint. Why are we stuck in position?"

Konev said, "I'm on Albert's side. Diffusion probably isn't a passive leakage. There's some sort of interaction between the diffusing object and the barrier through which the diffusion takes place—except that no one knows what the interaction might be exactly. Especially here, where we face the blood-brain barrier."

"We're here at the barrier," said Dezhnev. "You're the brain expert. Can you look around and tell us how this diffusion works?"

"No, I can't. But glucose is one molecule that gets through the blood-brain barrier easily. It must because it is the brain's sole fuel for energy. The trouble is that while the ship is as small as a glucose molecule, it *isn't* a glucose molecule."

"Are you getting at something, Yuri," said Boranova, "or is this a lecture?"

"I'm getting at something. We had the ship become uncharged in order to lunge into the joint, but why leave it uncharged now? Can it be given the charge pattern of a glucose molecule? If so, it will *be* a glucose molecule as far as Shapirov's body is concerned. I suggest you order it done, Natalya."

Kaliinin did not wait for the order. She said, "It is done, Natalya."

(They each addressed Boranova, Morrison noted. Each still maintained the fiction of the other's nonexistence.)

Dezhnev said, "And the joint's pressure decreases at once. It recognizes a friend, so it bows politely and steps aside. My father's mother, long may I keep her memory, would have cried out, 'Black magic,' and at once would have hidden beneath the bed."

"Arkady," said Boranova, "increase the power of the engines and pass through before the joint notices that underneath the glucose pattern is something that is not glucose."

"Yes, Natalya," said Dezhnev.

Morrison said, "This one is yours, Yuri. Your suggestion was just right. In hindsight I see that I should have thought of that, too, but the fact is, I didn't."

Konev said gruffly, as though finding praise something he couldn't handle, "It was nothing. Since the brain lives on glucose, we got down to glucose size. Eventually, we would have had to have a glucose pattern, and as soon as you asked the question why we weren't diffusing when we should have been, I realized we needed the pattern already."

Dezhnev said, "Members of the expedition, we are through the joint. We are out of the bloodstream. We are in the brain."

53.

IN the brain, thought Morrison, but not in a brain cell. So far they had only passed from the intercellular space between the cells of the capillary wall, into the intercellular spaces of the brain where the support structures existed that maintained the form and interrelationships of the nerve cells, or neurons. Remove them and the cells would squash into amorphous masses, pulled together by gravity and unable to maintain any sensible function.

It was a jungle, made up of thick viny threads of collagen. (This was the nearly universal animal connective protein that fulfilled the function of cellulose in plants, less cheaply, since it was protein rather than carbohydrate, but far more flexibly.) Through the eye of ultraminiaturization, those collagen threads, totally invisible without an electron microscope, looked like tree trunks, leaning this way and that in a world in which gravity was of little importance.

There were finer and still finer threads. Morrison knew that some of them might be elastin and that the collagen itself might come in subtly different varieties. If he could see the whole in a wider view, from a less-miniaturized standpoint, he would have been able to detect order and structure. At this level, however, it was chaotic. One couldn't even see far in any direction; the overlapping fibers blocked vision.

Morrison became aware that the ship was moving very slowly. The four others were each staring around in wonder. Either they had not expected this (Morrison hadn't, for he had been too interested in the electrical properties of the brain to think much concerning its microanatomy) or, if they had, they had nevertheless failed to visualize it.

Morrison said, "How do you expect to find your way to a neuron? Does anybody know?"

Dezhnev was the first to answer, "The ship can only move straight ahead, so we move straight ahead until we get to a cell."

"How do we move straight ahead through this jungle? If we can't steer the ship, how do we move around obstacles?"

Dezhnev rubbed his chin thoughtfully. "We don't move around, we push around. The ship will move past one of those objects and there will be more friction on the contact side than on the other, so our path bends, like a comet rounding the sun." He smiled. "Cosmonauts do that when they use gravity to skim around a satellite or planet. We'll do it to skim around those things."

Konev said morosely, "Those things are collagen fibers."

Morrison said, "Some of them are pretty thick. You won't always pass by. You'll hit one head-on and stay there and if you can only move forward, what will you do? This ship was designed only for the bloodstream. We're helpless out of it with nothing to carry us along."

Boranova interposed. "Arkady, you have three microfusion engines and the jets, I know, are arranged at the rear at the apices of an equilateral triangle. Can you fire only one of them?"

"No. One contact controls all three."

"Yes, Arkady, that is how it is now. But you designed the ship and you know the details of its controls. Is there anything you can do to modify them so that you can fire them one at a time?"

Dezhnev took a deep breath. "Everyone told me over and over again that I must cut corners, that I must save the budget, that I must do nothing to irritate the bureaucrats."

"Aside from that, Arkady, is there anything you can do?"

"Let me think. It means jury-rigging. It means finding something to make switches out of, and extra wire, and who knows if it will work or how long it will work if it does, and if we won't end up worse than we are. —I see what you mean, though. If I can fire only one of the engines, it will set up an unbalanced thrust."

"You'll be able to steer then, depending on which you fire."

"I'll try, Natalya."

Morrison said angrily, "Why didn't you think of this when we were in the wrong capillary? It might have saved me the small trouble of nearly dying trying to turn the ship by hand."

Dezhnev said, "If you hadn't so promptly suggested turning the ship by hand, we might have thought of it—but it wouldn't have been a good idea."

"Why not?"

"We were in the current of the bloodstream. The ship is carefully streamlined to take advantage of it and its surface is designed to allow water to flow past it without turbulence, which makes it all the harder to turn out of the current. It would have taken much longer than turning by hand—and very much more energy. The narrow confines of the capillary must be remembered, too. Here, there is no current and because we've been so miniaturized there is a great deal of room."

"Enough," said Boranova. "Get to work, Arkady."

Dezhnev did so, rummaging through a tool chest, removing a cover plate and studying the control details within, maintaining through it all a kind of incoherent muttering.

Konev, his hands clasped behind his neck, said, without turning, "Albert, tell us about those sensations you received."

"Sensations?"

"You were telling us about them just before we got the news from the Grotto that we were located in the correct capillary. I'm talking about the sensations you experienced when you were trying to analyze the thought waves."

"Ah," said Morrison and caught Kaliinin's eye.

Very slightly, she shook her head. Very tentatively, a warning finger crossed her lips.

Morrison said, "Nothing to tell. I had vague sensations I couldn't describe in any objective way. It could well have been my imagination. Certainly those whom I tried to tell about it were convinced it was."

"And you never published anything about them?"

"Never. I merely mentioned it in passing at conventions and that was bad enough. If Shapirov and you heard of it, it was through word of mouth only. If I had published, that would have come as near to scientific suicide as I would ever want to be."

"Too bad."

Morrison looked briefly toward Kaliinin. She had nodded very slightly, but said nothing. —Clearly, she couldn't say anything without being overheard by the entire ship.

Morrison looked around carelessly. Dezhnev was lost in his work, clucking to himself. Konev stared straight ahead, lost in whatever tortuous thoughts he happened to have. Boranova, behind Kaliinin, was studying the screen of her computer carefully and was making notes. Morrison did not try to read them—he could read English upside down, but he hadn't come to that pitch of ease with Russian.

Only Kaliinin, to his left, was looking at him.

Morrison pressed his lips together and then shifted his computer into a word-processing mode. It did not have a Cyrillic adjunct, but he spelled out the Russian words in phonetic Roman lettering. WHAT IS WRONG?

She hesitated, probably not very much at home in Roman. Then her own fingers flashed and the neat Cyrillic on her screen read: DON'T TRUST HIM. SAY NOTHING. It was erased at once.

Morrison wrote: WHY?

Kaliinin said: NOT EVIL, BUT PRIORITY, CREDIT. WILL DO ANYTHING, ANYTHING, ANYTHING.

The words were gone and she looked away firmly.

Morrison considered her thoughtfully. Was it only the vengefulness of a woman betrayed?

It didn't matter, in any case, for he had no intention of talking about anything that he hadn't already given away, either in a paper or by word of mouth. He himself was not evil, but where priority and credit were concerned, he might not do anything, anything, anything, but he would do a great deal.

Still, there was nothing to be done at that moment. Or one thing, perhaps, which was completely aside from the point, but which was beginning, just beginning, to occupy his mind to the exclusion of other things.

He turned to Boranova, who was still staring at her instrument and tapping her fingers softly against the arm of her seat in thoughtful concentration.

"Natalya?"

"Yes, Albert?" She did not look up.

"I hate to introduce a note of ugly realism, but"—his voice lowered to near-soundlessness—"I'm thinking of urinating."

She looked up at him, a corner of her lips twitching very slightly, but avoiding the smile. She did not lower her voice. "Why think of it, Albert? Do it."

Morrison felt like a little boy raising his hand for permission to leave the room—unreasonably so, he knew. "I don't like to be the first."

Boranova frowned, almost as though she were the teacher in the case. "That is quite silly and, in any case, you are not. I have already taken care of such a need in myself." Then, with a faint shrug, "Tension tends to increase urgency, I have frequently found."

Morrison had frequently found that, too. He whispered, "It's all very well for you. You're there in the back seat alone." And he nodded slightly in the direction of Sophia.

"So?" Boranova shook her head. "Surely you don't wish me to improvise a curtain for you? Shall I place my hand over her eyes." (Kaliinin looked in their direction in surprise.) "She will ignore you, I'm sure, out of decency and out of a feeling that in short order she will wish you to ignore her."

Morrison was keenly embarrassed, for Kaliinin was now looking at him with obvious understanding. She said, "Come, Albert, I held you naked in my lap. What room need one make for modesty now?"

Morrison smiled weakly and made a little thank-you gesture.

He tried to remember how to manage the waste lid on his seat, but once he remembered, he found that it slid open with a small but definite click. (Those irritating Soviets! Backward always in small ways. It might easily have been designed to open noiselessly.)

He also managed to loosen the electrostatic seam along his crotch and then found himself worrying whether he would manage to close it unobtrusively afterward.

Morrison felt the current of air at the moment the waste lid opened and it felt uncomfortably cold against his bare skin. He sighed with a tremendous relief when he was done, then he managed to close the seal along the crotch and sat there, panting. He realized that he must have been holding his breath.

"Here," said Boranova brusquely. He stared, for a moment, at what she was holding, then recognized it as a small sealed towel. He tore open the seal, found the towel within moistened and scented and rubbed his hands with it. (The Soviets were learning small elegances, obviously—or decadences, depending on whether finickiness or impatience won the battle for domination within you.)

And then Dezhnev's throaty voice sounded loudly, very loudly, in Morrison's ear after all the whispering he had been engaged in. "That's done now."

"What's done?" asked Morrison angrily, automatically assuming the reference was to his bodily functions.

"The individual firing of the motors," said Dezhnev, making a there-you-are gesture with both hands in the directions of the ship's controls. "I can fire any one, or two, or all three, if I wish. Absolutely certain—I think."

"Which is it, Arkady?" said Boranova waspishly. "Is it quite certain or is it a matter of opinion?"

"Both," said Dezhnev. "It is my opinion that I am absolutely certain. The trouble is that my opinion isn't always right. My father used to say—"

"I think we ought to try it out," said Konev, cutting off Dezhnev's father, perhaps in the full realization he was doing so.

"Of course," said Dezhnev. "That goes without saying, but as my father used to say"—he raised his voice as though determined not to be again subverted—"'the sure thing about anything that goes without saying is that someone is bound to say it.' —And you might as well know—"

He paused momentarily and Boranova said, "What might we as well know?"

"Several things, Natasha," said Dezhnev. "In the first place, steering will take a lot of energy. I've done my best, but the ship is not designed for this. For another—well, I can't communicate with the Grotto now."

"Can't communicate?" said Kaliinin, her voice rising to a near squeak in what was either surprise or indignation.

Boranova's voice marked her as definitely indignant. "What do you mean, we can't communicate?"

"Come, Natasha, I can't wire up the motors separately

without wires, can I? The best engineer in the world can't make wires out of nothing and can't manufacture silicon chips out of nothing, either. Something had to be dismantled and the one thing I could dismantle without disabling the ship was communications. I told them that out in the Grotto and there was a lot of shrieking and complaining, but how could they stop me? So now we can steer, I think—and we can't communicate, I know."

54.

THERE was silence as the ship began to move. The surroundings were utterly different now. In the bloodstream, there had been a heaving medley of objects—some crawling ahead of the ship, some slowly drifting behind, depending on eddies and streamlining, Morrison supposed. There was the *feeling* of movement, if only because the markings on the walls—fatty plaques in the arteries, tiling in the capillaries, slipped steadily backward.

Here, in intercellular space, however, there was stasis. No motion. No feeling of life. The tangle of collagen fibers seemed a forest primeval, built up of trunks only, without leaves, without color, without sound, without motion.

Once the ship pushed forward through the viscous intercellular fluid, however, everything began to move backward. The ship slipped toward and through a V-shaped meeting of fibers and, as they passed through, Morrison had the plain impression of a loose spiral making its way upward along each collagen fiber, the spiral being more marked on the thinner of the two.

Up ahead was a thicker fiber still, a monarch of the collagen jungle.

"You'll have to turn, Arkady," said Konev. "Now's the time to test it."

"All right, but I'll have to lean over. I don't have the controls neatly at my fingertips. There's a limit to improvisation." He leaned forward, groping at a level about that of his calves. "I do not relish the thought of having to do this constantly. It is hard on a man of portly habit."

"You mean a man who is fat," said Konev ill-naturedly.

"You have let yourself go flabby, Arkady. You should lose weight."

Dezhnev straightened up. "Very well. I will stop right now, go home, and begin to lose weight. —Is this a time, Yuri, to lecture me?"

"It is not a time for you to get emotional either, Arkady," said Boranova. "Steer!"

Dezhnev bent over, suppressing a grunt. Slowly, the ship turned rightward in a gentle arc; or, to judge more literally by appearance, the thick collagen fiber drifted leftward as it approached—as did everything else.

"You will hit it," said Konev. "Turn more sharply."

"It won't turn more sharply," said Dezhnev. "Each motor is only so far off-center and I can't change that."

"Well, then, we will hit it," said Konev, an edge of anxiety in his voice.

"Then let us hit," said Boranova angrily. "Yuri, do not go into panic over inconsequentials. The ship is tough plastic; that fiber is undoubtedly rubbery."

And as she spoke, the prow of the ship began to pass the collagen fiber, with little room to spare. Watching through the port side of the ship, it was clear that the broadening beam of the ship would make contact. When the fiber was nearly level with Kaliinin's seat, it happened. There was no scraping sound, only a very soft hiss could be detected. Not only was the fiber rubbery, as Boranova had said, so that it compressed slightly under the force of the collision, then rebounded, pushing the ship a trifle away—but the slimy intercellular fluid served as a cushion and a friction reducer.

The ship continued to move and turned leftward in the direction of the fiber.

Dezhnev said, "I shut off the motor as soon as I saw we were about to make contact. This leftward turn we're going through now is a friction turn."

"Yes," said Konev, "but what if you had wanted to turn in the other direction?"

"Then I would have used the motor. Or, considerably earlier in our progress, I would have made a turn toward a graze with the fiber to the right. That fiber would have turned us rightward. The main thing, in any case, is to use the motors as little as possible and the fibers as much as possible. In the first place, we don't want to consume our supply of energy too rapidly. In the second place, the rapid output of energy increases the chances of spontaneous deminiaturization."

"What!" cried Morrison. He turned to Boranova. "Is that true?"

"It's not an important effect," said Boranova, "but it's true. The chances go up a bit. I should say that conservation is the more important of the two reasons for saving energy."

But Morrison could not repress his anger. "Don't you see how ridiculous—no, criminal—this whole situation is? We're in a ship that simply isn't up to the task and everything we do makes it worse."

Boranova shook her head. "Albert, please. You know we have no choice."

"Besides," said Dezhnev, grinning, "if we manage to do the job in this unsuitable ship, think how much more remarkable that will make us. We will be heroes. Authentic heroes. We will surely get the Order of Lenin—each one of us. It will be a foregone conclusion. And if we fail, it is comforting to think that we will be able to explain it as the ship's fault."

"Yes. Soviet heroes, win or lose, all of you," said Morrison. "And what will I be?"

Boranova said, "Remember, Albert, you will not be neglected if we succeed. The Order of Lenin has been given to foreigners on a number of occasions, including many Americans. Even if you should not want the honor for some reason, the success of your theories will be established and you may receive a Nobel Prize before any of us do."

"We're in no position to count our chickens," said Morrison. "I shall refrain from composing my Nobel acceptance speech for just a while, thank you."

"Actually," said Kaliinin, "I wonder if we're in a position to reach a neuron."

"What's the difficulty?" asked Dezhnev. "We can move and steer and we're outside the capillary and in the brain. Just out there is a neuron, any number of them, billions of them."

"Just out where?" Kaliinin asked. "I don't see any neurons. Just collagen fibers."

Dezhnev said, "How much of this intercellular fluid do you think there is?"

"A microscopic thickness," said Kaliinin, "if we were normal in size. However, we're the size of a glucose molecule and, relative to ourselves, there may be a kilometer's distance or more to the nearest neuron."

"Well, then," said Dezhnev, "we'll move our ship a kilometer. It may take a little time but it can be done."

"Yes, if we could move in a straight line, but we're in the middle of a dense jungle. We have to turn and twist around this fiber and that and, in the end, we may travel fifty kilometers by our own measurement and find ourselves back at our starting point. We're just going to be blundering through a maze and we won't reach a neuron except by sheerest accident."

"Yuri has a map," said Dezhnev, sounding a little nonplussed. "Yuri's cerebro-whatever—"

Konev, frowning, shook his head. "My cerebrograph shows me the circulatory network of the brain and the cell pattern, but I can't expand it to the point where it will indicate our position in the intercellular fluid between cells. We don't know that sort of fine detail and we can't get out of cerebrography any more than we can put into it."

Morrison looked through the wall of the ship. In all directions, the collagen fibers could be made out, overlapping and blocking them in. In no direction could the eye see through them very far and in no direction was there any sign of anything but fiber upon fiber.

No nerve cells! No neurons!

CHAPTER 13

CELL

*The wall that says "Welcome, stranger"
has never been built.*
                    —Dezhnev Senior

55.

BORANOVA'S nostrils flared slightly and her dark eyebrows hunched together, but her voice remained calm.

"Arkady," she said, "You will travel forward in as straight a line as possible. Curve to a minimum extent and, if you can, curve left and right alternately. And, since we're in a three-dimensional situation, up and down alternately."

"It would get confusing, Natasha," said Dezhnev.

"Of course it will, but perhaps it won't get completely confusing. We may not be able to travel ruler-straight, but maybe we won't go in circles, spirals, or helixes either. And sooner or later we should reach a cell."

"Perhaps," said Dezhnev, "if you deminiaturize the ship a little bit—"

"No," said Boranova.

"Wait, Natasha. Think about it. If we deminiaturize a bit, then there will be less space to travel. We grow larger, the space between blood vessel and neuron grows smaller." He made eloquent gestures with his hands. "You understand?"

"I understand. But the larger we get, Arkady, the more

238

difficult it will be to pass between the fibers. The neurons of the brain are well-protected. The brain is the only organ to be completely encased in bone and the neurons themselves, which are the most irregular in the body, are well-packed with intercellular material. Look for yourself. It's only if we're down to the size of a glucose molecule that we can make our way through and around the collagen without, perhaps, doing drastic damage to the brain."

At this point, Konev committed the unusual act of turning in his seat, looking upward as he turned to his left so that his glance passed over Kaliinin before meeting Boranova's eyes. He said, "I don't think we have to travel onward completely blind—completely at random."

"How otherwise, Yuri?" asked Boranova.

"Surely the neurons give themselves away. Each has nerve impulses running its length periodically and at very short intervals. That might be detected."

Morrison frowned. "The neurons are insulated."

"The axons are—not the cell bodies."

"But it is the axons where the nerve impulse is strongest."

"No, it is the synapses where the nerve impulse may be strongest and they are not insulated, either. The synapses ought to be sparking all the time and you ought to be able to detect it."

Morrison said, "We couldn't in the capillary."

"We were on the wrong side of the capillary wall at the time. —Look, Albert, why are you arguing the matter? I'm asking you to try to detect brain waves. That's why you're here, isn't it?"

"I was kidnapped," said Morrison violently. *"That's* why I'm here."

Boranova leaned forward. "Albert, whatever the reason, you're here and Yuri's suggestion is a reasonable one. —And, Yuri, must you always be confrontational?"

Morrison found himself shaking with anger and for a moment he wasn't sure why. Konev's suggestion was indeed reasonable.

Then it occurred to him that he was being asked to put his theories to the test under conditions which would allow him no escape. He was on the very border of a brain cell that was magnified with respect to himself to mountainous proportions. He might be asked next to make his test inside, actually inside, such a cell. And if he did—and if he failed—under what blanket of argument and excuse could he hide from the fact that his work was wrong and had always been wrong?

He was angry, surely, at being thrust into this uncomfortable corner by circumstance and not at Konev particularly.

He was aware of Boranova waiting for him to say something and of Konev maintaining his incandescent stare.

Morrison said, "If I detect signals, I will detect them from all sides. Except for the capillary we have just left, we're surrounded by uncounted numbers of neurons."

"But some are closer than others," said Konev, "and one or two would be closest of all. Can't you detect the direction from which the signals will be the strongest? We can home in on that signal."

"My receiving device isn't equipped to determine directional signals."

"Ah! Then Americans, too, make use of devices that are equipped for specific purposes and do not prepare for emergency needs. It is not merely the ignorant Soviets who—"

"Yuri!" said Boranova sternly.

Konev swallowed. "I suppose you'll tell me I'm confrontational again. —In that case, Natalya, *you* tell him to think of a way of devising something that will tell him the direction from which the strongest signals are coming."

"Please, Albert, make the attempt," said Boranova. "If you fail, we shall just have to blunder our way through this collagen jungle and hope we come upon something before too long."

"We're blundering onward even as we speak," put in Dezhnev almost cheerfully, "but I still see nothing."

Still angry, Morrison activated his computer and put it into the brain wave reception mode. The screen flickered, but it was only noise—though the noise was more prominent than it had been within the capillary.

Until now, he had always used leads that involved micropositioning inside a nerve. Where was he to put the leads now? He had no nerve to put them into—or, rather, he was already inside the brain, which made the whole matter of positioning anomalous. Perhaps, though, if he let the leads (made as stiff as possible) rise in the air and spread apart like a pair of antennae, they might play the part. At their present size, the spread would be tiny and could scarcely be useful but—

He doubled and redoubled the leads and they stood up in long loops, looking very much like the insect antennae that had first given them their names. He then focused and sharpened reception as well as he could and the flickering on the screen suddenly broke into deep narrow waves—but only for a moment. Involuntarily, he let out a cry.

"What happened?" said Boranova, startled.

"I received something. Just a flash. —But it's gone."

"Try again."

Morrison looked up. "Listen. All of you. Quiet. Working this thing is difficult and I manage best when I can concentrate entirely. Understood? No noise. Nothing."

"What was it you received?" said Konev softly.

"What?"

"Like a flash. You received something like a flash. May we know what it was?"

"No. I don't know what I received. I want to listen again." He looked behind him to the left. "Natalya, I'm in no position to give orders, but you are. I am not to be disturbed by anyone, particularly by Yuri."

"We will all be quiet," said Boranova. "Proceed, Albert. —Yuri, not one word."

Morrison looked sharply to his left, for there had been a soft touch on his hand. Kaliinin was looking at him keenly and there was a small smile on her face. She mouthed words in an exaggerated fashion and he managed to catch the Russian: "Pay no attention to him. Show him! Show him!"

Her eyes seemed to glitter. Morrison could not help but smile warmly in response. She might be motivated entirely by a desire for vengeance against the man who had abandoned her, but he enjoyed the look of assurance and faith that was present in her eyes.

(How long ago had it been since a woman had looked at him with pride and with trust in his abilities? How many years ago had it been since Brenda had lost hers?)

A spasm of self-pity shook him and he had to wait for a moment.

Back to the device. He tried to shut out the world, shut out his condition, think only of his computer, only of the tiny fluctuations in the electromagnetic field produced by the interchange of sodium and potassium ions across the neuronic membrane.

The screen flashed again, steadied, and resolved into a pattern of low peaks and valleys. Carefully, barely daring to touch the keys, Morrison threw in an expansion directive. The peaks and valleys spread out, the edges sliding off the screen. On the single peak and valley left remaining, there was a fuzzy smaller wiggle.

It's recording the waves, he thought, afraid to say so, afraid even to think it with any intensity, lest the slightest physical or mental effect suffice to blank it out.

The minor wiggle—the skeptic waves, as he called them— went out of focus and back in, never quite sharpening.

Morrison wasn't surprised. He might be detecting the fields of a number of cells that didn't quite duplicate each other. There was also the insulating effect of the plastic wall of the ship. There was the eternal shaking of Brownian motion. There might even be the interfering charge of atom groupings outside the miniaturization field.

The wonder was that he had gotten waves at all.

Slowly he made hand contact with the antennae—slid his fingers up and down, first one hand, then the other, then both in unison, then both in opposite directions. Then he bent the antennae gently, this way and that. There were sharpening and fuzzing of the skeptic waves, but he didn't know, for certain, exactly what he was doing that resulted in the sharpening.

And then, at a certain point, the tiny waves sharpened acutely. A little to one direction and another they fuzzed, but in one particular direction they were sharp. He tried to keep his hands from trembling.

"Arkady," he said.

"Yes, my American magician," said Dezhnev.

"Curve left and a little upward. I don't want to talk too much."

"I'll have to curve around the fibers."

"Curve slowly. Too fast and I'll lose the focus."

Morrison fought to keep his eyes from flickering leftward toward Kaliinin. Just one look at her face and one inevitable thought of her prettiness would be distraction enough to fuzz out the screen. Even the thought of distraction was itself distracting enough for the thought wave to flicker.

Dezhnev was curving the ship in the gentle arc that was all that the offset motors would manage and slowly Morrison shifted the antennae to suit. Occasionally he muttered a brief whispered direction: "Up and right," "Down," "A little left."

Finally he gasped, "Straight ahead."

It should get easier, he thought, as they got closer, but he couldn't relax until a neuron was actually in sight. And, through the obscuring collagen thicket, that was not likely to be until they were nearly on top of it.

Concentrating on only one subject was as tiring as clenching a muscle and leaving it clenched. He had to introduce just a bit of quick variation. He had to think of something else, but something neutral, something that would, for a while, leave his mind unclenched. So he thought of his broken family because he had thought of them so often that the image had faded and lost effect somehow. It was a photograph that was growing bent and gray and he could snap out of it quickly and return to the single-minded contemplation of the skeptic waves.

Then—without warning and overwhelmingly—another thought invaded his mind. It was a sharp mental picture of Sophia Kaliinin, looking younger, prettier, and happier than she had ever seemed to him in the short time he had known her. And with that picture came a tumbling of love and frustration and jealousy that left him weak.

He had not been consciously aware of any of these feelings, but who knew what unconscious thoughts and emotions might be hidden there in his own brain cells? Kaliinin? Did he feel that way about her? So quickly? Or was it the abnormal tensions of this fantastic voyage into the brain that had brought about fantastic responses?

It was only then that he noticed that the screen had fuzzed out completely. He was about to shout a warning to Dezhnev to stop the motors while he concentrated and tried to recapture the waves when Dezhnev's voice boomed out.

"There it is, Albert. You guided us to the cell like a bloodhound. Congratulations!"

"Also," said Boranova, gazing at Konev's lowering countenance, "congratulations to Yuri for coming up with the idea and persuading Albert to make the effort."

Konev's face relaxed and Dezhnev said, "But now, how do we get inside?"

56.

MORRISON stared at the vista ahead with interest. What he saw was a vast ridged wall stretching up and down, right and left, as far as the ship's light made it possible to see. The ridges were themselves broken up into domes so that, on closer inspection, the wall seemed to be a checkerboard with each square bulging outward. There were ragged extensions jutting outward between the bulges, like thick, short, and branching ropes that gave the wall an appearance of being tattered.

Morrison, with some effort, allowed for his own miniaturization and grasped the fact that the bulges were the ends of molecules (of phospholipids, he assumed) that made up the cell membrane. He realized with some dismay just what it meant for the ship to be the size of a glucose molecule. The cell was an enormous object; by present ship measure, it must be many kilometers across.

Konev had been staring at the cell membrane also, but emerged from his thoughtful contemplation sooner than Morrison did.

"I'm not sure," said Konev, "that this is a brain cell—or, at least, a neuron."

"What else can it be?" said Dezhnev. "We're in the brain and that's a cell."

Konev made no visible attempt to smother the disgust in his expression as he said, "There is more than one kind of brain cell. The neuron is the important cell, the chief agent of the mind. There are ten billion of them in the human brain. There are also some ten times as many glial cells of several kinds, which serve supporting and subsidiary functions. They are considerably smaller than the neurons. On the basis of chance, then, it is ten to one that this is a glia. The thought waves are in the neurons."

Boranova said, "We can't be guided simply by chance, Yuri. Can you tell in some definitive way whether this is glia or a neuron without involving statistics?"

"Not just by looking at it, no. From this size, all I see is a small section of a cell membrane and in such a case one cell looks like another. We'll have to become larger and get a more panoramic view. —I presume we can become larger now, Natalya. After all, we're through what you called the collagen jungle."

"We can deminiaturize, if necessary," said Boranova, "but increasing size is more tedious and risky than decreasing it. An increase means the generation of heat and must be done slowly. Is there any alternative?"

Konev said tartly, "We might try Albert's instrument again. Albert, can you tell us if the skeptic waves you can detect are coming from straight ahead or from a slightly different direction?"

Morrison hesitated. Before his instrument had fuzzed out at a time just before the cell had been sighted, there had been the Kaliinin vision and he didn't want it back. It was too embarrassing, too upsetting. Surely, if his mind hid and suppressed emotions, it was because they were better hidden and suppressed.

He said uncertainly, "I'm not sure—"

"Try it," said Konev and all four Soviets were now looking at Morrison earnestly.

With an inward shrug, Morrison put his computer into action. After some consideration, he said, "I get the waves, Yuri, but not as strongly as I did on the way here."

"Do they get stronger in another direction?"

"Slightly, from a more upward direction, but I must warn you again that the directional abilities of my device are very primitive."

"Yes, like this ship you complain about. —Here is what it seems to me has happened, Natalya. Coming here, we were able to detect a neuron directly above the top of a glia that lay before it. When he saw the glia, Arkady naturally steered for it and its bulk now masks the neuron and we get the thought waves more dimly."

"In that case," said Boranova, "we must go over the glia to the neuron."

"And in *that* case," said Konev, "I say again that we must deminiaturize. At our present glucose size, the distance we must pass in moving over the glia may well prove to be a hundred or a hundred and fifty kilometers. If we increase in length ten times, say to the size and mass of a small protein molecule, we would reduce the apparent distance to merely ten or fifteen kilometers."

Kaliinin said in an abstracted voice, as though what she had to say bore no relationship to what had just been said, "We will have to be our present size to get into the neuron, Natalya."

And, after a short pause, as though disengaging himself from the possibility of directly answering the remark, Konev said, "Of course. Once we reach the neuron, we readjust our size to whatever seems best."

Boranova sighed and seemed lost in her own thought.

Konev said with unaccustomed gentleness, "Natalya, we'll have to change size eventually. We can't stay glucose size forever."

"I hate to deminiaturize oftener than I must," said Boranova.

"But we *must* in this case, Natalya. We cannot spend hours cruising along a cell membrane. And deminiaturizing tenfold at this stage involved a very low absolute energy change."

Morrison said, "Is it that starting the deminiaturizing process might initiate an uncontrolled and explosive continuation?"

Boranova said, "There's nothing wrong with your intuition, Albert. Without knowing anything about miniaturization theory, you manage to grasp the point. Once started, it is safest to allow the deminiaturization to continue. Stopping it involves a certain risk."

"So does remaining at glucose size for hours longer than we need," said Konev.

"True," said Boranova, nodding her head.

Dezhnev said, "Shall we put it to a vote and come to a people's democratic decision?"

At this, Boranova's head snapped up and her dark eyes seemed to flash. Her heavy jaws set firmly and she said, "No, Arkady. It is my responsibility to make the decision and I will increase the size of the ship." Then, abandoning the air of majesty, she said, "Of course you can wish me well."

Dezhnev said, "And why not? It would be the same as wishing all of ourselves well."

Boranova bent over her controls and Morrison grew quickly tired of trying to watch. He couldn't actually see what she was doing, wouldn't understand that she was doing if he did see it, and there was the mundane fact that his neck was beginning to ache with the effort to keep it turned. He looked forward and found Konev peering at him over *his* shoulder.

"About the skeptic wave detection," said Konev.

"What about the skeptic wave detection?" said Morrison.

"When we were making our way to this cell through the collagen jungle—"

"Yes yes, what about it?"

"Did you get any—images?"

Morrison remembered that tearing vision of Sophia Kaliinin. Nothing like it existed in his mind now. Even when he thought of it as it had then been, it now roused no response. Whatever it was in his mind, it seemed to have been reached only under the intense stimulation of concentrated skeptic waves; and whatever it was, he was not going to describe it to Konev—or to anyone else, for that matter.

He temporized, "Why should I have sensed any images?"

"Because you did on occasion when you analyzed skeptic waves at normal-size intensities."

"You're assuming that analysis during miniaturization would produce greater intensities or possess greater image-producing powers."

"It's a reasonable assumption. But did you or didn't you? The question doesn't involve theorizing. I'm asking about an observation. Did you get any images?"

And Morrison sighed inwardly and said, "No."

Konev continued his sidewise peering (under which Morrison felt himself grow a little restless and rather more than a little irate), then said softly, *"I did."*

"You did?" Morrison's eyes widened in honest surprise. Then, more cautiously, "What did you sense?"

"Not much, but I thought you might have gotten it more clearly. You were actually holding and manipulating your detector and it is probably more adapted to your brain than mine."

"Just what was it you got? Can you can describe it at all?"

"A kind of flicker that moved into and out of awareness. It seemed to me that I saw three human figures, one larger than the others."

"And what did you make of that?"

"Well, Shapirov had a daughter whom he adored and she

had two children whom he also adored. I imagine that in his coma he may have been thinking of them, or remembering them, or being under the delusion that he was seeing them. Who knows what goes on in a coma?"

"Do you know his daughter and his grandchildren? Did you recognize them?"

"I was seeing them, as it were, through translucent glass in the twilight. It was all I could do to sense three figures." He sounded disappointed. "I had hoped you would see it more clearly."

Morrison, thinking hard, said, "I neither saw, nor sensed, anything like that."

Konev said, "Of course, things should be sharper once we are inside a neuron. It is not images we must sense, in any case. We want to hear words."

"I've never heard words," said Morrison, shaking his head.

"Of course not," said Konev, "since you worked with animals who don't use words."

"True," said Morrison. "Just the same, I once managed to run some tests on a human being, though I never reported it. I sensed no words then or images either."

Konev shrugged it off.

Morrison said, "You know, under the circumstances, it might be natural for Shapirov's mind to be full of family—if we accept your interpretation of what you thought you sensed. What would the chances be that he would be thinking of some esoteric extension of miniaturization mathematics?"

"He was a physicist. Even his family came second to that. If we can sense words out of those skeptic waves, they'll be words dealing with physics."

"You think that, do you?"

"I am positive."

The two fell quiet and for a few minutes there was no sound in the ship. Then Boranova said, "I've deminiaturized the ship to protein size and I have brought the process to a halt."

A moment passed and then Dezhnev, with an unaccustomed tightness to his throaty voice, said, "Are things all right, Natasha?"

Boranova said, "The mere fact that you can ask the question, Arkady, is an answer in the positive. Deminiaturization has stopped without incident."

She smiled, but there was a definite trace of perspiration glistening at her hairline.

57.

THE surface of the glial cell still stretched out as far as the eye could see into the dimness beyond the reach of the ship's light, but it had changed in character. The domes and ridges had faded out into a fine texture. The ropes that had extended from between the domes had become threads nearly impossible to see as the ship sped along the surface.

Morrison's attention was, for the most part, on his computer, as he watched to see that the skeptic waves did not decline in intensity, but, periodically, he could not help but drift away from that and gaze at the panorama outside.

Occasionally, there would emerge from the surface of the cell the typical dendritic processes of a nerve cell—even one that was merely a subsidiary glial cell. They branched and subbranched like a tree in winter, growing out of the cell membrane.

Even at the new and larger size of the ship, the dendrites were large when they emerged from the cell. They were like tree trunks, which, however, narrowed rapidly and were clearly flexible. Lacking the rigidity of the cartilage fibers, they swayed in the eddies set up by the ship's progress through the extracellular fluid. They swayed, indeed, at the ship's approach and Dezhnev rarely had to do anything to avoid them. They would bend out of line and the ship would pass them safely.

Collagen fibers were fewer in the immediate neighborhood of the cell and, thanks to the larger size of the ship, were much thinner and more fragile. On one occasion, Dezhnev either did not see one looming directly ahead of the ship or did not care that it was. The ship brushed past it in a way that brought it just outside Morrison's seat. He flinched at the grating collision, but the ship was in no way damaged. It was the collagen fiber that bent, then snapped and dangled free. Morrison's head turned and his eyes followed the broken fiber for the second or so that it remained in view before floating away.

Boranova must have seen it, too, and watched Morrison's reaction, for she said, "There's no reason for concern. There are trillions of those fibers scattered through the brain, so that one more or less doesn't matter. Besides, they heal—even in a brain as badly damaged as poor Shapirov's."

"I suppose so," said Morrison, "yet I can't help but think we are crashing without any right through an infinitely delicate mechanism not meant for technological invasion."

"I appreciate your feeling," said Boranova, "but hardly anything in the world seems to have been brought into being by geological and biological processes with any apparent prevision of human interference. Humanity does a great deal of wrong to Earth and to life, some of it wittingly. —Incidentally, I'm thirsty. Are you?"

"Definitely," said Morrison.

"You'll find a cup in the little recess under your right armrest. Pass it back."

She distributed water to all five, saying matter-of-factly, "There's no shortage of water, so if you want seconds, say so."

Dezhnev looked at his cup distastefully, while keeping one hand on the controls. He sniffed at it and said, "My father used to say: 'There is no drink like pure water, provided one realizes that it is alcohol that is the purifying agent.'"

"Yes, Arkady," said Boranova. "I am quite sure your father purified his water frequently, but here on the ship, with your hands on the controls, you will have your water unpurified."

"We must all go through privations now and then," said Dezhnev, who then downed his water and made a face.

It might have been the taste of the water that caused Kaliinin to fumble between her legs. It took a moment for Morrison to realize that it was her turn to urinate and he turned his head toward the window and waited to see if another collagen fiber might go flying.

Boranova said, "I suppose, strictly speaking, it's lunchtime, but we can do without. Still—"

"Still what?" asked Dezhnev. "A good plate of piping hot borscht with sour cream?"

Boranova said, "What I have smuggled in against regulations are bits of chocolate—high-calorie, zero-fiber."

Kaliinin, who had disposed of her small damp paper towel and was shaking her hands to dry them, said, "It will rot our teeth."

"Not immediately," said Boranova, "and you can rinse your mouth with a little water to reduce the sugar residue. Who wants one?"

Four hands went up, Kaliinin's not the last. Morrison welcomed his gladly. He was fond of chocolate in any case and sucked at it to make it last longer. The taste reminded him poignantly of his boyhood in the outskirts of Muncie.

The chocolate was gone when Konev said to Morrison in a low voice, "Have you sensed anything while we've been skimming past the glial cell?"

"No," said Morrison. (He hadn't.) "Have you?"

"I thought I did. The phrase 'green fields' crossed my mind."

Morrison could not prevent himself from saying "Hmm" and for a while remained lost in thought.

"Well?" said Konev.

Morrison shrugged. "Phrases go through one's mind all the time. You hear something out of the corner of your ear, so to speak, and sometime later it penetrates your consciousness; or some stream-of-consciousness thoughts invade your mind and one phrase surfaces; or you can have an auditory hallucination of some sort."

"It crossed my mind when I was looking at your instrument and concentrating."

"You wanted to be aware of something, I suppose, and something promptly obliged by flitting through your mind in response. You get the same effect in dreams."

"No. This was real."

"How can you tell, Yuri? —I didn't sense any such thing. Did anyone else sense it, do you suppose?"

"They wouldn't. No one else was concentrating on your machine. Perhaps no one else in the ship had a brain sufficiently like yours to sense on your wavelength, so to speak."

"You're just guessing. Besides, what does the phrase mean?"

"Green fields? Shapirov had a house out in the country. He would remember the green fields."

"He might have merely supplied the image. You would supply the words."

Konev frowned, paused a moment, then said in a clearly hostile manner, "Why are you so opposed to the possibility of getting a message?"

Morrison allowed himself to be equally hostile. "Because I've been burned by reporting such sense perceptions. I've been ridiculed long enough and I have become cautious. An image of a woman and two children doesn't tell us anything. Neither does a phrase like 'green fields.' If you report it, how can you possibly tell it from a self-generated image or phrase? Now listen, Yuri, a hint, to be useful, must, however vaguely and indirectly, tie in with the quantum-relativity relationship. That we can report. Anything less than that is not compelling; it won't force belief. It will only succeed in hurting us. I speak from experience."

Konev said, "What, then, if *you* succeed in hearing something vital, something that bears on our project? Will you perhaps keep it to yourself?"

"Why should I? If I sense something in physics relating to miniaturization, I would lack the background to understand it and keeping it to myself would get me nowhere. If some useful result is shared between us, this computer remains my machine and it is activated by my theory. I am the one who will get the major share of the credit. I won't keep it to myself, Yuri. Both my self-interest and my honor as a scientist will keep me from doing that. —And what about you?"

"Of course I'll share whatever I sense. I have been doing so just now."

"I don't mean 'green fields.' That is nonsense. Suppose you sense something very significant and I don't. Might it not occur to you that the knowledge would be a state secret, as miniaturization itself is? Would you then tell me that knowledge and risk the wrath of your Central Coordinating Committee."

They had been speaking in whispers, heads together, but Boranova's ears picked up the key word. "Politics, gentlemen?" she asked frostily.

Konev said, "We're discussing the possible uses of Albert's instrument, Natalya. If I learn something of importance from Shapirov's skeptic waves and Albert does not, he thinks I will keep it from him under the excuse that it is a state secret."

Boranova said, "It well may be."

Konev said mildly, "We need Albert's cooperation. It is his machine and his program and I am sure he knows how to work it at less than perfect efficiency. If he is not completely assured of our honesty and goodwill, he may arrange to have us sense nothing. I am willing to share anything that I sense if he will do the same."

"The Committee may disapprove, as Albert himself pointed out," said Boranova.

"Let it. I don't concern myself with it," said Konev.

"I'll prove I love you, Yuri," interposed Dezhnev with a chuckle. "I won't quote you."

Kaliinin said, "Natalya, I agree that we should be honest with Albert, since we must ask him to be honest with us. Using his own device with which he has experience, he is far more likely to come up with something useful than we are. A policy of quid pro quo is likely to be far more to our advantage than to his. —Isn't that so, Albert?"

Morrison nodded. "I've been thinking precisely that and would have mentioned it if it looked as though you were going to tell me that it was against government policy to be honest with me."

Boranova said, "Well, let us await events." The tension died down.

Morrison remained busy with his own thoughts, watching his machine only in abstraction.

And then Dezhnev said, "There's another cell just ahead —a kilometer or two. It looks as though it might be larger than the one we've been passing. Is that a neuron, Yuri?"

Konev, who seemed to have been in a brown study of his own, snapped to attention. "Albert, what does your machine say? Is that a neuron?"

Morrison was already handling his device. "It must be," he said. "I've never seen the skeptic waves this sharp."

"Good!" said Dezhnev. "Now what?"

58.

KALIININ looked thoughtfully at the cell surface below. She said, "Natalya, we'll have to miniaturize to glucose size again. Arkady, get us in among the dendrites so that we can get down to the surface of the cell body.''

Morrison watched the surface also. The dendrites were much more elaborate than those on the glia. The nearest one branched and branched again until it looked like a fuzzy frond vanishing beyond the reach of ship's light. Others, farther away, were fuzzier and smaller.

Morrison suspected that the fuzziness was at least partly the result of Brownian motion. Surely there couldn't be much of that, however. Probably each final strand of the branchings—each twig—met a similar twig or some neighboring neuron to form that intimate near-touch called a synapse. The wavering of the twig would not be strong enough to break the contact or the brain couldn't do its work.

Dezhnev had the ship approach the surface of the cell body, slowly slithering past the nearest dendrite (he was learning to handle the unbalance of the individual engines with a certain finesse, Morrison thought) and, as he did so, it seemed to Morrison that the surface of the neuron was changing character.

Of course, it had to, for the ship was miniaturizing again. The ridges in the cell surface were becoming more prominent and were dividing into domes. Between the phospholipid domes the hairs were becoming ropier. Receptors, thought Morrison. Each one of them was designed to link on to a particular molecule that would be useful to the neuron and certainly glucose would be the most useful of those.

The downward change was considerably more rapid than the upward change. Absorbing energy was simple, while the energy release of deminiaturization was dangerous. Morrison understood that well by now.

Kaliinin said, frowning in concern, "I don't know which receptors are for glucose, but a great many of them must be. Skim across them slowly, Arkady—very slowly. If we're caught, I don't want to tear loose—or to tear them loose, either.''

"No problem, little Sophie," said Dezhnev. "If I shut off the motors, the ship stops at once. It can't push through the giant atoms that surround us at all easily. Too viscous. So I just give it a touch of energy, enough to shoulder our way past the molecules of water, and we'll tiptoe across the receptors.''

" 'Through the tulips,' " said Morrison, looking at Konev.

"What?" said Konev, looking both annoyed and puzzled.

"It's a phrase that went through my head. There's an old show tune called 'Tiptoe Through the Tulips With Me,' In English, the words are—"

"What nonsense are you speaking?" snapped Konev.

"I'm trying to point out that whenever someone says 'tiptoe' to me, I automatically hear the phrase 'through the tulips' in my mind. If I happen to be concentrating on my computer when someone says 'tiptoe,' I will still hear the phrase in my mind and it will not mean that I am getting it from the skeptic waves on the computer. Do you take my meaning?"

"You're talking emptily," said Konev. "Leave me alone."

But he looked shaken, Morrison thought. He had taken the meaning.

They were now moving parallel to the surface of the neuron. The receptors were moving gently and Morrison realized that he couldn't tell which were empty and which had attached themselves to some of the molecules moving through the extracellular fluid with them.

He tried to concentrate on those molecules. There seemed to be glitterings in the fluid which might have been the light of the ship's beacon reflected from molecules, but none of it showed up well. Even the surface of the cell membrane wasn't actually *clear* if you looked at it directly. It was more the surrealistic impression of a surface than an actual one— too few photons were being reflected and too few were reaching them on their small scale.

Still, by the glitter, he could make out a kind of grittiness in the fluid they were passing through (water molecules, surely) and among them, now and then, something wormy— twisting, turning, closing up, then opening again. The immediate neighborhood of the ship was, of course, within the miniaturization field, so that atoms and molecules of the standard-size world were constantly shrinking as they entered— and expanding again as they left. The number of atoms doing so must be enormous but the energy change that resulted, even totaled over that number, were small enough so that it did not drain the ship perceptibly, or bring about spontaneous deminiaturization, or do any damage. —Or, at least, it *seemed* to do no damage.

Morrison tried not to think about it.

Boranova said, "I don't mean to question your ability, Sophia, but please check and make sure the ship has the electrical pattern of glucose."

"I assure you it does," said Kaliinin.

And as though to give notice that that was indeed so, the ship seemed to twist in mid-fluid, judging by the sudden shift in view through the walls.

Under ordinary conditions, such a twist would have thrown every person on the ship hard against the wall or the seat arm. Mass and inertia, however, were at virtually zero and there was only a faint swaying, hardly distinguishable from that which they associated with Brownian motion.

Kaliinin said, "We've attached ourselves to a glucose receptor."

"Good," said Dezhnev. "I've turned off the motor. Now what do we do?"

"Nothing," said Kaliinin. "We let the cell do its work and we wait."

The receptor did not actually make contact with the ship. This was good, for had it come any closer it would have entered the miniaturization field and its tip would have collapsed. As it was, there was a close meeting of electrical fields only, negative to positive and positive to negative. The attractions were not the full ionic attractions but the lesser ones that resembled hydrogen bonds. It was enough to hold, but weak enough to allow the ship to pull away somewhat, as though it were connected to the receptor by rubber bands rather than by grappling hooks.

The receptor stretched the length of the ship and was irregular in outline, as though it were embracing a pattern of bulges along the plastic hull. The hull was smooth and featureless to the eye, of course, but Morrison was quite certain that there was an electric field that bulged in just the locations where the hydroxyl groups would be in the glucopyranose structure, the bulges taking on just the shapes they would in the natural molecule.

Morrison looked out again. The receptor virtually blanked out vision on the side of the ship along which it lay. If he looked beyond the receptor, however, he could see a farther stretch of the neuron's surface, seemingly without end, for it vanished beyond the reach of the ship's light.

The neuronic surface seemed to be heaving slightly and he could see greater detail. Among the regular domes of the rank and file of phospholipid molecules, he caught occasional glimpses of an irregular mass, which he guessed to be a protein molecule that ran through the thickness of the cell membrane. It was to these molecules that the receptors were attached, which did not surprise Morrison. He knew that the receptors must be peptides—chains of amino acids. They were part of the thread of a protein backbone, sticking outward, each different receptor made up of different amino acids in a specific order so designed as to possess an electric field pattern matching (in opposing attractions and physical shape) that of the molecule it was designed to pick up.

Then, even as he watched, it seemed to him that the receptors were moving toward him. He could see them now in greater numbers and could also see that those numbers were still increasing. The receptors and the protein molecules to which they were attached seemed to be swimming through the phospholipid molecules (with a film of cholesterol molecules underneath, Morrison knew), which opened before and closed behind.

"Something's happening," said Morrison as he felt the ship's own motion through the tiny drag of inertia that remained to them at their thoroughly negligible mass.

59.

KONEV said, "The surface is gathering us in."

Dezhnev nodded. "It looks like it's doing this." He held up his thick and callused hand, cupping it.

"Exactly," said Konev. "It will invaginate, make a deeper and deeper cup, narrowing the neck and finally closing it, and we will be inside the cell." He seemed quite calm about it.

So was Morrison. They wanted to be inside the cell and this was the way it was done.

The receptors continued coming together, alongside each one of them some molecule—some *real* molecule—and in among them the feigning molecule of the ship. The cell's surface, like Dezhnev's cupped hand, closed upon them entirely and drew them in.

"Now what?" said Dezhnev.

"We're in a vesicle inside the cell," said Kaliinin. "It will grow more acid and the receptor will then detach itself from us. It and all the receptors will then return to the cell membrane."

"And we?" persisted Dezhnev.

"Since we are recognized by our electric field as a glucose molecule," said Kaliinin, "the cell will try to metabolize us— break us up into smaller fragments and extract energy from us."

Even as she spoke, the peptide receptor fell away, uncoiling.

"Is that a good idea, having it metabolize us?" asked Dezhnev.

"It won't," said Morrison. "We'll be attached to an appropriate enzyme molecule which will find that we don't react as expected. We won't take on a phosphate group, so it will be helpless and will probably release us. We're not *really* a glucose molecule."

"But if the enzyme molecule releases us, won't another enzyme molecule of the same type attach itself to us and try again—and so on indefinitely."

"Now that you mention it," said Morrison, rubbing his chin and absently noticing the bristles grown since his morning shave, "it may be that the first molecules won't let us go, I suppose, if we won't do the expected."

"A fine situation," said Dezhnev indignantly, slipping into his local dialect of Russian, as he always seemed to do when excited, and which Morrison always had a bit of difficulty in following. "The best we can expect is that an enzyme molecule either holds us forever all by himself or holds us forever in a relay race as we pass from one enzyme to another indefinitely. —My father used to say: 'To be saved from the jaws of a wolf by a hungry bear is no great cause for gratitude.' "

"Please notice," said Kaliinin, "that no enzyme molecule has attached itself to us."

"Why is that?" asked Morrison, who had, indeed, noticed that.

"Because of a slight change in electric charge pattern. We had to mimic a glucose molecule to get into the cell, but once in, we don't have to be one anymore. In fact, we *must* mimic something else."

Boranova leaned forward. "Won't any molecule we mimic be liable to metabolic change, Sophia?"

"Actually, no, Natalya," said Kaliinin. "Glucose—or any other simple sugar in the body—belongs to a certain molecular configuration, so that we call it D-glucose. I've simply altered the pattern to its mirror image. We have become L-glucose and there isn't an enzyme that will touch us now, any more than any of us are likely to put a right shoe on a left foot. —Now we can move about freely."

The vesicle which had formed on their introduction to the cellular interior had broken up and Morrison gave up as hopeless any attempt to follow what was going on. Fragments around him were enveloped by much larger enzyme molecules that seemed to embrace them and then relax. Presumably, an altered victim of the enzymatic squeeze was set free to be embraced again by another enzyme.

It was all happening at once and, Morrison knew, this was only the anaerobic portion of the process (in which no molecular oxygen was used.) It would end by breaking up the glucose molecule, with its six carbon atoms, into two three-carbon fragments.

A little energy would be produced in this fashion and the fragments would be shunted to the mitochondria for the completion of the process *with* the use of oxygen; a process in which the universal energy-transfer molecule adenosine triphosphate (or ATP, for short) would be invested in order to get things started and, in the end, be produced once more in quantities substantially greater than the investment.

Morrison felt the urge to drop everything and to find a way into a mitochondrion, the small energy factory of the cell. After all, the fine details of mitochondrial processes had *still* not been worked out—but then he pulled away almost angrily at the thought. The skeptic waves came first. He shouted that to himself, as though trying to force a realization of priorities onto an overly curious brain that was threatening to diffuse its interests.

Apparently, the same thought occurred to Konev, for he said, "We're finally inside the neuron, Albert. Let's not be tourists. What do you find in the way of skeptic waves now?"

CHAPTER 14

AXON

*Those who say "A penny for your thoughts"
are usually being overgenerous.*
                                    —*Dezhnev Senior*

60.

MORRISON bristled at Konev's order. (It had definitely been that.)

He indicated his resentment by refusing to respond at all for a while. He continued to stare out into the interior of the neuron and could distinguish nothing he recognized. He could see fibers, convoluted plates, hulks of uncertain size and of no clear shape. What's more, he had a strong feeling that there was a skeletal presence in the cell that held the larger objects—the organelles—in place, but that the ship was slipping past it all too quickly, as though it were in a river racing downstream. The feeling of motion was far stronger here than in the bloodstream, for though there were small objects (debris?) that moved along with them, there were larger objects that apparently remained in place and that they passed rapidly.

Finally Morrison said, "Look, Yuri, we're moving so quickly that the motion is likely to distort the skeptic waves badly."

Konev snarled, "Are you mad? We're not moving quickly

at all. We're just drifting with the intracellular stream that serves to make certain that the small molecules are all made available to the organelle structure of the cell. The movement is very slow on the normal scale; it seems fast only on our miniaturized scale. Do I have to teach you cellular physiology?"

Morrison bit his lips. Of course. He had again forgotten how miniaturization distorted his perception. And again Konev was completely right.

"It might be better, though," said Morrison, fighting for self-respect, "if we changed back to D-glucose and allowed an enzyme to snatch us up. The combined size would slow us down and make it easier to pick up the waves."

"We don't have to slow down. The nerve impulse travels at a minimum of two meters per second in real velocity and in apparent velocity at our size that's about seventy times the real speed of light. As compared with that, our speed, however great it seems, is trivial. Even if we are moving at the apparent speed of a rocket ship, to the nerve impulse we seem virtually motionless."

Morrison lifted his arm in surrender and felt furious with Konev. There was such a thing as being *too* right. He cast a quick sidewise glance at Kaliinin, with the uncomfortable feeling that she would be showing her contempt. She met his glance soberly and with no trace of a sneer. In fact, her shoulders lifted slightly as though to say (Morrison imagined), "What do you expect of a savage?"

Boranova (Morrison glanced over his left shoulder) seemed oblivious to the exchange. She was busy with her instrument and Morrison wondered what she could be so intent on, considering that the ship's engines were off and they were merely drifting with the current.

As for Dezhnev—with the engines off—he was the one crew member who, in truth, had nothing to do at the moment (except to keep half an eye at the material up ahead in case of an unexpected emergency).

He said, "Come, Albert, study the skeptic waves and give us some answers. Then we can leave this place. It's extremely exciting being inside a cell for those who like it, but already I am quite certain I have seen enough. My father used to say: 'The most exciting part of any trip is reaching home again.' "

Boranova said, "Arkady—"

"Yes, Natasha."

"Save a few words for tomorrow." Morrison noticed the trace of a smile on her lips.

"Certainly, Natasha. I suspect an attempt at sarcasm, but I shall do as you say." And though he snapped his mouth shut with an exaggerated click of his teeth, he began to hum very quietly to himself, a tune in the minor mode.

Morrison felt a little astonished. They had been in the ship now for a little less than five hours—but it felt the equivalent number of days, perhaps years. Yet, unlike Arkady and despite his earlier feelings of terror, he was not ready to leave Shapirov's body. He felt a strong urge to explore the cell and his thoughts rested on the possibility.

Kaliinin must have been thinking along similar lines, for she said in a soft, introspective tone, "What a shame to be the first people inside the most complex of all living cells and to do nothing at all about investigating it properly."

"That is exactly—" began Morrison, then thought better of it and let the words dangle.

Konev swung his arm as though he were driving off hordes of insects. "I can't understand this. We are in the cell and we came here for a specific purpose. Albert, focus on the skeptic waves."

"I am doing so," said Morrison sharply. "In fact, I have done so. —Look!"

Konev twisted his head, then unclasped himself, so that he could turn around and peer over the back of his seat. He stared at Morrison's small screen and said, "The waves seem sharper."

"They *are* sharper. They're more intense and they show finer oscillations than I've ever seen. Come to think of it, I wonder how fine they can get. Sooner or later, an oscillation, if fine enough, will represent the wobbling of a single electron—and then we have to take into account the uncertainty principle."

"You forget. We're miniaturized and Planck's constant is nine orders of magnitude smaller for us than it is under standard conditions."

"*You* forget," protested Morrison, eager to catch the other in a misstep this time, "that the waves are reduced by that much before they reach us. Those waves are exactly where they should be relative to the uncertainty principle, therefore."

Konev hesitated a bare moment. "It doesn't matter. We're looking at something now and there's no perceptible uncertainty blurring. What does it mean?"

"It supports my theory," said Morrison. "This is exactly what I ought to see inside a cell if my interpretation of skeptic wave activity is correct—"

"That's not what I mean. We began with the assumption that your theory was correct. Now it's no longer an assumption, it's a demonstrated fact, and I congratulate you. But what does it mean? What do those skeptic waves show Shapirov to be thinking?"

Morrison shook his head. "I have no data—zero data—on the correlation of such waves and specific thoughts. It would take years to gather such a correlation, if it could be done at all."

"But perhaps the skeptic waves, when they're clear and intense, produce an inductive effect on *your* brain. Are you getting any of your famous images?"

Morrison thought for a moment, then shook his head, "None!"

From behind him came a quiet voice, "I'm getting something, Albert."

Morrison turned. "You, Natalya?"

"Yes, it's odd—but I am."

Konev demanded, "What are you getting, Natalya?"

Boranova hesitated, concentrating. "Curiosity. Well, it's not exactly an image of anything. Just an impression. I feel curiosity."

"And so you might," said Morrison. "It needs no impression from outside to produce such a feeling under these circumstances."

"No no. I know what my own thoughts and impressions are like. This is imposed from outside."

Morrison said, "Do you feel it right now?"

"Yes. It comes and goes a little, but I feel it right now."

"All right. What about now?"

Boranova looked surprised. "It stopped suddenly. —Did you turn off your machine?"

"I turned it down. Now, you tell me when you feel the sensation and when you don't." He turned to look at

Kaliinin, intending to tell her to say or do nothing that would indicate when he turned the machine down or up, but she was staring out at the cell, obviously lost in the marvel of watching the interior of a neuron. He wondered if, at the moment, she heard—or cared—what was going on.

He turned away and said, "Natalya, close your eyes and concentrate. Just say 'on' when you get the sensation and 'off' when you don't."

For several minutes, she complied with his suggestion.

Morrison said to Konev, "Does the machine make a noise when it is turned down or up? Is there anything you can hear or sense?"

Konev shook his head. "I'm not aware of anything."

"Then there's no mistake. She's getting the sensation only when the machine is on."

Dezhnev, who, unlike Kaliinin, had followed everything, said, "But why?" His eyes narrowed. "The brain waves are there whether your machine detects them or not. She should get the feeling of curiosity all the time."

"No no," said Morrison. "My device filters out all the components but the actual skeptic waves. Without the machine, she just gets a confused mass of sensations, responses, correlations, and miscellany of all kinds. With the machine, she gets only the skeptic waves, which further demonstrates the usefulness of my theory."

"I don't get anything at all," said Dezhnev, frowning. "Doesn't that destroy your theory?"

Morrison shrugged. "Brains are complicated mechanisms. Natalya gets it. You don't. For that matter, neither do I. Maybe this particular skeptic wave component fits something in Natalya's brain, not in ours. I'm not going to be able to explain everything at once. —Do you get anything, Konev?"

"No," he answered, as discontented as Dezhnev had been. "Yet I obtained impressions when we were outside the neuron."

Morrison shook his head and said nothing.

Konev burst out, "Can't you get anything but just a vague feeling of curiosity, Natalya?"

Boranova, "No, Yuri, I can't. Not at this moment. But you remember Pyotr Shapirov. He was curious about everything."

"I remember, but that doesn't help. Albert, in what direction are we moving?"

Albert said, "Downstream. It's the only direction in which we can move."

"No no." Then, in sudden anger, "Is that a joke? Are you trying to be funny?"

Morrison said, "Not at all. You asked in what direction we were going. What other answer could I have given you? Surely the compass directions have no meaning here."

Konev said, "All right. Sorry. The stream goes this way here. On the other side of the cell, it goes the other way. It's a circulation. But the nerve impulse goes one way only, from the dendrites to the axon. Are we on the side of the cell that's taking us in the same direction as the nerve impulse or in the other direction?"

"Does it matter?" said Morrison.

"I think it does. Can your device tell you in which direction the impulse is traveling?"

"Yes, certainly. There should be a slight shift in the shape of the waves, depending on whether they are meeting the device head-on or from the rear."

"And?"

"And we're moving in the direction of the impulse."

"Good! A stroke of luck. We're heading for the axon, then."

"So it would seem."

Boranova said, "And if we are heading for the axon?"

Konev said, "Natalya, think! The skeptic waves travel along the surface of the cell. The cell here is wide and relatively large. The skeptic waves spread out over a large surface and are weakened in intensity. As the cell approaches the axon, it narrows. The axon itself is long, a very long tube compared to the cell—and very narrow. The waves must concentrate enormously as they race along that tube and they must grow more intense. What's more, the axon is insulated by a thick myelin sheath, so that the wave energy will not be lost to the outside, but will be kept tightly within the axon."

Boranova said, "You think, then, that we can receive more effectively in the axon?"

"Much more effectively. If you can detect curiosity now, it should be overwhelming in the axon. And you might be able to detect what Shapirov is curious about."

"It may turn out to be totally unimportant," said Morrison thoughtfully. "What if he's curious about why he should be lying there and not moving?"

"No," said Konev sharply, "that would not interest him. I knew Shapirov well. You didn't."

Morrison nodded. "That's true enough."

"All his waking time was consumed with the miniaturization process," said Konev. "All his dreams, too, I suspect. And toward the end, in the last few weeks before the—the accident took place, he was working, thinking, dreaming of the connection between quantum and relativity, thinking of how to make miniaturization and deminiaturization energy-free and stable."

"Surely," said Morrison, "if that were the case, he must have given some hints as to some of the details of his thinking."

"No, he was a child in some ways. We knew *what* he was thinking of, but not whether he was making progress or in what direction. What he loved to do was to present it to us whole, complete. —Remember, Natalya, how he loved to do that? He did that with miniaturization itself. When he finally wrote his paper—it was a young book—"

Morrison said casually, "Where was it published?"

Konev sneered. "You know it wasn't published. It had a limited circulation to those who had to know. It's nowhere where *you're* likely ever to see it."

Boranova said, "Yuri, don't be needlessly insulting. Albert is a fellow crew member and a guest. He is not to be treated as a spy."

Konev said, "If you say so, Natalya. Nevertheless, if Shapirov is curious, so intensely curious that Natalya gets that message, it can be only about the quantum-relativity connection. If we can get some details about that, any details at all, we'll have a starting point and can continue."

"And you think we'll get those details in the axon?"

"Yes, I'm sure of it." Konev clenched both fists as though preparing to get a stranglehold on the facts.

Morrison looked away. He was *not* sure of it. Increasingly, it was beginning to look to him as though matters were moving in another direction altogether and that that was just as well—"

He tried not to show it, but he was as excited as Konev was.

61.

DIM objects to either side loomed up ahead, drifted to one side, left or right, and fell behind. Ribosomes? Golgi apparatus? Fibrils of one sort or another? Morrison could not tell. From the vantage point of small molecule size, nothing, not even the sharpest, most familiar intracellular object, would look familiar, let alone recognizable.

They were racing through a strange land of indefiniteness and Morrison could not, no matter how he tried, picture his surroundings as those with which he was familiar from electron micrography.

He wondered if, somewhere beyond where the light of the ship's beam extended, there would be the endless volume of the cell's nucleus. Imagine being within submicroscopic distance of it and yet never seeing it.

He concentrated on the immediate surroundings. It seemed to him, once again, that he ought to make out the water molecules that made up 98 percent of all the molecules in the cell, that huge percentage being the direct consequence of the fact that they were just about the smallest molecules there.

He could not be sure. Focus his eyes though he did and as tightly as he could, what he saw was only a faint glitter—a photon, perhaps, bouncing off such a molecule and flashing back toward his eye. At best, he would only see one or two from any given water molecule.

He was suddenly aware of Kaliinin's head, bending toward his. Her hair brushed his face and he noticed, as he had once or twice before, the fresh scent of her shampoo.

She said, "This is terrible, Albert."

Her breath was a little strong and Morrison flinched before he could stop himself.

She noticed, for her fingers came up sharply, covering her mouth, and she mumbled, "I'm sorry."

Morrison shook his head slightly. "My own breath isn't exactly a bed of roses. —Tension, nothing much to eat. A drink of water might help, Natalya."

One drink set off everybody, of course, in a chain reaction. Kaliinin fingered a small white pellet. "Peppermint drop?"

Morrison held out his hand and smiled. "Is it permitted?"

Kaliinin's eye flickered back toward Boranova and she gave a Who-cares shrug. Having passed the drop to Morrison, Sophia popped another in her mouth.

Then she said again, "This is terrible, Albert."

"What is, Sophia?"

"How can we pass through this cell without examining it in detail?"

"We have a specific mission."

"Yes, but no one may be back within a brain cell for many years. Perhaps, never. When, in the future, someone will read that this ship and this crew merely raced through, looking neither to right or left, what barbarians they will think we must have been."

She was whispering very softly and their heads were bent close together. Morrison found himself rather enjoying it.

Had he grown so calloused to the threat of the situation— the constant skirting along the edge of the abyss of spontaneous deminiaturization, the possibility of split-second death at any moment—that he could take joy from the trivial fact that his lips were so close to the pretty face of a woman?

Well, why quarrel with that? Let the nearness anesthetize him, so that he might for a moment forget.

Morrison remembered the sharp image he had had so brief a time before of a happy, smiling, beautiful girl. He had not recognized the thought as his own, so unexpectedly had it come out of nowhere, and it didn't return, even now, but he remembered it distinctly and the memory squeezed at his heart with a warm feeling.

He had the momentary impulse to kiss her lightly, just a touch upon the cheekbone with his lips—and fought it down. If she decided to take it amiss, he would feel like an incredible fool.

Morrison said gently, "The people of the future will know we had a mission. They will understand."

"I wonder," Sophia said, then paused and sent a quick and almost fearful look in the direction of Konev, who as always sat stiff and detached at any sign of speech or even motion from Kaliinin.

She turned to her computer, switched it to the word-processor mode, and tapped out in rapid Russian: YURI IS A FANATIC WHO SACRIFICES EVERYTHING TO HIS MANIA. THERE IS NO CHANCE OF READING THOUGHTS, BUT HE PERSUADES EVERYONE. She blanked it, then tapped out: WE ARE HIS VICTIMS and blanked it at once.

For "we," read "I," thought Morrison sadly. He looked at his own instrument hesitantly. It seemed to him that the thought waves, which he had dimmed to low, were growing more intense. Morrison looked out as though he might be able to tell just how near the axon they now were, but, of course, there was no way of knowing.

He blanked the radiation, switched to word-processing, and printed out in Roman-lettered Russian: HE, TOO, IS HIS VICTIM.

Kaliinin at once printed savagely: NO. I DON'T BELIEVE PEOPLE ARE THEIR OWN VICTIMS.

Morrison thought sadly of his one-time wife, his two children, his own inability to present his theory persuasively, or, alternatively, to walk away from it, and tapped out: I BELIEVE WE ARE EACH OF US MORE A VICTIM OF OURSELVES THAN OF ANYONE ELSE and returned it quickly to the thought-wave mode.

He sucked in his breath sharply. The waves on his screen had risen high in intensity despite the fact that the device was still at low.

Morrison opened his mouth to comment on the fact, but Dezhnev made that unnecessary. "Yuri," he said, "the cell membrane is curving in and we're curving in with it."

That would account for it, thought Morrison. The cell was narrowing in toward the axon and the skeptic waves were being enormously concentrated. His device, having filtered out everything else, would radiate the wave function of the skeptic waves throughout the interior of the ship. And with what results?

Konev said with delight, "We'll see what happens now. Albert, keep your machine working at top intensity."

Boranova said, "I hope that whatever happens gives us our answer or at least a start to our answer. I have grown tired waiting."

"I don't blame you," said Dezhnev. "As my father used to say: 'The longer it takes to get to a point, the blunter it turns out to be.' "

It seemed to Morrison that every line of Konev's stiff body now betokened excitement and expectant triumph—but Morrison did not join in that expectation.

62.

MORRISON stared outward. They were well into the axon now and being carried along it by the fluid stream within the cell.

In the real world, the axon was an excessively thin fiber, but in the microminiaturized world of the ship, it might be the equivalent of a hundred kilometers across. As for its length, it was much, much longer than the cell itself. Going from one end to the other of the axon might very well be the equivalent of a trip from the Earth to the moon and back a couple of dozen times over. On the other hand, their apparent speed on the microminiaturized scale must seem, to themselves, to be a respectable fraction of the speed of light.

There was no indication of that incredibly rapid speed, however. The ship was moving with the current and there was far less in the way of macromolecules or organelles in the axon than there had been in the cell body. If there were structural fibers withstanding the current and remaining motionless with respect to the cell membrane, the current swept them past those too rapidly for them to be visible, even if a sizable number of photons were reflected from them—which, of course, they were not.

So he gave up. There was nothing to look at outside.

He ought, in any case, to be looking at his screen. The skeptic waves were becoming even more intense, he could see. It had grown difficult to wipe out the nonskeptic material. It was so strong that it flooded the computer's receiving capacity.

What's more, the tight, elaborate vibration of the skeptic waves had become a series of irregular spikes. Even at full expansion, it was clear he wasn't getting all the detail that existed. Morrison had a clear vision of the necessity of a laser printout clear enough to be placed under a microscope.

Konev had unclasped himself and had half lifted himself over the back of his seat so that he might stare at the screen.

He said, "I haven't seen it like that before."

Morrison replied, "Nor have I and I have been studying skeptic waves for nearly twenty years. *Nothing* like this."

"I was right, then, about the axon?"

"Absolutely, Yuri. The waves have concentrated themselves beautifully."

"And the meaning, then?"

Morrison spread out his hands helplessly. "There you have me. Since I have never seen anything like this, I obviously can't interpret it."

"No no," said Konev impatiently. "You keep concentrating on the screen and I keep thinking about induction. Our own minds are the true receptors—by way of your machine. What do *you* receive? Images? Words?"

"Nothing," said Morrison.

"That's impossible."

"Are you getting anything?"

"It's your machine. Adjusted to you."

"You've had images before, Yuri."

Dezhnev's voice broke in dryly, "My father used to say: 'If you want to hear, you must begin by listening.'"

Boranova said, "Dezhnev Senior is correct. We can receive nothing if we fill our minds with contention and shouts."

Konev drew a deep breath and said with a softness that was most uncharacteristic of him, "Very well, then, let us concentrate."

An unnatural quiet fell over the ship's crew.

Then Kaliinin said, breaking the silence rather timidly, "There is no time."

"No time for what, Sophia," said Boranova.

"I mean that's the phrase I sensed: 'There is no time.'"

Morrison said, "Are you saying that you received it from Shapirov's skeptic waves?"

"I don't know. Is that possible?"

Boranova said, "A moment before I had the same thought. It occurred to me that a better way of tackling the problem might be to study the recorded skeptic waves on the screen and to wait for sudden changes. It might be the change of pattern rather than the pattern itself that would produce an image. But then I thought that the waiting might be an enormously long-drawn-out affair and for that we lacked the time."

"In other words," said Morrison, "you thought, 'There is no time.'"

"Yes," said Boranova, "but it was my own thought."

"How can you know, Natalya?" said Morrison.

"I know my own thoughts."

"You also know your own dreams, but sometimes dreams arise out of external stimuli. Suppose you receive the thought 'There is no time.' Because you are not accustomed to receiving thoughts, you quickly build up a line of free association that makes it reasonable for you to feel that you have had the thought yourself."

"That may be so, but how does one tell, Albert?"

"I'm not sure, but Sophia apparently sensed the same phrase and we might ask if she were thinking something independently that would give rise to the phrase as a matter of course."

"No, I was not," said Kaliinin. "I was trying to keep my mind empty. It just came in."

"I didn't sense anything," said Morrison. "How about you, Yuri?"

Konev shook his head, frowning ferociously at his failure. "No, I didn't."

"In any case," said Morrison thoughtfully, "it needn't mean anything. Natalya felt it might be an idle thought that arose out of a series of previous thoughts in a natural way and with none but the most superficial meaning. Even if the thought had arisen in Shapirov's mind, it might be equally superficial there."

"Perhaps," said Konev, "but perhaps not. His whole life and mind were bound up in the problems of miniaturization. He would be thinking of nothing else."

"You keep saying that," said Morrison, "but, actually, that is romantic nonsense. No one thinks of nothing else. The most lovesick Romeo in history could not concentrate on his Juliet forever. A twinge of colic, a distant sound, and he would be distracted at once."

"Nevertheless, we must take anything Shapirov says as possibly significant."

"*Possibly,*" said Morrison. "But what if he were trying to work out the extension of the miniaturization theory and decided to moan he had no time, that there was insufficient time to complete his work?"

Konev shook his head, more, it seemed, to brush off distraction than in a clear negative. He said, "How about this? What if it seemed to Shapirov that any miniaturization that involved an increase in the speed of light proportional to the decrease in Planck's constant would involve a change that was instantaneous, that took no time. And, of course, as the speed of light increased vastly, so would the inevitable speed of a massless—or nearly massless—object. He would, in effect, abolish time and could say to himself proudly, 'There is no time.'"

Boranova said, "Very farfetched."

"Of course," said Konev, "but worth thinking about. We must record every impression we get, however dim, however apparently meaningless."

"I plan to do precisely that, Yuri," said Boranova.

Konev said, "Then quiet again. Let's see if we can get anything more."

Morrison concentrated fiercely, his eyes half-buried under jutting eyebrows, but those same eyes were fixed on Konev, who sighed and said in a whisper, "I get something over and over—'nu times c equals m sub s.'"

Morrison said, "I got that, too, but I thought it was 'm times c square.'"

"No," said Konev tightly. "Try again."

Morrison concentrated, then, quite abashed, said, "You're right. I get it, too: 'nu times c equals m sub s.' What does it mean?"

"Who can say at first glance? However, if this is in Shapirov's mind, it means something. We can assume that nu is radiational frequency, c the speed of light, and m sub s is the standard mass—that is, the mass at rest under ordinary conditions. In the light of—"

Boranova's arms lifted with an admonitory forefinger upraised. Konev stopped short and said uncomfortably, "But that is neither here nor there."

Morrison grinned. "Classified material, eh, Yuri?"

And then Dezhnev's voice sounded with an unaccustomed petulance to it. "How is it," he said, "that you are hearing all these things about time and standard mass and whatnot and I sense nothing? Is it that I am not a scientist?"

Morrison said, "I doubt that that has anything to do with it. Brains are different. Maybe they come in different types the way blood does. Blood is blood but you can't always transfuse one person's blood into another. Your brain may be sufficiently different from Shapirov's so that there is no sensory crossover."

"Only mine?"

"Not *only* yours. There may be billions of minds that can pick up nothing from Shapirov. You'll notice that Sophia and Natalya can pick up the same things, which Yuri and I cannot —and vice versa."

"Two men and two women," grumped Dezhnev, "and I am what?"

Konev said impatiently, "You are wasting our time, Arkady. Let's not endlessly discuss every tiny thing we pick up. We have more to hear and little time to do it in. If you concentrate a little harder, Arkady, you, too, may sense something."

Silence!

It was broken occasionally by a soft murmur from one or another who reported sensing an image or a scrap of words. Dezhnev contributed only one thing: "I sense a feeling of hunger, but it may be my own."

"Undoubtedly," said Boranova dryly. "Console yourself with the thought, Arkady, that when we get out of here, you will be allowed seconds and thirds of every dish and unlimited vodka."

Dezhnev grinned almost lasciviously at the thought.

Morrison said, "We don't seem to come across anything mathematical or even out of the ordinary. I insist that even Shapirov must have the great majority of his thoughts concerned with trivia."

"Nevertheless," grunted Konev under his breath, "we listen."

"For how long, Yuri?"

"Till the end of the axon. Right down to the end."

Morrison said, "Do you then intend to run into the synapses or will you double back?"

"We will go as close to the synapses as possible. That will bring us into the immediate neighborhood of the adjoining nerve cell and the skeptic waves may be even more easily sensed at that crucial point of transfer than anywhere else."

Dezhnev said, "Yes, Yuri, but you are not the captain. — Natasha, little flower, is that what you wish, too?"

Boranova said, "Why not? Yuri is right. The synapse is a unique spot and we know nothing about it."

"I ask only because half our power supply has now been consumed. How long dare we continue to remain within the body?"

"Long enough," said Boranova, "to reach the synapse, certainly."

And silence fell once more.

63.

THE ship continued to move along the enormous length of the axon and Konev dictated the actions of the others more and more.

"Whatever you get, report. It doesn't matter whether it makes sense or not, whether it's one word or a paragraph. If it's an image, describe it. Even if you think it's your own thought, report it if there's the slightest doubt."

"You'll have meaningless chatter," said Dezhnev, apparently still annoyed at his nonreceiving brain.

"Of course, but two or three meaningful hints will pay all. And we won't know what's meaningful until we examine everything."

Dezhnev said, "If I sense something I think isn't mine, do I throw it in, too?"

"You, especially," said Konev. "If you're as insensitive as you seem to think, anything you do get may be particularly important. Now, please, no more talk. Every second of conversation may mean we miss something."

And there began a period of disjointed phrases out of which, in Morrison's opinion, it was impossible to make sense.

One surprise came when Kaliinin said suddenly, " 'Nobel Prize!' "

Konev looked up sharply and almost responded—then, as though realizing who had said it, he subsided.

Morrison said, trying not to sound mocking, "Did you get that, too, Yuri?"

Konev nodded. "At almost the same time."

"That's the first crossover between a man and woman,"

said Morrison. "I suppose Shapirov had his mind on it in connection with his extension of miniaturization theory."

"Undoubtedly. But his Nobel Prize was sure for what he had already done in miniaturization."

"Which is classified and therefore unknown."

"Yes. But once we perfect the process, it will no longer be unknown."

"Let's hope so," said Morrison sardonically.

Konev snapped, "We are no more secretive than you Americans."

"All right. I'm not arguing," but Morrison grinned broadly at Konev, who was peering over his shoulder at him, and that seemed to irritate the younger man even further.

At one point, Dezhnev said, " 'Hawking.' "

Morrison's eyebrows lifted in surprise. He had not expected this.

Boranova said, looking displeased, "What is this, Arkady?"

"I said, 'Hawking,' " said Dezhnev defensively. Out of nowhere it popped into my mind. You told me to tell you anything that did."

"It is an English word," said Boranova, "that means 'spitting.' "

"Or 'selling,' " said Morrison cheerfully.

Dezhnev said, "I don't know enough English to know that word. I thought it was someone's name."

"So it was," said Konev uncomfortably. "Stephen Hawking. He was a great English theoretical physicist of over a century ago. I was thinking of him, too, but I thought it was my own thought."

Morrison said, "Good, Arkady. That might be useful."

Dezhnev's face split with a grin. "I'm not altogether useless, then. As my father used to say: 'If the words of a wise man are few, they are nevertheless worth listening to.' "

An interminable half hour later, Morrison said gently, "Are we getting anywhere at all? It seems to me that most of the phrases and images tell us nothing. 'Nobel Prize' tells us, reasonably enough, that Shapirov thought of winning one, but we know that. 'Hawking' tells us that that physicist's work was significant, perhaps, in connection with the extension of miniaturization, but it doesn't tell us why."

It was not Konev who rose to the defense, as Morrison

would have expected, but Boranova. Konev, who might have been readying himself for a response, seemed willing, on this occasion, to let the captain bear the weight.

Boranova said, "We are dealing with an enormous cryptogram, Albert. Shapirov is a man in a coma and his brain is not thinking in a disciplined or orderly fashion. It is sparking wildly, those parts of it that remain whole, perhaps randomly. We collect everything without distinction and it will all be studied by those of us with a deep understanding of miniaturization theory. They may see meaning where you see none. And a bit of meaning, in one corner of the field, may be the start of an illumination that will spread to all parts of it. What we are doing makes sense and it is the proper thing to do."

Konev then said, "Besides, Albert, there is something else we can try. We are approaching a synapse. This axon will end eventually and split up into many fibers, each of which will approach but not join with the dendrite of a neighboring neuron."

"I know that," said Morrison impatiently.

"The nerve impulse, including the skeptic waves, will have to jump the tiny gap of the synapse and, in doing so, the dominant thoughts will be less attenuated than the others. In short, if *we* jump the synapse, too, we will reach a region where we may, for a while at least, detect what we want to hear with less interference from trivial noise."

"Really?" asked Morrison archly. "This notion of differential attenuation is new to me."

"It's the result of painstaking Soviet work in the area."

"Ah!"

Konev fired up at once, "What do you mean, 'Ah!'? Is that a dismissal of the value of the work?"

"No no."

"Of course it is. If it's Soviet work, it means nothing."

"I just mean that I haven't read or heard anything about it," Morrison said in defense.

"The work was done by Madame Nastiaspenskaya. I presume you've heard of her."

"Yes, I have."

"But you don't read her papers, is that it?"

"Yuri, I can't keep up with the English-language literature, let alone with—"

"Well, when this is over, I'll see that you get a collection of her papers and you may educate yourself."

"Thank you, but may I say that on the face of it I think the finding is an unlikely one. If some types of mental activity survive a synapse better than others, then, considering that there are many hundreds of billions of synapses in the brain, all constantly in use, the final result would be that only a tiny proportion of thoughts would survive at all."

"It's not as simple as that," said Konev. "The trivial thoughts are not wiped out. They continue at a lower level of intensity and don't decline indefinitely. It's just that, in the immediate neighborhood of a synapse, the important thoughts are, for a time, relatively strengthened."

"Is there evidence for this? Or is it only a suggestion?"

"There's evidence of a subtle nature. Eventually, with miniaturization experiments, that evidence will be hardened, I'm sure. There are some people among whom this synapse effect is much stronger than average. Why else can creative individuals concentrate so hard and so long, if they are not less distracted by trivia? And why, on the contrary, are brilliant scholars traditionally absentminded?"

"Very well. If we find something, I won't quarrel with the rationale."

Dezhnev said, "But what happens when we come to the end of the axon? The stream of fluid we're riding will just make a U-turn at that point and carry us back again against the opposite wall of the axon. Do I force my way through the membrane?"

"No," said Konev. "Of course not. We'd damage the cell. We'll have to take on the electric charge pattern of acetylcholine. That carries the nerve impulse pattern across the synapse."

Boranova said, "Sophia, you can give the ship an acetylcholine pattern, can't you?"

"I can," said Kaliinin, "but aren't the acetylcholine molecules active on the outside of the cell?"

"Nevertheless, the cell may have a mechanism for ejecting them. We'll try."

And the trip along the seemingly endless axon continued.

64.

SUDDENLY the end of the axon was in sight. There was no hint, no warning.

Konev noticed it first. He was watching and he knew what he was watching for, but Morrison gave him full credit. He himself was watching, too, and knew what he was watching for, and yet did not see it when it came.

To be sure, Konev was in the front seat, while Morrison had to stare past Konev's head. That was not much of an excuse either.

In the curiously ineffective light of the ship's beacon, it was clear that there was a hollow ahead and yet the current was beginning to veer away from it.

The axon was beginning to break off into branches, into dendrites like those at the other end of the neuron, at the end where the nucleated cell body was. The axonian dendrites at the far end of the cell were fewer and thinner, but they were there. Undoubtedly, a portion of the cellular stream flowed into it, but the ship was in the main stream that curved away and they could take no chances.

They would have to push into the first dendrite encountered—if it could be done.

"There, Arkady, there," cried Konev, pointing, and it was only then that all the rest realized they were reaching the end of the axon. "Use your motors, Arkady, and push over."

Morrison could make out the soft throbbing of the motors as they edged the ship toward the side of the stream. The dendrite toward which they aimed was a tube that was slipping sideways, a huge tube at their size scale, so huge they could only see a small arc of its circumference.

They continued to edge closer to it and Morrison found himself leaning toward the dendrite, as though adding body English could improve matters.

But it was not a matter of reaching the tube itself, merely moving over an eddying section of fluid, a rushing of water molecules that quieted into gentle circles and then slipped beyond into another stream that was curving off in another direction.

The ship made the transition and was suddenly plunging forward into the tube opening.

"Turn off the motors," said Konev excitedly.

"Not yet," grumbled Dezhnev. "We may be too near the countercurrent emerging from this thing. Let me slip over a bit closer to the wall."

He did so, but that did not take long. They were now essentially moving with the current, not against it. And when Dezhnev did finally shut off the engine and pushed back his damp, graying hair, he heaved a great breath and said, "Everything we do consumes a ton of energy. There's a limit, Yuri, there's a limit."

"We'll worry about that later," said Konev impatiently.

"Will we?" said Dezhnev. "My father always said: 'Later is usually too late.' —Natalya, don't leave all this to Yuri. I don't trust his attitude toward our energy supply."

"Calm yourself, Arkady. I will take care to override Yuri if it becomes necessary. —Yuri, the dendrite is not very long, is it?"

"We will come to the ending in short order, Natalya."

"In that case, Sophia, please see to it that we are ready to adopt the acetylcholine pattern at a moment's notice."

"You'll give me the signal, then?" said Kaliinin.

"I will not have to, Sophia. I'm sure that Yuri will whoop like a Cossack when the end is in sight. Shift the pattern to acetylcholine at that moment."

They continued sliding along the final tubular remnant of the neuron they had entered a considerable time before. It seemed to Morrison that, as the dendrite continued to narrow, he could see the wall arc above him, but that was illusion. Common sense told him that even at its narrowest, the tube would appear to be a few kilometers across at their present molecular size.

And, as Boranova had foreseen, Konev lifted his voice in a great cry, probably quite unaware that he was doing so. "The end is ahead. Quick. Acetylcholine before we're swept around and back."

Kaliinin's fingers flickered over the keyboard. There was no indication from inside the ship that anything about it had changed, but somewhere up ahead was an acetylcholine receptor—or, more likely, hundreds of them—and the patterns meshed, positive to negative and negative to positive, so that the attraction between ship and receptor was sharp and great.

They were pulled out of the stream and melted into and through the wall of the dendrite. For a few minutes they continued to be pulled through the intercellular medium between the dendrite of the neuron they had just left and the dendrite of the neighbor neuron.

Morrison saw almost nothing. The ship, he felt, was sliding along—or through—a complex protein molecule and then he noticed the formation of a concavity, as when the ship had first entered the first neuron.

Konev had unclasped himself so that he could stand up. (Quite obviously, he was too excited to feel this was something he could do sitting down.)

He said, almost stuttering, "Now, according to the Nastiaspenskaya hypothesis, the filtering out of the important thoughts is most evident immediately after the synapse. Once the cell body is approached, the difference fades. So once we are in the neighboring dendrite, open your minds. Be ready for anything. Say whatever you hear out loud. Describe any images. I'll record everything. You, too, Arkady. Albert, you, too. —We're in now. Begin!"

CHAPTER 15

ALONE!

*Good company robs even death
of some of its terrors.*
—*Dezhnev Senior*

65.

MORRISON watched what followed with a certain detachment. He did not intend to participate actively. If something forced itself into his mind, he would respond and report it. It would be unscientific not to.

Kaliinin, at his left, looked grim and her fingers were idle. He leaned toward her and whispered, "Have you got us back as L-glucose?"

She nodded.

He said, "Are you aware of this Nastiaspenskaya hypothesis?"

She said, "It's not in my field. I've never heard of it."

"Do you believe it?"

But Kaliinin was not to be trapped. She said, "I'm not qualified either to believe or disbelieve, but *he* believes it. —Because he wants to."

"Do you sense anything?"

"Nothing more than before."

Dezhnev was, of course, silent. Boranova occasionally produced a crisp word or two, which, however, seemed to Morrison's ears to lack conviction.

Only Konev seemed to maintain enthusiasm. At one point, he cried out, "Did anyone get that? Anyone? 'Circular rhythm.' 'Circular rhythm.'"

There was no direct answer and, after a while, Morrison said, "What does that mean, Yuri?"

Konev did not answer. —And even he grew quiet after a while and was reduced to staring blankly ahead as the ship moved onward in the fluid stream.

Boranova asked, "Well, Yuri?"

Konev said rather hoarsely, "I do *not* understand it."

Dezhnev said, "Yuri, little son, it may be this is a bad neuron and isn't doing much thinking. We'll have to try another and maybe another. The first one may have been simply beginner's luck."

Konev looked at him angrily. "We don't work with single cells. We're in a group of cells—a million of them or more—that are a center of creative thought by Albert's theory. What one of them thinks, they all think—with minor variations."

Morrison said, "That's what I believe I have shown."

Dezhnev said, "Then we don't go looking from cell to cell?"

"It would be no use," said Morrison.

"Good," said Dezhnev heavily, "because we don't have the time and we don't have the energy. So what do we do now?"

In the silence that followed, Konev said again, "I do *not* understand it. Nastiaspenskaya could *not* be wrong."

And now Kaliinin, with great deliberation, unclasped herself and stood up.

She said, "I want to say something and I don't want to be interrupted. Natalya, listen to me. We have gone far enough. This is an experiment that perhaps had to be done, even though, in my opinion, it was sure to fail. Well, it *has* failed."

She pointed a slim finger briefly at Konev, without looking at him. "Some people want to alter the Universe to their liking. Whatever is not so, they would *make* so by sheer force of will—except that the Universe is beyond any person's will, squeeze he ever so hard.

"I don't know if Nastiaspenskaya is correct or not. I don't know if Albert's theories are correct or not. But this I know

—what they think, and what any neuroscientist thinks about the brain generally, must be about a reasonably normal brain. Academician Shapirov's brain is not reasonably normal. Twenty percent of it is nonfunctioning—dead. The rest must be distorted in consequence and the fact that he has been in a coma for weeks shows that.

"Any reasonable human being would realize that Shapirov cannot be thinking in normal fashion. His brain is an army in —in disarray. It is a factory in which all the equipment has been jarred loose. It is sparking randomly, emitting broken thoughts, scattered pieces, splinters of memory. Some men" —she pointed again—"won't admit it because they believe that if they only insist loudly enough and strongly enough, the obvious will retreat and the impossible will somehow come into being."

Konev had now also unclasped and was also standing. He turned slowly and looked at Kaliinin. (Morrison was astonished. Konev was actually looking at her. And on his face there was no visible sign of anger or hatred or contempt. It was a hangdog look, with a touch of self-contempt in it. Morrison felt sure of this.)

Yet Konev's voice was steady and hard as he looked away from Kaliinin and turned to Boranova, addressing her.

"Natalya, was this point made before we embarked on this voyage?"

"If you mean, Yuri, did Sophia say all this to me before this moment?—She did not."

"Is there any reason we should be plagued with crew members who have no faith in our work? Why should such a person have agreed to come on this voyage?"

"Because I am a scientist," shot back Kaliinin and she, too, addressed Boranova. "Because I wanted to test the effect of artificial electrical patterns on biochemical interaction. That has been done, so that for *me* the voyage was a success, and for Arkady, since the ship has handled as it should, and for Albert, since the evidence for his theories is stronger now, I gather, than it was before we came here, and for you, Natalya, since you brought us down here and, presumably, will bring us back safely again. But for one"—pointing at Konev—"it has been a failure and the mental stability of he who has failed would be greatly helped by the frank admission of that failure."

(She's getting back at him with a vengeance, thought Morrison.)

But Konev did not crumple under Kaliinin's forceful attack. He remained surprisingly calm and he said, still to Boranova, "That is not so. That is the reverse of what is true. It was clear from the start that we could not expect Shapirov to think as he did when he was in full health. It was entirely likely we would get bits and pieces of meaning intermingled with meaninglessness and trivialities. That we did. I was hoping to get a higher percentage of meaning in this new neuron immediately past the synapse. There we failed. That makes the task before us more difficult, but not impossible.

"We've got well over a hundred phrases and images we've salvaged from Shapirov's thinking. Don't forget *'nu* times *c* equals *m* sub *s,'* which must be significant. There's no possible reason to think of that simply as a triviality."

Boranova said, "Have you thought, Yuri, that it is possible that that fragment of a mathematical expression represents something Shapirov tried and found wanting?"

"I have thought of it, but why should it stick in his mind, in that case? It is certainly worth investigating. And how much of what seems to be trivial or meaningless would not be so if even one phrase or image gave us a necessary hint. With each step forward, other things might more easily fall into place. We certainly have no reason *as yet* to declare this voyage a failure—or any part in it."

Boranova nodded slightly. "Well, let's hope you're right, Yuri, but, as Arkady has already asked, what do we do now? What, in your opinion, ought we to do now?"

With great deliberation, Konev said, "There's one thing we haven't tried yet. We've tried detection outside the neuron, inside the neuron, inside the axon, inside the dendrites, past the synapse, but, in every single case, we have tried it inside the ship, inside its presumably insulating walls."

"In that case, then," said Boranova, "are you suggesting that we make the attempt outside the ship and within the cell fluid itself? Remember, such an observer would still be inside a plastic suit."

"A plastic suit is not as thick as a plastic ship and the insulating effect would presumably be less. Besides, the computer itself need not be inside the suit."

Morrison said with gathering alarm, "Who do you have in mind for this?"

Konev looked at him coolly. "There is only one possibility, Albert. The computer is your design and is made to match your brain. You are, of necessity, the most sensitive to Shapirov's thoughts. It would be foolish in the highest degree to send out anyone else. I have *you* in mind for this, Albert."

66.

MORRISON'S stomach clenched tightly. Not that! He couldn't be asked to do it again!

He tried to say so, but his mouth seemed to have dried completely and instantaneously and he could make no sound other than a throaty hiss. It flashed through his mind that he had been beginning to enjoy the feeling of not being a coward, of wandering, by ship, through the brain cell fearlessly— but he was a coward, after all.

"Not that!" he cried out, but it wasn't his voice; it was higher by an octave. It was Kaliinin.

She had turned around to face Boranova, holding herself down in her seat with knuckles standing out whitely.

"Not that, Natalya," she cried again passionately, her chest heaving in excitement. "It's a cowardly suggestion. Poor Albert has been out there once already. He nearly died and if it hadn't been for him we might still be lost in the wrong capillary and we might never have reached this cell block at all. Why should he have to do that again? It is surely someone else's turn and since *he* wants it done"—no one questioned who "he" was—"let *him* do it. He should not ask it of someone else."

Morrison, beneath his own fright, wondered faintly if Kaliinin's emotion was due to a growing affection for him or a determination to oppose at every point any strong wish of Konev's. There was a corner of Morrison's mind that was pragmatic enough to be certain it was the latter.

Konev's face had grown slowly redder as Sophia spoke. He said, "There's no *cowardice* here." (He spat out the word, making it quite plain that that was what had most offended him.) "I am making the only possible suggestion. If I go out there, which I am perfectly willing to do, it can only be with Albert's device, which won't work as well for me as it would for him. We cannot choose this one or that one according to whim. It must be the one who can get the best results and there is no question, in that case, who it must be."

"True," said Morrison, finding his voice now, "but there is no reason to suppose that reception will be better outside the ship than inside."

Konev said, "There is no reason to think the reverse, either. And as Dezhnev will tell you, our energy supply—and therefore our time—is decreasing. There is no room for delay. You'll have to leave the ship as you did before—and now."

Morrison said in a low voice, which he hoped would make the remark final, "I'm sorry. I will not leave the ship."

But Boranova had apparently made up her mind. "I'm afraid you'll have to, Albert," she said gently.

"No."

"Yuri is right. Only you and your device can give us the information we need."

"I am certain there'll be no information."

Boranova held out her two hands, palms upward. "Perhaps not, but we can't leave that a matter of conjecture. Let us find out."

"But—"

Boranova said, "Albert, I promise you that if you do this one thing for us, your part in all this will be reported honestly when the time comes for open publication. You will be known as the man who worked out the correct theory of thought, the man who developed the device that could exploit that theory properly, the man who saved the ship in the capillary, and the man who detected Shapirov's thinking by bravely venturing into the neuron, as earlier he had ventured into the bloodstream."

"Are you implying that the truth will not be told if I refuse?"

Boranova sighed. "You force me to play the role of villainess openly. I would rather you had been satisfied with the implication. —Yes, the truth need not be told. That, after all, is the only weapon I hold against you. We cannot very well turn you out of the ship by force, since there is no advantage in your merely being outside. You must also sense poor

Shapirov's thought and for that we must have your willing cooperation. We will reward you for that, but only for that."

Morrison looked around at his crewmates' faces, searching for help. Boranova—steadily studying him. Konev—staring him down imperiously. Dezhnev—looking awkward, not willing to commit himself either way. And Kaliinin . . . his only hope.

Morrison gazed at her thoughtfully and said, "What do you think, Sophia?"

Kaliinin hesitated, then said in a voice that did not tremble, "I think it is wrong to threaten you in this way. A task like this should be performed voluntarily and not under duress."

Dezhnev, who had been humming very softly to himself, now said, "My old father used to say: 'There is no duress like one's own conscience and it is that which makes life so needlessly bitter.'"

"My conscience doesn't trouble me in this matter," said Morrison. "Shall we put it to a vote?"

"It wouldn't matter," said Boranova. "I am the captain and in a case like this I alone have the vote."

"If I am out there and sense nothing, would you believe me?"

Boranova nodded. "I would. After all, you might so easily invent something that would sound useful if you wished us to be suitably grateful. If you come back with nothing or with trivia, I believe I would have a greater tendency to believe that than if you instantly claimed you had heard something of great importance."

Konev said, "I am not likely to be fooled. If he comes in with something that seems important, I will be able to tell if it truly is. And now, surely, we have had enough discussion. Let's go!"

And Morrison, his heart beating and his throat tightening, managed to say, "Very well, I will go—but only for a brief time."

67.

MORRISON, of his own accord, stripped himself of his cotton garment. The first time (was it really only a couple of hours before?) it had seemed to be a violation of modesty; this second time it was almost routine.

He was quite aware, as with Kaliinin's help he struggled into the suit, how easily he could suck in his abdomen. Despite a good breakfast, ample water, and a piece of chocolate, his stomach was empty and he was glad it was. He felt a twinge of nausea as the suit enclosed more and more of his body and to throw up, once enclosed, would have been unbearable. Just before enclosure, he refused another piece of chocolate with what was almost a shudder.

They put his computer into his sheathed hands and Boranova said to him loudly, "Can you work it?"

Morrison heard her without too much difficulty. He knew he wouldn't hear her once he was outside the ship. He balanced the essentially weightless computer in one hand and struck the keys carefully and rather gracelessly with the other. He shouted back, "I think I can manage."

Then, rather clumsily, they tied the computer to both his wrists with firm knots of tough plastic twine (probably the same material of which the suit and the ship itself were made).

"So you don't lose it," Boranova called out.

Out into the air lock he went. He felt himself embraced by it, then pressured as the air in it was withdrawn, and then he was outside the ship.

Outside again. For only a brief time, he had warned the rest, but what good was that? How could he enforce that, if the others within the ship refused to let him back in? Already, he was sorry he had let himself be talked out of the ship by *any* threat, but dared not articulate the thought. It would do him no good.

Morrison tucked the computer under his left arm, partly because he did not entirely trust the plastic twine that secured it and partly because he wanted to protect it from the cellular contents as much as possible. He felt the surface of the ship for some spot where the electric charge on his suit would adhere to a charge of opposite nature on the ship's hull.

Morrison found one that allowed him to keep his back on the ship. The electric field did not hold him tightly and there was considerable give. Still, he was the size of an atom and it might be difficult to concentrate electric charge on a portion of him.

Or would it be? Wouldn't the electrons that were the source of the charge be microminiaturized as well? He felt—and resented keenly—his ignorance of miniaturization theory.

He was little aware of his motion along the intracellular stream, for everything was moving along with him. He found himself, however, the center of a shifting and ever-changing panorama. With the thinner plastic of the suit between himself and the scene, with the beacon of his own suit turning here and there as he moved his head and felt the headpiece twist (a little resistantly) with it, he could make out more.

There was the knobbiness of the water molecules rubbing against each other, like dimly seen balloons. He could see them brush past him slowly, this way or that, and largely ignore him. Occasionally, one would cling for a moment, an electric charge meeting an opposite charge on his suit, so that they clutched at him and released their hold only lingeringly. It was almost as though a molecule occasionally yearned for him but couldn't manage to turn the wish into deed.

Among these were larger molecules, some as large as the ship, some far larger still. He could see them only because light glinted off them here and there in changing, prismatic fashion. He did not *see* them; his mind built them up out of what he could glimpse. That he could do this at all was the result of his knowing a good deal about the contents of the cell to begin with, or thought he did. It might also, he thought, simply be his imagination.

It even seemed to Morrison that he could make out the skeleton of the cellular interior; the large structures that remained in place while the fluid stream passed them and that gave the cell its more or less fixed shape. These structures seemed to go by so quickly he could barely take note of them before they were gone. They alone gave him the impression of the rapid movement of the intercellular stream that carried the ship and him along with it as it weaved in gentle swoops around those fixed structures.

All this observation had not taken very long, but it was enough. It was time that he now turned his attention to his computer.

Why? It would detect nothing. Morrison was sure of it, but

he couldn't act on that belief, however strongly he felt it. He might be wrong, perhaps, and he owed it to the others—and to himself, too—to make the effort.

He tried clumsily to adjust the computer to maximum sensitivity, barely able to handle the keys correctly and relieved that the self-contained power pack in the computer worked properly. He concentrated hard in order to sense and tap the currents of thought passing by.

The device did its work. The water molecules drifted by it as gently and untouchingly as they drifted by him and, disregarding them, his computer portrayed the skeptic waves more purely etched, more steep and clear, more finely detailed, than he had ever before seen them. But for all that, he sensed nothing but a faint hissing whisper that produced neither words nor images but only sadness.

Wait! How did he know the whisper was sad? Surely that was merely a subjective judgment on his part. Or was he detecting an emotion? Was the partially brain-dead, totally comatose Shapirov sad? Would it be surprising if he were?

Morrison looked over his shoulder, back at the ship. Surely what he was detecting was enough. He was registering sad nothingness and nothing more. Should he signal now to be pulled in? Would they be willing to do so? And if they brought him in and if he told Boranova that he had sensed nothing, would not Konev tell him angrily that he had been out there only two minutes, that he hadn't given it a chance? Would Konev not demand he go out again?

And if he waited longer?

Actually, he *could* wait longer. At this stage of miniaturization (or for whatever cause), he did not feel any particular heat.

But if he waited longer—another two minutes, or five minutes, or an hour, for that matter—Konev would still say, "Not enough."

He could make out Konev looking out toward him, his expression dark and glowering. Kaliinin was directly behind him, since she had unclasped herself and moved over into what had been Morrison's seat. She was staring outward anxiously.

He caught her eyes and she seemed about to signal to him, but Boranova leaned forward and pushed her shoulder firmly. Kaliinin moved back to her own seat at once. (She had to, Morrison told himself, for her job was to keep an eye on the charge patterns of the ship and of himself right now and she could not—must not—abandon that job, no matter what her anxiety over him.)

For the sake of completeness, Morrison tried to catch Dezhnev's eye, but the angle required was too great for the twisting ability of his headpiece. He caught, instead, Konev motioning in what seemed, clearly, an interrogative gesture.

Morrison looked away petulantly, making no attempt to give information, and became aware of something in the distance looming toward him at a great speed. He could make out no details, but he automatically winced as he waited for the current to carry the ship and himself around it.

It came straight on like a juggernaut and Morrison cowered toward the hull of the ship.

The ship did evade the object, but not by much and as the looming monster passed him Morrison felt himself drawn outward and toward it.

It flashed through his mind that Kaliinin had put some random electric charge on his suit and that whatever it was he was passing, by the most miserable of coincidences, had a charge that exactly complemented his own.

Under normal circumstance, that would not have mattered. The ship and the structure passed each other at such a speed that no attraction could have sufficed to rip him loose, but he was a tiny object with neither mass nor inertia and, for a moment, he felt—stretched—as though the structure and the ship disputed ownership. The ship, it seemed to his appalled eyes, briefly faltered and then was pushed loose by the current.

Morrison had been peeled off by the object and the ship, still continuing with the current, moved off so rapidly that it was lost to sight at once. One second it was with him, the next second it was totally gone.

Before he had time to realize what had happened, he was alone and helpless—an atom-sized object in a brain cell. His only faint attachment to life and reality—the ship—was forever gone.

68.

SOME minutes must have been lost to Morrison. During that time, he had no conception of where he was or of what had happened. He was conscious only of absolute panic, of the conviction that he was on the point of death.

When life continued, Morrison was almost sorry. If that moment had been death, it would have been all over. Now he still had to wait for it.

How long would his air last? Would heat and humidity crawl on, even if more slowly than before, inexorably, just the same, perhaps. Would his light give out before he did and would he have to die in utter darkness as well as utterly alone? He thought, quite madly, How will I know when I'm dead if it's absolutely dark before and absolutely dark thereafter? (He thought of Ajax' prayer to Zeus that if he had to meet death, let it be in the light of day. And, with this Morrison thought hopelessly, And with one person, at least, to hold one's hand.)

What to do, then?

Just wait?

What had gone wrong, anyway?

Ah, he was not yet dead. The fear had receded enough to allow room for a little curiosity—and a will to fight and *live*.

Could he somehow get loose from this thing? It seemed disgraceful, somehow, to die like a fly stuck in amber. —And every moment the ship was getting farther away. Almost at once he thought, It's already too far away for me to be caught, no matter what I do.

The thought drove him to frenzy and Morrison writhed with all his might, trying to break loose. It did no good and it occurred to him that he was wasting energy and increasing the heat within the suit.

He slid his hands upward along the misty structure that held him, but his hands bounced away. Like charges repel each other.

He reached along it—right, left, up, down. Somewhere there was the opposite charge. He might be able to seize hold then and try to tear the structure apart. (Why were his teeth chattering? Fright? Desperation? Both?)

His right hand clicked shut as it was attracted to a portion of the structure. He clenched hard, trying to push past the mere charge and tear at the atomic arrangement itself—if there *was* any atomic arrangement that had meaning aside from the charge itself.

For a moment, Morrison felt the structure resist a too-tight grip with a kind of rubbery rebound. And then, without warning, it crumbled in his hand. He stared in amazement at his hand, trying to make out what had happened. There was no tearing, ripping, or wrenching sensation. It seemed to him that a portion of the structure had simply disappeared.

Morrison tried again, groping here and there, until another portion vanished. What was happening?

Wait awhile! The miniaturization field extended beyond the ship slightly, Boranova had said. It would extend beyond the suit, too. When he squeezed as hard as he might, some of the atom he was touching would miniaturize and, in so doing, it would lose its normal architecture and break loose from the atoms to which it had formerly been bonded. Anything he touched—if he could touch it hard enough—would miniaturize.

Any atom or portion thereof that he miniaturized in this way would become a point-sized particle with far less mass than an electron. It would take off at nearly the speed of light, pass through matter as though that matter weren't there, and be gone.

Could this be so? It *had* to be so. Nothing else he could imagine would make sense.

And even as he thought this, Morrison began to push his hands and feet violently against the imprisoning material—and broke loose.

He was no longer glued to the structure. He was an independent body coursing along the intercellular stream.

It didn't stop the ship from being forever out of reach, but he was at least on its trail. (Foolish! Foolish! What good was it to be on its trail? On his own scale, he was dozens of kilometers from the ship—if not scores.)

Another thought struck him and staggered him. He had been miniaturizing atoms to get free, but such miniaturization required an input of energy. Not much at this stage, since there was so little mass to remove, but where would the energy come from?

It had to come from the suit's own miniaturization field. Every atom that miniaturized weakened the field, therefore. How much had he weakened it, then, by getting loose?

And was that why he wasn't feeling the heat? Had the miniaturization of his surroundings soaked up some of the heat as well as of the energy of the miniaturization field? No, that couldn't be so, for he hadn't felt much in the way of heat even before he began breaking loose.

Yet another thought struck him, making his position more desperate still. If he had broken loose from the structure at the expense of the energy of his field—if his field had been weakened—then he would have deminiaturized slightly. Was that the reason for spontaneous deminiaturization?

Boranova had talked of the possibility of such spontaneous deminiaturization. The possibility of that increased, the smaller the miniaturized object was. —And he was now small.

As long as he had been on the ship, he had been part of the overall miniaturization field of the ship. He was part of a molecule-sized object. While he was part of the cytoskeleton of the cell, he was part of an even larger object. But now he was alone, separate, part of nothing beyond himself. He was an atom-sized object.

He was much more likely, now, to deminiaturize spontaneously, except that it wouldn't be spontaneous—it would be the weakening of the field by the miniaturization of surrounding normal objects.

How could he tell if he were deminiaturizing? If he were, the process would proceed at an exponential rate. He would be deminiaturizing slowly at first, but as he grew larger he would affect a larger volume of surrounding material and he would grow larger at a faster rate, then still faster, and finally it would be an explosion and he would die.

But what did it matter if he were deminiaturizing? If he were, then, in a brief time—seconds merely, at most—he would be dead and it would happen too quickly to make any impression upon him. One moment he would be alive and the next moment there would be nothingness.

How could he ask for a better death? Why should he want to know a second earlier that it was going to happen?

Because he was alive and he was human—and wanting to know was what made an object alive and human.

How could he tell?

Morrison stared at the dim glinting around him, at the moving swell of the water molecules, turning and shifting around him in a kind of slow motion as both he and they moved along the intercellular stream.

If he were increasing in size, they should seem to be decreasing, and vice versa.

Morrison stared. They *were* decreasing in size, getting smaller. Was this death? Or his imagination?

Wait, were the water molecules *increasing* in size? Swelling? Getting larger? Ballooning? If so, it must follow that he was getting smaller.

Would he shrink to the size of a subsubatomic particle? A subelectron? Would he go streaking off at the speed of light and explode when he was halfway to the moon, dying in a vacuum before he had time to know he was in a vacuum?

No, the molecules were shrinking, not expanding—

Morrison closed his eyes and took a deep breath. He was going mad. Or was he beginning to experience brain damage?

Better to die, then. Better death altogether than a dead brain and living body.

Or were the water molecules pulsating? Why should they pulsate?

Think, Morrison, think. You're a scientist. Find an explanation. Why should they pulsate?

He knew why the field might weaken—its tendency to miniaturize the surroundings. Why should it strengthen?

It would have to gain energy to strengthen. From where?

What about the surrounding molecules? They had more random heat energy per volume than he had because they were at a higher temperature. Ordinarily, heat should flow from the surroundings into his suit until his suit and he himself would be at blood temperature and he would die of his own inability to rid himself of the heat he had accumulated, as he almost had on his earlier venture outside the ship.

But there was not only the heat energy intensity of his body; there was also the energy of the miniaturization field. And, as he was struck randomly by the water molecules, energy need not flow into him in the form of heat, but in the form of miniaturization activation. The field would grow more intense and he would shrink.

This must be true at all times when a miniaturized object was surrounded by normal objects of higher temperature. The energy might flow from the surroundings to the miniaturized object either as heat or as field intensity. And it must be that the smaller the object, the more intensely miniaturized, the more it was the field that gained the energy and not the object itself.

Probably the ship, too, was pulsating, growing larger and smaller constantly, but to an extent not great enough to notice. Still, that was why the Brownian motion hadn't increased as far as it might have and that was why the air-conditioning could perform its function with less strain. The miniaturization field formed a cushion in both cases.

But he—Morrison, alone in the cell—was much smaller, possessing less mass, and for him the energy inflow went far more into miniaturization than heat.

Morrison's fists clenched helplessly. He let go of the computer and didn't care. Undoubtedly, the others, Boranova and Konev certainly, knew of this and might have explained it to him. Once again they let him go into danger without warning him.

And now that he had worked it out for himself—what good did it do him?

He opened his eyes suddenly.

Yes, there were pulsations. Now that he knew what to expect, he saw them. The water molecules were expanding and contracting in an irregular rhythm as they gave up energy to the field and then extracted energy from it.

Morrison watched it with a stupefied swaying rhythm and he found himself muttering soundlessly: "Larger, smaller, larger, smaller, larger, smaller."

It could only get so large, he thought. The expansion mirrored his own contraction and there was only so much energy to be pushed into him to power that contraction. The cellular contents had a temperature only so high. On the other hand, they could take large quantities of energy from him, and once they took enough, what was left would go more and more quickly, and he would explode.

Therefore, when the water molecules expanded in size (and he himself was growing smaller) he was safe. He would not grow very small. When the water molecules contracted in size, however (and he himself was growing larger), he was not safe. If the water molecules continued to contract until they were too small to see that meant he would be expanding toward instantaneous explosion.

"Larger, smaller—smaller—*stop contracting!*"

Morrison let his breath go, for the molecules were expanding again.

Over and over! Each time—would the contraction stop?

It seemed to be playing with him and it didn't matter anyway. No matter if it brought him to the brink of destruction, then snatched him away, and if it did it a million times over, it wouldn't matter. Sooner or later, his air would be gone and he would die a slow, suffocating death.

Better a quick death, surely.

69.

KALIININ was screaming. She was the first to realize what had happened and she choked on her words.

"He's gone! He's gone!" she shrieked.

Boranova was unable to stop herself from asking the obvious question. "Who's gone?"

Kaliinin turned wide eyes on her and said, "Who's gone? How can you ask who's gone? *Albert* is gone."

Boranova stared blankly out at the spot where Morrison had been and now wasn't. "What happened?"

Dezhnev muttered hoarsely, "I'm not sure. We cut a corner closely. Albert, attached to the outside of the ship, introduced an asymmetry, perhaps. I tried to steer the ship away from—from whatever it was, but it didn't respond properly."

"A fixed macromolecular organelle," said Konev, who looked up now after having buried his face in his hands, "scraped him off. We've got to get back to him. He may have the information we need."

Boranova by now clearly understood the situation. She unclasped herself with a quick movement and stood up. "Information?" she said tightly. "Is that what you feel the loss of, Yuri? Information? Do you know what's going to happen now? Albert's miniaturization field is isolated and he's only atom-sized. The chance of his undergoing spontaneous deminiaturization is at least fifty times ours. Given enough time, the chance will become too good. Information or not, we must get him. If he deminiaturizes, he will kill Shapirov and he will kill us."

Konev said, "We're just arguing motivation. We both want him back. The reasons why are secondary."

"We should never have sent him out," said Kaliinin. "I knew it was wrong to do so."

"It is done," said Boranova gruffly, "and we must proceed from that point. Arkady!"

"I'm trying," said Dezhnev. "Don't teach a drunkard to hiccup."

"I'm not trying to teach you anything, old fool. I'm ordering you. Turn around. Back! Back!"

"No," said Dezhnev. "Let this old fool tell you that's ridiculous. Do you want me to make a U-turn and buck the current? You want me to try to force my way upstream?"

Boranova said, "If you just stand still, the stream will bring him to us."

"He is adhering to something. He will not be brought to us," said Dezhnev. "What we must do is turn to the other side of the dendrite and let the return stream carry us back."

Boranova put both hands to her head and said, "I apologize for calling you an old fool, Arkady, but if we go back by the counterstream we'll miss him."

"We have no choice," said Dezhnev. "We lack the energy to try to make our way against the stream we're in."

Konev said, sounding a bit weary but reasonable, "Let Arkady do as he wishes, Natalya. We will not lose Albert."

"How can you know that, Yuri?"

"Because I can hear him. —Or, rather, sense him. —Or, rather, sense Shapirov's thoughts by way of his instrument, bare and uninsulated in the cell."

There was a momentary silence. Boranova, clearly astonished, said, "Are you getting something?"

"Of course. In that direction," said Konev, pointing.

"You can tell the direction?" said Boranova. "How?"

"I'm not sure how. I just feel— It's in that direction!"

Boranova said, "Arkady, do as you were planning."

"I am doing it regardless of what you say, Natasha. You may be captain, but I am navigator with death staring me in the face. What have I to lose? As my old father would say: 'If you are dangling from a rope over an abyss, don't bother snatching at a coin that falls out of your pocket.' —It would be better if I had a real steering mechanism than this system of trying to maneuver three off-center engines."

Boranova had stopped listening. She peered into the darkness uselessly and said, "What is it you hear, Yuri? Shapirov's thoughts tell us—what?"

"Nothing at the moment. It is just noise. Anguish."

Kaliinin muttered, as though to herself, "Do you suppose part of Shapirov's mind knows he's in a coma? Do you suppose part of his mind feels trapped and is clamoring to get out? Like Albert—trapped? Like we ourselves—trapped?"

Boranova said sharply, "We are not trapped, Sophia. We can move. We will find Albert. We will get out of this body. Do you understand, Sophia?" She reached for the other woman's shoulders, her fingers digging deeply.

Kaliinin winced. "Please. I understand."

Boranova turned to Konev. "Is that all you get? Anguish?"

"But strongly." Then, curiously, staring at Boranova, "Do you sense nothing?"

"Nothing at all."

"But it is so strong. Stronger than anything I felt when Albert was in the ship. It was right for him to move outside."

"But can't you make out any actual thoughts? Words?"

"Perhaps I am too far. Perhaps Albert hasn't got his machine properly focused. And you really sense nothing?"

Boranova shook her head decisively and glanced briefly at Kaliinin, who said in a low voice (rubbing one shoulder), "I sense nothing, either."

And from Dezhnev came a discontented, "I never get any of these mysterious messages."

"You got 'Hawking.' Albert suggested there might be different brain types as there are different blood types and that he and I might be of the same type. He may be right," said Konev.

Boranova said, "From what direction does the sensation come now?"

"From there." This time Konev pointed much closer to the fore end of the ship. He said, "You are turning, aren't you, Arkady?"

"I am," said Dezhnev, "and I'm now fairly close to the doldrums between the two streams. I am planning to edge

only slightly into the counterstream so that we head back, but
not too quickly.''

"Good," said Boranova. "We don't want to miss him.
—Yuri, can you judge the intensity? Is it getting stronger?"

"Yes, it is." Konev seemed a bit surprised, as though he
had not noticed the rise in intensity until Boranova had mentioned it.

"Is it imagination, do you think?"

"It might be," said Konev. "We haven't really gotten any
closer to him. We're just making a turn. It's almost as if he's
approaching us."

"Perhaps he's washed off whatever he adhered to or
forced himself loose. In that case, the current *would* carry him
to us, if we're forcing a turn and staying essentially in the
same place.''

"Perhaps."

"Yuri," said Boranova vehemently, "you just concentrate
on the sensation. Keep Arkady aware at all times of the direction from which it comes, which means you will have to be
pointing toward Albert steadily. —Arkady, as you get closer
to Albert, you will have to turn toward the original stream
again and get into it as close to his position as possible. Then
once we're moving together, it will be easy to drift closer by
use of our motors.''

"Easy for one who's not controlling the motors," growled
Dezhnev.

"Easy or difficult," said Boranova, her formidable eyebrows hunching low, "do it. If not— No, there is no 'If not.'
Do it.''

Dezhnev's lips moved, but no sound came and silence fell
upon the ship—except for the unheard flood of sensation that
entered Konev's mind but left the other minds empty.

Konev remained standing, facing in the direction from
which it seemed to him the sensation was coming. He muttered once, "Definitely stronger." Then, after several moments, "It seems to me I can almost sense words. Maybe, if
he comes close enough—''

His expression grew even more strained, as though it were
trying to force the sensation, to cram it into his mind, while
taking the noise apart and separating it into words. His finger
kept pointing rigidly and he said finally, "Arkady, begin

curving back into the doldrums and be ready to plunge into the original stream. —Quickly. Don't let him pass us."

"As quickly as the motors will let me," said Dezhnev. Then, in a lower voice, "If I could maneuver this ship by the same magic with which the rest of you hear voices—"

"Head straight for the membrane," said Konev, ignoring the remark.

It was Kaliinin who saw the spark of light first. "There he is!" she cried out. "That's the light of his suit."

"I don't have to see it," said Konev to Boranova. "The noise is like a volcanic eruption in Kamchatka."

"Still noise, Yuri? No words?"

"Fright," said Konev, "incoherent fright."

Boranova said, "If I were aware in any way of being trapped in a comatose body, it would be precisely how I would feel. —But how has he come to realize it now? Earlier we did make out words and even quiet and peaceful images."

Dezhnev said, panting a little in the excitement of the chase, which had him unconsciously holding his breath, "It may be something we've done with this ship. We've stirred up his brain."

"We're too small," said Konev with contempt. "We can't even stir up this one cell noticeably."

"We're coming up to Albert," said Dezhnev.

"Sophia," said Boranova, "can you detect his electrical pattern?"

"Faintly, Natalya."

"Well, throw everything you've got into something complementary that will attract him tightly."

"He seems a little large, Natalya."

"He's oscillating, I'm sure," said Boranova grimly. "Once you attach him to the ship, he'll become part of our general miniaturization field and his size will adjust. Quickly, Sophia."

There was a slight bump as Morrison was electronically pulled against the side of the ship.

CHAPTER 16

DEATH

Once the sun sets, it grows dark;
don't let that catch you by surprise.
—Dezhnev Senior

70.

MORRISON could not later recall anything that took place—either just before or just after his return to the ship. Try as he might, he did not remember seeing the ship coming for him at any time, nor did he recall the moment of transfer, nor the removal of his plastic suit.

Going far enough back, he remembered the despair and loneliness of waiting to explode and die. Going far enough forward, he remembered looking up at the concerned face of Sophia Kaliinin bending over him. There was nothing in between.

Hadn't this happened already? The two incidents, joined by Kaliinin's care for him, were separated by several hours in time, but melted into one.

He said in a hoarse and almost unintelligible voice, "Are we headed in the right direction?" He said it in English.

Kaliinin hesitated, then answered slowly, also in English and with a moderately heavy accent, "Yes, Albert, but that was some time ago, when we were in the capillary. You came

303

back and then went out a second time. We are in a neuron now. Remember?"

Morrison frowned. What was all this?

Slowly, in bits, his memory returned. He closed his eyes and tried to get it all straight. Then he said, "How did you find me?" He spoke in Russian now.

Konev said, "I sensed—quite strongly—the thought waves of Shapirov as it came through your instrument."

"My computer! Is it safe?"

Konev said, "It was still attached to you. Did *you* make out actual thoughts?"

"Actual thoughts?" Morrison stared at him fuzzily. "What actual thoughts? What are you talking about?"

Konev was clearly impatient, but he set his lips tightly together and then said, "I could make out Shapirov's thought waves reaching me across the cell by way of your device, but there were no actual words or images."

"What did you sense, then?"

"Anguish."

Boranova said, "The rest of us sensed nothing at all, but it seemed to us that what Yuri described was the anguish of a mind that knew it was in a comatose trap, that knew it was a prisoner. Did you sense anything more specific than that?"

"No." Morrison looked down upon himself and realized that he was sprawled across two seats, his head was in the crook of Kaliinin's arms, and that he was in his one-piece cotton suit. He tried to struggle upright. "Water, please."

He drank thirstily, then said, "I don't recall hearing anything or sensing anything. In my position—"

Konev said sharply, "What has your position to do with it? Your computer was transmitting information. I sensed it at a considerable distance. How would it be possible for you not to sense anything?"

"I had other things to think about, Yuri. I was lost and I was sure of death. Under the circumstances, I paid no attention to anything else."

"I can't believe that, Albert. Don't lie to me."

"I am not lying to you. —Madame Boranova." He managed to pronounce the name very formally. "I demand that I be treated in a courteous manner."

"Yuri," said Boranova sharply. "Don't make accusations. If you have questions to ask, ask them."

Konev said, "Then let me put it this way. I sensed a great deal of emotion, even though I was far from the instrument in terms of our miniaturized state. You, Albert, were right on top of your device and it was keyed to your brain, not mine. Our brains are of similar type, presumably, but they are not identical and you can sense on your instrument more sharply than I can. How is it possible, then, that I could sense so much and that you should nevertheless claim to have sensed nothing?"

Morrison said strenuously, "Do you think I had time or inclination for sensing? I was swept away from the ship. I was separated, alone, lost."

"I understand that, but you need make no special effort to sense. The sensations would invade your mind despite anything that might be taking place."

"I received no sensations just the same. What filled my mind was that I was alone and I was going to die. How is it possible you don't understand that? I thought I would heat up and die, as I almost did the first time." A sudden doubt assailed him and he looked across at Kaliinin. "There were two times, weren't there?"

"Yes, Albert," she said softly.

"And then I realized I wasn't heating up. Instead, it seemed to me that I was growing larger and smaller—oscillating. I was involved in some sort of miniaturization transfer in place of heat transfer. Is that possible, Natalya?"

Boranova hesitated, then said, "That effect follows naturally from the field equations of miniaturization. It has never been tested, but apparently you confirmed it while out there."

"It seemed to me that my surroundings were oscillating in size, that the water molecules all around me were expanding and contracting, and it seemed to me to be more logical that it was I who was oscillating, rather than that everything else was."

"You were correct and what you report is valuable. One might argue from this that the turmoil of the event to you was not without its compensation in a larger sense."

Konev said indignantly, "Albert, you tell us that you were perfectly capable of careful and rational thought out there—and yet you expect us to believe that you sensed nothing?"

Morrison raised his voice. "Can't you understand, you

monomaniac, that it was this very careful and rational thought, as you call it, that filled my mind to the exclusion of everything else? I was in absolute terror. I expected, with each contraction of the molecules around me, that contraction would continue indefinitely, which would mean, in actual fact, that I would expand indefinitely; that, in other words, I would undergo spontaneous deminiaturization and explode and die. I was not in the least concerned with sensing thought waves at that moment. If any had forced themselves on me, I would, in my condition then, have ignored them. That is the truth."

Konev twisted his face into an expression of scorn. "If I had an important job to do and if a firing squad had their weapons trained on me, then in the few moments before they fired, I would still concentrate on my job."

Dezhnev muttered, "As my father used to say: 'Anyone can hunt a bear fearlessly when the bear is absent.'"

Konev turned on him fiercely, "I've had enough of your father, you old drunkard."

Dezhnev said, "Repeat that to me when we are safely back in the Grotto and you will then find you are hunting the bear when the bear is present."

Boranova said, "Not another word, Yuri. Are you intent on quarreling with everyone?"

"Natalya, I'm intent on doing my job. Albert must go out again."

"No," said Morrison in terror. "Never."

Dezhnev, who glared at Konev less than lovingly, said, "A hero of the Soviet Union is heard from. *He* must do *his* job, so Albert must go out into the cell again."

Boranova said, "Dezhnev is right, Yuri. You boast that even a firing squad would not interrupt your duty. Go out once, then, as Albert has done twice."

Konev said, "It is his machine. It is keyed to his brain."

"So I understand," said Boranova, "but you, as you yourself say, have the same brain type. At least you could sense what he sensed. Certainly you sensed the skeptic waves when he was lost in the intercellular current. And you were at a distance. With the machine in your very hand and yourself outside, you would gather data of your own, which should be more valuable to us, in any case. Of what use would it be to have Albert's keener perception if you insist on disbelieving whatever he says?"

All were staring at Konev now. Even Kaliinin managed to look at him at intervals through her long lashes.

Then Morrison coughed slightly and said, "I'm afraid I urinated into the suit. A little. Not much, I think. Terror has its price."

"I know," said Boranova. "I've drained it and cleaned it as well as I could. That shouldn't stop Yuri. A little bit of urine residue will surely not stop the dedication to duty of a man like him."

Konev said, "I resent this clumsy sarcasm on the part of all of you, but I'll go out into the cell. Do you really think I'm afraid of doing that? My only thought to the contrary has been that Albert is the best receiver. Still, I am second-best, certainly, and if he will not do it, then I will, provided—"

He paused and Dezhnev said, "Provided the bear is not there, eh, Yuri, my hero."

Konev said bitterly, "No, old sot, provided that I am held firmly to the ship. Albert was torn loose because he was attached feebly, a poor job on the part of the one in charge of that department. I want no poor jobs done on me."

Kaliinin said to no one, her eyes on her fingertips, "Albert must have struck a structure in such a way as to exactly fit it, electrically speaking. The chance of that happening was very low. Even so, I shall try to make use of an odd pattern on the ship and the suit in order to reduce the odds as far as I can manage."

Konev nodded. "I'll accept that," he said to Boranova. Then, to Morrison, "You say there is no heat transfer?"

Morrison said, "None that I could detect. Just size oscillation."

"Then I won't bother removing my garment."

Boranova said, "You understand, Yuri, that you won't stay out long. We cannot stretch the risk of deminiaturization indefinitely."

"I understand," said Konev and with Morrison's help he clambered into the suit.

71.

MORRISON looked through the hull of the ship and watched Konev.

Twice it had been the other way around. He had been outside looking in. (And for a while, that second time, he had been nowhere looking nowhere.)

Morrison felt a little chagrined that Konev seemed so composed. Konev did not turn to look into the ship. He held Morrison's computer in his hands, following Morrison's hasty instructions on the elementary aspects of expanding and focusing. He seemed entirely intent on his job. Was he really that icily brave? Would he continue to concentrate even if he were ripped loose as Morrison had been? Probably —and Morrison felt ashamed of himself.

He looked at the others on the ship.

Dezhnev remained at his controls. He had to stay near the membrane of the cell. He had suggested moving into the doldrums between the two streams. Nearly motionless as they would then be (probably turning in a slow eddy, actually), they would not risk the kind of accident that had torn Morrison loose. Konev had vetoed that at once. It was along the membrane that the skeptic waves moved and he wanted to be near them.

Dezhnev had also suggested turning the ship upside down. Up and down made no difference here in the cell, any more than it did in outer space. By turning upside down, the air lock would be on the side of the ship away from the membrane and that might keep Konev away from cytoskeletal structures.

That merely angered Konev. He pointed out that such structures might be anywhere in the cell and that, in any case, he did not want the bulk of the ship between himself and the membrane.

So he was out there, in just the way he wanted, and Dezhnev, paying close attention to his controls, whistled very softly to himself.

Boranova watched her instrument, looking up only occasionally to gaze thoughtfully at Konev. Kaliinin was fidgety.

It was the only word. Her eyes shifted toward Konev a hundred times and they shifted away as many times.

Boranova said suddenly, "Albert, it's your instrument. Do you think Yuri can work it? Do you think he's getting anything?"

Morrison smiled briefly. "I preset it for him. There isn't much further for him to do and I explained the focusing. Just the same, I know he isn't getting anything, Natalya."

"How can you know that?"

"If he were to sense something, I would overhear it—or oversense it, perhaps I should say—as he oversensed me when I was out in the stream. I sense nothing; absolutely nothing."

Boranova looked surprised. "But could that be? If he sensed something when you held it, why shouldn't he sense something when he holds it?"

"Perhaps conditions have changed. Consider that all this agony that Konev says he detected when he followed my machine's broadcast of Shapirov's thoughts to me. That was not characteristic of what we heard before."

"I know. It had been almost idyllic before. Green fields. Mathematical equations."

"Can it be, then, that the living part of Shapirov's brain, if it is capable of consciousness, has just recently recognized its comatose position, that it has done so in the last hour, perhaps—"

"Why should that have happened in the last hour? That's too much of a coincidence that it should do so now, just as we are in the brain."

"Perhaps we have stimulated the brain by actually being in it, and brought the realization about in consequence. Or, perhaps it *is* a coincidence. The funny thing about coincidences is that they *do* happen. —And perhaps the realization that struck him with anguish not long ago has now caused him to sink into silent apathy."

Boranova looked uncertain. "I still can't believe that. Do you really think Yuri's not getting anything?"

"Nothing of any significance. I am quite certain."

"Perhaps I should call him in."

"I would if I were you, Natalya. He's been out nearly ten minutes. If he isn't getting anything, that's time enough."

"But what if he's getting something?"

"Then he'll refuse to come in. You know Konev."

Boranova said, "Tap on the hull of the ship, Albert. You're nearest his face."

Morrison did so and Konev looked in their direction. His face was blurred through the plastic headpiece but he wore an unmistakable frown. Boranova gestured for him to come in.

Konev hesitated, then nodded, and Morrison said to Boranova, "There's your proof."

Konev was brought in and they could see his face was flushed. They unbuckled his helmet and he drew in a deep breath.

"Whew! That's good. It was getting a little warm out there. Since I was attached to the ship, the size oscillation was less than I expected and the heat transfer was perceptible. — Help me get the rest of this plastic armor off."

Boranova said in a sudden small spasm of hope, "Is *that* why you were ready to come in? The heat?"

"That was certainly the chief reason."

"Did you sense anything, Yuri?"

And Konev scowled and said, "No. Not a thing. Nothing."

Morrison lifted his head. A muscle in his right cheek twitched briefly, but he did not smile.

72.

"WELL, Natasha, little captain," said Dezhnev with an air of faded bonhomie. "What do we do next? Any ideas?"

He received no answer. In fact, no one seemed to notice that he had spoken.

Konev was still mopping away at his chest and at the back of his neck. His look at Morrison had no bonhomie in it at all. His dark eyes smoldered. "There was a great deal of transmission out there when you were outside the ship."

"If you say so," said Morrison coldly, "but I told you that I don't remember a thing about it."

"Maybe it does make a difference who holds the device."

"I don't believe that."

"Science is not a matter of belief, but of evidence. Why don't we see what happens when you go out holding your own device exactly as I did? We'll have you bound firmly so that you don't come loose again and you can stay out the same ten minutes I did. No more."

Morrison said, "I won't do it. That's already been tried."

"And I sensed Shapirov's thoughts—even if you say you didn't."

"You did not sense his thoughts. You sensed only emotion. There were no words."

"Because you let go of the device. You admitted that yourself. Try it now, without letting go."

"No. It won't work."

"You were frightened because you were torn loose. This time you will not be torn loose, as I was not. You will not be frightened."

"You underestimate my capacity for terror, Yuri," said Morrison, shrugging.

Konev looked disgusted. "Is this a time to joke?"

"I'm not joking. I'm easily terrified. I lack your—whatever."

"Courage?"

"All right. If you want an admission I lack courage, I'll admit it."

Konev turned to look at Boranova. "Natalya. You are the captain. Direct Albert to try once more."

"I don't think I can *direct* him under these conditions," said Boranova. "As he himself has said, what good will it do if we combine our strength, force him into the suit, and shove him out? If he is incapable of doing anything, we'll get nothing out of it. However, I can *ask* him. —Albert."

"Save your breath," said Morrison wearily.

"Once more. Not more than three minutes by the clock unless you get a transmission."

"We won't. I'm convinced we won't."

"Then only three minutes to prove the point."

Morrison said, "To what end, Natalya? If I get nothing, Yuri will say I am deliberately misadjusting my computer. If there is no trust between us, we will accomplish nothing in any case. How would it be, for instance, if I displayed Konev's conviction that to disagree is to lie? I say I sensed nothing of either Shapirov's thoughts or emotions when I was alone in the intracellular stream. Konev said he sensed a great deal. Who else did? Did you, Natalya?"

"No. I sensed nothing."

"Sophia?"

Kaliinin shook her head.

"Arkady?"

Dezhnev said in an aggrieved tone, "I do not seem to be able to sense very much."

Morrison said, "Well, then, Yuri stands alone. How are we to know he really sensed anything? I shall not be as unkind as he is. I shall not accuse him of lying—but isn't it possible that his wild desire to sense something caused him to imagine he had?"

Konev's face was white with anger, but his voice, except for a slight tremor, was cool enough. "Forget all that. We have spent hours in this body and I'm asking for one last observation, one last experiment, that may justify all that has gone before."

"No," said Morrison. "Last pays all. I've heard that before."

Boranova said, "Albert, this time there will be no mistake. One *last* experiment."

Dezhnev said, "It would have to be a last experiment. Our power supply is lower than I would like it to be. Finding you was costly, Albert."

"Yet we did find you," said Konev, "and without counting the cost. *I* found you." He suddenly smiled tightly and fiercely. "And I wouldn't have found you if I did not detect the transmissions emanating from your device. It would have been impossible. There's the proof that what I sensed was not imaginary. And since I found you, pay me back."

Morrison's nostrils flared. "You came after me because my explosion would have killed you all in a matter of minutes, perhaps. What payment do you expect for your anxiety to save your own li—"

The ship rocked violently without warning. It swayed heavily and Konev, who had been standing, tottered and caught at the back of his seat.

"What was it?" called out Boranova, clutching with one hand at her own control device.

Kaliinin bent over her computer. "I caught a glimpse, but you can't tell in this light. It may have been a ribosome."

"A ribosome," repeated Morrison in astonishment.

"Why not? They're scattered all over the cell. They're the protein-manufacturing organelles."

"I know what they are," said Morrison indignantly.

"So it landed us a blow. Or rather, as we skimmed along, we landed it a blow. It doesn't matter which way you look at it; we just had a giant piece of Brownian motion."

"Worse than that," said Dezhnev, pointing outward in horror. "We're not getting heat transfer, we're getting field oscillation."

Morrison, staring in despair, recognized the phenomenon he had seen when alone in the cell. The water molecules were expanding and contracting—visibly so.

"Stop it! Stop it!" shouted Konev.

"I'm trying to," said Boranova through tight lips. "Arkady, shut off the jets and make all the power available to me. —Shut off the air-conditioning, lights, everything!"

Boranova bent over the tiny glow that marked her battery-powered computer.

Morrison could see nothing except for the light from Boranova's computer and, in the seat next to him, Kaliinin's. He could not see, in the otherwise total darkness of a cell buried in the interior of a brain, the water molecules swelling and subsiding.

There was no uncertainty about it, however. He could feel the jarring in the pit of his stomach. It was not the water molecules that were oscillating, after all. It was the miniaturization field that was—and the objects that were buried in it —and he himself.

Each time the ship expanded (and the water molecules seemed to contract), the field converted some of its energy to heat and he could feel the flush that swept over him. Then, as Boranova forced energy into the field, squeezing it into contraction, the heat vanished. For a while, he could feel the oscillations slow and subside.

But then they began to grow wilder and he knew that Boranova was failing. She could not fend off the spontaneous deminiaturization that was on the way and, in ten seconds, he knew he would be dead. He—and all of them, and the body in which they were buried—would be an exploding puff of water vapor and carbon dioxide.

He felt dizzy. He was going to faint and, in his pusillanimous way, he would thus anticipate death by a second and his last recognizable emotion would be one of intense shame.

73.

THE seconds passed and Morrison didn't faint. He stirred a little. He should be dead by now, shouldn't he? (It was inevitable that the next thought should come: Can there be an afterlife after all? —He dismissed the possibility quickly.)

He was aware of someone sobbing. No! It was harsh breathing.

He opened his eyes (he hadn't realized they were closed) and found himself staring at Kaliinin in the dim light. Since all the energy available was being pumped into the effort to keep the ship from deminiaturizing, he saw her only by the glow of her own computer. He could make out her head bent over it, her hair in disarray, and her breath whistling sharply through her parted lips.

He looked around in a sudden renewal of hope and thought and life. The ship's oscillations seemed less extreme. They were settling downward into a kind of peace even as he watched.

And then cautiously, Kaliinin stopped and looked up sidewise at him, her face twitching into a painful smile. "It is done," she said in a hoarse whisper.

The light within the ship brightened slowly, almost tentatively, and Dezhnev uttered a huge shuddering sigh. "If I am not dead now," he said, "I hope to live yet a little while. As my father once said: 'Life would be unbearable if death were not worse yet.' —Thank you, Natasha. You may be my captain forever."

"Not I," said Boranova, her face looking very old—to the point where Morrison would not have been surprised to see white streaks in her black hair. "I simply couldn't pump enough energy into the ship. Was it something you did, Sophia?"

Kaliinin's eyes were closed now, but her breasts were still heaving. She stirred a little, as though reluctant to answer, reluctant to do anything but savor life for a time. Then she said, "I don't know. Maybe."

Boranova said, "What did you do?"

Kaliinin said, "I couldn't just wait for death. I made the ship the electric duplicate of a D-glucose molecule and hoped the cell would do the normal thing and interact with a molecule of ATP—adenosine triphosphate. In doing so, it gained a phosphate group and energy. The energy, I hoped, would go into reinforcing the miniaturization field. I then neutralized the ship and the phosphate group fell off. D-glucose again, another gain in energy, then neutral, and so on, over and over." She stopped to pant a bit. "Over and over. My fingers were working so fast, I didn't know if I were hitting the right keys or not—but I must have. And the ship gained enough energy to stabilize the field."

Boranova said, "How did you come to do that? No one has ever suggested in my hearing that this might—"

"Nor in mine," said Kaliinin. "Nor in mine. I was just wondering this morning before we got on the ship what I would do—or what anyone could do—if spontaneous deminiaturization began. We'd need energy, but if the ship couldn't pump up enough— I thought, Could the cell itself supply the energy? If it did, it would only be through ATP, which every cell has. I didn't know if it would work. I had to spend energy, forcing the electrical pattern on and off the ship, and I knew I might spend more than I got from ATP. Or the energy of the ATP might simply not affect the ship in such a way as to counter the deminiaturization. It was all such a gamble."

Dezhnev said softly, almost as though to himself, "As my old father would say: 'If you have nothing to lose, gamble freely.'" Then, briskly, he said, "Thank you, little Sophia. My life is yours from now on. I will give it to you at your need. I will go farther. I will even marry you if that would strike you as convenient."

"A chivalrous offer," said Kaliinin, smiling faintly, "but I wouldn't ask marriage of you. Your mere life—at need—would be quite enough."

Boranova was entirely herself now and she said, "This will be cited in detail in the final report. Your quick thinking and your quick action saved everything."

Morrison couldn't trust himself to make any speech at all. (Unaccountably, he felt near tears. —In gratitude for life? In admiration for Kaliinin?) All he could do was reach for Kaliinin's hand, put it to his lips, and kiss it. Then, after clearing his throat vigorously, he said with extraordinary mildness, "Thank you, Sophia."

She looked embarrassed, but did not draw her hand away immediately. She said, "It might not have worked. I didn't think it would work."

"Had it not," said Dezhnev, "we would be no deader."

Through all this, only Yuri Konev had not said a word and Morrison turned to look at him. He sat as he usually sat, very upright and very much turned away from them.

Morrison, finding his voice suddenly—and his anger—said, "Well, Yuri, what have you to say?"

Konev looked over his shoulder briefly and said, "Nothing."

"Nothing? Sophia saved the expedition."

Konev shrugged. "She did her job."

"Her job? She did much more than her job." Morrison leaned forward and reached wildly for Konev, grabbing his shoulder. "She invented the technique that saved us. And in doing so, she saved your life, you idiot. She's the reason you're still alive. You can at least thank her."

"I'll do as I please," said Konev, twitching his shoulder and then writhing out of Morrison's grasp.

Morrison's hands found their way around Konev's throat. "You miserable, egotistical barbarian," he grunted out, squeezing desperately. "You love her in your own insane way and you won't give her a kind word. Not one kind word, you piece of dirt."

Again Konev pulled himself loose and then the two were pummeling each other clumsily. They were half-trapped by the seats from which they had partly risen and neither could maneuver properly under zero-gravity conditions.

Kaliinin screamed, "Don't hurt him!"

He won't hurt me, thought Morrison, striving mightily. He had not been engaged in this kind of physical combat since he was sixteen and, he thought in embarrassment, he wasn't doing any better now.

Boranova's voice rang out sharply. "Stop it. Both of you." And they did. Both of them.

Boranova said, "Albert, you are not here to teach anyone manners. And Yuri, you need not labor to be a boor, it comes natural to you. If you do not wish to acknowledge Sophia's—"

Sophia said with an obvious effort, "I'm not asking for thanks—from anyone."

"Thanks?" said Konev angrily. "Let us all say thanks. Before the deminiaturization started, I was trying to get this American coward to thank us for rescuing him. I didn't want thanks in words. This isn't a dance floor. We needn't bow and curtsy. I wanted him to show his thanks by getting out there and trying to sense some of Shapirov's thoughts. He refused. Who is he to teach me how and when to say thanks?"

Morrison said, "I said before the deminiaturization that I wouldn't do it and I repeat that now."

Dezhnev interrupted and said, "We beat a dead horse here. We have consumed our energy supply as though it were vodka at a wedding. Between pursuits and deminiaturizations, we have very little to spare for the task of deminiaturizing under controlled conditions. We must get out now."

Konev said, "It would take very little energy to have this man go out for a couple of minutes and come in again. Then we can leave."

For a moment, Konev and Morrison stared at each other hostilely and then Dezhnev said in a voice that seemed drained of some of its life, "My poor old father used to say: 'The most frightening phrase in the Russian language is "That's odd."'"

Konev turned angrily and said, "Shut up, Arkady."

Dezhnev replied, "I mentioned that only because it is now time for me to say it: That's odd."

74.

BORANOVA pushed her dark hair back from her forehead (a bit wearily, Morrison thought, and noted the hair itself was clearly damp with perspiration). She said, "What is odd, Arkady? Let us not play games."

"The current flow of the cellular material is slowing."

There was a brief silence, then Boranova said, "How can you tell?"

Dezhnev said heavily, "Natasha, dear, if you sat in my seat you would know that there are fibers crisscrossing the cell—"

"The cytoskeleton," put in Morrison.

"Thank you, Albert, my child," said Dezhnev with a grand wave of his hand. "My father used to say: 'It is more important to know the thing than the name.' Still, never mind. The whatever-you-call-it doesn't stop the cell flow and it doesn't stop the ship, but I can see it glint past. Well, it's glinting past more slowly now. I assume the fibers don't move, so I take it we're slowing. And since I'm not doing anything to slow the ship, I assume that it is the intracellular flow that is really slowing. —This is called logic, Albert, so you don't have to educate me on that point."

Kaliinin said in a small voice, "I think we have damaged the cell." She sounded conscience-stricken.

Morrison took it so and said, "One brain cell gone, more or less, won't hurt Shapirov in any way, especially in the condition he's in. I wouldn't be surprised if the cell were gone, though. After all, the ship came after me in a furious race, I imagine—and I thank you all again for that—and it probably vibrated itself nearly to death and must have vibrated the entire cell as well."

Konev said, frowning darkly, "That's mad. We're molecule-sized—and a small molecule at that. Do you suppose anything we can do, whether moving or jiggling, is going to damage an entire cell?"

Morrison said, "We don't have to reason it out, Yuri. It's an observed fact. The intracellular stream is stopping and that isn't normal."

"In the first place, that's just Arkady's impression," said Konev, "and he's no neurologist—"

"Do I have to be a neurologist to have eyes?" demanded Dezhnev hotly, one arm raised as though to strike at the younger man.

Konev cast a brief glance at Dezhnev, but made no other acknowledgment of his remark. He said, "And besides, we don't know what is normal in a living brain cell from this level of observation. There may be calms and eddies in the flow, so that even if something like this is observed, it might be only temporary."

"You're whistling past the graveyard, Yuri," said Morrison. "The fact is, we can't use this cell any more and we don't have sufficient remaining energy to wander around searching for another cell."

Konev ground his teeth. "There must be *something* we can do. We *can't* give up."

Morrison said, "Natalya, make the decision. Is there any point in investigating this cell any further? And are we in a position to seek out another cell?"

Boranova raised her hand and bowed her head in a moment of thought. The others turned to look at her and Konev seized the opportunity to grasp Morrison by the upper arm and pull him closer. His eyes were dark with hostility. He whispered, "How is it you think I am in *love* with—" he jerked his head in Kaliinin's direction. "What gives you the right to think so? Tell me that."

Morrison looked at him blankly.

At this point, Boranova spoke, but it was not to answer Morrison's question. She said mildly, "Arkady, what is it you are doing?"

Dezhnev, who was bent over his controls, lifted his head. "I am rearranging the wiring back to what it was. I am hooking up communications again."

Boranova said, "Have I told you to do that?"

Dezhnev said, "Necessity has told me to do that."

Konev said, "Does it occur to you it will be impossible to steer?"

Dezhnev growled and said in sullen irony, "And does it occur to you that there may be no more steering to do?"

"What is the necessity that drives you, Arkady?" said Boranova patiently.

Dezhnev said, "I don't think it's this cell alone that is out of order. The temperature around us is going down. —Slowly."

Konev sneered. "By your measurements?"

"No. By the ship's measurements. By the background infrared radiation we're getting."

"You can't tell anything by that," said Konev. "At our size, we get very few infrared photons. The level would vary all over the lot."

Dezhnev nodded at Konev and said, "Like this." His hand waved up and down frenetically. "Still, it can wave up and down like a rowboat in a typhoon and yet do so at a lower and lower average level." And his hand sank ever lower as it continued its trembling.

Boranova said, "Why should the temperature be dropping?"

Morrison smiled grimly. "Come on, Natalya. I think you know why. I *know* that Yuri knows why. Arkady must find out and for that reason necessity is forcing him to put back communications."

An uncomfortable silence fell, except for Dezhnev's occasional grunts and muttered expletives as he struggled with the ship's wiring.

Morrison gazed out at the surroundings, which he could once again see in the usual unsatisfactory fashion now that ship's lighting had been restored. There were the usual dim glitter of molecules, large and small, that traveled with them. Now that Dezhnev had mentioned it, he saw the occasional reflection of light from a line that stretched across the path before them and then moved over (or under) and behind at express speed.

These were, undoubtedly, very thin collagen fibers that preserved the shape of the irregular neuron and kept it from converting itself into a roughly spherical blob under the pull of its own surface tension. Had he been watching for it, he would have noticed it before. It occurred to him that Dezhnev, as navigator, had to watch for everything and, in the entirely unprecedented situation in which the ship found itself, Dezhnev had had no guide, no instruction, no experience to let him know what to watch for. There was no question but that Dezhnev's task had placed him under greater tension than the others had allowed for.

Certainly, to Morrison himself, Dezhnev had been taken for granted as the least of the five. Not fair, Morrison thought now.

Dezhnev had straightened up now. He had an earphone in one ear canal and said, "I should be able to establish communication." He said, "Are you there? Grotto. —Grotto."

Then he smiled. "Yes. We are, to this point, safe. —I'm sorry, but as I told you, it was either communicate or steer. —How is it at your end? —What? Repeat that, more slowly. —Yes, I thought so."

He turned to the others. "Comrades," he said, "Academician Pyotr Leonovich Shapirov is dead. Thirteen minutes ago, all vital signs ceased and our task now is to leave the body."

CHAPTER 17

EXIT

*If trouble were as easy to get out
of—as into—life would be one sweet song.*
—Dezhnev Senior

75.

A GRAY silence fell over the ship.

Kaliinin buried her face in her hands and then, after a long moment, broke the silence by whispering, "Are you sure, Arkady?"

And Dezhnev, blinking hard to hold back tears, said, "Am *I* sure? The man has been on the brink of death for weeks. The cellular flow is slowing, the temperature is falling, and the Grotto, which has him wired with every instrument ever invented, says he is dead. What is there to be but sure?"

Boranova sighed. "Poor Shapirov. He deserved a better death."

Konev said, "He might have held out another hour."

Boranova said with a frown, "He did not pick and choose, Yuri."

Morrison felt chilled. Until now he had been conscious of some surrounding red corpuscles, of a specific speck of inter-cellular region, of the interior of a neuron. His environment had been circumscribed to the immediate.

Now he looked out of the ship, through its transparent

plastic walls, at what appeared to him, for the first time, to be thickness upon thickness of matter. On their present scale, with the ship the size of a glucose molecule and himself not much more than the size of an atom, the body of Shapirov was larger than the planet Earth.

Here he was, then, buried in a planetary object of dead organic matter. He felt impatience over the pause for mourning. Time for that later, but meanwhile— He said in a voice that was perhaps a little louder than it ought to have been, "How do we get out?"

Boranova looked at him in surprise, eyes widening. (Morrison was certain that in her grief for Shapirov the thought of leaving had been momentarily buried.)

She cleared her throat and made a visible effort to be her usual businesslike self. She said, "We must deminiaturize to some extent, to begin with."

Morrison said, "Why only to begin with? Why not deminiaturize all the way to normality right now?" Then, as though to forestall the inevitable objection, "We will inflict damage on Shapirov's body, but it is a dead body and we are still alive. Our needs come first."

Kaliinin looked at Morrison reproachfully. "Even a dead body deserves respect, Albert, especially the dead body of a great scientist like Academician Pyotr Shapirov."

"Yes, but surely not to the extent of risking five lives." Morrison's impatience was growing. Shapirov was only someone he had known by distant reputation and peripherally—to Morrison he was not the demigod he seemed to be to the others.

Dezhnev said, "Aside from the question of respect, we are enclosed by Shapirov's cranium. If we expand to fill that cranium and then try to crumble the cranium by the effect of our miniaturization field, we will lose too much energy and deminiaturize explosively. We must first find our way out of the cranium."

Boranova said, "Albert is right. Let's begin. I will deminiaturize to cell size. Arkady, have the people in the Grotto determine our exact position. Yuri, make sure you locate that position accurately on your cerebrograph."

Morrison stared out the hull at the distant cell membrane —a brighter and more continuous sparkle, one that was visible through the occasional flicker of light from the intervening molecules.

The first indication of deminiaturization was the fact that the molecules—subsided. (It was the only word Morrison could think of to describe what happened.)

It was as though the little curved swellings that filled the space around them—and which Morrison's brain constructed out of twinklings rather than saw directly—shrank. It was for all the world as though they were balloons with the air being let out of them until the surroundings seemed relatively smooth.

But even as the liquid around them grew smooth, the large macromolecules in the distance—the proteins, the nucleic acids, the still larger cellular structures—also shrank and, in doing so, grew more distinct. The sparks of light they reflected were more closely spaced.

The cell membrane itself seemed to be approaching and it, too, could be seen more clearly. It came closer still and yet closer. The ship was, after all, in a narrow dendrite that projected from the cell body itself and if the ship was going to enlarge to the size of a cell, it would have to grow much larger than this mere projection.

It was clear that the membrane was going to collide with the ship and Morrison automatically clenched his teeth and steeled himself for the shock of impact.

There was none. The membrane came closer and closer and then simply separated and was not there. It was too thin a structure and too lightly bound to withstand the consequences of being forced into a miniaturization field. Though the ship was deminiaturizing to an extent, it was still far, far smaller than the normal world around it and the molecules of the membrane, on entering the field and shrinking, lost contact with each other so that the integrity of the whole vanished.

Morrison watched everything after that with fascination. The surroundings seemed chaotic until, as objects continued to shrink, he began to recognize the intercellular jungle of collagen that they had encountered before entering the neuron. That jungle continued to shrink, in its turn, until the collagen trunks and cables became nothing more than twine.

Boranova said, "And that is all. We will want to be able to fit within a small vein."

Dezhnev grunted. "That is all under any circumstances. Our remaining energy supply is not great."

Boranova said, "It will last until we find our way out of the cranium, surely."

Dezhnev said, "We can hope so. However, you're only the captain of the ship, Natasha; you are not the captain of the laws of thermodynamics."

Boranova shook her head as though in reproof and said, "Arkady, have them determine our position—and don't lecture me."

Konev said, "I'm certain, Natalya, that it is not terribly important to determine our position. It cannot be measurably different from what it was when we left the capillary. All our wanderings since have merely taken us to a nearby neuron and from that to a neighboring neuron. The difference in position on even an ordinary microscopic scale is scarcely measurable."

And then, after a wait of several minutes, the position came through and Konev said, "As I told you."

Morrison said, "What's the good of the position, Yuri? We don't know which way we're headed and we can only go in whatever direction that might be. Now that communications are restored, we can't steer."

Konev said, "Well, then, since there is only one way in which we can head, we will head in that direction. I'm sure that Arkady's father had a saying concerning that."

Dezhnev said at once, "He used to say: 'When only one course of action is possible, there is no difficulty in deciding what to do.'"

"You see?" said Konev. "And we will find that whatever direction we go in, we will find a way out. Move ahead, Arkady."

The ship moved forward, ploughing through the now fragile threads of collagen, splashing through a neuron, and cutting across a thin axon. (It was hard to believe they were recently inside one of those axons and that it had seemed like a highway a hundred kilometers across.)

Morrison said dryly, "Suppose that Shapirov was still alive when it became necessary for us to leave his body. What would we have done?"

"What do you mean?" said Boranova.

"I mean, what alternative is there to this? Would we not

have had to determine our position? And to do that, would we not have had to establish communications? And once that was done, would we not have been able to move in only one direction—forward? Would we not have had to deminiaturize in order not to have to travel the equivalent of tens of thousands of kilometers, but merely the equivalent of a few kilometers? In short, in order to get out, would we not have had to push our way through the living neurons of a living Shapirov, as we are now pushing our way through dying and dead ones?"

Boranova said, "Well—yes."

"Where, then, is the respect for a living body? After all, we actually hesitated to violate the integrity of a dead one."

"You must understand, Albert, that this is an emergency operation with an inadequate ship. We have no choice. And, in any case, it is not like your suggestion that we deminiaturize completely in the brain, smashing the cranium and leaving Shapirov headless. Our present course, even if Shapirov was alive, would destroy a dozen neurons—or possibly a hundred—and that would not have been likely to make Shapirov's condition appreciably worse. Brain neurons are continually dying throughout life—like red corpuscles."

"Not quite," said Morrison grimly. "Red corpuscles are continually replaced. Neurons never are."

Konev interrupted, his voice rather loud, as though he were impatiently overriding the idle talk of others. "Arkady, stop. We need another position determination."

There was at once a dead silence within the ship, one that continued—as though any speech might interfere with the measurements being made in the Grotto or might hamper the concentration of those making the measurements.

Finally Dezhnev whispered the measurements to Konev, who said, "Confirm them, Arkady. Make sure you have them right."

Morrison unclasped himself. He was still virtually without mass, but there was distinctly more of it than there had been when they were maneuvering within the cell. He pulled himself cautiously upward, so that he could see the cerebrograph over Konev's shoulder.

There were two red spots on it, with a thin red line connecting them. The map displayed on the screen condensed a bit, the two dots shrinking toward each other, and then it expanded again in a different orientation.

Konev's fingers worked busily over the computer keys and the map grew double and uninterpretable. Morrison knew, however, that Konev could view it through a device that would render it stereoscopic, displaying a third dimension.

Konev laid down that device and said, "Natalya, this time chance is on our side. Wherever we are and in whatever direction we were traveling, we'd be bound to encounter a small vein sooner or later. In this case, it is sooner. We are not far away and we will strike it in such a way that we will be able to enter."

Morrison heaved an internal sigh of relief, but could not help saying, "And what would you have done if chance had dictated a vein very far away?"

Konev said coolly, "Then I would have had Dezhnev break communications again and steer to a closer one."

Dezhnev, however, turned to stare at Morrison, made a grimace of disagreement, and mouthed the words, "Not enough energy."

"Move forward, Arkady," said Boranova peremptorily, "and get to the vein."

After a few minutes, Dezhnev said, "Yuri's map is right, which I wouldn't have bet on with any enthusiasm. That's it ahead."

Morrison found himself staring at a curving wall reaching into the indefinite haze upward and downward and with just a faint suggestion of tiling to it. If it was a vein, it was as yet not very far removed from a capillary. Morrison wondered uneasily if the ship would be able to fit inside it.

76.

BORANOVA said, "Is there any way, Sophia, that you can give the ship an electric charge pattern that will slip us into the vein?"

Kaliinin looked doubtful and Morrison, holding up his hand, said, "I don't think so, Natalya. The individual cells may not be entirely dead even now, but certainly the organization within them has been destroyed. I don't think any cell in the body can take us in by pinocytosis or by any other means."

"What do I do, then?" said Dezhnev unhappily. "Force my way in?"

"Of course," said Konev. "Lean against the vein wall. A small bit of it will then miniaturize and disintegrate and you can move in. You won't have to use your motors much."

"Ah," said Dezhnev, "the expert speaks. The vein will miniaturize and disintegrate at the expense of our field and that would take energy, too—more energy than forcing our way in would."

"Arkady," said Boranova, "don't be angry. This is not the time for it. Use your motors moderately and take advantage of the first weakening of the vein wall through miniaturization to burst through. Using both techniques will consume less energy than either separately."

"We can hope so," said Dezhnev, "but saying so doesn't make it so. When I was little, my father said to me once: 'Vehemence, my little son, is no guarantee of truth.' He told me this when I swore with great earnestness that I had not broken his pipe. He asked me if I understood the statement. I said I didn't and he explained it to me very carefully. Then he walloped me."

"Yes, Arkady," said Boranova, "but move in now."

Konev said, "It's not as though you're going to flood the brain with blood. It wouldn't matter now that Shapirov is dead, but, as it happens, the blood isn't flowing now. Virtually nothing will leak."

"Ah," said Dezhnev, "this raises an interesting point. Ordinarily, once we enter a vein, the blood flow would carry us in a particular direction. Without blood flow, I must use my engines—but in which direction must we go?"

"Once we penetrate at this point," said Konev calmly, "you will turn to the right. So my cerebrograph says."

"But if there is no current to turn me to the right and if I enter at an angle to the left?"

"Arkady, you will enter at an angle to the right. My cerebrograph tells me that, too. Just push in, will you?"

"Go ahead, Arkady," said Boranova. "We have no choice but to rely on Yuri's cerebrograph."

The ship moved forward and, as the prow touched the vein wall, Morrison could feel the slight vibration of the laboring motors. And then the wall simply gave and pulled away in all directions and the ship was inside.

Dezhnev stopped the motors at once. The ship moved in at a rapidly slowing pace, rebounded off the far wall (maintaining contact so briefly as to cause no damage that Morrison could see), and straightened out with the long axis of the ship along the enormous tunnel of the vein. The ship's width was better than half the width of the blood vessel.

"Well," said Dezhnev, "are we pointed in the right direction? If we're not, there's nothing to be done. I can't back up. We fit the vein too tightly for Albert to get out and turn us around and we have an insufficient remaining supply of energy to miniaturize further and make such a turn possible."

"You're pointed in the right direction," said Konev sternly. "Just get moving and you'll find out soon enough. The vessel will get larger as we move."

"Let's hope it does. —And if it does, how far do we have to travel before we can move out of the body?"

"I can't say yet," said Konev. "I have to follow the vein on my cerebrograph, consult with the people in the Grotto, and arrange for the insertion of a hypodermic needle into the vein as close as possible to the position in which we'll be when we emerge from within the cranium."

Dezhnev said, "May I explain that we cannot move on forever. What with miniaturizing and deminiaturizing, with steering at very low efficiency, with wrong capillaries, and with chasing after Albert when he was lost, we have used up much more energy than we had counted on using. We had much more energy than we thought we'd need, but, even so, we've almost used it all."

Boranova said, "Do you mean we're out of energy?"

"Just about. Haven't I been telling you this for quite a while?" said Dezhnev. "Haven't I been warning you we were running low?"

"But how low are we? Are you saying we don't have enough to carry us out of the cranium?"

"Ordinarily, we would have plenty for that, even now. If we were in a living vein, we could count on a blood current sweeping us along. But there is no current. Shapirov is dead and his heart isn't beating. That means I'll have to force my way through the bloodstream with my motors going and the cooler the stream gets, the more viscous it will become, the harder the motors will have to work, and the more rapidly the energy supply will run out."

Konev said, "We have only a few centimeters to go."

Dezhnev said furiously, "Only a few? Less than the width of my palm? Really? At our present size, we've got *kilometers* to go."

Morrison said, "Should we deminiaturize further, then?"

"We can't." Dezhnev was now speaking very loudly. "We don't have the energy for it. Uncontrolled deminiaturization takes no energy; it *releases* energy. But *controlled* deminiaturization— Look, Albert, if you jump out of a high window, you will reach the ground without effort. But if you want to survive the ordeal and if you want to be lowered slowly while you hang on to a rope, that takes a great deal of effort. Understand?"

Morrison muttered, "I understand."

Kaliinin's hand stole to his and squeezed it gently. She said in a low voice, "Don't mind Dezhnev. He grumbles and howls, but he'll get us there."

Boranova said, "Arkady, if vehemence doesn't guarantee truth, as you told us just now, neither does it guarantee a cool head and a solution. Rather, the reverse. So why don't you just push your way along the vein and perhaps the energy will last until we reach the hypodermic."

Dezhnev scowled and said, "It's what I will do, but if you want me to keep a cool head, you must let me get rid of some heat."

The ship began to move and Morrison thought to himself: Every meter we go is a meter closer to the hypodermic needle.

It didn't make much sense as a comforting thought, since to fail to reach the needle by a small distance might be as fatal as to fail by a large distance. Yet it worked to slow the beat of his heart and it gave him a sense of accomplishment as he watched the wall slide rapidly backward.

The red corpuscles and platelets seemed far more numerous now than they had been in the arteries and capillaries on the way in. Then there had been a blood flow and there had been only the relatively few objects in their immediate neighborhood that had moved along the flow with them. Now the various formed bodies were largely motionless and the ship moved past what seemed countless numbers, squeezing them right and left and leaving them behind, bobbing, in their wake.

They even passed an occasional white cell, large and globular and quiescent. Now, though, they were totally unresponsive to the presence of a foreign object speeding by. In one case, the ship simply whipped through a white cell and left it sprawling behind.

Konev said, "We are going in the right direction. The vein is now distinctly wider than it was."

And so it was. Morrison had noticed that without managing to grasp the significance. He had been too intent on simply moving.

He felt a small surge of hope. To have been going in the wrong direction would have been total disaster. The vein would have narrowed and burst, leaving them adrift in gray matter with, perhaps, insufficient fuel to find and reach another vein.

Konev was taking down something that Dezhnev was repeating to him. He nodded and said, "Have them confirm those figures, Arkady. —Good!"

He spent some time with his cerebrograph and then said, "Listen, they know the vein we're in and they will be inserting a hypodermic needle at a specific spot that I have marked off on the cerebrograph. We will reach it in half an hour or a little less. —Can you keep going for half an hour, Arkady?"

"More likely a little less. If the heart was beating—"

"Yes, I know, but it isn't," said Konev. Then he said, "Natalya, may I have whatever records you have concerning what we have sensed of Shapirov's thought processes? I am going to send the raw data—complete—out to the Grotto."

Boranova said, "You mean in case we don't make it out."

"That's exactly what I mean. This material is what we went in for and there's no reason to have it perish with us if we can't get out."

"That's a proper attitude, Yuri," said Boranova.

"Provided," said Konev, his voice suddenly taking on a tinge of anger, "the data has any value at all." Briefly, he glared at Morrison.

Konev then bent toward Dezhnev and together the two began electronically transmitting the information they had collected, computer to computer, from tiny to large, from inside a vein to the outside world.

Kaliinin was still holding Morrison's hand, perhaps as much for comfort to herself as to him, Morrison thought.

He said in a low voice, "What happens, Sophia, if we run out of energy before we reach the needle?"

She lifted her eyebrows briefly and said, "We'll just have to remain passively in place. The people in the Grotto will try to reach us wherever we are."

"We won't deminiaturize explosively as soon as the energy is gone, will we?"

"Oh no. Miniaturization is a metastable state. You remember we explained that. We'll stay as we are indefinitely. Eventually—sometime—this chance pseudo-Brownian motion of expanding and contracting will set up spontaneous deminiaturization, but that might not be for— Who knows?"

"Years?"

"Possibly."

"That won't do us any good, of course," said Morrison. "We'll die of asphyxiation. Without energy, we won't be able to recycle our air supply."

"I said the people in the Grotto would try to reach us. Our computers will still be working and they can home in on us, cut to the vein and into it, and spot us electronically—or even visually."

"How can they find one cell among fifty trillion?"

Kaliinin patted his hand. "You are in a pessimistic mood, Albert. We're an easily recognizable cell—and a broadcasting one."

"I think I would feel better if we find the hypodermic needle now and they don't have to look for us."

"So would I. I am merely pointing out that running out of energy and *not* finding the needle is not the ultimate end."

"And if we *do* find it?"

"Then we are drawn out and the Grotto's own energy sources will be applied to the task of deminiaturizing us."

"Can't they do it now?"

"We're too closely surrounded by masses of unminiaturized material and it would be too difficult to focus the deminiaturizing field with sufficient accuracy. Once we are out and visible to them, the conditions will be entirely different."

At this point, Dezhnev said, "Have we transmitted everything, Yuri?"

"Yes. Everything."

"Then it is my duty to tell you that I have only enough energy to continue moving this ship for five minutes. Perhaps less, but certainly not more."

77.

MORRISON, Kaliinin's hand still in his, squeezed convulsively and the young woman winced.

Morrison said, "I'm sorry, Sophia."

He released her hand and she rubbed it vigorously.

Boranova said, "Where are we, Yuri? Can we get to the needle?"

"I should say yes," said Konev. "Slow down, Arkady. Conserve what energy you have."

"No, believe me," said Dezhnev. "At the present speed, I am cutting through the blood with comparatively little turbulence, thanks to the streamlining and surface characteristics of the ship. If I slow down, there'll be more turbulence and energy waste."

Konev said, "But we don't want to overshoot the mark."

"We won't. Any time you want me to cut the motors, we begin to slow down at once because of the blood viscosity. As we slow down, the turbulence builds, we slow down faster, and in ten seconds we're motionless. If we had our normal mass and inertia, the rapid pace of slowing would plaster us all up against the front of the ship."

"Stop when I tell you, then."

Morrison had risen and was looking over Konev's shoulder again. The cerebrograph, he judged, must be at enormous expansion, perhaps at maximum. The thin red line that had marked the path of the ship by dead reckoning was now thick and was approaching a small green circle, which, Morrison surmised, must represent the position of the hypodermic needle.

But it was dead reckoning and it could be off a bit. Konev was alternating his gaze between the cerebrograph and the view up ahead of the ship.

"We should have aimed for an artery," Morrison said suddenly. "They're empty after death. We wouldn't have had to waste energy on viscosity and turbulence."

Konev said, "Useless idea. The ship cannot progress through air." He might have gone on, but at this point he stiffened and cried out, "Stop, Arkady! Stop!"

Dezhnev hit a knob hard with the heel of his hand. It moved inward and Morrison felt himself sway gently forward as the ship slowed and stopped almost at once.

Konev pointed. There was a large circle, glowing with an orange light. He said, "They're using fiber optic methods to make sure the tip glows. They said I wouldn't miss it."

"But we *have* missed it," said Morrison tightly, "We're looking at it, but we're not there. To get into it, we have to turn—and that means that Dezhnev has to unhook communications again."

"No use," said Dezhnev. "I have enough power in my engines to have kept us going another forty-five seconds maybe, but I certainly do not have enough to start us moving from scratch. We are at this moment dead in the water and cannot move again."

"Well, then?" began Morrison with what was almost a wail.

"Well, then," said Konev, "there is another kind of motion that *is* possible. That hypodermic needle has intelligence at the other end. Arkady, tell them to push it in very slowly."

The orange circle expanded slowly, becoming slightly elliptical.

Morrison said, "It's going to miss us."

Konev made no reply to that, but leaned over toward Arkady to speak directly into the transmitter. The orange ellipse became, for a moment, more markedly elliptical, but this ceased after a bark from Konev. It became nearly circular after that. The needle was close now and was pointing at them.

And then there was sudden motion everywhere. The faint outlines of the red corpuscles and the occasional platelet, moved, and converged toward and through the circle. And the ship was moving, too.

Morrison looked up and around as the orange circle moved past them neatly on all sides, then slipped behind the ship, shrank rapidly, and disappeared.

Konev said with grim satisfaction, "They've sucked us in.

From this point on, we sit quietly. They will handle everything."

78.

NOW Morrison did his best to wash away thought, to close his mind. Either he would be brought back to the standard world, to normality, to reality, or he would die in a microblink and the rest of the Universe would go on without him—as it would do, in any case, in twenty years, or thirty, or forty.

He shut his eyes firmly and tried to respond to nothing, not even to the beating of his heart. At one point he felt a light touch on his left hand. That would have to be Kaliinin. He withdrew his hand—not suddenly in rejection, but slowly, as though simply to say: "Not now."

At another point, he heard Boranova say, "Tell them, Arkady, to evacuate Section C, to put in strictly long-distance controls. If we go, there is no point in carrying anyone with us."

Morrison wondered if Section C were indeed evacuated. He would evacuate if he were ordered to or even if he were not ordered to, but there might be those lunatics who would be anxious to be on the spot when the first crew to explore a living body returned safely. —So they could tell their grandchildren, he supposed.

What happened to such people, he wondered, if they ended up not having grandchildren—if they died too young to see them—if their children chose never to have children—if the—

Dimly, he was aware that he was deliberately immersing himself in nonsense and trivia. One can't really think of nothing and especially not if one has spent a lifetime devoting one's self to thought, but one can think of something utterly unimportant. There are, after all, so many more possible thoughts that are unimportant rather than important, trivial rather than vital, nonsensical rather than sensible, that—

He might even have fallen asleep. Thinking about it afterward made him feel certain he had. He wouldn't have thought it would be possible to be so cold-blooded, but it wasn't cold blood; it was weariness, relief from tension, the feeling that someone else was making decisions, that he himself might be totally relaxed at last. And perhaps (although he didn't want to admit it), it had all been too much and he had simply passed out.

And again he felt a light touch on his left hand and this time it did not go away. He stirred and opened his eyes on something that looked like ordinary illumination. Too ordinary—it hurt his eyes. He blinked rapidly and they watered.

Kaliinin was looking down at him. "Wake up, Albert!"

He wiped at his eyes, began to make the natural interpretation of his surroundings, and said, "Are we back?"

"We are back. All is well. We are safe and we're waiting for you. You're nearest the door."

Morrison looked back at the open door and started to his feet, rising a few inches and sinking back. "I'm *heavy.*"

Kaliinin said, "I know. I feel like an elephant myself. Just get up slowly. I'll help you."

"No no, that's all right." He fended her off. The room was crowded. His vision had cleared to the point where he could see the crowd, face upon face, looking toward him, smiling, watching. He did not want them—Soviet citizens, all—to see the sole American helped to his feet by a young Soviet woman.

Slowly, a little drunkenly but by himself, he rose to his feet, stepped sidewise to the door and very carefully let himself down to a small flight of stairs. Half a dozen pairs of arms reached out to help him, utterly disregarding his words: "It's all right. I don't need help."

Then he said sharply, "Wait!"

Before stepping to solid ground, he turned and looked past Kaliinin, who was right behind him.

"What is it, Albert?" she asked.

He said, "I was just taking a last look at the ship because I don't intend *ever* to see it again—not at a distance, not in films, not in any form of reproduction."

Then he was on normal ground again and the others followed. It was with relief that Morrison saw that every one of them was helped down.

There would then have been some sort of impromptu celebration, but it was Boranova who stepped forward, looking distinctly disheveled and much unlike her usual calm, well-cared-for self—all the more so since she was wearing the thin cotton coverall that did very little to hide the mature lines of her body.

"Fellow workers," she said, "I'm sure there will be appropriate ceremonies at some reasonable time to mark this fantastic voyage of ours, but please, we are in no condition to join you now. We must rest and recover from an arduous time and we beg your indulgence."

They were all led off to wild shouts and frantic waving and only Dezhnev had the presence of mind to take a glass offered to him that contained something that was either water or vodka and Morrison, for one, had no doubt as to which of the alternatives was, in fact, the case. The broad smile on Dezhnev's damp face as he sipped made it certain.

Morrison said to Kaliinin, "How long were we on the ship?"

"I think it was over eleven hours," said Kaliinin.

Morrison shook his head. "It seemed more like eleven years."

"I know," she said, smiling slightly, "but clocks lack imagination."

"One of Dezhnev Senior's aphorisms, Sophia?"

"No. One of my own."

"What I want," said Morrison, "is a chance at the bathroom, and a shower, and fresh clothes, and a good dinner, and a chance to shout and scream, and a good night's sleep. In that order, I think, especially with the bathroom coming first."

"You'll have it all," said Kaliinin, "as will the rest of us."

And they did and the dinner seemed to Morrison to be particularly satisfactory. Throughout their stay on the ship, tension had managed to suppress his appetite, but such things are merely deferred and hunger was gnawing with a vengeance once Morrison felt truly safe, truly comfortable, truly clean, and truly clothed.

The main course at the dinner was a roast goose of enormous size which Dezhnev carved, saying, "Be abstemious, my friends, for as my father used to say: 'Eating too much kills more quickly than eating too little.'"

Having said this, he served himself a much larger helping than he served anyone else.

The one outsider present was a very blond tall man, who

was introduced as the military commander of the Grotto, something which could be seen at once, since he was in full uniform with a spate of decorations. The others seemed extraordinarily polite to him and extraordinarily uncomfortable at the same time.

Throughout the meal, Morrison felt the tension returning. The commander looked at him often, with unsmiling gravity, but said nothing to him directly. Because of the commander's presence, he felt uable to ask *the* important question and then, finally, when he might have raised it after the commander's departure, he suddenly found himself too sleepy. He would not be able to argue it out properly if there were any complications.

And when he finally managed to tumble into bed, his last semiconscious thought was that there *would* be complications.

79.

BREAKFAST was late and Morrison found that it was for two. Only Boranova joined him.

He was mildly disappointed, for he had looked forward to the presence of Sophia Kaliinin, but when she failed to appear, he decided not to ask after her. There were other questions he would have to ask.

Boranova looked tired, as though she had not had enough sleep, but she looked happy, too. Or perhaps (Morrison thought) "happy" was too strong a word. Contented, rather.

She said, "I had a good talk with the commander last night and there was a two-way video call with Moscow. Carefully shielded. Comrade Rashchin himself spoke with me and was clearly pleased in the highest degree. He is not a demonstrative man but he told me that he had been in touch with events all yesterday and that, during the interval in which we were not in communication with the outside world, he had been unable to eat or to do anything but pace back and forth. That, perhaps, was an exaggeration. He even said he had wept with joy at hearing that we were all safe and that may be true. Undemonstrative men can be emotional when the dam breaks."

"It sounds good for you, Natalya."

"For the whole project. You understand that, according to

the tentative schedule under which we had worked, we were not expected to launch a voyage into a living human body for at least five years. To have done so with a grossly inadequate ship and to have come out of it alive is viewed as a great triumph. Even the bureaucracy in Moscow understood the emergency under which we labored."

"I doubt that we really got what we were after."

"You mean Shapirov's thoughts? That was, of course, Yuri's dream. On the whole, it was fortunate that he talked us all into following that dream. We would never have attempted the voyage otherwise. Nor does the failure of the dream dim our feat. Had we failed to return alive, we can be sure that there would have been much criticism of our folly in attempting the matter. As it is, though, we are the first to have entered a living human body and to have returned alive —a Soviet first that will stand forever in history. There will be no non-Soviet feat of the sort for years and our Soviet leadership is well-aware of that and very satisfied. We are assured of the money we will need for a considerable time, I imagine, provided we can come up with a spectacular feat now and then."

She smiled broadly at this and Morrison nodded and smiled politely with her. He cut away at the ham omelet he had requested and said, "Would it have been diplomatic to emphasize that an American was one of the crew? Was I mentioned at all?"

"Come, Albert, don't think so ill of us. Your feat in turning the ship by hand at the risk of your life was mentioned with emphasis."

"And Shapirov's death? That will not be blamed on us, I hope?"

"The death is understood to have been unavoidable. It is well-known that he was kept alive as long as he was by advanced medical methods only. I doubt that it will be mentioned to any great extent in the records."

"In any case," said Morrison, "the nightmare is over."

"The nightmare? Come, give yourself a month or two and it will seem an exciting episode that you'll be glad you experienced."

"I doubt it."

"You'll see. If you live to witness other such voyages,

you'll be delighted to say, 'Ah, but I was on the very first,' and you'll never tire of telling the story to your grandchildren."

That's the opening, thought Morrison. Aloud, he said, "I see you assume that I will see my grandchildren someday. What happens to me once we're finished with breakfast, Natalya?"

"It will be out of the Grotto for you and back to the hotel."

"No no, Natalya. I want more than that. What follows *that?* I warn you that if the miniaturization project is going to go public and if there's a parade in Red Square, I don't intend to be part of it."

"Parades are out of the question, Albert. We're a long way from going public, although we're closer to it by far than we were the day before yesterday."

"Let me put it baldly then. I want to go back to the United States. Now."

"As soon as possible, certainly. I imagine there will be pressure from your government."

"I should hope so," said Morrison dryly.

"They would not have been willing to have you back before you had a chance to help us or"—her eyes looked into his rather sternly—"from their point of view, spied on us. But now that you have done your part—and I'm sure they will be aware of that somehow—they will demand you back."

"And you must send me back. You promised that over and over."

"We will keep our promise."

"Nor need you think I have spied on you. I have seen nothing you have not let me see."

"I know that. Yet, when you return to your own country, do you imagine that you will not be questioned exhaustively on what you have seen?"

Morrison shrugged. "That was the consequence you must have accepted when you brought me here."

"True and we won't let it keep us from returning you. It is quite certain you won't be able to tell your people anything they don't already know. They poke their noses into our affairs carefully and skillfully—"

"As your people poke their noses into ours—" said Morrison with some indignation.

"Undoubtedly," said Boranova with a negligent wave of her hand. "Of course, you will be able to tell them of our success, but we don't really object to their knowing. To this day, Americans insist on believing that Soviet science and technology is second-class. It will do us good to teach them a lesson in this. One thing, though—"

"Ah," said Morrison.

"Not a large thing, but a lie. You must not say we brought you here by force. In any public mention of this matter, you must state—if the question arises—that you came here voluntarily, in order to test your theories under conditions not available to you elsewhere in the world. It is a totally likely thing. Who would disbelieve you?"

"My government knows otherwise."

"Yes, but they will themselves urge you to tell the lie. They are as little eager as we are to plunge the world into a crisis over this. Aside from the fact that crises between the United States and the Soviet Union would instantly antagonize the rest of the world against both of us in these so-called good new days, the United States will no more wish to admit they had let you be taken than we would to admit we had taken you. Come, Albert, it is a small thing."

Morrison sighed. "If you return me now, as you say you will do, I will keep quiet about this small matter of kidnapping."

"You use the conditional. You say 'if.'" Boranova was grim. "You clearly find it troublesome to believe me to be a person of honor. Why? Because I am a Soviet. Two generations of peace, two generations of getting along, and your old habits persist. Is there to be no hope for humanity?"

"Good new days or not, we still don't like your system of government."

"Who gives you the right to judge us? We don't like yours, either. —But never mind. If we begin to quarrel, that will spoil what should be a happy day for you—and what *is* a happy day for me."

"Very well. We will not quarrel."

"Then let us say good-bye now, Albert, and someday we will meet again under more normal circumstances I am sure." She held out her hand to him and he took it. She went on, "I have asked Sophia to escort you back to the hotel and to make the arrangements for your leaving. You will not object to that, I'm sure."

Morrison pressed her hand strongly. "No. I rather like Sophia."

Boranova smiled. "I had sensed that somehow."

80.

IT *was* a happy day for Boranova and her exhaustion did not prevent her from enjoying it.

Exhaustion! How many days of rest, how many nights of sleep, how long a stretch at home with Nikolai and Aleksandr would it take to cure that?

But she was alone now and for a period of time there would be nothing to do. Seize the moment!

Boranova stretched out luxuriously on the couch in her office and gave herself over to a curious jumble of thought— now a commendation from Moscow, with a promotion, all mixed up with days on the beach at Crimea with her husband and son. It became almost real as she slept and dreamed that she was pursuing little Aleksandr as he marched firmly into the cold waters of the Black Sea in heedless lack of concern over the possibility of drowning himself. She was carrying a drum that she was beating wildly in order to attract the attention he stubbornly refused to give her.

And the vision broke apart and faded and the drumbeat was a hammering at the door.

She rose with a confused effort, smoothed the blouse she was wearing, and strode to the door in hasty concern. This turned to fury when she threw it open and found Konev frowning darkly, his fist raised to renew his assault.

"What is this, Yuri?" she said indignantly. "Is this your way of announcing yourself? There are signals."

"Which no one answered, though I knew you to be within."

Boranova motioned him in with a quick gesture of her head. She was not anxious to see him and he was not a pleasant sight.

She said, "Haven't you slept at all? You look awful."

"I haven't had time. I've been working."

"At what?"

"At what do you suppose, Natalya? At the data we obtained yesterday in the brain."

Boranova felt her anger seep away. After all, it was Konev whose dream this had been. The success of survival was sweet for everyone but Konev. Only he felt the failure.

She said, "Sit down, Yuri. Try to face it. The thought analysis didn't work—and it couldn't. Shapirov was too far gone. Even as we went in, he was on the point of death."

Konev looked at Boranova blankly, as though totally disregarding her words. "Where is Albert Morrison?"

"There's no use in hounding him, Yuri. He did what he could, but Shapirov's was a dying brain. —Listen to me. It was a dying brain."

Again that blank look. "What are you talking about, Natalya?"

"The data we got. The supposed data that you're struggling with. Let it go. The voyage has been a marvelous success even without it."

Konev shook his head. "A marvelous success *without* it? You don't know what you're saying. Where is Morrison?"

"He's gone, Yuri. It's finished. He's on his way back to the United States. As we promised."

Konev's eyes opened wide. "But that's impossible. He can't go. He *mustn't* go."

"Well, now," said Boranova calmly. "What are *you* talking about?"

Konev rose to his feet. "I went over the data, you *stupid* woman, and it's all plain. We must keep Morrison. At all costs, we must keep him."

Boranova's face reddened. "How dare you insult me, Yuri? Explain yourself at once or I will have you suspended from this project. What is this new mad fixation of yours on Albert?"

Konev lifted his hands halfway upward, as though impelled by an overwhelming desire to strike out at something, with nothing present to strike at.

He gasped, "I'm sorry, I'm sorry. I withdraw the adjective. But you must understand. All through our stay in the brain—all the time we were trying to tap Shapirov's thoughts—Albert Morrison was lying to us. He *knew* what was happening. He *must* have known and he carefully led us in the wrong direction. We must have him, Natalya, and we must have his device. We can *never* let him go."

CHAPTER 18

RETURN?

*The trouble with triumph is that
you may be on the other side.*
    —Dezhnev Senior

81.

MORRISON was doing his best to keep his feelings under control. There was a natural elation. He was going to go home. He was going to be free. He was going to be safe. Much more than that, he would—

But he dared not think of that climactic bit as yet. Yuri Konev was fearfully intelligent and already suspicious. Morrison's thoughts, if Konev concentrated on them, might give themselves away in his facial expressions somehow.

—Or were they just playing with him? That was the other side of the coin.

Were they planning to break his spirit and turn him to their own uses? It was an old trick, to raise hopes and then dash them—far worse than having no hope at all at any time.

Would Natalya Boranova do such a thing? She had not hesitated to take him forcibly when he would not come willingly. She had not hesitated to threaten to destroy his reputation forever to get him on the ship. How much farther would she go? Would she stop at nothing?

His heart bounded with a marked relief when Sophia

Kaliinin appeared. Surely *she* would not be party to such a deception.

He believed that even more firmly when she smiled at him, looking happier than he had ever seen her. She took his hand and tucked it under her arm.

"You'll be going home now. I'm so glad for you," she said and Morrison could not make himself believe that those words—their intonation, her expression—were all part of a careful lie.

Nevertheless, he said cautiously, "I *hope* I'm going home."

And she said, "You are. —Have you ever been on a skimmer?"

For a moment, Morrison stumbled on the Russian word, then used a translated English phrase. "Do you mean an SPF? A solar-powered flyer?"

"This is a Soviet design. Much better. It has light engines. You can't always trust the sun."

"But why a skimmer, then?" They were moving briskly toward the passageway that would lead them out of the Grotto.

"Why not? We'll be at Malenkigrad in fifteen minutes and since you've never been in a Soviet skimmer, you'll love it. It will be one more way of celebrating your return."

"I'm a little nervous of heights. Will it be safe?"

"Absolutely. Besides, I couldn't resist. We're in a wonderful situation now and I don't know how much longer it will last. Whatever we want we get—for the moment. I said, 'A skimmer is what we will want,' and they smiled all over their faces and said, 'Why, certainly, Dr. Kaliinin. It will be waiting for you.' Day before yesterday, I would have had to fill out a proof-of-need form for a plate of borscht. Today I am a hero of the Soviet Union—unofficially, as yet. We all are. You, too, Albert."

"I *hope* I won't be expected to stay for the official ceremonies," said Morrison, still cautious.

"The official ceremonies will be confined to the Grotto, of course, and won't be elaborate at all. Your scroll will undoubtedly be forwarded to you. Perhaps our ambassador can give it to you in a quiet Washington ceremony."

"Not necessary," said Morrison. "I would appreciate the honor, but getting it in the mail is all I really want."

They had turned down a corridor that Morrison had not

taken before and then walked long enough to make him wonder uneasily where they might be going. No need to have worried, Morrison thought as they emerged into a small airfield.

There was no mistaking the skimmer. It had long wings, glittering with a layer of photovoltaic cells along their entire upper surface, very much as American SPFs had. The American planes, however, relied on the solar panels entirely. The skimmer he saw had small rotors—gasoline-powered, no doubt—as assists. Kaliinin might present that as a Soviet improvement but Morrison suspected that the Soviet photovoltaic cells were not as efficient as the American ones.

A mechanic was standing near the skimmer and Kaliinin approached him with long, confident strides. "How does it test out?"

"Sweet as a dream," said the mechanic.

She smiled and nodded, but as he stepped away she muttered to Morrison, "I'll check it out anyway, of course. I've seen dreams that turned into nightmares."

Morrison studied the skimmer with a mixture of interest and apprehension. It looked like the skeleton of a plane, with everything somehow thinner and longer than it should be. The cockpit was tiny, like a soap bubble under the huge flap of wings and the long backward extension of a thin skeletal structure.

Kaliinin had to bend herself nearly double to climb in. Morrison watched her as she fiddled with the controls. Then, after what seemed a considerable lapse of time, she taxied it down the field, turned it, and came back. She raised the rotos and let them turn slowly and eventually everything was shut down and she got out.

"It's working nicely," she said. "The fuel supply is adequate and the sun is shining brilliantly. One couldn't ask for more."

Morrison nodded and looked around. "One could ask for the pilot. Where is he?"

Kaliinin froze at once. "Where is *he?* Is there some sexual requirement for the task? I pilot my own skimmer."

"You?" exclaimed Morrison quite automatically.

"Yes, I! Why not? I have my license and I qualify as a master pilot. Get in!"

"I'm sorry," stammered Morrison. "I—I rarely fly and piloting anything through the air is almost a mystical thing to me. I just assumed that a pilot didn't do anything but piloting and that if someone did anything else, he couldn't be a pilot. Do you know what I mean?"

"I'm not even going to try to figure it out, Albert. Get in."

Morrison climbed in, following her directions and doing his best not to damage his head on any portion of the skimmer—or, perhaps, damaging the skimmer.

He sat in his seat, staring in horror at the skimmer's open side to his right. "Isn't there a door to close?"

"Why do you want a closed door? It would spoil the wonderful feeling of flight. Strap yourself in and you'll be perfectly safe. —Here, I'll show you how. —Are you ready now?" She was in the seat beside him, looking quite confident and pleased with herself. They were crowded into contact and that much at least Morrison found rather soothing.

"I'm resigned," he said. "That's as close as I can get to ready."

"Don't be silly. You're going to love this. We'll use the motors to rise."

There was a high-pitched throb of the small engine and a rhythmic slap as the rotors began to spin. Slowly the skimmer rose and—as slowly—it turned. It canted to one side while turning and Morrison found himself leaning out over the open side and straining precariously against the strap that held him. He barely managed to fight off the strong impulse to throw his arms around Kaliinin for nothing more than utterly nonerotic security.

The skimmer straightened and Kaliinin said, "Now, listen," as she turned off the engine and threw in a switch labeled, in Cyrillic—SOLAR. The throb ceased and the rotors slackened as the forward propeller began to turn. The skimmer moved slowly and almost silently forward.

"Listen to the quiet," whispered Kaliinin. "It's like drifting on nothing."

Morrison looked down uneasily.

Kaliinin said, "We won't fall. Even if a cloud passed over the sun or if a circuit failure put the photovoltaic cells out of action, there is enough power in the storage components to bring us across kilometers, if necessary, to a safe landing. And if we ran out of power, the skimmer is more than half a glider and it would still settle down to a safe landing. I don't think I could force the craft into a crash even if I tried. The only real danger is a strong wind and there's none of that now."

Morrison swallowed and said, "It's a gentle motion."

"Of course. We're not going much faster than an automobile would go and the sensation is much pleasanter. I love it. Try to relax and look at the sky. There's nothing as peaceful as a skimmer."

He said, "How long have you been doing this?"

"When I was twenty-four, I got my master's license. So did Yu— So did *he.* Many a peaceful summer afternoon we spent in the air in a skimmer like this. Once we each had a racing skimmer and marked out lover's knots in the air." Her face twisted slightly as she said that and it occurred to Morrison that she had obtained a skimmer for the short hop to Malenkigrad only for the sake of a momentary reliving of memories and for no other reason.

"That must have been dangerous," he said.

"Not really—if you know what you're doing. Once we skimmed along the foothills of the Caucasus and *that* might have been dangerous. A wind squall can easily smash you into a hillside and that wouldn't be fun at all, but we were young and carefree. —Though I might have been better off if that had happened."

Her voice trailed away and for a moment her face darkened, but then an inner thought seemed to illuminate her into a smile.

Morrison felt his distrust mounting again. Why did the thought of Konev make her so happy, when she could not bear to look at him when they were together in the miniaturized ship?

Morrison said, "You don't seem to mind talking about him, Sophia." Then, deliberately, he used the forbidden word, "About Yuri, I mean. It even seems to make you happy. Why is that?"

And Kaliinin said between her teeth, "It's not sentimental memories that makes me happy, I assure you, Albert. Anger and frustration and—and heartbreak can make a person vicious. I want revenge and I am mean-spirited enough—well, human enough—to enjoy it when it comes."

"Revenge? I don't understand."

"It's simple enough, Albert. He deprived me of love and

my daughter of a father when I had no way of striking back. That did not bother him as long as he had his dream of bringing miniaturization to practical low-energy fruition so that he might become, at a bound, the most famous scientist in the world—or in history."

"But he failed at that. We didn't get the necessary information from Shapirov's brain. You know we didn't."

"Ah, but you don't know *him.* He never gives up; he's driven by the Furies. I've seen him, fleetingly, looking at you, after the voyage through Shapirov's body was done. I know his looks, Albert. I can tell his thoughts even from the droop of an eyelid. He thinks you have the answer."

"Of what was in Shapirov's brain? I don't. How could I?"

"It doesn't matter whether you do or not, Albert. He *thinks* you do and he wants you and your device with a greater yearning than he ever wanted anything in his life; certainly more than he wanted me or his child. And I'm taking you away from him, Albert. With my own hands I am taking you out of the Grotto and will watch you leave for your own country. And I will see him sicken to death of frustrated ambition."

Morrison stared at her in astonishment as the skimmer moved along in response to her rock-steady hand at the controls. He had not thought that Kaliinin was capable of wearing an expression of such consuming and malignant joy.

82.

BORANOVA had listened to Konev's emotional and breathless account and felt herself carried along by the wave of his utter conviction. That had happened before, when he had been convinced that Shapirov's dying mind could be tapped and that Morrison, the American neurophysicist, was the key to doing that. She had been swept along then and she tried to resist it now.

She said finally, "That sounds quite mad."

Konev said, "What's the difference what it sounds like if it's true?"

"Ah, but is it true?"

"I am certain."

Boranova muttered, "We need Arkady here to tell us that

his father assured him that vehemence was no guarantee of truth."

"Neither is it a guarantee of the reverse. If you accept what I say, you must also see that we can't let him go. Certainly not now and possibly not ever."

Boranova shook her head violently. "It's too late. There's nothing to be done. The United States wants him back and the government has agreed to let him go. The government can't very well backtrack now without bringing about a world crisis."

"Considering what is at stake, Natalya, we must surely risk it. The world crisis will not explode. There will be loud talk and much posturing for a month or two and then if we have what we want, we might let him go if absolutely necessary—or we might arrange an accident—"

Boranova rose to her feet angrily. "No! What you are suggesting is unthinkable. This is the twenty-first century, not the twentieth."

"Natalya, whatever century this is, we face the question of whether the Universe is to be ours—or theirs."

"You know you're not going to convince Moscow that that is what is at stake. The government has what it wants, a safe voyage into and out of a body. At the moment it's all they want. They never understood that we wanted to read Shapirov's mind. We never explained that."

"*That* was a mistake."

"Come, Yuri. Do you know how long it would have taken to persuade them that Albert would have to be taken forcibly if he did not come voluntarily? They would not have wanted to risk a crisis—even as much a crisis as they now face, which is a minor one indeed. You will now be asking them to face a much larger one. Not only will you fail but you will encourage them to look into the matter of the arrival of Albert here and I don't think we can afford that."

"The government is not all one piece. There are many high officials who are convinced that we are too eager to give in to the Americans, that we pay too high a price for the occasional pat on the head we receive. I have people to whom I have entry—"

"I have long known that you have. That's a dangerous game you play, Yuri. Better men than you have been caught up in that sort of intrigue and have come to deplorable ends."

"It's the chance I must take. In a case like this, I can turn the government around. But we must have Albert Morrison in our own hands if we're to do it. Once he's gone, it will be all over. —When is he supposed to be leaving?"

"Nightfall. Sophia and I agreed that, for the sake of avoiding obtrusiveness and of needlessly provoking those who tend to be against accommodation with the Americans, night is better than day."

He stared at her, eyes opening widely enough so that they almost seemed protuberant. "Sophia?" he said harshly. "What's she got to do with it?"

"She's in charge of the details of returning Albert. She requested it."

"She requested it?"

"Yes. I imagine she wished to be with him for an additional while." With a touch of spite, she added, "Perhaps you didn't notice it, but she rather likes the American."

Konev sneered in disgust. "Not a bit of it. I know that devil. I know her if I know anything at all—every thought in her head. She's getting him away from *me*. Sitting right next to him in the ship, watching his every move, she must have guessed his importance and she means to deprive *me* of him. She won't wait for nightfall. She'll hurry him off at once."

He rose and left the room at a run.

"Yuri," Boranova called after him. "Yuri, what do you intend to do?"

"Stop her," floated back the answer.

She gazed after him thoughtfully. She could stop *him*. She had the authority. She had the means. And yet—

What if he was right? What if what was at stake was indeed nothing less than the Universe? If she stopped him, everything—*everything*—might be handed over to the Americans. If she let him go, there might be a crisis of an intensity that hadn't been dreamed of in generations.

She had to come to a decision at once.

She began again.

If she stopped him, she would have *done* something. If he then turned out to have been right, the blame for having stopped him and having lost the Universe would rest squarely on her. If he turned out to be wrong after being stopped—her action would be forgotten. There is nothing dramatic about a mistake that is not made.

If she did nothing to stop him, however, then all was on Konev's head. If he somehow prevented Morrison's return to the United States and if the government were then humiliatingly forced to release him, it would be Konev who would be blamed. Boranova would lose nothing, for he had dashed off without telling her what he was going to do and she could reasonably claim she had not dreamed he would try to subvert the known intention of the government. She would be in the clear. If, on the other hand, he prevented Morrison's return and proved to be right and the government won the battle of wills that followed, she could claim the credit of having done nothing to stop him. She could say that it had been with her permission that he had worked.

Well, then, if she stopped him, the worst was blame, the best was neutral. If she did nothing, the best was credit, the worst was neutral.

So Boranova did nothing.

83.

MORRISON decided that Kaliinin was right. As the minutes passed, he grew less uncomfortable in the skimmer and even began to experience a feeble pleasure.

He could see the ground clearly through the open latticework that made up the chassis of the craft. It was about thirty meters below (he judged) and moving smoothly backward.

Kaliinin sat at the controls, completely absorbed, though it didn't seem to Morrison that she had much to do. Presumably, it was skill and patient observation that made it possible for her to keep the skimmer on track without minute-by-minute adjustment.

He said, "What happens if you find yourself moving into a headwind, Sophia?"

She said without taking her eyes from the controls, "Then I would have to use the engine and waste fuel. If it were a fresh wind, it wouldn't pay to use a skimmer at all. Fortunately, today is ideal skimmer weather."

Morrison began to feel something that was almost well-being for the first time since having left the United States—

no, since a considerable length of time before that. He began to picture himself back in the United States; it was the first time he had dared to do so.

He asked, "What happens after we reach the hotel in Malenkigrad?"

"Car to the airport," said Kaliinin crisply, "and then you'll board a plane to America."

"When?"

"Tonight, according to schedule. I'll try to get it done more quickly."

Morrison said with what was almost joviality, "Anxious to get rid of me?"

And to his surprise, the answer came back at once. "Yes. Exactly."

He studied her face in profile. The look of studied hatred had long since vanished, but there was a settled anxiety about her expression that caused Morrison to quiver. The picture of himself back in the United States began to fade around the edges.

He said, "Is anything wrong, Sophia?"

"No, nothing wrong now. It's just that I expect that—*he* will come after us. The wolf is in pursuit, so I must get you away quickly if I can."

84.

THE city of Malenkigrad lay below them, although it was not exactly a city. Small in name, it was small in fact and it raveled off in all directions into the flat countryside.

It was the bedroom community for the people working on the miniaturization project and during the day—now—it seemed all but deserted. There was a moving vehicle here and there, occasionally a pedestrian, and, of course, children playing in the dusty streets.

It occurred to Morrison that he had no way of knowing where, in the mighty stretch of land that made up the Soviet Union, Malenkigrad and the Grotto might be. It wasn't in the birch forest or in the tundra. The early summer was warm and the ground looked semiarid. He might be in central Asia or in the steppes near the European side of the Caspian. He could not say.

The skimmer was dropping now, more gently than an elevator. Morrison would not have believed that so soothing a descent could be possible. Then the wheels touched the ground and they braked to a nearly instant halt. They were in the rear of the hotel, a hotel the small size of which he could appreciate when it was seen from the air.

Kaliinin left the skimmer with a lively jump and motioned to Morrison, who emerged more sedately.

He said, "What happens to the skimmer now?"

She answered carelessly, "I'll pick it up on my return and take it back to the Grotto field if the weather holds. Come, let's go around to the front and I'll get you into your room, where you can rest a little and where we can plan the next step."

"The room with the soldiers watching me, you mean."

She said impatiently, "There'll be no soldiers watching you. We're not afraid of your trying to escape *now*." Then, with a quick glance around, she added, "Though I'd rather have the soldiers, actually."

Morrison looked about, too, a bit anxiously and decided he'd rather *not* have the soldiers. It occurred to him that if Konev came to reclaim him, as Kaliinin clearly feared he might do, he might easily come with soldiers at his back.

And then Morrison thought: Or is this really something to fear? She has a thing about Yuri. She'll believe anything of him.

The thought did not quiet him, however.

Morrison had not seen the hotel in broad daylight from outside; he had not had the leisure to study it in any case. It occurred to him that it was probably used only by visiting officials and special guests—such as he himself, if he could lay claim to the category. He wondered if, small as it was, it was ever full. Certainly, the two nights he had spent here had been quiet indeed. He recalled no noise in the corridors and the dining room, when he had eaten there, had been all but empty, too.

It was at the moment he thought of the dining room that they approached the front entrance and there, to one side, sitting in the sun and poring over a book, was a stoutish woman with reddish-brown hair. She was wearing half-spectacles, perched low on her nose. (Morrison was surprised at that bit of archaism. It was rare to see glasses in these days when eye-molding was routine and normal vision had truly become normal.)

It was the glasses and the studious look on her face that changed her appearance so that Morrison might easily not have recognized her. He would not have, perhaps, if he had not just thought of the dining room. The woman was the waitress to whom he had appealed for help three evenings before and who had failed him—Valeri Paleron.

He said austerely, "Good morning, Comrade Paleron." His voice was stiff and his expression unfriendly.

She did not seem discomfited by this. She looked up, removed her glasses, and said, "Ah, Comrade American. You are back safe and sound. Congratulations."

"For what?"

"It is the talk of the town. There has been an experiment that was a great success."

Kaliinin, her face like thunder, said sharply, "That should not be the talk of the town. We need no wagging tongues."

"What wagging tongues?" said the waitress with spirit. "Who here does not work at the Grotto or have a relative there? Why should we not know of it and why should we not speak of it? And can I fail to hear? Must I stop my ears? I cannot carry a tray and put my fingers in my ears, too."

She turned to Morrison. "I hear that you did very well and are greatly praised for it."

Morrison shrugged.

"And this man," the waitress said, turning to the frowning and increasingly impatient Kaliinin, "wished to leave before he had the chance to participate in the great deed. He turned to me for help in his scheme to leave—to me, a waitress. I reported him at once, of course, and that made him unhappy. Even now, see how he glares at me." She wagged her finger at him. "But consider the favor I did you. Had I not prevented you from doing whatever it was they were trying to have you do, you would not now be the great success you are, the toast of Malenkigrad and perhaps even of Moscow. And the little Tsaritsa here surely loves you for it."

Kaliinin said, "If you do not stop this impudence immediately, I shall report *you* to the authorities."

"Go ahead," said Paleron, her hands on her hips and her eyebrows lifting. "I do my work, I am a good citizen, and I have done nothing wrong. What can you report? —And there is a fancy car here for you, too."

"I saw no fancy car," said Kaliinin.

"It is not in the parking lot, but on the other side of the hotel."

"What makes you think it is for me?"

"You are the only important persons to approach the hotel. For whom, then, should it be? For the porter? For the desk clerk?"

"Come, Albert," said Kaliinin. "We are wasting our time." She brushed past the waitress, doing this so closely that she stepped on her foot—perhaps not by accident. Morrison followed meekly.

"I hate that woman," muttered Kaliinin as they walked up the flight of stairs to Morrison's second-floor room.

"Do you think that she is an observer of this place on behalf of the Central Coordinating Committee?" asked Morrison.

"Who knows? But there is something wrong with her. She is possessed by a devil of impudence. She does not know her place."

"Her place? Are there class distinctions, then, in the Soviet Union?"

"Don't be sarcastic, Albert. There are supposedly none in the United States, either, but you have them surely. And so do we. I know what the theory is, but no person can live by theory alone. If Arkady's father didn't say that, he should have."

They walked up one flight of stairs to what had been Morrison's room earlier in the week and apparently still was. Morrison viewed it with mild distaste. It was a room without charm, though the sunlight made it seem less gloomy than he remembered it to be and, of course, the prospect of returning home was enough to add glitter to anything.

Kaliinin sat in the better of the two armchairs in the room, her legs crossed, the upper leg swinging in short arcs. Morrison sat down on the side of the bed and watched her legs thoughtfully. He had never had good occasion to admire his own calmness under pressure and it seemed to him rather unusual to watch someone be more nervous than he himself was.

He said, "You seem greatly troubled, Sophia. What is wrong?"

She said, "I told you. That woman Paleron troubles me."

"She can't upset you that much. What's wrong?"

"I don't like waiting. The days are long now. It will be nine hours until sunset."

"It's amazing that it's only a matter of hours. The diplomatic maneuvering could have continued for months." He said so lightly enough, but the thought gave him a cold feeling in the pit of his stomach.

"Not in a case like this. I've seen it work before, Albert. The Swedes are involved. It's not an American plane that's coming. Having an American plane land deep in Soviet territory is still something our government shies away from. But the Swedes— Well, they serve as an intermediary between the two nations by common consent and they tend to work hard to defuse any possibility of friction."

"In the United States, we consider Sweden lukewarm toward us at the best. I think we'd prefer to have Great Britain—"

"Oh come, you might as well say Texas. As it is, Sweden may be lukewarm toward you, but she is considerably less than that toward us. In any case, it's Sweden and their principle always is that if it is necessary to defuse a situation, it is best to defuse it swiftly."

"It seems quite swift to me. Certainly, I'm the one who should be in the greater hurry, since it is I who am most anxious to leave. Why should a few hours matter to you?"

"I've told you. *He* is after us." She ground out the pronoun.

"Yuri? What can he do? If your government is giving me up—"

"There are elements in the government who might easily not wish to give you up and our—friend—knows some of these well."

Morrison raised a finger to his lips and looked around.

Kaliinin said, "Are you worried about being bugged? That's another American spy novel myth. Bugs are so easily detected these days and so easily scrambled— I carry a small detector myself and I've never spotted one."

Morrison shrugged. "Then say what you wish."

"Our friend is not a political extremist himself, but he

finds he can use those in high office who are. There are extremists in America, too, I suppose."

"Those who think our policy toward the Soviet Union is too mild?" Morrison nodded. "I've met a few."

"Well, then, there you are. His ambition consumes him and if extremism will advance his plans, then he is prepared to be an extremist."

"Surely you don't think he can arrange some sort of coup in Moscow and put the diehards in control and do it all in time to stop me from leaving for home this evening?"

"You've got it the wrong way around, Albert. If he could somehow prevent you from leaving and precipitate a crisis, he may be able to persuade some in the government to stand firm and delay your leaving for a long time. He can be very persuasive, our friend, when he is in the full grip of his mania. He can sway even Natalya."

Kaliinin fell into a silence and bit at her lower lip. Finally she looked up and said, "He hasn't given up on you and he won't. I'm sure of it. I've got to get you away."

She rose suddenly and paced up and down the room with short, quick steps, looking as though she were trying to force the Universe into turning her way. She stopped in front of the door, listened, then jerked it open suddenly.

Valeri Paleron, her bland expression shifting rapidly into surprise, had one fist raised, as though she were about to knock.

"What do you want?" said Kaliinin tightly.

"I?" said the waitress. "I want nothing. It is a question of whether *you* do. I have come to ask if you would like some tea."

"We have not asked for any."

"I did not say you have. I come out of courtesy."

"Then go out of courtesy. And do not return."

Paleron, reddening, looked from Kaliinin to Morrison and said between her teeth, "Perhaps I interrupt a tender moment."

"Leave!" said Kaliinin. She closed the door, waited long enough to count to ten in a deliberate manner (her lips moving soundlessly), and then flung it open again. No one was there.

She closed the door and locked it, walked to the opposite

end of the room, and said in a low voice, "She had been out there, probably, for quite some time. I heard feet shuffling."

Morrison said, "If high-tech bugging is passé, then I suppose there is a premium on old-fashioned eavesdropping."

"Ah, but for whom?"

"Do you suppose she does it for Yuri? It doesn't seem likely that he would have the money to hire spies—or does he?"

"It might not take much money. A woman like that might do it for pleasure."

There was silence for a moment and then Morrison said, "If it's possible that you're beset by spies, Sophia, why not come to America with me?"

"What?" She seemed not to have heard him.

"You might be in trouble for getting me out, you know."

"Why? I have official papers that will place you on the plane. I am under orders."

"That might not save you if a scapegoat is needed. Why not just get on the plane with me, Sophia, and come to America?"

"Just like that? What would happen to my child?"

"We'll send for her afterward."

"*We'll* send for her? What are you suggesting?"

Morrison flushed slightly. "I'm not sure. We can be friends, certainly. You'll need friends in a new country."

"But it can't happen, Albert. I appreciate your kindness and concern—or pity—but it can't happen."

"Yes, it can. This is the twenty-first century, not the twentieth, Sophia. People may move about freely anywhere in the world."

"Dear Albert," said Kaliinin, "you do tend to live in theory. Yes, people can move about, but every nation has its exceptions. The Soviet Union will not allow a highly trained scientist with experience in miniaturization-related fields to leave the country. Think about it and you'll see that that's reasonable. If I *do* accompany you, there will be an immediate Soviet protest, a sure claim that I have been kidnapped, and there will be a loud howl from all corners of the world that I be sent back in order to avoid a crisis. Sweden will act as quickly for me as she has for you."

"But in my case, I *was* kidnapped."

"There'll be many who will believe I was—or who might

prefer to believe it—and I will be sent back by the United States, as you are being sent back by the Soviet Union. We've papered over, in this fashion, dozens of crises over the last six decades or so—and isn't that better than war?"

"If you *say,* firmly and frequently, that you want to stay in the United States—"

"Then I never see my child again and my life may be at risk, too. Besides, I don't *want* to go to the United States."

Morrison looked surprised.

Kaliinin said, "Do you find that hard to believe? Do you want to stay in the Soviet Union?"

"Of course not. My country—" He stopped.

She said, "Exactly. You talk endlessly about humanity, about the importance of a global view, but if we scrape you down to your emotions, it's your country. I have a country also, a language, a literature, a culture, a way of life. I don't want to give it up."

Morrison sighed. "As you say, Sophia."

Sophia said, "But I cannot endure it here in this room any longer, Albert. There's no use waiting. Let us get into the car and I'll drive you to where the Swedish plane is waiting."

"It probably won't be there."

"Then we'll wait at the airport, rather than here, and we'll at least be certain that as soon as it arrives you can board it. I want to see you safely gone, Albert, and I want to see *his* face afterward."

She was out the room and clattering down the stairs. He followed hastily. He was, in truth, not sorry to be going.

They strode along a carpeted corridor and through a door that led directly out to the side of the hotel.

There, pulled up close to the wall, was a highly polished black limousine.

Morrison, a little breathless, said, "They're certainly supplying us with deluxe transportation. Can you drive that thing?"

"Like a dream," said Kaliinin, smiling—and then came to a full and sudden halt, her smile forgotten.

Around the corner of the hotel stepped Konev. He, too, halted and for long moments they did not stir, either of them —as though they were a pair of Gorgons, each of whom had frozen into stone at the glance of the other.

85.

MORRISON was the first to speak. He said a little huskily, "Have you come to see me off, Yuri? If so, good-bye. I'm leaving."

The phrases sounded false in his own ears and his heart was pounding.

Yuri's eyes shifted just enough to glance quickly at Morrison and then moved back to their original position.

Morrison said, "Come, Sophia."

He might as well have said nothing. When she spoke—finally—it was to Konev. "What do *you* want?" she demanded harshly.

"The American," said Konev in a tone no softer than hers. "I'm taking him away."

"Don't. We need him. He has deceived us." Konev's voice was becoming quieter.

"So you say," said Kaliinin. "I have my orders. I am to take him to a plane and see that he gets in. You cannot have him."

"It's not I who must have him. It's the nation."

"Tell me. Go on and tell me. Say that Holy Mother Russia needs him and I'll laugh in your face."

"I'll say no such thing. The Soviet Union needs him."

"You care only for yourself. Step out of my way."

Konev moved between the two others and the limo. "No. You don't understand the importance of his staying here. Believe me. My report has already gone to Moscow."

"I'm sure and I can guess to whom it's going, too. But old gruff-and-grumble won't be able to do anything. He's a blowhard and we all know that. He won't dare say a word in the Presidium and if he does, Albert will be long gone."

"No. He's not going."

Morrison said, "I'll take care of him, Sophia. You open the limo door." He felt himself trembling slightly. Konev was not a large man, but he looked wiry and he was clearly determined. Morrison did not believe himself to be a successful gladiator under any conditions and he certainly didn't feel like one now.

Kaliinin lifted her hand, palm turned toward Morrison.

"Stay where you are, Albert." She then said to Konev, "How do you intend to stop me. Do you have a gun?"

Konev looked surprised. "No. Of course not. Carrying a hand weapon is illegal."

"Indeed? But I have one." She drew it from her jacket pocket, a small thing almost enclosed in her fist, its small muzzle gleaming as it edged through the space between her first and second fingers.

Konev backed away, eyes widening. "That's a stunner."

"Of course. Worse than a gun, isn't it? I thought you might interfere, so I'm prepared."

"That's also illegal."

"Then report me and I'll plead the need to fulfill my orders against your criminal interference. I will probably get a commendation."

"You *won't*. Sophia—" He took a step toward her.

She took a step back. "No closer. I'm ready to shoot and I might do so even if you stand where you are. Just keep in mind what a stunner does. It scrambles your brain. Isn't that what you once told me? You'll be unconscious and you'll wake up with partial amnesia and it may take you hours to recover or even days. I've even heard that some people never *quite* recover. Imagine if your magnificent brain should not *quite* regain its fine edge."

"Sophia," he said again.

She said, through almost closed lips, "Why do you use my name? The last time I heard you use it, you said, 'Sophia, we will never speak again, never look at each other again.' You are now speaking to me, looking at me. Go away and keep your promise, you miserable ——" (She used a Russian word that Morrison didn't understand.)

Konev, white to his lips, said a third time, "Sophia— Listen to me. Believe that every word I have ever said is a lie, but listen to me now. That American is a deadly threat to the Soviet Union. If you love your country—"

"I'm tired of loving. What has it gotten me?"

"And what has it gotten me?" whispered Konev.

"You love yourself," said Kaliinin bitterly.

"No! You kept saying that, but it's not so. If I have some regard for myself now, it is because only I can save our country."

"You believe that?" said Kaliinin, wondering. "You really believe that? —You are mad to do so."

"Not at all. I know my own worth. I couldn't let *anything* deter me—not even you. For the sake of our country and my work, I had to give you up. I had to give up my child. I had to tear myself in two and throw the better half of myself away."

"*Your* child?" Kaliinin said. "Are you claiming responsibility?"

Konev's head bent. "How else could I drive you away? How else could I be sure I would work unimpeded? —I love you. I have always loved you. I have known all along it was my child and that it could be no one else's."

"Do you want Albert so much?" Her stunner did not waver. "Are you willing to say that it is your child—say you love me—believe I will, for that, give you Albert—and then deny it all again? How low an opinion you must have of my intelligence."

Konev shook his head. "How can I convince you? —Well, if I deliberately threw it all away, I can't expect to get it back again, can I? Will you, in that case, give me the American for the sake of our nation and then throw *me* away? Would you let me explain the need for him?"

"I wouldn't believe the explanation." Kaliinin threw a quick glance in Morrison's direction. "Do you hear this man, Albert?" she said. "You don't know with what cruelty he cast my daughter and me aside. Now he expects me to believe that he loved me all along."

And Morrison heard himself say, "That much is true, Sophia. He loves you and he has always loved you—desperately."

Kaliinin froze for a moment. Her free left hand gestured at Morrison while her eyes remained fixed on Konev. "How do you know that, Albert? Did he lie to you, too?"

But Konev shouted in excitement, "He *knows*. He admits it. Don't you see? He sensed it with his computer. If you now let me explain, you will believe everything."

Kaliinin said, "Is this true, then, Albert? Do you confirm Yuri?"

And Morrison, too late, clamped his mouth shut, but his eyes gave him away.

Konev said, "My love has been unwavering, Sophia. As

much as you have suffered, so much have I. But give me the American and there will be no more of it. I will no longer ask that I be spared any chance of hindrance. I will do my work and have you and the child, too, whatever the cost may be—and may I be cursed if I don't manage both."

Kaliinin stared at Konev, her eyes suddenly swimming in tears. "I want to believe you," she whispered.

"Then believe. The American has told you."

As though she were sleepwalking, she moved toward Konev, holding the stunner out to him.

Morrison shouted, "Your orders—to the plane!" He rushed wildly at them.

But as he did so, he collided heavily with another body. Arms were around him, holding him closely, and a voice in his ear said, "Take it easy, Comrade American. Do not attack two good Soviet citizens."

It was Valeri Paleron, who held him in a strong and unbreakable grip.

Kaliinin clung as closely to Konev, though with different effect, the stunner still gripped loosely in her right hand.

Paleron said, "Academician, Doctor, we could become conspicuous here. Let us go back to the American's room. Come, Comrade American, and come quietly or I will be compelled to hurt you."

Konev, catching Morrison's eye, smiled tightly in absolute triumph. He had it all—his woman, his child, and his American—and Morrison saw his dream of returning to America pop like a soap bubble and vanish.

CHAPTER 19

TURNAROUND

In the true triumph, however, there are no losers.
—Dezhnev Senior

86.

MORRISON sat in the hotel room that he had, for some fifteen minutes, thought he would never see again. He was close to despair—closer, it seemed to him, than he had been even when he was alone and lost in the cellular stream of the neuron.

What was the use? Over and over again, he thought this, as though the phrase were reverberating in an echo chamber. He was a loser. He had always been a loser.

For a day or so, he had thought that Sophia Kaliinin had been attracted to him, but, of course, she hadn't. He had been nothing more than her weapon against Konev and when Konev had called to her—beckoned to her—she had returned to him and had then no further use for her weapons, either for Morrison or for her stunner.

He looked at them dully. They were standing together in the sunlight streaming through the window—they in the sunlight, he in the shadow, as it must always be.

They were whispering together, so lost in each other that Kaliinin seemed unaware that she was still holding the stunner. For a moment, her knees bent as though she was going to get rid of its weight by dropping it on the bed, but then Konev said something and she was all attention and again unaware of the stunner's existence.

Morrison called out hoarsely, "Your government will not endure this. You have orders to release me."

Konev looked up, his eyes brightening slightly, as though he were being persuaded, with difficulty, to pay attention to his captive. It was not, after all, as though he had to watch Morrison in any physical sense. The waitress, Valeri Paleron, was doing that most efficiently. She stood a meter from Morrison and her eyes (somehow amused—as though she enjoyed the job) never left him.

Konev said, "My government need not concern you, Albert. It will change its mind soon enough."

Kaliinin raised her left hand as though to object, but Konev enclosed it in his.

"Do not be concerned, Sophia," he said. "Information at my disposal has been forwarded to Moscow. It will make them think. They will get back to me on my personal wavelength before long and when I tell them we have safely secured Morrison, they will take action. I am sure they will have the persuasive power to make the Old Man see reason. I promise you that."

Kaliinin said in a troubled voice, "Albert!"

Morrison said, "Are you getting ready to tell me that you are sorry, Sophia, that you crossed me out of existence at one word from the man you seemed to have hated?"

Kaliinin reddened. "You are not crossed out of existence, Albert. You will be well-treated. You will work here as you would have worked in your own country, except that here you will be truly appreciated."

"Thank you," said Morrison, finding some small reservoir of the sardonic inside himself. "If you feel happy for me, of what importance is my feeling for myself?"

Paleron intervened impatiently, "Comrade American, you talk too much. Why do you not sit down? —*Sit down.*" (She pushed him into a chair.) "You may as well wait quietly, since there is nothing else you can do."

She then turned to Kaliinin, around whose shoulders Konev's right arm was protectively placed. "And you, little Tsaritsa," she said, "are you still planning to place this fine lover of yours out of action that you hold this stunner so

menacingly in your hand? You will be able to embrace him
the more tightly if both arms are free."

Paleron reached for the stunner Kaliinin was holding and
Kaliinin gave it up without a word.

"Actually," said Paleron, looking curiously at the stunner,
"I am relieved at having it. In the paroxysm of your newfound love, I feared you might shoot in all directions. It
would not be safe in your hands, my little one."

She moved back to the vicinity of Morrison, still studying
the stunner and turning it in various ways.

Morrison stirred uneasily. "Don't point it in my direction,
woman. It may go off."

Paleron looked at him haughtily. "It will not go off if I
don't want it to, Comrade American. I know how to use it."

She smiled in the direction of Konev and Kaliinin. Relieved of the weapon, Kaliinin now had both arms around
Konev's neck and was kissing him with quick, gentle touches
of her lips against his. Paleron said in their direction, but not
really to them, for they weren't listening, "I know how to use
it. Like this! And like this!"

And first Konev, then Kaliinin crumpled.

Paleron turned toward Morrison. "Now help me, you idiot, we must work quickly."

She said it in English.

87.

MORRISON had difficulty understanding. He simply stared at
her.

Paleron pushed his shoulder as though she were trying to
awaken him from a deep sleep. "Come on. You grab the
feet."

Morrison obeyed mechanically. First Konev and then
Kaliinin were lifted onto the bed, from which Paleron had
stripped the thin blanket. She stretched both of them out
along the narrow confines of the single mattress, then
searched Kaliinen in a quick, practiced way.

"Ah," she said, staring at a sheet of folded paper, whose
close-set print marked it indelibly as something written in
governmentese. She flipped it into the pocket of her white
jacket and continued the search. Other items came to light—

a pair of small keys, for instance. Quickly she went over Konev, plucking a small metallic disc from the inner surface of his lapel.

"His personal wavelength," she said and placed that, too, into her pocket.

Finally she retrieved a black rectangular object and said, "This is yours, isn't it?"

Morrison grunted. It was his computer program. He had been so far gone he had not been aware that Konev had taken it from him. He clutched at it frantically now.

Paleron turned Kaliinin and Konev toward each other, propping them so that they would not fall apart. She then placed Konev's arm around Kaliinin and covered the two with the blanket, tucking it in under each to help keep them in place.

"Don't stare at me like that, Morrison," she said when she was done. "Come on." She seized his upper arm in a firm grip.

He resisted. "Where are we going? What's happening?"

"I'll tell you later. Not a word now. There is no time to lose. Not a minute. Not a second. Come." She ended with soft fierceness and Morrison followed her.

Out of the room they went, down the stairs as softly as she could manage (he following and imitating), along the carpeted corridor, and out to the limousine.

Paleron opened the front door on the passenger side with one of the keys she had obtained from Kaliinin's pocket and said brusquely, "Get in."

"Where are we going?"

"Get in." She virtually hurled him into the limo.

She settled quickly behind the wheel and Morrison resisted the impulse to ask her if she knew how to drive. It had finally gotten through to his stunned mind that Paleron wasn't simply a waitress.

That she had played the part of one, however, was made plain by the faint odor of onions still clinging to her and mixing rather infelicitously with the richer and pleasanter odor of the limo's interior.

Paleron started the engine, looked around the parking area, which was deserted except for a cat going about some business of its own, and moved out over a sandy patch to the path that led to the nearby road.

Slowly the limo picked up speed and when it finally reached the ninety-five kilometer-per-hour mark, it was moving along a two-lane highway on which, occasionally, an automobile, moving in the other direction, passed them. Morrison found himself capable of thinking normally again.

He glanced back earnestly through the rear window. A car, far behind them, was turning off at an intersection they had passed some moments before. No one appeared to be following them.

Morrison then turned to watch Paleron's profile. She seemed competent but grim. It was clear to him now that she was not only no waitress by true profession but was very likely no Soviet citizen. Her English had a strong urban accent that no European would learn in school or could pick up in a way that would be true enough to fool Morrison's ear.

He said, "You were waiting there outside the hotel, reading a book, so that you would see Sophia and myself when we came."

"You got it," said Paleron.

"You're an American agent, aren't you?"

"Shrewder and shrewder."

"Where are we going?"

"To the designated airport where the Swedish plane will pick you up. I had to get the details on that from Kaliinin."

"And you know how to get there?"

"Yes, indeed. I've been in Malenkigrad for considerably longer a period than your Kaliinin has been here. —But tell me, why did you tell her this man, Konev, was in love with her? She was just waiting to hear that from a third person. She *wanted* it confirmed and you did that for her. In that way, you handed over the whole game to Konev. Why did you do it?"

"For one thing," said Morrison mildly, "it was the truth."

"The *truth?*" Paleron, looking bemused, shook her head. "You don't belong in the real world. You sure don't. I'm surprised no one knocked you on the head and buried you long ago—just for your own good. Besides, how do you know it's the truth?"

Morrison said, "I know. —But I was sorry for her. She saved my life yesterday. She saved all our lives yesterday. For that matter, Konev saved my life, too."

"You all saved each other's life, I suppose."

"Yes, as a matter of fact."

"But that was yesterday. Today you started fresh and you shouldn't have let yesterday influence you. She would never have taken up with him again if it weren't for your dumb remark. He could have sworn himself purple about loving her and all the rest of that rubbish and she wouldn't have believed him. She *dared* not. Be made a fool of again? Never! She would have stunned him to the ground in another minute and then you told her, 'Why, yes, kid, that there guy loves you,' and that's all she needed. I tell you, Morrison, you shouldn't be out without your keeper."

Morrison stirred uneasily. "How do you know all this?"

"I was on the floor in the back seat of this car, ready to go with you and Kaliinin and to make sure she took you there. And then you pulled your dumb trick. What was there to do but grab you and keep you from being stunned down, then get you back to the room where we could have some privacy, and after that get hold of the stunner somehow?"

"Thank you."

"That's all right. —And I made them look like a loving couple, too. Anyone coming in will be bound to say, 'Excuse me,' and leave quickly—and that will give us more time."

"How long will it be before they're conscious again?"

"I don't know. It depends on how accurately I placed the radiation and what each state of mind was and who knows what else. But when they do come back, it will take them some time to remember what happened. I'm hoping that in their position, the first thing they'll remember is that they're in love. That would preoccupy them for a while. Then when they do get around to remembering you and what it was that was being done with Moscow, it will be too late."

"Are they going to be permanently damaged?"

Paleron cast a quick look at Morrison's concerned face. "You're worried about them, aren't you? Why? What are they to you?"

"Well . . . shipmates."

Paleron made an inelegant sound. "I guess they'll recover okay. They might be better off if some of that supersensitive edge is ground off. They can get together and make a nice family then."

"And what's going to happen to you? You'd better get on the plane with me."

"Don't be a jackass. The Swedes wouldn't take me. They've got orders to take one guy and they'll test you to make sure you're the right one. They'll have records of your fingerprints and your retina pattern, right out of the files of the Population Board. If they take the wrong person or an additional person, that'll be a new incident and the Swedes are too smart for that."

"But then what will happen to you?"

"Well, for starters, I'll say you got hold of the stunner and rayed them both, then held the stunner on me and made me take you to the airport because you didn't know its location. You ordered me to stop outside the gates, then stunned me down and tossed the stunner into the car. Early tomorrow, I'll make my way back to Malenkigrad, like I was coming out of a stunning."

"But Konev and Kaliinin will deny your story."

"They weren't looking at me when they were stunned and almost no one remembers the actual moment of stunning, anyway. Besides, the Soviet Government knows that they ordered you returned and if you *are* returned, then anything Konev will tell them about you will do him no good. The government will accept the *fait accompli.* It's rubles to kopeks or, better, dollars to kopeks that they'll prefer to forget the whole thing—and I'll just go back to waitressing."

"There's bound to be some suspicion clinging to you."

"Then we'll see," she said. *"Nichevo!* What will be, will be." She smiled faintly.

They continued to travel along the highway and Morrison finally said with a touch of diffidence, "Shouldn't we speed it up a little?"

"Not even by a kilometer per hour," said Paleron firmly. "We're going at just under the speed limit and the Soviets have every centimeter of the highway radarized. They have no sense of humor about the speed limit and I don't intend to spend hours trying to get out of a police station because I wanted to save fifteen minutes reaching the plane."

It was past noon now and Morrison was beginning to feel the mild, premonitory pinches of hunger. He said, "What was it that Konev told Moscow about me, do you suppose?"

Paleron shook her head. "Don't know. Whatever it was, he got a response on his personal wavelength. It signaled about twenty minutes ago. You didn't hear?"

"No."

"You wouldn't last long in my business. —Naturally, they got no answer, so whoever Konev was talking to in Moscow will try to find out why. Someone will find them and then they'll figure you're on the way to the airport and someone will chase out after us to see if you can be headed off. Like Pharaoh's chariots."

"We don't have Moses to part the Red Sea for us," muttered Morrison.

"If we get to the airport, we'll have the Swedes. They won't give you up to anybody."

"What can they do against the Soviet military?"

"It won't be the Soviet military. It will be some functionary, working for an extremist splinter group, who will try to bluff the Swedes. But we have official papers giving you up to them and they won't be bluffed. We just have to get there first."

"And you don't think we should go faster?"

Paleron shook her head firmly.

Half an hour later, Paleron pointed and said, "There we are and we have the breaks. The Swedish plane is in early and has landed."

She stopped the car, pressed a button, and the door flew open on his side. "You go on alone. I don't want to be seen, but listen—" She leaned toward him. "My name is Ashby. When you get to Washington, tell them that if they think it's time for me to get out—I'm ready. Got it?"

"I've got it."

Morrison got out of the car, blinking in the sunlight. In the distance, a man in uniform—not a Soviet uniform, as nearly as he could tell—waved him forward.

Morrison broke into a run. There were no speed limits on running and though he could see no one in pursuit he would not have been surprised to see someone rise out of the ground to stop him.

He turned, waved a last time in the direction of the car, thought he saw an answering wave, and continued to run.

The man who had gestured to him advanced, first at a walk, then at a run, and caught him as he all but fell forward. Morrison could see now that he was wearing a European Federation uniform.

"May I please have your name?" said the man in English. His accent, to Morrison's infinite relief, was Swedish.

"Albert Jonas Morrison," he said and together they walked toward the plane and the small group waiting to check his identity.

88.

MORRISON sat at the plane window, tense and exhausted, staring downward at the land fleeing east. A lunch, consisting largely of herring and boiled potatoes, had soothed the inner man but scarcely the inner mind.

Had the miniaturized trip through the bloodstream and brain yesterday (only yesterday?) twisted him forever into a mental attitude of apprehension of imminent disaster? Would he never again be able to accept the Universe as friendly? Would he never walk through it in serene consciousness that no one and no thing wished him harm?

Or had there merely been insufficient time for him to recover?

Of course, common sense told him that there was reason not to feel completely safe yet. That was still Soviet earth under the plane.

Was there still time for Konev's ally in Moscow, whoever he might be, to send out planes after the Swedes? Was he powerful enough to do so? Would Pharaoh's chariots take to the air and continue the pursuit?

For a moment, his heart failed him when he actually saw a plane in the distance—then another.

He turned to the stewardess, who sat across the aisle from him. He did not have to ask the question. She apparently read his anxious expression accurately.

"Federation planes," she said, "as escort. We've left Soviet territory. The planes are Swedish-crewed."

Then, when they passed over the English Channel, American planes joined the escort. Morrison was safe from the chariots, at any rate.

His mind did not let him rest, however. Missiles? Would someone actually commit an act of war? He tried to calm himself. Surely no man in the Soviet Union, not even the Soviet Executive himself, could make such a move without consultation and no consultation would take less than hours or perhaps days.

It couldn't be.

Still, it wasn't until the plane had landed on the outskirts of Washington that Morrison could allow himself to feel that it was over and that he was safely in his own country.

89.

IT was Saturday morning and Morrison was recovering. He had attended to his creature needs. He had had breakfast and had washed. He was even partly dressed.

Now he lay in bed on his back, arms behind his head. It was cloudy outside and he had only half-clarified the window because he wanted a sense of privacy. In the hours after he had disembarked from the plane and had been rushed to his present place of concealment, there had been enough official crowding around him to make him wonder a bit if he was any better off in the United States than he had been in the Soviet Union.

The doctors had finally finished their probing, the initial questions had been asked and answered, even during dinner, and they had finally left him to his sleep in a room that was, in turn, inside something that resembled a fortress for the depth of its security.

Well, at least he didn't have to face miniaturization. There was always that thought to comfort him.

The door signal flashed and Morrison reached over his head, feeling the bedboard for the button that would clarify the one-way patch on the door. He recognized the face that appeared and pushed another contact that allowed the door to be opened from the outside.

Two men entered. The one whose familiar face had been at the one-way patch said, "You remember me, I hope."

Morrison made no move to get out of bed. He was the center now around which all revolved, at least temporarily, and he would take advantage of that. He simply raised his arm in casual greeting and said, "You're the agent who wanted me to go to the Soviet Union. Rodano, isn't it?"

"Francis Rodano, yes. And this is Professor Robert G. Friar. I imagine you know him."

Morrison hesitated and then courtesy swung his feet off the bed and lifted him to his feet. "Hello, Professor. I know of you, of course, and have seen you on holovision often enough. I'm pleased to make your personal acquaintance."

Friar, one of the "visible scientists" whose photographs and HV appearances had made him familiar to most of the world, smiled tightly. He had a round face, pale blue eyes, an apparently permanent vertical crease between his eyebrows, ruddy cheeks, a sturdy body of average height, and a way of looking around him restlessly.

He said, "You, I take it, are Albert Jonas Morrison."

"That's right," said Morrison easily. "Mr. Rodano will vouch for me. Please sit down, both of you, and forgive me if I continue to relax on the bed. I have about a year's relaxation to catch up on."

The two visitors sat down on a large couch and leaned toward Morrison. Rodano smiled a bit tentatively. "I can't promise you much relaxation, Dr. Morrison. At least for a while. Incidentally, we have just received word from Ashby. Do you remember her?"

"The waitress who turned the tables? Yes, indeed. Without her—"

"We know the essentials of the story, Morrison. She wants you to know that your two friends have recovered and are apparently fond of each other still."

"And Ashby, herself? She told me she was ready to leave if Washington thought it best. I reported that last night."

"Yes, we'll get her out one way or another. —And now I'm afraid we must bother you again."

Morrison frowned. "How long will this keep up?"

"I don't know. You must take it as it comes. —Professor Friar, won't you take over?"

Friar nodded. "Dr. Morrison, do you mind if I take notes. —No, let me rephrase that. I am going to take notes, Morrison."

He plucked a small computer keyboard of advanced design out of his briefcase.

Rodano said mildly, "Where will these notes go, Professor?"

"To my recording device, Mr. Rodano."

"Which is where, Professor?"

"In my office at Defense, Mr. Rodano." Then, with some

irritation under the other's continuing stare, "Into my *safe* in my office at Defense and both the safe and the recording device are well-coded. Does that satisfy you?"

"Proceed, Professor."

Friar turned to Morrison and said, "Is it true that you were miniaturized, Morrison. You, personally?"

"I was. At my smallest, I was the size of an atom while part of a ship the size of a glucose molecule. I spent better than half a day inside a living human body, first in the bloodstream, then in the brain."

"And this is true? No chance of an illusion or trickery?"

"Please, Professor Friar. If I were tricked or hypnotized, my testimony now would be worthless. We can't proceed unless you recognize the fact that I am in my right mind and can be relied on to report events that correspond reasonably well with reality."

Friar's lips pressed together and then he said, "You are right. We must make assumptions to begin with and I will assume you are sane and reliable—without prejudice to further reconsideration of such assumptions."

"Of course," said Morrison.

"In that case"—and Friar turned to Rodano—"we begin with one great and important observation. Miniaturization *is* possible and the Soviets do indeed have it and make use of it and can miniaturize even living human beings without apparent harm to them."

He turned back to Morrison. "Presumably, the Soviets claim to miniaturize by reducing the size of Planck's constant."

"Yes, they do."

"Of course they do. There's no other conceivable way of doing it. Did they explain the procedure by which that was done?"

"Certainly not. You might as well make the assumption that the Soviet scientists I dealt with are as sane as we are. They wouldn't carelessly give away anything they don't want us to know."

"Very well, then. Assumption made. Now tell us exactly what happened to you in the Soviet Union. Do not tell it as an adventure story, but only as the observations of a professional physicist."

Morrison began to talk. He was not entirely sorry to do so.

He wanted to exorcise it and he didn't want the responsibility of being the only American to know what he knew. He told the story in detail and it took hours. He did not finish until they were sitting at a lunch delivered by room service.

Over dessert, Friar said, "Let me summarize, then, as best I can from memory. To begin with, miniaturization does not affect time flow, nor the quantum interactions—that is, the electromagnetic, weak and strong interactions. The gravitational interaction is affected, however, and decreases in proportion to mass, as it naturally would. Is that so?"

Morrison nodded.

Friar went on. "Light—and electromagnetic radiation, generally—can cross into and out of the miniaturization field, but sound cannot. Normal matter is weakly repelled by the miniaturization field but, under pressure, normal matter can be made to enter it and be itself miniaturized, at the expense of the energy of the field."

Morrison nodded again.

Friar said, "The more miniaturized an object becomes, the less energy is required to miniaturize it further. Do you know if the energy requirement decreases in proportion to the mass remaining at any particular stage of miniaturization?"

"That would certainly seem logical," said Morrison, "but I don't recall anyone mentioning the quantitative nature of that phenomenon."

"To go on, then. The more miniaturized an object, the greater the chance of its spontaneous deminiaturization—and that refers to the entire mass within the field, rather than to any component part. You, as a separated individual, were more likely to deminiaturize spontaneously than you would as part of the ship. Is that right?"

"That was my understanding."

"And your Soviet companions admitted that it was impossible to maximize and to make things more massive than they are in nature."

"Again, that was my understanding. You must realize, Professor Friar, that I can only repeat what I was told. They might have deliberately misled me or they may have been wrong because they had insufficient knowledge themselves."

"Yes yes, I understand. Do you have any reason to believe they were deliberately misleading you?"

"No. It seemed to me they were being honest."

"Well, perhaps. Now, the most interesting thing to me is that Brownian motion was in balance with miniaturization oscillation and that the greater the degree of miniaturization, the greater the shift in balance toward oscillation and away from ordinary Brownian motion."

"That is an actual observation of my own, Professor, and doesn't rest merely on what I was told."

"And that shift of balance has something to do with the rate of spontaneous deminiaturization."

"That is my own thought. I cannot state it as fact."

"Hmm." Friar sipped thoughtfully at his coffee and said, "The trouble is that all this is superficial. It tells us about the behavior of the miniaturization field, but nothing about how the field is produced. —And in decreasing the value of Planck's constant, they leave the speed of light untouched, you say?"

"Yes, but that, as I emphasized, means that maintaining the miniaturization field costs enormously in energy. If they can couple Planck's constant with the speed of light, increasing the latter as they decrease the former— But they don't have that yet."

"So they say. It was in Shapirov's mind, supposedly, but you were unable to get it out."

"That's right."

Friar remained lost in thought for a few minutes, then shook his head. "We'll go over everything you've said and deduce what we can from it, but I fear it won't help."

"Why not?" asked Rodano.

"Because none of it goes to the heart. If someone who had never seen a robot or heard anything about any of its component parts were to report a robot in operation, he could describe how the head and limbs moved, how the voice sounded, how it obeyed orders, and so on. Nothing he could observe would tell him how a positronic brainpath works or what a molecular valve is. He would not even have an inkling that either exists, nor would those scientists who would work from his observations have any.

"The Soviets have some technique to produce the field and we know nothing about it, nor does anything Morrison can tell us help us there. They might have published material that led up to it, not aware that something crucial was in the making—that was what happened in the mid-twentieth century, when early work on nuclear fission was published before it was understood that it ought to be kept secret. The Soviets didn't make that mistake with miniaturization, however. Nor have we succeeded in retrieving information concerning the matter through espionage or by the luck of having some key personnel on the other side defect and come to us.

"I will consult with my colleagues on the Board, but on the whole, Dr. Morrison, I'm afraid that your adventure in the Soviet Union, however daring and praiseworthy has—except for your confirmation that miniaturization does exist—been useless. I'm sorry, Mr. Rodano, but it might as well not have happened."

90.

MORRISON'S expression did not change as Friar advanced his conclusion. He poured himself a little more coffee, added cream judiciously, and drank it without haste.

Then he said, "You're quite wrong, you know, Friar."

Friar looked up and said, "Are you trying to say that you know something about the production of the miniaturization field? You had said that—"

"What I'm going to say, Friar, has nothing at all to do with miniaturization. It has everything to do with my own work. The Soviets took me to Malenkigrad and the Grotto in order that I might use my computer program to read Shapirov's mind. It failed at that, which is perhaps not surprising, considering that Shapirov was in a coma and near death. On the other hand, Shapirov, who had a remarkably penetrating mind, referred to my program as a 'relay station' after he had read some of my papers. That's what it turned out to be."

"A relay station?" Friar's face took on a look of puzzled distaste. "What does that mean?"

"Instead of tapping Shapirov's thought, my programmed computer, once inside one of Shapirov's neurons, was acting as a relay, passing thought from one of us to another."

Friar's expression became one of indignation. "You mean it was a telepathic device."

"Exactly. I first experienced that when I was aware of an

intense emotion of love and sexual desire for a young woman who was on the miniaturized ship with me. Naturally, I assumed it was my own feeling, for she was a very attractive woman. Nevertheless, I was not aware of any conscious feeling of that sort. It was not until several other instances of the sort that I realized I was receiving the thoughts of a young man on board ship. He and the young lady were estranged, but the passion between them existed, nevertheless."

Friar smiled tolerantly. "Are you sure you were in condition, on board the ship, to interpret these thoughts properly? After all, you were under tension. Did you also receive similar thoughts from the young lady?"

"No. The young man and I exchanged thoughts, involuntarily, on several occasions. When I thought of my wife and children, he thought of a woman and two youngsters. When I was lost in the bloodstream, it was he who picked up my sensations of panic. He assumed he had detected Shapirov's miseries by way of my machine—which remained in my possession when I was adrift—but those were my feelings, not Shapirov's. I did not exchange thoughts with either woman on board, but they exchanged thoughts with each other. When they tried to catch Shapirov's thoughts, they detected similar words and feelings—from each other, of course—which the young man and myself did not."

"A sexual difference?" said Friar skeptically.

"Not really. The pilot of the ship, a male, received nothing at all, either from the women or from the other men, though on one occasion, he did seem to get a thought. I couldn't say from whom. My own feeling is that there are brain types, as there are blood types—probably only a few—and that telepathic communication can be most easily established among those of the same brain type."

Rodano interposed softly, "Even if all this is so, Dr. Morrison. What of it?"

Morrison said, "Let me explain that. For years I've worked to identify the regions and patterns of abstract thought within the human brain with some unremarkable success. Occasionally, I would catch an image, but I never interpreted that properly. I thought it was coming from the animal on whose brain I was working, but I now suspect that they came when I was fairly close to some human being who was in the grip of strong emotion or deep thought. I never noticed that. My fault.

"Nevertheless, having been stung by the general indifference and downright disbelief and ridicule of my colleagues, I never published the matter of catching images, but modified my program in an attempt to intensify it. Some of those modifications were never published, either. Thus, I entered Shapirov's bloodstream with a device that could more nearly serve as a telepathic relay than anything I had ever had before. And now that, at last, my thick head has absorbed exactly what it is that I have, I know what to do to improve the program. I am sure of that."

Friar said, "Let me get this straight, Morrison. You are telling me that, as a result of your fantastic voyage into Shapirov's body, you are now certain you can so modify your device as to make telepathy practical?"

"Practical to an extent. Yes."

"That would be an enormous thing—if you could demonstrate it." The skepticism in Friar's voice did not disappear.

"More enormous than you perhaps think," said Morrison with some asperity. "You know, of course, that telescopes, whether optical or radio, can be built in parts over a wide area and, if they are coordinated by computer, can achieve the function of a single large telescope, one much larger than can practically be built in a single piece."

"Yes. But what of that?"

"I mention it as an analogy. I am convinced that I can demonstrate something of the same sort in connection with the brain. If we were to have six men united telepathically, the six brains would, for the time, act as one large brain and, in fact, be beyond human in intelligence and in the capacity for insight. Think of the advances in science and technology that could be made, advances in other fields of human endeavor as well. We would, without going through the tedium of physical evolution or the danger of genetic engineering, create a mental superman."

"Interesting, if true," said Friar, obviously intrigued and as obviously unconvinced.

"There is a catch, though," said Morrison. "I performed all my experiments on animals, placing leads from my computer into the brain. That was—and as I see now, must be—not at all precise. No matter how we refine it, we will have only a crude telepathic system at best. What we need is to invade a brain and place a miniaturized and properly programmed computer in a neuron, where it can act as a relay. The telepathic process will then be sharpened enormously."

"And the poor person on whom you inflict this damage," said Friar, "will eventually explode when the device deminiaturizes."

"An animal brain is much inferior to the human brain," said Morrison earnestly, "because of the fact that the animal brain has fewer neurons, less intricately ordered. The individual neuron in a rabbit's brain may, however, not be significantly inferior to a human neuron. A robot could be used as a relay."

Rodano said, "American brains working in tandem could, then, work out the secret of miniaturization and perhaps even beat the Soviets at the task of coupling Planck's constant to the speed of light."

"Yes," said Morrison enthusiastically, "and one Soviet scientist, Yuri Konev, who was the shipmate who shared thoughts with me, caught on to this, as I did. It was for that reason that he tried to hold on to me and to my program in defiance of his own government. Without me and my program, I doubt that he can duplicate my work for a long time, perhaps not for many years. This is not really his field."

"Continue," said Rodano. "I'm beginning to get a feeling for this."

Morrison said, "This is the situation, then. Right now, we've got a kind of crude telepathy. Even without miniaturization, it may help us forge ahead of the Soviets, but it may not. Without miniaturization—and without the establishment of a properly programmed computer in an animal neuron as a relay—we can't be sure of accomplishing anything.

"The Soviets, on the other hand, have a crude form of miniaturization. They may, in the ordinary course of investigation, find a way of linking quantum theory and relativity theory to make a truly efficient miniaturization device, but that might take a very long time.

"So if we have telepathy but not miniaturization, and if they have miniaturization but not telepathy, it may be that we may win after a long period of time—or they may win. The nation that wins has, in a sense, an unlimited speed of travel and the Universe will belong to it. The nation that loses will wither—or at least its institutions will wither. It would be good for us if we win the race, but it is they who may win and the process of racing may force the breakdown of two generations of an uneasy peace and lead to an all-destructive war.

"On the other hand, if we and the Soviets are willing to work together and, both of us, to use telepathy as refined and strengthened by a miniaturized relay station in a living neuron, we may achieve, in combination and in a very short time, what amounts to antigravity and infinite speed. The Universe will belong to both the United States and the Soviet Union; indeed, to the whole globe, to Earth, to humanity.

"Why not, gentlemen? No one would lose. Everyone would gain."

Friar and Rodano stared at him in wonder. Friar finally said, swallowing hard, "You make it sound good, *if* indeed you have telepathy."

"Do you have the time to listen to my explanation?"

"I have all the time you want," said Friar.

It took some hours for Morrison to explain his theory in detail. Then he leaned back and said, "It's almost dinnertime. Now I know that you—and others as well—will be wanting to interview me and that you will all want me to set up a system which will demonstrate the practicality of telepathy and that that will keep me busy for—well, for the rest of my life, for all I know, but I must have one thing now."

"What's that?" asked Rodano.

"Some time off to begin with. Please. I've gone through enough. Give me twenty-four hours—from now until dinnertime tomorrow. Let me read, eat, think, rest, and sleep. Just one day, if you don't mind, and thereafter I will be at your service."

"Fair enough," said Rodano, rising. "I will arrange that if I can and I suspect I can. The twenty-four hours is yours. Make the most of it. I agree that you'll have precious little time to yourself thereafter. And from now on, for quite a while, resign yourself to being the most strictly guarded person in America, not excluding the President."

"Good," said Morrison. "I'll call for a dinner for one."

91.

RODANO and Friar had finished their own dinner. It had been an unusually silent meal in an isolated and guarded room.

Once it was over, Rodano said, "Tell me, Dr. Friar, do you think Morrison is right in this matter of telepathy?"

Friar sighed and said cautiously, "I will have to consult with some of my colleagues who are more knowledgeable concerning the brain than I am, but I feel he is right. He is very convincing. —And now I have a question for you?"

"Yes?"

"Do you think Morrison was correct as to the necessity of cooperation between the United States and the Soviet Union in this matter?"

There was a lengthy pause and finally Rodano said, "Yes, I think he's right there, too. Of course, there'll be howls from every direction, but we can't risk the Soviets getting there first. Everyone will see that. They'll have to."

"And the Soviets? Will they see it, too?"

"They'll have to, also. They can't risk us getting there first. Besides, the rest of the world will undoubtedly get wind of what is going on and they will clamor for a piece of the action and demand that no new cold war be started. It may take some years, but in the end we will cooperate."

Rodano then shook his head and said, "But do you know what really strikes me as peculiar, Professor Friar?"

Friar said, "What in this whole course of events can possibly strike you as *not* peculiar?"

"Nothing, I suppose, but what strikes me as *most* peculiar is this. I met Morrison last Sunday afternoon to urge him to go to the Soviet Union. At the time, my heart sank. He struck me as a man without guts, as a zero, as a wimp, as someone who wasn't even bright except in an academic sense. I didn't think he could be relied on to accomplish *anything*. I was simply sending him to his death. So I thought—and so I said to a colleague the next day—and, so help me, so I still think. He's nothing and it's simply a miracle that he survived and that's only thanks to others. And yet—"

"And yet?"

BANTAM BOOKS
GRAND SLAM SWEEPSTAKES
Win a new Chevrolet Celebrity . . .
It's easy . . . It's fun . . . Here's how to enter:

OFFICIAL ENTRY FORM

Three Bantam book titles on sale this month are hidden in this word puzzle. Identify the books by circling each of these titles in the puzzle. Titles may appear within the puzzle horizontally, vertically, or diagonally . . .

Bantam's titles for August are:

OMAMORI

FANTASTIC VOYAGE II

RICH AND RECKLESS

In each of the books listed above there is another entry blank and puzzle . . . another chance to win!

Be on the lookout for Bantam's September titles: IT'S ALL IN THE PLAYING, FLASHBACK, SO MANY PROMISES. In each of them, you'll find a new puzzle, entry blank and GRAND SLAM Sweepstakes rules . . . and yet another chance to win another brand-new Chevrolet automobile!

MAIL TO: GRAND SLAM SWEEPSTAKES
Post Office Box 18
New York, New York 10046

Please Print

NAME _____

ADDRESS _____

CITY _____ STATE _____ ZIP _____

OFFICIAL RULES

NO PURCHASE NECESSARY.

To enter identify this month's Bantam Book titles by placing a circle around each word forming each title. There are three titles shown above to be found in this month's puzzle. Mail your entry to: Grand Slam Sweepstakes, P.O. Box 18, New York, N.Y. 10046.

This is a monthly sweepstakes starting February 1, 1988 and ending January 31, 1989. During this sweepstakes period, one automobile winner will be selected each month from all entries that have correctly solved the puzzle. To participate in a particular month's drawing, your entry must be received by the last day of that month. The Grand Slam prize drawing will be held on February 14, 1989 from all entries received during all twelve months of the sweepstakes.

To obtain a free entry blank/puzzle/rules, send a self-addressed stamped envelope to: Winning Titles, P.O. Box 650, Sayreville, N.J. 08872. Residents of Vermont and Washington need not include return postage.

PRIZES: Each month for twelve months a Chevrolet automobile will be awarded with an approximate retail value of $12,000 each.

The Grand Slam Prize Winner will receive 2 Chevrolet automobiles plus $10,000 cash (ARV $34,000).

Winners will be selected under the supervision of Marden-Kane, Inc., an independent judging organization. By entering this sweepstakes each entrant accepts and agrees to be bound by these rules and the decisions of the judges which shall be final and binding. Winners may be required to sign an affidavit of eligibility and release which must be returned within 14 days of receipt. All prizes will be awarded. No substitution or transfer of prizes permitted. Winners will be notified by mail. Odds of winning depend on the total number of eligible entries received.

Sweepstakes open to residents of the U.S. and Canada except employees of Bantam Books, its affiliates, subsidiaries, advertising agencies and Marden-Kane, Inc. Void in the Province of Quebec and wherever else prohibited or restricted by law. Not responsible for lost or misdirected mail or printing errors. Taxes and licensing fees are the sole responsibility of the winners. All cars are standard equipped. Canadian winners will be required to answer a skill testing question.

For a list of winners, send a self-addressed, stamped envelope to: Bantam Winners, P.O. Box 711, Sayreville, N.J. 08872.

"There will be born to the Royal House one who is dead
yet will live, who will die again and live again.
And when he returns, he will hold in his hand
the destruction of the world . . ."

THE DARKSWORD TRILOGY
by
Margaret Weis and Tracy Hickman

☐ **Forging the Darksword** (26894-5 • $3.95/$4.95 in Canada)
begins the adventures of the angry young Joram, born into
a world where his lack of magic powers means an instant
death sentence. When he meets the catalyst Saryon, destiny
makes them allies and they find themselves delving into
ancient technology, forging a sword capable of absorbing
magic.

☐ **Doom of the Darksword** (27164-4 • $3.95/$4.95 in
Canada) Determined to learn the truth of his heritage,
Joram travels to the royal city of Merilon. There he finds
not only the answers to his questions but treachery in the
palace and a battle for the throne.

☐ **Triumph of the Darksword** (27406-6 • $3.95/$4.95 in
Canada) Rising to power he never dreamed of, Joram finds
himself faced with the greatest challenge of his life: leading
the people of Thimhallan against powerful and ruthless
invaders.

Buy **Forging the Darksword, Doom of the Darksword** and
Triumph of the Darksword now on sale wherever Bantam
Spectra books are sold, or use this page to order:

Bantam Books, Dept. SF82, 414 East Golf Road, Des Plaines, IL 60016

Please send me the books I have checked above. I am enclosing
$_____ (please add $2.00 to cover postage and handling). Send
check or money order—no cash or C.O.D.s please.

Mr/Ms _____

Address _____

City/State _____ Zip _____

SF82—8/88

Please allow four to six weeks for delivery. This offer expires 2/89.
Prices and availability subject to change without notice.

BANTAM
SHOP-AT-HOME
C·A·T·A·L·O·G

Special Offer
Buy a Bantam Book
for only 50¢.

Now you can have Bantam's catalog filled with hundreds of titles plus take advantage of our unique and exciting bonus book offer. A special offer which gives you the opportunity to purchase a Bantam book for only 50¢. Here's how!

By ordering any five books at the regular price per order, you can also choose any other single book listed (up to a $5.95 value) for just 50¢. Some restrictions do apply, but for further details why not send for Bantam's catalog of titles today!

Just send us your name and address and we will send you a catalog!

BANTAM BOOKS, INC.
P.O. Box 1006, South Holland, Ill. 60473

Mr. Mrs. Ms. _____
_____ (please print)

Address _____

City _____ State _____ Zip _____

FC(A)—10/87

Please allow four to six weeks for delivery.